^aMost Unusual Duke

SUSANNA ALLEN

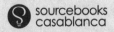

sourcebooks
casablanca

Published by Sourcebooks Casablanca, an imprint of Sourcebooks
P.O. Box 4410, Naperville, Illinois 60567-4410
(630) 961-3900
sourcebooks.com

Printed and bound in Canada.
MBP 10 9 8 7 6 5 4 3 2 1

Prologue

THE SLEUTH GATHERED AROUND THE CEREMONIAL CIRCLE, and Arthur felt sick.

Nothing had been done to prepare the grove for use, not in the way his father had taught him: the bears had not processed from the four quarters as was required; there were neither torches to lead their way nor bonfire to anchor the sacred space. They had hardly known to gather as the clan's connection was so weak: their Alpha had rushed out of his study, and they had responded to the faint call through the foundering connection. They gathered in darkness as the moon waned; the stink of fear emanated from those present as their Alpha was challenged for dominion over the Osborn sleuth.

His father's sleuth. His father, the Alpha who battled for his life, for their lives, for Arthur's life and his right to this clan. He who was the heir presumptive but unable to Change.

He was six years old. His Shift would not come upon him for another year.

The snarls erupting from the challenger were unlike anything Arthur ever heard. He had grown up in peace and near isolation, his family's daily existence following the age-old ways of their kind: the children stayed with the mothers, and the fathers wandered, challenging each other to build greater numbers of offspring and expand their power…and yet what use was power when the fathers never stayed for long in the homes they built, if they wandered far and wide and were rarely there to play with their cubs? Mummy once tried to explain that the dukedom of Osborn was amongst the most fortunate of sleuths, as they had a fine, big home and were strong in number, but it mattered little if Papa was forced to roam now and then to keep up appearances. Mum said he would prefer to be with them, but Arthur wasn't convinced this was so.

Would the usurper have hesitated to call for a challenge if the clan's Beta was here? It was the Beta's duty to act as the voice of reason, but Papa's Second was off chasing a mating partner of his own. Arthur knew what mating was, even if the grown-ups didn't know he did. He knew his parents were *vera amorum*; that meant they were fated mates, they were special, but it didn't matter in the fight against this horrible Shifter who came from abroad and saw what his father built and wanted it for his own.

Arthur wanted to toss his accounts, to hide behind his mum's skirts and cry. But his mother was dead and his father was weak because his heart was in pieces and Arthur was too young to come to his aid.

The bears circled and snapped at each other for ages. *Maybe nothing will happen after all*, Arthur thought, as one bear leaped forward and the other retreated, back and forth, back and forth. Maybe when one of them got tired, he who was vanquished would bare his throat in obeisance, in surrender, and it would be done. Nobody would die, not even the horrible Shifter.

On some silent signal known only to them, the combatants rose on their hind legs and crashed together with a sound like thunder, the very earth shaking from the impact. They wrestled as Arthur and his little brother Garben sometimes did when they played at being their bear selves, but they never hurt each other, not the way these grown males were. This would not end without blood spilled on the ground.

Arthur looked around the circle. The females were large enough and strong enough to defend them, to support their Alpha, but if they intervened they would shame him. This seemed stupid to Arthur, whose father rolled out of the way of the challenger's claws at the very last moment. The males of their number in their prime were not present; ranging as far and wide as they did, and as weak as the *sentio* was, they would never have been alerted in time to come to their Alpha's aid. There were only two elder males among them, who were ancient and nearly toothless and, if their daily complaints were anything to go by, would welcome their release to Valhalla.

The females formed a closed rank on the edge of the circle to protect their young. Arthur, his brother, and one of their sleuth-mates, little Charlotte, were concealed as best as could be in their human skins; the few children who could Change were not allowed to do so. Even if they were of an age to Shift on their own, a child's essential self, their bear Shape, could be held back by their mum. It was a gift from the goddess, a way to keep the young safe.

Safety in the sleuth had been on a razor's edge since Arthur's mum's death and his father's decline. Papa refused to mate again, refused to dishonor his *vera amoris* by taking up with any of the willing females. He vowed to fuel the *sentio* with the memory of their fierce love, but his grief was more powerful than his resolve and greater than his once-great strength. Day by day the connection between every member of the sleuth weakened in concert with their Alpha's vigor.

The combatants dropped down onto their fours. When a bear bunched on his back feet and pushed, it leant even more force to his shoulder to help him strike down his foe; he could then use his front claws to rake at the soft underbelly and position his fangs for the killing strike. Each bear sought to use the strength of the other against his adversary, looking for an opening, a weakness, a drop in the defense, and it came.

His father stumbled. Arthur could see the exhaustion in his eyes, even after so short an engagement; he fell on his belly and was too slow, too slow. The usurper opened his jaws, clamped his teeth on the back of Papa's neck, and shook and bit and clawed. The sound of the crack of bone, the snap of neck reverberated throughout the grove. Arthur heard Charlotte's gasp and Ben's whimper, and he grabbed them by the arm and pulled them away from the edge of the circle as the usurper rose on his back legs and roared, demanding obeisance, demanding honor be shown to him for his triumph.

It was a hollow victory. In the instant of killing the Alpha, Hallbjorn might command the sleuth through brute force, but he did not command its essence: the *sentio* snuffed out like a candle in the wind. Unable to challenge in turn but refusing to expose their necks to the usurper, the sleuth scattered, the four paths leading out of the circle dividing their escape. The females grabbed the youngest by the scruffs of their necks; older children were chivvied onto the backs of the adults to hold on for their lives as they fled into the night.

The usurper thrashed about on his hind legs, roaring with rage; Charlotte clung to Ben, both pale and frightened and weeping; Arthur hid his face in the fur of the female on whose back he rode.

In the myths of every species, the Alpha child of a wronged father swore revenge and wreaked it at the appropriate time to take his rightful place.

Arthur made an entirely different vow.

One

WOLVES. SO BLOODY DRAMATIC.

Arthur Humphries, Duke of Osborn, leaned against a silk-covered wall in the Viscount Montague's ballroom. He was present under extreme duress, thanks to a strongly worded missive from his cousin, and now the evening wanted only this: an eruption of romance from Alfred, Duke of Lowell. Rumors had reached even him, in his ambulatory rustication, of His Grace's abduction of the Honorable Felicity Templeton. Those who knew that Lowell was a *versipellis*, a Shapeshifter, realized the duke had finally found his fated mate and reeled with the news she was *homo plenus*—a human. The majority of society were appalled that the peer had run off with an utter nobody rather than snatching up a diamond of the first water or, at the very least, a female of better breeding than Baron Templeton's only offspring.

When he heard of the scandal surrounding the freshly dubbed "Fallen Felicity," Arthur had dismissed it as fourth-hand tittle-tattle with no truth in it. On the contrary: it appeared to be much ado about something, and the drama would play out before the entire world.

The lady's entrance had been sensational enough, with her arrival so late as to challenge fashionability; added to that, her presence devolved into a confrontation with an uncle regarding a dispute about a will. Arthur rubbed his shoulder against the wall as Alfred blathered on about legacies and titles and Odin knew what, but he had to admit to admiration for Lowell's control. Here, in a mansion full of humans, a wolf dared to show his temper and managed to hold his essential self at bay. Nary a claw edged his fingertips; not a sight of his scruff threatened to unfurl.

Miss Templeton turned to face her uncle and the onlookers; in so doing she gave the duke her back. *She must know what he is and yet she shows no fear*, Arthur thought. Brave little human. Standing up to loathsome relations as well as holding her own with a powerful Shapeshifter? She would make a fine Alpha female, human or not.

Upon a further outbreak of choler over some title or other, the King's guard entered without fanfare and laid hands on the lady's uncle; a smattering of applause accompanied the snarling and shouting of the man as he was forcibly escorted out.

That was that, then. Thrilling in its way, Arthur supposed, and rather more gripping than the current bill at Covent Garden. *The Blind Beggar of Bethnal Green* had nothing on the Alpha Duke of Lowell Hall. Nevertheless, Arthur could not comprehend why George had demanded his attendance when the prince himself was nowhere to be seen. Had the Regent appeared at what even Arthur knew was a middling ball, it would set an alarming precedent.

Arthur's presence was sensational in its own right, enough to send the matchmaking mamas into the boughs. No duke of the realm was safe from those trading on the Marriage Mart, not even when the holder of such an august title was as large and rough around the edges as himself. His attire was not in the first stare, as his love of tailors was nonexistent; he could not say how old his coat was nor his trousers, only that they had taken as many a turn around a ballroom as he. *Turn* was overstating the matter: more like held up as many a wall.

A mama determined upon a coronet for her offspring would discount his costume as a rectifiable deficiency, but only the hardiest of matchmakers would overlook his idiosyncratic coiffure. His hair was styled after Brummell's Brutus but was infinitely richer in density and perfectly complemented his meticulously tended sideburns. A dollop of *pomade de nerole*—its bitter orange scent a familiar comfort—kept his unruly curls in control.

It was a pity a beard was so far out of fashion that even Arthur was clean-shaven, and yet he often toyed with the idea of cultivating the appearance of a Hussar. Had he been a second son—and a human, Freya forbid—he would have leapt at a commission, at the chance to live off the King's shilling, released from the albatross of his title, a woman in every port…no, that was the Navy. The Navy then, sailing the high seas, at the mercy of the elements, free of the land and his ties to it, of the responsibilities that loomed in his consciousness, that he denied, even though doing so left him so, so—

Alone, his bear muttered.

Hush, Arthur scolded. He pushed himself away from the wall and wandered the edges of the throng. He noticed his customary cultivars of scuttlebutt were poking at the hot coals of this latest spectacle and hoped the imminent Duchess of Lowell had the emotional fortitude to outlast the relentless judgment of these biddies. He himself was at his happiest far from London, away from the endless scrutiny and the machinations of the *beau monde*. Once Ben and Charlotte had wed, he'd begun his social hibernation, nipping in the bud the notion of reestablishing the Osborn sleuth. He was doing them a service. There were more than a few of the old guard near enough to their homeplace to provide his brother's growing family with hearth and home.

Did his brother go about? He felt a pinch in his chest at the thought of Ben moving through society, the cheeky Charlotte at his side, winkling out the ton's deepest secrets with no effort at all. Arthur breathed in sharply—they were not here this evening, were they? He would not put it past Georgie to orchestrate some sort of reunion, where Arthur could not in good conscience flee in an instant. His long-ago oath was secure in his self-made aloofness, and he would not rescind it. Tonight's event would come to a close, and he would return to his natural habitat.

Not natural, chided his bear.

Chosen habitat, Arthur retorted.

Wretched choice. The bear rolled in his aura and showed Arthur his back.

It is the choice our kind have made for eons. Why he quarreled with his creature he did not know. He would like to offer this as an example to any human who thought animals were easily led or lesser in reasoning. His essential self was able to argue with the best. *A male bear does not remain with his sleuth, and that is that.*

Animali puris *ways are not our ways,* the bear countered. *The new generation has put them aside.* Even though the humans in his vicinity could not hear his bear growl, they obeyed an unconscious atavistic instinct and hurried away.

Arguing logic with his essential self was a losing game, and yet he continued: *My father observed the law. You were not there.*

I was yet to be roused, but I was there. The bear rubbed up against him, nosed him in the aura around his head, for comfort, in sorrow. *I am here now. The time has come.*

Never, Arthur retorted.

Now, his creature murmured.

Both he and his bear were rendered speechless as Lowell went down on one knee. Holy Freya and all her Valkyries, never say he was going to—yes, there it was, a ring and a plea. The females as one looked about to swoon and the males as though they'd cheerfully run the duke through, hanging be damned.

Mate, his bear sighed.

With a human? Arthur scoffed. Surely that was not possible.

His bear insisted: *They are mates.*

You needn't be getting any ideas.

Want ours.

Was there anything worse than ursine obstinance? *No human female would have us, you great hairy numpty,* Arthur said. *We are landless, homeless—*

We are none of that, his bear snarled. *For you have only to embrace the legacy of our parents—*

Arthur growled and set loose a flurry of debutantes. *You know nothing of what you speak—*

He turned to leave, uncertain of his ability to hold to his manskin, and nearly plowed down a footman decked out in royal livery.

"Your Grace." The servant bowed. "His Highness desires your presence."

"Does he indeed?" So George was here, then. The footman gestured, and Arthur sighed. "Lead on."

Two

Dukes. Infernal attention seekers.

Beatrice, widow of the Marquess of Castleton, watched as Miss Templeton's uncle was taken by force from the ballroom. Surely a family dispute was best settled at home rather than in front of the whole world? Added to the spectacle, Beatrice knew the Duke of Lowell for what he was and marveled at his boldness. The *ton* deemed him uncivilized enough, but were they to discover exactly how barbaric he was, she did not like to think how they would react.

Lowell turned to Miss Templeton. It would appear this performance had not concluded. "Before we were so rudely interrupted, you mentioned something about the next dance?"

"I believe it is a waltz," she replied, her voice sounding clear as a bell throughout the room. "Would you do me the honor?"

"Would you do me an even greater honor?" The duke dropped to one knee before her, and yet another gasp flew through the gathering, Beatrice's only reaction a tightening of fingers on her fan. Her ears rang as the duke proceeded to propose to the overcome Miss Templeton. Snapping open her fan, she wafted it before her face until she reclaimed her composure. Lowell opened his palm; Beatrice saw it contained a ring. "Felicity," he said, "I offer this as a symbol of my pledge to revere you above all others, as a symbol that our joined lives will shine as brightly as these gems, do you tell me you accept my troth and consent to be my wife."

"I accept," Miss Templeton replied. "Alfred."

He rose and slipped the ring over the fourth finger of her left hand, held that hand in both of his, kissed the back of it and led his betrothed to the dance floor. The orchestra began to play, and

Beatrice wondered at herself, at the hint of a tear in her eye, at the painful beating of her heart. How astonishing, after what she'd been through, that a romantic impulse stirred within her breast.

She stood as still as one of the marble columns that lined the perimeter of the floor. Showy and offering no structural support, they gave the illusion of presence to what was a mundane ballroom. She felt akin to them, those useless props, as her title and consequence was as much of an illusion, her very person a construction. Her face was a cipher, a remote mask she had donned very early in her marriage. She had always been ladylike and composed; she now felt petrified, turned to stone, forbidding and formidable no matter her apparent femininity.

Beatrice's figure had always been considered the apex of womanly design. She was small, pleasingly rounded in the correct places, with skin as pale as milk and hair as golden as a freshly minted guinea. How keen she had been to make her come-out, knowing she was a pattern card of female perfection. Pride goeth before a disastrous marriage, and she had enjoyed Incomparable status for a very short time before the alliance with Castleton was made.

The mask descended every day of that marriage, a shield of ice, her armor against the world, against her husband. Her cornflowerblue eyes shone as guileless as a milkmaid's until one was close enough to see the hauteur in them. Her skin was as pale as the day she debuted but now gave the impression of ice, not youth. The chill embedded itself into the marrow of her bones, and there was nothing in this world able to melt it.

A plague of rakes milling about the room cast thoughtful looks in her direction, and she faced them down; the last thing she needed was one of their scurrilous lot, emboldened by Lowell's effort, dropping to one knee before her. It happened often enough in private and was easily thwarted with an indomitable dispassion that sent the importunate suitor straight back out the door. She had to credit their audacity, as it was known she had the ear of the prince regent, although no one knew why. Naturally, they speculated she was his mistress. Let them; she was secure in the hold she had over His Highness, and it had nothing to do with the pleasures of the flesh.

She attached herself to a coterie of dowagers who muttered to one another as they watched the soon-to-be ducal couple waltz, Miss Templeton's gown showing to its best advantage, the skirt opening and closing like the petals of a lily as Lowell swept her around the floor. A whimsical nod to Felicity's days as a wallflower? She would make a formidable duchess, and Beatrice applauded her *sangfroid* and sense of humor.

They were acquaintances, not bosom friends, as it would do neither woman credit in society should they seek to deepen their friendship. A marchioness of means paying particular attention to an Honorable of no means to speak of would draw too much notice, and she knew Felicity wished—or had done—to remain as unnoticeable as possible. Did the woman know to whom she pledged her troth? Or, rather, to what? Miss Templeton did not give the impression she lacked wits. Had Lowell revealed himself to her, revealed the beast he held within? Perhaps a coded letter of felicitation was required. A cryptic yet informative missive to put her on her guard.

The most terrifying thing Beatrice learned in her marriage to the Marquess of Castleton may now come in useful.

To wit: she knew how to recognize a wolf-creature on sight. She would instruct Miss Templeton how to discern them, from the lightness of their gait, the glint in their eyes, eyes that appeared to change color depending on their mood, and their ability to hear through the very walls, never mind at a distance. She would tell her friend to be aware, to beware: these creatures, though not the horrors to be found in the pages of a Gothic novel, were perhaps more alarming as they walked amongst the *ton* undetected.

Was Lowell as beastly as Castleton? The duke was not like him in aspect, but what of his nature? Beatrice hoped he was not. She had long held the duke in high regard as he had not maligned his sister, Lady Phoebe Blakesley, for fleeing England rather than wed the monster to whom Beatrice herself had been given. How much the worse it must have been for the lady, who would have known what lay in her future. How lucky to have such a brother. How Beatrice had often longed for one like the Duke of Lowell.

She did not lack brothers, but as the first girl born after four boys, she soon became household custodian, with her father and his sons playing at being lords of the manor and her mother weakened unto near incapacity due to yearly confinements. As soon as Beatrice reached the age of reason, she took on responsibilities beyond her years. The boys did not know what anything was worth in money, from a bun in a teashop to a year of their tenants' rents, and yet they had a fortune to draw upon, to join their clubs and purchase their overbred steeds, thanks to her. Beatrice struck a perfect balance between parsimony and extravagance, between strictures and indulgences, wrought from hard-won experience in learning to judge the weather and the harvest and the mood of the cook and the perspicacity of the butler. She managed it, even as a girl still in the schoolroom, even as her mother produced three more brothers and one last, darling sister, even as she sought her father's approval and did not find it.

It never failed to astonish her that she wanted a family of her own, and yet she did. She yearned to raise useful sons and confident daughters, to be honored as a capable helpmeet, to take on the mantle of wife and make it good, better, best.

Beatrice had accepted Castleton with that in mind, and it spectacularly had not come to pass.

She'd heard that Lowell had a female chamberlain. She herself would make a prodigious chamberlain, had acted as one in all but name before being set aside like a porcelain shepherdess on a side table. In an underused parlor. In the back of a great house. She was only to look beautiful when her husband wished to gaze upon her, to be composed and flawless as she waited upon her lord to pay her his addresses. And what addresses they had been.

Why Castleton chose her was beyond comprehension. Knowing what she did now, regarding the circles he moved in, it made little sense that the marquess had not yet plucked another bride from amongst his own kind. Perhaps her father and he shared a club? Castleton would have sought an instantaneous solution to his failed nuptials; from her father's point of view, it was past time she was auctioned off. Auctioned she was, though the great sum she garnered for her family would not go far without her there to husband it.

Beatrice snorted to herself, without a wrinkle on her visage to betray her. *Husband, indeed.* As if she'd seek out another one of those. Despite her small stature and general bosominess, once she set aside her blacks she was well able to fend off the fortune hunters, the impecunious suitors who attempted to gain her hand and her wealth with promises of carnal delights. She faced down the highest among them, the prince himself, and succeeded beyond her wildest dreams. She moved through society after years of isolation, in the *ton* but not of it, enjoying notoriety if not prestige, even as the novelty began to pall...

Why ought she remain in society? Beatrice had nothing to prove and nothing to gain. Did she merely seek to poke the *beau monde* in the eye with her independence and her iciness? She knew they called her Lady Frost behind her back, and it touched her not a jot. What need had she to remain as the cynosure of these silly people who had no idea what they harbored in their midst? She would leave, taking her secrets with her, leave London, make a start by leaving this ball—

A servant in royal livery hove into view and bowed before her.

The intake of breath as this was witnessed soughed around her like a wintry wind. Beatrice ostentatiously accepted the proffered slip of paper. She read it, implacable. She nodded infinitesimally to the footman and followed him out of the ballroom, a gale of gossip in her wake.

Three

THE FOOTMAN LED ARTHUR DOWN ONE CORRIDOR AFTER another, the manor's humble facade belying a warren of halls and doors. Muffled sounds of illicit coupling emitted from behind more than one of those doors until the lit sconces reduced in number and they entered a shadowy conservatory.

The lady of the house was inordinately fond of orchids.

As they approached a small dais hosting a daybed and a work basket, another door opened, and they were joined by a human female, haughty in bearing—none other than Lady Frost. She was directed to stand at his left and took her place without so much as a glance at his person. *Ton* gossip had it she was a "special friend" of George's, although, if Arthur recalled correctly, His Highness preferred his females to be comfortable in frame and cozy in nature.

This little bit would not be to the royal taste. The lady gave the impression of ten stone of imperiousness contained in a two-stone saddlebag. Arthur was not sure he'd ever seen so small a human adult; he doubted her nose came up to his sternum. Her blonde hair was caught up in a tight matronly twist, but the sober coiffure did nothing to dim its golden brightness even in the low light. Her *embonpoint* was impressive considering her stature, and yet she had no bum to speak of. An urge bubbled up in Arthur to tease her about it; in the first instance, nothing ever bubbled up within him, ever, and in the second—there was no second. Why in the name of Freya would he tease a female of any species? His bear snorted and sniffed and rolled in his aura, searching for something, Arthur knew not what.

Down, you, he scolded. *This is neither the time nor the place.*

Curious, curious, his bear muttered.

What is? Arthur leaned in a fraction and scented nothing of interest.

Nothing where something ought to be, his creature responded.

He was prepared to lecture his bear on philosophical fatuity when yet another door opened, this one at the back of the dais, presumably leading directly from the garden. His Royal Highness, the Prince Regent George IV, entered, done up in his usual finery; the light of the few candles caught on the embroidery rioting up and down his coat, depicting a leap of hares. His pantaloons were as tight as pantaloons could be, and Arthur suspected he would need to be cut out of them at the end of the evening. He discerned the hand of Lady Jemima Coleman in the royal vesture, although it was not widely known she was responsible for the *habillements* of several highly ranked personages, the prince not least among them. That snippet of tittle-tattle would rock more than one foundation.

He was torn out of his musings regarding Georgie's wardrobe as Lady Frost dropped into so deep a curtsy it was surely derisive. There was a flavor to the abject obeisance that implied its excessive depth served to shore up the uncertain authority of its object. She curled as naturally as the branches of the orchids surrounding them, her chin touching her chest as she lowered to the floor. Arthur managed the most cursory of bows and exposed his neck, as was the Shifter way, not wishing to draw attention from her audacity.

George remained on the dais, and his stillness could be confused for patience if one was unfamiliar with his temperament. He had taken note of the lady's barbed intent as he did not bid either release their displays of respect. Arthur's neck was beginning to suffer from fatigue; how was the lady managing? He suspected she would not waver and wondered what inspired her scorn.

The moment drew out, a demonstration of princely pique. Arthur raised his head to glare at George, who sighed and said, "Rise, ma'am." She did so, as effortlessly as she lowered, and resumed her posture, gloved hands folded at her waist, fan and reticule dangling from a wrist, visage devoid of clues as to her thoughts.

"I find myself on the horns of a dilemma," George announced. He paused for effect as if inviting his audience press him to continue.

Arthur dared. "Do you, Your Highness? And in those pantaloons?"

"I assure you it is no laughing matter, Arthur," the Prince continued languidly but was betrayed by a slight flush beneath his ears.

"Horns, you say? Anyone we know?" In for a penny, and it was a pound of censure he would accrue for even obliquely alluding to their secret, given the presence of the human female.

"His Grace the Duke of Lowell is now betrothed, as you have both witnessed," George said. "One hopes he and his lady will be fruitful and multiply, growing his estate in stature and consequence, as can only prove fortuitous for those of our kind."

"The titled kind. Dukes and princes and such like." Arthur tipped his head as subtly as he was able down to his left. His silly punning was one thing, but how did Georgie dare speak so loosely before Lady Frost?

"And yet the greater the strength consolidated by Lowell," George continued, "the greater the need that it be matched by his betters. Such as we, Arthur."

"We are cousins," he said to the lady, who did not give the appearance of attending to a word he or His Highness had said.

"Are you unknown to one another? The Marchioness of Castleton, I am pleased to present to you Arthur, Duke of Osborn. Or is it Dowager Marchioness? Is that more in line if not entirely fitting?"

Only one paying as close attention as Arthur would detect the lady's flinch.

"I do believe one is a dowager if widowed, despite a lack of progeny," George went on, indelicate, thoughtless. Arthur's bear lifted his head, as stunned as the man at their regent's lack of manners. "There was, however, knowledge aborning."

"His Highness refers to my awareness of the peculiarities to be found in his and Castleton's unique…ancestry." The marchioness flicked her gaze at Arthur for a heartbeat. "And yours, I presume. As his cousin."

"Quite right, ma'am, quite right." Georgie was always at his most dangerous when his voice softened as it did now, a bored whisper. It boded ill for the interlocutor.

"I marvel at your *sangfroid*, Georgie." Arthur noted the wince on his cousin's face at the nickname and hoped he drew fire from the female.

"I am not fond of diminutives," George said, and the air changed, a frisson of his *dominatum* priming the air like lightning about to strike. The prince dropped any pretense of indolence. "I am not fond of relations who do not uphold the family name, of high-ranking peers who do not do their duty to their nation and their species. I am not fond of secrets," and here Arthur and his bear snorted in reckless unison, "nor of secret-keepers who are well placed to wreak havoc. I am especially not enamored of the thought of Lowell's pack rising in status by the day."

"I have no care for status." Speaking of cold blood, the lady had apparently earned her sobriquet. She spoke as calmly as she would in turning down kippers for breakfast. "Nor for society, nor for threatening the royal slumber. I have decided to leave London and the *beau monde*—"

"You have decided?" George lifted his brows in disbelief.

"I have, Your Highness." Arthur moved closer to her side; she may know George's secret, but she would not bait him if she knew the potential violence of the regent's essential self.

"How very fortunate that our desires intersect." The force of the prince's will careered about the room. "As it were."

"As what were?" Arthur remembered being similarly at sea the first time he saw *Hamlet*. Disaster stirred underneath the exchanges, the words themselves anodyne yet sinister in intent.

"As my plans for the future and the parts you will play coincide." George ran a hand over an embroidered lapel. "You enjoy the theatre, do you not, Your Grace? I have heard tell of your attendance at the most popular revues of our day, here and abroad."

"Heard, had you? Have ears everywhere, do you?" Arthur felt his dormant *dominatum* rouse, unpracticed, raw, and he fought it down. His would make no match for Georgie's, and he would not risk the female coming to harm.

"Oh, yes." His Highness sighed. "For when my subjects near and dear to me fail to do their duty, it pains me, Arthur. Here." He laid a hand on his chest. "And we know how vital it is to command from a strong heart. It is time you did so."

———

The very large male—the Duke of Osborn—bristled and growled. Beatrice was well acquainted with the subtle change in the atmosphere that heralded the transformation from man to beast. It had emanated from the prince regent initially; she suspected the duke was not far behind.

"You have no say over the choices of the marchioness," the duke snarled, and Beatrice almost laughed. Everyone in this room had more say than she. Even the orchids had greater value.

"The lady knows better than you, Artie." The diminutive was delivered with pique. "And she knows her leverage over Us must inevitably come to an end."

A shiver ran down her spine. It was true: she was not so foolish as to have thought her protection would stretch to the end of her life. She had suspected she would be killed by one of these creatures in due course. Would the prince see to her end himself, or would he require his cousin to dirty his claws?

"There is a letter among my personal effects that reveals the secrets I kept, should I meet a mysterious end." She lied without compunction.

The result was an arched brow from the prince and a light touch on her elbow. "Our kind can scent an untruth," said the duke, who sounded regretful.

"Well played, nonetheless," said His Highness. "Secrets weigh equally heavily on the keeper. I will relieve you of your burden and elevate you at the same time, dear Beatrice, if I may."

"No. You may not." She would run, to America, to the Antipodes—

"Were you to flee you would not get far. My influence would precede you to the very ends of the earth." Beatrice met his gaze, as she was not meant to, as would be treasonous under any other circumstance that did not involve the knowledge she kept close. He looked vaguely apologetic as he continued. "Do you tell your tale, I will have your mental capacity questioned. I will see your fortune disappear in the snap of a finger. In addition, your family will fail to benefit from your candor. Is your youngest sister not about to make her debut? I will ensure she has the most disastrous of Seasons, at the hands of—"

"Monster." Beatrice set her shoulders. "Beast."

"Odin's breath, ma'am," the duke gasped.

"My formidable enemy." George smiled; Beatrice questioned his mental capacity, but even she would not say so, given the state of his father's. "My soon-to-be cousin by marriage."

Georgie could not mean that he and she… Arthur looked at the little female, who did not appear to have been caught by surprise. "Pardon me?"

"It is time your hibernation came to an end, cousin," Georgie said.

"I do not wish to marry, and I will not marry, and I will never marry." Arthur's boyhood vow sounded appropriately childish, and he did not care.

"I hope you do not intend to insult the lady," Georgie said. "Humans are quite the rage these days."

"*Homo plenus* or *versipellis*, I will not."

"I say you will." The air bristled again, a ripple, a threat. "I say you will throw off your naive rancor and take your place. Your clan awaits and must have its Alpha."

Thundering Thor, how could he use these words before her?

"Family is so important, is it not, ma'am?" George purred. "Arthur, only see how far the marchioness would go to protect them, and she only human." He would challenge Georgie on the spot did it not mean the utter destruction of the entire nation. "Such sentiment accorded to family ties is far more powerful amongst those of our kind, dear Beatrice. We, who must live two lives at once, require a strong bond with our kin or else we would weaken and die. Much the way Arthur's father weakened and—"

"Do not!" Arthur let his claws drop and snarled full force at the prince, uncaring if the lady fainted, uncaring if a brawl broke out between himself and his Regent. He need not worry as to the former: the marchioness looked at him with as little dismay as if he had sneezed.

"As I say. So important, the ties that bind. How swiftly you rush to defend your father's name." George cocked his head. "I wonder does such protection extend to a brother and the brother's wife and children?"

Dare he threaten Ben and Charlotte and the cubs? Her ladyship's epithets came to mind. *Monster. Beast.* "Leave them out of this," Arthur demanded, his bear looming in his aura.

"The family of an Alpha who will not take his rightful place and who have no true home of their own may find they are required, for their own good, to reside at Court," George continued, undaunted. "This would be a pity if the male and the female are a love match, as mates are not in one another's pockets under the royal roof. Such devotion is suited only to the lower orders. Thus, the husband will be separated from the wife, the wife made a lady of the Court, and we know how the royal dukes adore them."

"You. Will. Not." Arthur was that close to Changing; a light touch to his elbow checked him, and he was taken aback at the lady's daring and her perception.

"Won't I? And that is, of course, to say nothing of the children. A whelp of three, I believe?" George assumed a look of forlorn concern. "Court is no place for the young and needs must they be put into the care of nursemaids and governesses and tutors, perhaps out in the countryside or even as far away as the Hebrides."

"You will not separate a mother from her children," said the lady. Sweet Freya, this female had no sense of self-preservation. She stepped forward, which only resulted in making her even smaller before George, and yet her hands were in fists and the rage pouring off her was—

Breathtaking, swooned his bear.

"And how shall you stop me, ma'am?" With that, George called forth his *dominatum*.

The threat Beatrice had sensed, the terrifying quiver in the atmosphere, finally erupted and was nothing to what she'd experienced in her marriage. When the marquess raged and howled and by some class of dark art made the air unbreathable; when she felt her bones were on the verge of crumbling into dust, the stronger she stood and the calmer she remained, the less it affected her. Year after year, rage after rage, she strengthened and he weakened and she became invincible.

Or so she thought. The Prince of Wales had finer control of his ferocity and a greater ability to wield it. Beatrice's muscles trembled; her hands shook, and she swayed on her feet. The enormous duke put her behind him, and his shouts for the prince to desist sounded like he was underwater. The prince remained unmoved, and she forgot herself so far as to clutch at the coat of the man before her.

The duke fought back in the same fashion if not to similar effect: a wave of power radiated from him, but it was no match for His Highness's. If Beatrice had learned anything in life, it was how to choose a battle; she moved back to the duke's side, and grabbing his hand, finding strength there, she struggled through the life-sapping force and assumed her exaggerated curtsy once more.

The oppression lifted so quickly she well nigh fell over.

"How dare you, Georgie." The duke raised her up and took her hands, rubbed them, and she thought he may have growled, surprisingly not an offensive sound.

"It is my place to dare." The man who stood before them was not the fribble of the scandal sheets who spent the contents of the exchequer on ostentatious ensembles and myriad inamorata. The man who stood before them was not the sullen son of a king who would not pass on his crown in good time. The man who stood before them was not merely a man. "It is my place to secure the future of my subjects but, more importantly, of my family." He bowed to Beatrice as if he had not nearly suffocated her with his uncanny might. He turned back to the duke. "It is my duty to ensure you secure yours. It is time our generation take the reins. Alfred has done so, and now we follow suit."

"I will not challenge Hallbjorn." This name was not known to her, and it sounded quite foreign. Were they everywhere, these animal-people?

"I say it will not be required. He did not mate, he had no Second, the way is clear, and you will take it." A flash of that strange potency surged, and Beatrice could not help herself; she shuddered.

His Highness nodded, satisfied. "And the lady is not so safe as she would think. The fortune hunters you keep at bay, ma'am, merely take their lumps and in turn petition me, certain I will look upon one of them with favor and discharge you accordingly in a fit of boredom or caprice. I have only to say the word and make it so."

"We agreed," she began.

"We did, we did." He canted his head and regarded her from beneath lowered lids. "You have betrayed yourself by a knowing glance and, yes, a change in your scent one too many times. Our kind know you know our secret, and many of the old guard would see this problem solved in the time-honored way. Do you wish to die, ma'am?"

"I do not." Beatrice had survived Castleton, and she would survive this.

"There we have it." His Highness smiled, as icy an example as she had in her own arsenal. "Do you wish the lady to die, Arthur? For there is no other way to guarantee her safety."

The duke seethed but showed no sign of transforming into a wild animal. He glared at the prince for oceans of time, for a glacial age until he shook his head once, furious and curt.

Beatrice cleared her throat. "I insist that my fortune remain in my own keeping." Let it never be said she was backward in going forward.

"I do not want your money," the duke snapped.

Beatrice bestowed upon him her own class of frosty smile. "That is convenient, as you shall not have it."

"He will require it." His Highness fiddled with an elaborate cuff and sounded bored once more. "And he will return its value in kind."

"Obfuscation does not suit you, Georgie," the duke sneered.

"Oh, it does, Artie, it does." The royal footmen filed back into the room from various doors. "You will marry tomorrow, directly following Lowell's vows. What a lark! We shall make it a day of ducal nuptials in Carlton House."

"What a lark," the duke spat.

"We shall welcome you at the appointed time, ma'am, or shall I be presumptuous and say 'Your Grace'?" George gave her an affable nod. "My man Todd will organize both your departures and accompany you to your new residence, where he will remain and make himself useful. The Humphries family home, as you will soon see, wants freshening."

"It cannot be in any fit state to bring a wife," the duke said. "I have no fortune at my disposal—"

"You do, and you know how to draw upon it," the prince began.

"—and I would not force the foulest ruffian from the Seven Dials to bide there, much less a fine society lady."

"I choose a leaky roof over certain death," Beatrice said.

"This is no choice!" He flung his arms about rather dramatically for a person of his stature. "This is manipulation at its basest! How dare you, Georgie?"

"If not I, then who?" Beatrice felt a shadow of sympathy for the lengths the Regent had gone to enforce his will on this man. The duke's stubbornness was unlike any she had ever encountered.

"Your Grace," she began. Even to her ears, her voice was flat as freshly ironed chintz. "If nothing else, let us unite in our mutual misfortune and inability to cross one of such great rank. Let us negotiate terms for ourselves."

The duke stared at her, aghast. He scowled at the prince once more for good measure and then paused to bow to her before stalking off, slamming the door behind him.

"There. Not so much of a brute as to take his leave without manners." The prince crooked an elbow. "Shall we?"

"Oh, Your Highness, I am not equal to your magnificence." She curtsied again and held it, held it, held it, until she heard the huff of an incredulous laugh and the footsteps of her regent stride away and out the door.

Four

ARTHUR WATCHED THE DUKE OF LOWELL PACE THE BLUE Chamber in Carlton House, irritated by his fellow peer's eagerness. He too was a groom on this day, for all that he was unburdened by nerves. Now that he thought of it, however, his belly churned and his throat felt tight, like it was caught in a vise. Perhaps he'd had a bad kipper at breakfast.

Lowell's Beta, the Honorable Matthias Bates, once again assured his Alpha of his secure possession of the ring, cajoled him and teased him, and behaved as a good Second would: he was a friend and ally, the bulwark upon which the Alpha could rely.

If Arthur was admitting to anything, he envied the relationship between the two men. It was what he had assumed he would build with Ben before their lives fell apart, he as Alpha, Ben by his side. It was childish to wish things had transpired differently; there was little profit in imagining his brother as his Beta.

"To what do we owe the pleasure, Osborn?" Alfred asked.

"His Highness's decree." Ought he have dressed with greater attention? He dismissed the notion out of hand as there was no outdoing Alfred when it came to matters of *habiliment*. He chose not to mention his own imminent wedding.

"You were never one to adhere to George's directives too closely." Fair enough, and Alfred would know. The young Alphas of their generation and their retinues were often called to meet in the Royal Presence, but once childhood was left behind, so was such enforced frivolity. He hadn't been in the same room with the wolf until the Montague ball.

"Times change." He could hear himself, his response little better than a snarl, and he threw back his shoulders as though preparatory to fisticuffs. This was why he did not truck with other Alphas; they brought out the worst in him.

Bates cleared his throat. "Perhaps His Highness wishes His Grace to see what joy is in store when it is his time to mate and bond." Ha! No change there, then: Lowell's Second was always spewing oblique observations to trick the listener into disputing or clarifying, thereby inadvertently revealing incriminating information. Arthur was meant to jump at that like a trout for a worm; he would not give the blond wolf the satisfaction.

"Perhaps the Lowell Second is behind the times as usual." Arthur could not resist baiting the Beta. "Even as his Alpha looks to outshine the bride with his toilette."

"One would accuse those of the ursine persuasion of being sartorially unsophisticated," Matthias returned, "were it not for the example your cousin makes."

"Ah, now, Matthias," Lowell admonished, "diamonds do emerge from the rough."

"'Sweet are the uses of adversity which, like the toad, ugly and venomous, wears yet a precious jewel in its head.'" Arthur wasn't partial to *As You Like It*, but if the quote fit...

"Holy Venus, still at it with the Bard, are you?" Bates loathed the theatre to the exact degree Arthur adored it.

"Matthias, you risk maligning His Grace, for is not a 'good name in man and woman the immediate jewel of their souls'?" Lowell only just got the phrase out before he barked with laughter.

Matthias muttered about boils and plague sores, betraying his Shakespearean knowledge, and Arthur smirked. "Not as nervous as you were, eh, Lowell?"

Calling attention to the levity had the opposite effect on both dukes: Arthur returned to glaring out the window, and Alfred recommenced pacing until a door flew open and a flurry of footmen attended the entrance of Georgie and the bride and—oh, little Jemima Coleman. Arthur hadn't seen her in ages. She too had been one of Georgie's set growing up and a nursery friend of his own. Word had it she was as thick as thieves with the soon-to-be Duchess of Lowell, and the *on-dits* were proven true by her presence. The flamboyant prelate Georgie laid on cleared his throat and began the human marriage service with a flourish of his little book. As he spoke his vows, Lowell's *dominatum* flared to life but not with the accompanying force…ah. It was the pack's *sentio* he called forth, the ineffable connection from heart to heart that bonded a clan. Wedding his *vera amoris*, even under human conditions, was a profound enough act to strengthen the ties between the Alpha and those in his care, even from this distance, despite the *homo plenis* nature of his mate.

Little wonder Georgie was concerned.

The closing words were spoken, and if Arthur wasn't mistaken, Alfred visibly restrained himself from kissing his duchess. That fancy bishop would likely combust.

"And thus falls another fine lord." George sighed. "It is almost too, too much to be borne. Is it not, Jemmikins? Unbearable?"

"Stuff it, Georgie." Jemima looked piqued beyond measure. The prince reached out and pinched her side, causing her to flap about like a mad thing. She'd always been ticklish. Arthur noted Bates's absorption with the lady's reaction, and with the lady in general, and wondered what lay in that direction. And why Georgie was making terrible ursine puns. Had he not revealed his true nature to the new Duchess of Lowell? He wondered at the royal reticence given Georgie's looseness of tongue before Lady Frost.

"Shall we, my dear?" Lowell could not appear more besotted if he tried. "I thought to forego a wedding breakfast and make for the Hall. I intend we arrive in Sussex well before moonrise."

"I would prefer to celebrate there." The duchess cuddled into her husband's side and outshone the Lowell tiara for radiance. Holy Odin. Arthur had never thought such a mawkish thing in his life.

"I do hope you have a bottle of something nice in the coach, Lowell," said Georgie. "How very beastly of you, should you have nothing at hand to while away the miles to Sussex. Whatever shall you do otherwise?" And with that cheeky bon mot, the prince turned to leave and then paused. "Bates, Osborn, if you would." Arthur noted Bates's curious look, but he followed without a word, as Georgie bellowed for his secretaries and his valet, with the wedding party bowing and curtsying in his wake.

The anteroom they entered was little more than a cupboard in comparison to the extravagance of the lion's share of Carlton House. Speaking of lions: bereft though it was of the brooms and buckets it may have previously held, it contained yet another duke. Alwyn, Duke of Llewelyn, lurked in a corner as best he could in a space not conducive to concealment. His uncivilized behavior was forgivable, Arthur supposed, given Llewelyn had been held captive in an exotic animal menagerie for Odin only knew how long. The Welshman barely spoke and never Changed, which boded ill for his health. The lion Shifter was eccentrically bedecked in garments collected from a variety of centuries and color palettes, and if nothing else it made Arthur's ensemble look positively à la mode. He nodded to his peer and received a glare in return.

"Your Highness," intoned the bishop, who was now ignominiously squashed against the far wall, "I hardly think this the appropriate setting for a covenant of consequence to be undertaken."

"Do you desire a new roof or do you not, Cornelius?" George examined one of his frothy cuffs. As ever, the prince was dressed as if expecting his portrait to be painted. He appeared unsurprised by the lack of response to his query. "Everyone has his price, cousin," he said to Arthur. "What shall be yours?"

"Is yours a *sentio* as formidable as that of Lowell? Cousin?" Arthur, in turn, examined his less-than-elaborate cuff.

A favorite youthful pastime of Arthur's had been goading his hotheaded relation into his Change. Vain from birth and full of his own consequence due to his royal lineage, it was pure pleasure for Arthur to inspire such rage in Georgie he would forget himself enough to destroy one of his meticulous outfits. With age came greater control, and yet the bishop backed away as best he could, and Llewelyn snarled deep in his throat. George fought his reaction admirably, but even his impeccable control could not prevent a wave of choler rushing around the snug chamber.

What a contrast to Lowell's joyful service. A feral duke, a blackmailed bishop, an irate prince, and an ambivalent groom. His chest contracted; no more kippers for breakfast, so.

The door opened, and the bride—the frosty, unwilling bride—entered.

———

Do you wish to die, ma'am?

No, she did not.

Beatrice had spent the last night into the early morning considering her options and come to the natural conclusion she had none. Or one: marry the excessively robust Duke of Osborn, retire to wherever they were being sent, and count herself lucky she was allowed to keep control of the Castleton coffers. Not that there was anyone to dispute her claim. She had famously failed to produce an heir; he must have been the last of his line, else there would have been petitioners for the title. How little she had known of her first husband. How little she knew of her second.

Beatrice dressed in marked contrast to that long-ago farce in St. George's, pews overflowing with the spitefully curious, the heavy scent of lilies in the air more suited to a funeral. She had been supplied with a heavy veil, masking the truth of her soon-to-be spouse whom she had not met until she joined him at the altar. At the very least, this go-round she had clapped eyes on her husband-to-be, all twenty feet tall of him, with his immoderate hair and a voice that seemed to originate in the soles of his feet and reverberate through his chest.

Her carriage dress was of sober hue and two years out of fashion. The dark-blue cloth was high quality but serviceable, suitable for a journey of long duration; it buttoned up to her throat and ended in a deep, frilly collar. The skirt's voluminous ruffle, trimmed with a darker-blue satin, was a frippery the modiste insisted upon and Beatrice had not argued, as she had won the battle for a plain straight sleeve and a modest cuff.

Her one indulgence, on this day and in her life, was her hat. Anything that added to her meager height was to be embraced, and today's high-crowned Imperial bonnet answered. Of dove-gray satin embellished with ivory-colored French trim, three rows of ribbon each tied in an enormous flat bow, one atop the other. Its ribbons were wide and exceedingly long, fluttering all the way down to her knees, and edged with the same ivory; the entire confection was lined with an unexpected splash of violet.

Eschewing a reticule, she clutched a miser purse in her right hand.

She would begin as she intended to go on.

There was residual cheer in the corridor from Felicity's wedding, which she had been barred from attending. By contrast, there was an atmosphere of aggression in the antechamber in which her second round of vows were to be made, and it had all the hallmarks that often preceded Castleton's giving way to his beast. She stiffened her spine and stood as still as a held breath in the doorway until the tension dissipated. Georgie—she vowed to call him Georgie from now on; he deserved nothing less—looked at her with regret.

That would not do.

She began her curtsy, as fluid as water off a duck's back—

"No, ma'am, I forbid it." Georgie tugged on the hem of his riotously embroidered waistcoat. He had dressed with more ceremony than the bride. "By royal decree, the Duchess of Osborn is not to show such obeisance to any." He offered her his arm, which she could not refuse, and walked her the three steps to the groom's side. Standing next to Osborn was like standing beside a cliff face or a venerable oak. Was he as great in age as Castleton had been? He looked to be no more than thirty, but one could not tell with those of his kind. Would he remain youthful and imposing even as she aged and withered?

The prelate had taken his place and opened his little book, the prince looked at her beneath lowered lids, and the duke stared straight ahead. In addition to the famous Lord Brody, Lowell's steward, an eccentrically dressed person stood at her back. Something about his placement gave her a frisson of unease she smothered. "Do carry on," she prompted. There was no profit in drawing this out.

"Yes, Cornelius, do," Georgie said. And Cornelius did.

The ceremony did not earn the name; it was a transaction much as she used to have with the butler and cook in her childhood home. Near the end of the ordeal, His Highness handed a ring to the duke, who scowled at the prince and looked to rebel, but quickly gave in and slid it onto her finger. She received it with surprise, not having expected such a tribute. A golden stone set in silver glowed brightly; how it did so when there was no window to shed light upon it she did not know.

And then it was done.

"Alfred nearly bussed his new duchess in front of Cornelius," Georgie remarked, his playful salaciousness reasserting itself after having successfully seen to the ruination of the lives of two of his subjects.

The duke looked at Beatrice, and she turned away, pulling on her gloves. Bates bowed, as did the strange person; now that she got a good look at him, it was clear he was one of the animal-people. He scowled at all assembled and left without a word.

"As promised, here is Mr. Todd," the prince said, a small, gingery person at his side, yet another creature if his canny, bright gaze was anything to go by. He was little over a head taller than she, and the best term she could furnish to describe him was "pointy." Georgie went on: "You will be pleased to know he is at your disposal and well able for whatever he is called upon to do."

Beatrice nodded and accepted the aid of the footman who had taken charge of her pelisse. She buttoned its frogs and hoped the sharp eyes of those in attendance would not see her fingers tremble.

Georgie took his leave of them in a great rush of words and footmen and tailoring. She accepted the duke's elbow, duly offered, and called upon every year, every day, every hour of her hard-won composure as they followed Mr. Todd through Carlton House.

It was done. She was married again.

To a wild creature, again.

———————

Unlike Lowell, who no doubt departed with pomp out the North Front Gate and onto Pall Mall, Arthur and his bride were escorted to a nondescript portal and into a side yard.

"Why are you at my, er, our disposal, Todd?" Arthur inquired.

He received a small smile that betrayed sharp little teeth. "I am a general factotum and well able to supply any aid required," he said, without truly answering, and led them to a large carriage. Six heavy horses stood in the traces in front of a traveling chariot of unusual size, a nod to Arthur's comfort and the lady's by extension.

"Mr. Todd, I do not recognize the escutcheon," Lady Castleton—Her Grace—said.

"I leave that to your husband to relate," he murmured as a footman let down the steps.

"What's this, now?" Arthur pulled back the door and nearly tore it from its hinges. "Remove it," he growled at the sly creature.

"I cannot be seen to deface the property of the peerage." Bloody foxes. Always had a slippery way with a phrase.

"Are you not our factotum, Mr. Todd?" the duchess—would he truly call her "the duchess"?—inquired. Regardless of what Arthur called her, she was Lady Frost through and through. "Is His Grace's order not to be obeyed?"

"I walk a fine line," Todd replied, deferential. "As we are still on royal ground, I fear my fealty is spoken for, Madam." He smiled in apology, hazel eyes glittering, and joined the baggage carts that Arthur assumed, in his general factotum-ness, Todd had organized.

Madam. Hmm.

A footman handed her into the vehicle, and she settled on the bench facing the horses, as was only correct. Arthur sighed and heaved his great bulk into what had been a spacious interior until he put himself into it. There was nowhere to set his feet but to each side of—of Madam, a posture implying an intimacy they did not enjoy.

Nor would ever enjoy. How did one go about proposing a white marriage so soon after the legal fact? Small wonder the humans employed solicitors to negotiate contracts and such in advance of the ceremonies. Although…he recalled the Countess of Liverford had taken out notices in the broadsheets declaring her agreements null and void after ten years of marriage and due to the earl's profligacy and suspected pox. She had retired to the Continent in high spirits and with full pockets, a cicisbeo on each arm.

That juicy scrap of gossip did not elevate his spirits as it ought. Would Arthur live out his days in company with a stranger? He suspected there was a marked contrast between the chosen solitude of his last several decades and the purposeful evasion of another who lived in close proximity. It did not bode well for a comfortable existence.

He hoped Arcadia's wood had not been razed. He would take it for his sanctuary.

Hiding place, scoffed his bear.

Ah, it's you, is it? His bear had been oddly quiet throughout the morning. *Done with your brown study?*

The bear ignored his query. *Why has she no scent?*

Arthur's nostrils flared. Nothing. *She is not our mate; there is nothing to scent.*

There is nothing to scent, and thus we do not know if she is our mate. With that, his bear retreated once more.

"Thus," was it? Arthur sniffed again. It was odd, now that he was alerted to it. From flowers in a hedgerow to clothes in a press, everything had a fragrance signature, and Madam had none, or at least nothing that betrayed her true essence. He remembered Ben's being astringent and healthful and Charlotte's heavily influenced by sealing wax and ink.

Madam's clothes smelled of lavender, likely due to the sachets ladies used in their wardrobes, but there was nothing he found common with a human of her age and station, nothing that spoke to pursuits with paints or embroidery (yes, even thread had a signature), nothing of a lapdog or a house cat or a—

"You may have ridden if you wished." The coach turned out of the city gate and headed south.

Madam opened the slats covering one of the windows and fixed her gaze outward as they tooled past the first instance of pastoral terrain to be found so close to Town. "Horseback does not appeal," she said, every sinew of her body conveying dismissiveness.

"Ladies of your station are known to be avid equestriennes."

She glanced at him the way she might at a cushion. "There is no love lost between myself and such beasts."

"All" beasts, implied. He experienced reluctant admiration for her gift in making statements imbued with layers of meaning. Whereas he—

"I prefer plain speaking, Madam." Yes, *Madam* would do very well.

"Shall we speak plainly?" Her cool tone dared him to do so; her composure was combative, in the same way her curtsy to Georgie was the height of defiance. In contrast to this fierce control, she was so small and so delicately blond she looked like a confection, like a little cake. A confection soberly iced, it was true, and full of salt, it had to be said, but her severe traveling costume only served to set off her youthful looks—

What age was she? When had she wed that mephitic wolf? Had she done so directly after she came out, she could not be more than two and twenty. He discerned from her presence and dress at that infernal ball she was no longer in mourning. Had she mourned Castleton? Thoughts of her come-out led to those of the sister Georgie had promised to destroy. Had she other siblings?

"I am one of only two," he said.

"Two?" The eyebrow facing him arched like a swallow on the wing.

"I have one. Sibling." She turned and blinked at him once. The judgment rendered in that gesture! It was her version of claws or a swat with a paw. She was a salty little cake with claws. His bear threw off his sulk to howl with laughter. "I was merely... We know nothing about one another. I thought to myself, has Mada—have you any siblings."

"I am the middle child of nine."

"Brothers? Or sisters?"

"Four elder boys, myself, three more boys, and the youngest, my sister."

"The one about to make her debut." Arthur was pleased to demonstrate he remembered that.

Madam was not pleased to hear it. "The one Georgie threatened me with to secure my compliance, yes."

"Georgie?" He laughed. "When did he give you permission to make free with his childhood name?"

"I took it myself." Little clawed spitfire cake. "Do you know where we are going?"

"Yes." Two could play this game. He did not elaborate. She blinked again and resumed her avid attention to the passing scenery. His bear rolled about with glee, presumably at Madam's audacity. Whose side was he on? "Arcadia is in the Borough of Waverley," Arthur said, his voice launching into the enclosed space like a cannonball.

"That is near to Lowell Hall." Madam betrayed herself by tightening her hand on her tiny purse.

"Are you acquainted with the duke?" His bear sat up, suspicious.

"I am acquainted with the duchess," she corrected. "I count her as a friend, such as one may be on the fringes of society." She looked down at her lap. "They are a love match."

"My younger brother married for love."

"How unusual." Madam's tone betrayed an utter lack of curiosity.

"Indeed," Arthur agreed, unwilling to surrender. "They were promised from the cradle as children often are, but it transpired they were fated mates."

"Such as your kind are."

"As we can be. As humans can be." He wasn't entirely sure about that last.

"Barring the claws and teeth."

"I would not dispute that so readily, my lady." Arthur sat forward with relish. "Surely you have heard the *on-dits* regarding Viscount Wallace and his lady? She has taken to wearing unfashionably high-necked gowns to hide his love bites—"

"I do not care for tittle-tattle, Your Grace." Her tone called to mind moors in the depths of December.

Arthur sat back, daunted at last. "It is fortunate then you will not meet your sister-in-law, for she sups of scandal broth the very moment it has been spooned out." He took a page from her book and looked out the opposite window.

Why would they not meet? Beatrice wondered. Was he ashamed of her? He would not be the first of her husbands to feel so, despite this new specimen being as far from the previous as it was possible to be. Castleton had been wiry and graying and slightly stooped; by contrast the duke exuded rude good health. His robust form was as diffidently adorned as the night they met, and yet even the least tutored eye would discern the faultless quality of his attire. Nor could she cast aspersions on his grooming; his hair betrayed profound attention paid to it. It was thick and carefully coiffed with pomade, likely the source of the scent of bitter orange pervading the carriage. It rivaled the tresses of any debutante who had been told it was her finest feature.

She was conscious of his legs bracketing her skirts, aware that his posture made her heart flutter. She knew better than to give in to that fluttering as she knew his kind could detect it, marking her as prey. The deep breathing she undertook to slow its pace only served to draw the delicious citrus scent deeper into her lungs, causing havoc in her petticoats, which was not acceptable. Or expected. The very notion she would find this stranger pleasing in any way was surely the first step on the road to misfortune.

Beatrice turned her attention to his hands, an even graver error. Her brothers cultivated themselves as Pinks of the ton, and their hands exhibited their utter unfamiliarity with work of any kind. The same could not be said of the duke's, although what he turned them to she could not fathom.

Would she address him as "Duke"? "His Grace"? "Osborn"? She knew one thing she could not name him. "*Vera amoris,*" she murmured.

"Who, now? Oh, my brother." The duke flexed a thigh so powerfully it rustled her skirt. "You know our ways." He flexed his other thigh; both were the approximate size of a tree in its middle years. "How was it that you came to Castleton's attention?" he asked.

"Myself specifically or a human in general?" She played with the ring beneath her glove. "I imagine my father and he were known to one another, as men of our class can be. After Lady Phoebe… departed on her travels, my father offered me in her place."

"Had he not thought to discover why the lady…departed on her travels?" His tone was gentle but incredulous. "Castleton was widely known to be unstable at best."

"Indeed? Who amongst your kind would have thought to inform my father without explaining who Castleton was, in essence?" She had stopped asking herself this years ago. "It would have made no odds. The bride price was high and Castleton able to pay it."

"And your marriage, what was its duration?" Both thighs flexed. Honestly, there was no call for it.

"Near to five years." Given his professed love of gossip, she was shocked he did not know this.

"And you were not blessed with offspring."

"I was not." Her flat tone did not reflect the familiar tightening in her chest.

The duke's oversized arms crossed over his massive chest. "One does wonder was he able."

"One does wonder you dare allude to such." What an uncouth observation. Out of the corner of her eye, she watched him think, his jaw tensing and relaxing, his brows drawing together and apart. Was he conversing with himself? Or was he consulting with his creature? He then exclaimed: "We will, of course, undertake a white marriage."

"Naturally, Your Grace." She infused as much frost as she was able into her reply.

Naturally. For she was an unnatural female, barren and of no use. Particularly to a creature that presumably expected great swathes of offspring, like the animals they were.

Very well. She would be a figurehead rather than a failed broodmare. She would take on the mantle of duchess and use her position to help her sister find a true love of her own. She would live in Town during the season and retreat to the country for the rest of the year. It was an arrangement many had made before her and many would make after. She would not expect any differently. She was not unique.

She was not special.

⸻

Arthur's bear growled at his ham-handedness. That was not the most propitiously timed demand, on the heels of his poorly worded reflection on Castleton's ability to bring forth young. For that lack could be laid entirely at his door. He did not know if Madam had sought a child of that creature or if any offspring was better than none. He had no way of knowing and certainly no skill in divining the truth. Had Madam any female companionship? A confidante at least? Freya only knew what class of society was to be found wherever Castleton's lands lay. Was it Yorkshire or even further north—

"Northumberland, was it?"

"Castleton's holding?" She navigated his conversational shoals with aplomb. "Adolphus Place is in North Sunderland and quite remote. We did not enjoy acquaintance with anyone of any species, and the servants were all of your kind."

"He had no pack? No Beta, no Gamma?"

"I do not understand these terms."

"*Versipellis*," and it was the first time Arthur used the term plainly, "require a hierarchy to survive and thrive. Castleton, as an Alpha, ought to have had a Beta, or Second, and a Gamma, or Third. These would allow him the vital work of holding his pack together, to reserve his strength for necessities of protection. A Beta is charged with being the Alpha's go-between in matters of pack business, and a Gamma is in charge of the direct grievances of the rest."

"There were no such things." Madam gave him her full attention. "Where does one find such people, the Beta and the Gamma?"

"Often from within the foundation family. Unlike humans, a spare is not a total loss as a creature. He often takes on the role of Second." If only his father had had a brother. If only the bears of his father's time had reproduced more prolifically.

"And if the second child was a daughter?"

"It is not a role for females."

"Is it not, Your Grace?" Madam took this less calmly than the "white marriage" remark. Her little hands clenched. "And yet Lowell has a woman who is quite close to hand—"

"Lowell is not the pattern card for Shifter behavior." Bloody wolf!

"Is he not? A pity. Although I suspected it was not the general way of your kind."

"Our kind?"

"Wolves."

We are not a wolf! his bear screeched like a fishwife. *Does she think all* versipelles *are wolves? Tell her I am no canine!*

I will tell her what I deem fit. "I see Castleton did not attend to your education."

"Oh, I learned," she said, the words bitter. Arthur found he did not like to see her plush, pink little mouth misshapen by resentment. "As dearly as the marquess sought to prevent it, I learned."

How had she discovered the secret? Arthur doubted she had been enlightened in a calm, pleasant manner. "Allow me, then. *Versipellian* hierarchy is not unlike that of human society, in that the strongest creatures are found at the apex and their charge is to devote themselves to the care and comfort of the majority."

"That is as unlike human society as I can imagine, Duke."

"Duke"? His bear snorted; it was somewhat preferable to "Your Grace," but not by much. "I take your point, Madam," he conceded.

"Is it better to compare it to class, then?"

Arthur suspected it took quite a lot for her to evince interest. "It is, in that the highest are those who have much in material terms, but unlike upper human classes, *versipellian* leaders have no function, no purpose, without having any in their care." He leaned forward, elbows on his knees, and her heartbeat increased measurably. Madam sat up straighter, if it was possible, and focused her attention on the stray lock of hair that was wont to fall on his brow. He tucked it back, and her heartbeat stuttered. Hmmm. "A true Alpha is but the servant of the greater good."

Madam looked out the window. Arthur shook his head so the lock fell again, and she slowly but surely plastered herself against the back of the bench. She cleared her throat. "And who are your Beta and Gamma?"

"I have neither." Arthur sat back. "I have no clan."

"Whyever not?" She turned back to him, genuine interest on her face. "You speak with passion regarding the hierarchy and the responsibilities of the Alpha and do not preside over a clan?"

Arthur took it in turn to sit back. "Did Georgie put you up to this?"

"Up to what?"

"To this, this insistence I take my responsibilities?"

"He did not. Nor have I done any such thing. Is this not a conversation?"

"It is an interrogation." His bear muttered and scolded him. "I will speak no more on this topic."

"As you please." Madam turned her face from him, her profile so impassive as to have been carved like one of Gunter's ice sculptures set as a centerpiece on a buffet at a levee. She tilted her head in a gesture very like her sardonic curtsying to princes. "Shall we discuss our favorite meals? Or colors?" He huffed. "No? Another time, perhaps."

The rest of the drive was undertaken in silence. They stopped twice for refreshment; the sun began its descent in midafternoon, as it did at the time of year, and though the journey would end in a matter of moments, it would yet stretch before them for decades. *Versipelles* lived far longer than the average human; Madam would be released from this unwanted alliance well before Arthur shuffled off his mortal coil—ah, Hamlet—and then he…

Would be free. To return to his hibernation and his exile.

In less time than it took him to sink into a dolorous mood, the carriage turned between two ivy-covered pillars lacking a gate, and in an uncharacteristic fit of expression, Madam gasped.

Five

BEATRICE GRABBED A HANGING STRAP FOR PURCHASE. THE vehicle rocked side to side as it negotiated the uneven surface of the drive, which needed not so much a raking as it did utter reconstruction. The coachman slowed to a crawl in deference to the horses as he guided them around one gaping hole after the next. What might once have been a grand avenue of oaks was uncared for, overgrown and untamed, with years of fallen leaves gone to mulch at their roots. The way to the manor was circuitous, like something out of a myth, the final obstacle the hero must traverse to achieve his triumph.

There was no triumph to be claimed. As the house came into view, she saw that the shrubbery flanking the terrace betrayed a lack of care, as did the stones of the terrace itself, as did the crumbling masonry of the building, as did the shattered windows on the first and second floors… It was three stories of desolation, topped by attics that surely suffered from the woeful state of the slates on the deteriorating roof. The hedgerows had lost shape, the lawn was a disgrace, and there were no tidy rows of servants lined up to greet them upon their arrival.

Beatrice took it in, as the coachman sang the horses down to a halt, as an outrider opened the door, lowered the steps, and handed her down, as she shook out her skirts and waited for the vast breadth of duke to join her.

She took it in, every brittle brick, every weed and bramble, every shattered pane, the general pall of disrepair and disregard, and contrary to reason, jubilation flooded her being.

Madam was seething, Arthur could tell. She stiffened as she looked the place over, taking in its decrepitude and disuse, spine rigid, bosom swelling, hand clenching the silly purse she carried. Her face was impassive, and yet he was certain she was infuriated.

He'd love to see her lose her composure, see that icy mien dissolve in fierce rage. He imagined her behind closed doors succumbing to true feeling, the rime of her public persona melting. Would she be as fiery in private as she was frosty in public? Why in the world were his thoughts trotting down this road? It must be the fault of his bear.

He got a grumble for his pains, the beast continuing his sulk.

Arthur gestured to the porch, and Madam processed up the shallow steps, happily finding the safest places to set her feet. Her tiny feet; they must be miniature if the rest of her was anything to go on, as delicate as her fingers were, and her button nose.

Arthur raised a hand to knock and saw the flinch, so minute and yet there. By the Gods, could he resurrect that poxed wolf he would, and see Castleton sent straight back to Helheim. Or whatever constituted the lupine infernal place. He opened his palm to bash against the door.

Moments passed as they waited for a response. The weather, which had become more threatening the farther they journeyed from Town, looked to be turning nasty as gray clouds rolled in from the west. Arthur banged on the door again and then tried the doorknob. His heightened hearing discerned a slow shuffle as he was about to put his shoulder to the bloody thing and render it into kindling.

A key turned in the lock, a laborious undertaking of scraping and tugging. The knob turned slowly, ominously, like the work of a specter in one of Mrs. Anchoretta Asquith's Gothic novels. A huff and groan put paid to that theory as the door creaked open to reveal a small man dressed in butler's livery dating from the seventeenth century. Worn velvet pantaloons were tucked haphazardly into felt knee boots; the man's waistcoat looked to have only ten of its required thirty buttons, and his ornate frock coat was threadbare. He was of a height with the duchess thanks to his profound stoop; a well-furrowed face beamed from beneath a decrepit wig.

"Master Artie!" The butler's face collapsed into even more wrinkles. "As I live and breathe!"

"It is a miracle you do so, Conlon," Arthur said. "You were ancient when Odin was a lad." He looked down at the duchess, astounded, as she had poked him inelegantly in the side.

"And is this…" Conlon's voice wobbled with emotion. "Oh my days, is this our new duchess? Your Grace," he intoned and started to bow, an undertaking that would likely take an hour or more.

"Please, Mr. Conlon, do not." Madam stepped forward, a warm look in her eye if not a smile on her face. Arthur consulted the heavens to see if a drove of pigs soared overhead. "I suspect you suffer from your joints, and I desire you not to exert yourself."

"It is the lumbago, ma'am," Conlon admitted.

"A tiresome affliction at this chill time of year," she soothed even as she maneuvered him into the foyer.

Which was currently employed as a manufactory for spider-webs. Madam cast her eye around, and Arthur anticipated a tirade. Instead, she patted the butler on his arm. "Conlon, I suspect we have caught you and the household by surprise," she said, her voice as gentle as the rain that now pattered on the windows. "We have a variety of cases and trunks the royal footmen will carry in if you would direct them to the ducal suite." Todd slipped in the door and hovered at her side.

"There's no ducal suite no more." A figure loomed in the dark of the corridor, her voice as raspy as the lock on the front door. "Ain't been no need in Arcadia for many a year."

"Is that any way to greet our new duchess, Morag?" Conlon's

neck tucked in and out of his collar in agitation as the woman, red-faced and black-haired, moved into the light.

"Freya help us. Morag?" Arthur exclaimed. "Have we a single servant under the age of one thousand in this household?"

"Your Grace." Madam turned to him. "It is a testament to the loyalty of this house's retainers that they continue in service, given they had none present to tend." She turned her back on him entirely, the little clawed spitfire cake of a minx that she was, a choice not lost on Conlon or Morag; both looked thrilled at her bravery. "Have I the pleasure of addressing the housekeeper of Arcadia? Due to His Highness's deep desire that we wed without delay, I doubt you were given sufficient warning of our arrival."

"I am the keeper of the house such as it is, Your Grace, such as it is a house and not a home." The most cursory of curtsies accompanied this reply.

"Another plain speaker. I comprehend it is the custom of this pack." No one dared reprove her incorrect application of the term. "Is the ducal suite habitable, or is it not?"

The housekeeper glared in Arthur's general direction. "It is not, ma'am, not since—"

"That will do, Morag," he interrupted. "Help Conlon and Todd see to our things."

"I pray you will avoid the stairs, Mr. Conlon," Madam said. "May I trouble you to ask Cook to lay on some tea?" The wee man beamed and creaked off down the corridor. Madam turned to the housekeeper. "Morag, this is Mr. Todd, royal factotum at our disposal. Please convene with him over the best placement of our things at this time."

She then cleared her throat. "If I may have a word, Your Grace."

Arthur preceded her to the door of a receiving room, which was not pulled shut as it was leaning against the wall of the corridor. The room itself was clear of dust as well as vacant of furnishings of any kind but for a lone footstool.

"Beginning as you intend to go on, Madam?" Arthur asked as she ran a finger over the mantelpiece. She offered no reaction to the state of her fingertip. "Coddling the help?"

"It is not coddling but respect for another human being. Or, or creature." Madam removed her gloves and her pelisse and held them in front of her like a shield. "He is rather small for a wolf."

Not a wolf! his bear howled. "Our sort come in many shapes and sizes."

"I presume this is the Osborn homeplace?"

"It holds that distinction."

"It appears to have been uninhabited for many years."

"You are the picture of perceptivity."

She opened her mouth to inquire further but seemed to think better of it. Pain or sadness moved across her features until they resumed their customary immobility.

That could not be right. What care had she for the state of this place and that it had no one to live in it? He didn't care, and it was his family home. Arthur turned away from the bright-blue gaze that seemed to peer straight into his soul. He kicked the footstool and scratched at the shredded silk covering a wall.

He heard her take a breath, pause, and then say: "I believe a cup of tea is required before another step is taken."

"I shall leave you to it, then. The kitchen is to the left, down a short hall, and then to the left again, if you condescend to take your refreshment there." Arthur bowed her out of the room as well as any royal footman and watched as she disappeared down the gloomy corridor.

He glared as a spider spun itself down into his line of sight and stopped himself swatting it away; it had a greater right to be within these walls than he.

He turned his attention to the shadows lurking at the first landing.

There was nothing for it, then.

The staircase leading up to the first floor seemed sound enough until Arthur put his foot through the second-to-last tread.

The runner in the corridor looked to be composed more of dust than yarn, and its edges bore the marks of mice of the *animali puri* variety. That they would dare enter the house of a Shifter was testament to the lack of predatory beasts under its roof.

More spiderwebs, dense as moss, hung from paintings listing on the walls, with several lying facedown on the floor.

The first door he attempted required the full force of his weight to breach. It was the family drawing room; he did not enter. He eschewed investigating the staterooms as well.

Each of the remaining portals on the first floor had an idiosyncrasy regarding their opening; in many cases there were no doors at all. He quailed to think Conlon and Morag had been reduced to using them for kindling. The interior of each room was a devastation of gouged walls and demolished furniture. The work of Hallbjorn, for who else would have wreaked such havoc? His bear remained mute, but not from spite, not now.

He did not ascend to the second floor to investigate the nursery that lay across the corridor from the ducal suite, nor those august rooms themselves, nor the portrait gallery that ran along the entire back of the house. He would put that off as long as he was able, as he would the third floor, which played host to the servants' quarters and—Holy Freya, the attics! If the exterior view was anything to go by, the attics were in a disastrous state, and if that proved to be the case... He poked at a warped bump of wallpaper, and his finger went straight through it to the plaster. Upon closer inspection, the walls buckled like the ripples in a pond. He could not bring himself to look at the ceiling.

Was the entire household to live on the ground floor like a trace of rabbits? He did not dwell on what those left behind had faced over the years. He clutched a hand to his chest where he felt a twinge. It was likely the kippers repeating on him. That was what it must be, this broken feeling in his chest.

Oh, yes, his bear said, sarcastic. *No more kippers for breakfast.*

———

"…and the breakfast room is over on the other side of the hall, made sense to someone back in old Elizabeth's day but it makes none now." Morag finished her discourse on the failings and deficiencies to be found in the halls of Arcadia with some relish.

While the ground floor of the manor was fairly respectable, what little Beatrice had seen could do with improvement. The reception room in which she had taken the duke to task was not designated as such, primarily due to the fact there was no one to receive. Was its purpose to contain a single footstool? Or merely to provide the cluster of spiders free rein to weave their webs?

Upon repairing to the kitchen, she was introduced to Mrs. Porter, the cook, bullish in aspect yet content in demeanor, and two housemaids. Ciara and Glynis were both small, dark, and if not elderly then at the very best aging. They tilted their heads at her, showing their necks, a custom she knew demonstrated respect by creatures of their kind. It was done now, however, with greater reverence than had any in Adolphus Place.

The maids painstakingly set the table for tea. Beatrice had assured them that there was no need to stir up another fire elsewhere, that there was nothing like a kitchen for homeyness. There was no other room fit to sit in anyway.

Beatrice took a sip of the brew Mr. Conlon laboriously poured out. She selected a slice of shortcake and reveled in its light and buttery texture. "This is delicious, Mrs. Porter."

"That'd be Ciara's doing," said the cook. "She's a dab hand with the baking."

"Well done, Ciara. I am not apprised of His Grace's opinion, but baked treats are my weakness."

The butler waxed lyrical on Master Artie's sweet tooth as Beatrice made inroads into the shortcake. He cut himself off as she reached for the teapot and served her once more.

"Thank you, Mr. Conlon." She brushed her fingertips on the scrupulously clean serviette. "I am impressed beyond measure by the care you have taken of this house. I see there is much left to do to bring it up to scratch. What of the lands? Is there a steward or chamberlain in His Grace's employ?"

"No need for either since there's no one to live in the cottages or tend the fields," Morag said.

"There is a need now, at the very least to restore Arcadia to its true stature," Beatrice said. "I shall call upon Mr. Todd, then, to take stock of the park and the surroundings."

"Some use he'll be, raiding the hen house." The housekeeper smirked.

"Hush, Morag," Mr. Conlon scolded. "You know the law."

"The law?" Beatrice's query was met with expressions showing a mixture of trepidation and appraisal. The women turned to the butler, who undertook the responsibility of explaining.

"I take it you are aware of our difference to you?" His voice was gentle, and she nodded.

"Among ourselves, we know who is who—" Glynis began.

"—and what is what," Ciara finished. "But even then we would not be so rude as to ask."

"We're not to tell a human but our species, except under special circumstances," Mrs. Porter added.

"Like as when a *homo plenus* marries one of us," Morag said. "I'd call that special, I would."

Beatrice looked at each. "Are you not wolves?"

The staff gasped as one. "Wolves!" Mr. Conlon's sleepy eyes widened. "Good lady, no. We are as many as there are *animali puri*."

"That's the common or garden sort of creature," Morag

explained. "You may discern a *versipellis*'s true nature from certain characteristics, and you may speculate, but private-like."

"Indeed. I do be passing slow, for example. My sort are." The butler's head retracted in and out of his shoulders. "For I am a turtle!" His little face crinkled with glee, and he clapped his tiny wrinkled hands.

"Ah!" Beatrice experienced delight for the first time in many days. "I vow to honor and respect this knowledge, Mr. Conlon."

"Wolves!" Morag exclaimed. "I am a moorhen, ma'am." She puffed out her impressive chest.

Mrs. Porter proved to be a cow and the maids, mice.

"This is unexpected." Beatrice took in the open faces before her. "All in Adolphus Place were wolves, from the marquess to the boot boy."

"That is a very old-fashioned way of going about things," Mr. Conlon said. "As the years have passed, many the like of us turtles and hens and pigs and mice have pledged our loyalty to a mightier species, and we are the safer for it."

What then was the duke that he should reign as Alpha? She would not reveal her ignorance of his creature.

How embarrassing he had not deigned to tell her.

How frightening he may be more dangerous than a wolf.

Morag snorted, an unlikely sound to emit from a hen. "We'll see to your education, ma'am, as it appears your husband has not. Not a surprise as he is loath to do what's expected of him."

"Morag, I do appreciate a dash of salt, but only when doled out with respect." The hen was testing to see how far she may push; Beatrice determined it was exactly this far. "I do hope my meaning is clear."

Against the odds, the housekeeper looked pleased to be put in her place. "Fair enough, ma'am, fair enough."

"Now." Beatrice accepted a serving of fresh biscuits frosted with lemony icing. "Have I anywhere to sleep this night?"

Some time later, Arthur found the kitchen empty, the remains of a plate of lemony biscuits among the detritus of tea things. Shameless, he licked a finger to clean up the crumbs. Hustle and bustle down the hall led him to what had once been the stillroom.

It was a hive of activity. Two royal postillions, unaccustomed to work inside the house, struggled with a table that Arthur could carry with one hand. Another followed with an upholstered chair, yet another with a jug and bowl. Todd brought up the rear carrying a small case.

"What goes on, Todd?" he demanded as the footmen swept past in a tottering phalanx.

"We are appointing the temporary ducal suite, Your Grace." The fox preceded him over the threshold.

He could say with confidence he had never set foot in this room as a child. It had been Ben's domain, and his brother considered Arthur little better than a bull in a china shop and banned him from the place. A wall of all-but-empty glass-fronted cases ranged down one side of the room, and a large hearth took up the other. It was not spacious and was rapidly becoming less so as another pair of royal footmen muscled in a variety of trunks. Conlon struggled to set a dressing screen in place, refusing the aid of the hovering Todd, while Morag shoved a table next to the hearth crossways and appeared satisfied with its placement.

"What is all this?" Arthur demanded. As if he didn't know.

"What is required in a sleeping chamber, Duke," Madam said. "It is the largest room and the only one unused for habitation. Thanks to the unflagging industry of your staff, it is clean and ready for our installment but for the—ah, thank you, over here, if you will." Madam directed the placement of the bed near to the window.

The bed.

There was only one bed.

The duke had taken one look at the room, at the bed, and fled.

Morag had snarled, while Mr. Conlon made excuses for His Grace's essential self likely needing release.

Morag mumbled something off-color, and Beatrice directed the rest of the room's arrangement to her liking until she was left alone to assess her surroundings. The chair set by the window looked as well as she'd envisioned. A footman had wrestled the sash open at her direction; how pleasant to have a footman at her direction. How thrilling to have a say in where the overstuffed Chesterfield library chair would be put, a mismatched ottoman for her feet. She chose to be gratified she was left alone and not required to bed down with a stranger, no matter he was her husband now.

A nightingale warbled, perched on the lowest branch of a nearby tree. She had not heard a night bird's song in years. Had Castleton's presence frightened the natural wildlife? Would Osborn's clear the lands of smaller creatures? Or what if...

"I don't suppose that is you, Duke?" Imagine such a large male becoming such a small thing. And that a miscellany of creatures should follow the lead of a songbird. "Forgive me, I know I am not meant to ask. Would you whisper a word in the ear of His Grace and tell him that not knowing the species of his creature is worse than knowing?"

She pulled the collar of her dressing gown tight around her throat and curled her legs beneath her. "Shall I tell you how I came to be in possession of this dreadful secret? It was a scene taken from the pages of a novel by Mrs. Anchoretta Asquith. A young bride, an isolated, moldering keep, the night of a full moon."

The bird chirped and flew to settle on the sill. A stirring in the underbrush near her window put her on guard. Perhaps His Grace was eavesdropping. What use his hearing this story was she did not know, but: "I had not received a marital visitation for the third night in a row. Not that I sought it out, not that I wanted that husband, but how I longed for a child. I was so timid, little bird, so innocent when I tapped upon his door. I heard him mumbling wildly, and if only I had turned away… I opened the door at the precise moment that he gave over his humanity to the creature. He was a man, a titled man, a marquess, and then he was…a wolf, a slavering, snarling wolf. He leaped for me, but his valet stopped him, his valet who was also a wolf."

She did not remember shutting the door, only the sound of two animal bodies throwing themselves against it, one to keep it shut, one to pursue her. She was so shocked she didn't even run but exited through the connecting room as cautiously as she had entered it and locked her bedchamber door behind her. She had the foresight to lock the one that gave onto the hall and shut her windows; she got under the covers and stared at the ceiling as she began to shake, uncontrollably, until dawn.

The bird tweeted a descant as though inquiring after the rest. "The next day, my sweet friend, the marquess did not even explain himself but rather threatened me via his valet and the housekeeper. Both were matter-of-fact about the consequences, called attention to my parents and siblings and suggested I keep my peace.

"To be fair, there was no one to tell, no one to believe me until Castleton died without issue and the servants fled after he was taken away for whatever obsequies his kind adhere to. No one to tell at all, until His Royal Highness the prince regent informed me that the title had gone into escheat and of the pittance that would comprise my widow's mite." She smiled, bitter, sour. "And then, suddenly, I had someone to tell."

Beatrice rose. "And now I have told you. I don't know if it matters if you keep it to yourself. I shall leave it to your discretion." The sash window moved smoothly and stayed open the few inches Beatrice deemed healthful for a good night's sleep; by contrast, the interior shutters did not budge, and drawing the curtains proved an arduous business. She smiled as the bird peeped what she chose to believe was its good night.

She did not see the nightingale hop from the windowsill, narrowly escaping the attacking claw that sought its doom.

Six

BEATRICE ROSE WITH THE LARK AS SHE HAD DONE EVERY DAY of her life. Pulling on her robe and sliding her feet into slippers, she tugged open the curtain hanging at the window. Due to their late arrival, she had not had the opportunity to take in the grounds behind the house. The back was in a state of wildness similar to the forecourt; there were none of the Italianate flourishes currently in fashion, no paths upon which to stroll between carefully cultivated box hedges and espaliered trees—nothing but a hill running down to a wood that loomed behind several rows of overgrown shrubs that may once have been topiary. She was aware the animal-people required wild places in which to exert themselves, but this outdid even Castleton's acreage.

Wild and untamed as it was, its chaotic nature appealed to her. Beatrice had gone to a variety of outdoor functions the *ton* laid on the moment a gleam of sunshine appeared in the sky and found their outdoor spaces to be as polished and remote as their ball-rooms and parlors. Like many who called themselves civilized, she often overlooked that she had been born and reared in the countryside; seeing the rolling lawn and the deep forest called her youth to mind. Her brothers relished being out of doors, and they had been the better for it after a day of running wild, splashing in the brook, climbing every tree in creation. The one near the still-room window was massive, likely an oak, its branches spread in what she fancied was a protective manner. She would look forward to it coming into bud.

What would she wear on her first day as mistress of Arcadia? She had more than one serviceable twill well able to stand up to a day's work taking inventory. Dressing without flair had become a habit as she had no acquaintance to call upon in North Sunderland and no need to impress anyone there. As difficult as—if nearly impossible—it was for a lady to dress herself, she managed; with no responsibilities and a loathing of helplessness, she had become her own lady's maid.

As well as chambermaid. It was not as if she'd never made a bed, accustomed to helping the nursery staff with their work. She shook out each layer of bedclothes and tucked the bottom sheet around the topmost mattress. This was filled with a high-quality flock while the lower two were filled with chaff. The linens were impeccably kept; she supposed the staff had little to occupy them but for the maintenance of simple things. The sheets had seen some use, but the seams held fast as she tested them. She pulled a woolen blanket flat and the large duvet on top of it. The pillow slips were, of course, the most worn as they had been fashioned as was customary out of sheets past their best use, but the weave of the fabric was very fine, and the softness was welcome. There was satisfaction to be gained from setting to rights what had been tumbled in sleep, even if it had only been herself. As ever.

Not that she'd entertained notions of a rousing marital life once she'd clapped eyes on Castleton at the altar in St. George's. It had taken every ounce of strength she could muster to stop herself from running hysterical from the church. She had been raised to do her duty—she had raised herself to do so, more like. In part, to prove she was not useless to her father, to show she would bring him honor when she went off to wed, and in equal part so she may have some feeling of worth in her own eyes. Little good it did her in the end, and the old frustration welled up. The last layer of bedclothes, a worn coverlet, almost tore beneath her hands.

Wallowing in the past would not do. No matter her unexpected desire to tell her sad history to the nightingale.

The bed was as crisp as when she'd made it herself the previous evening, to the false dismay of little Ciara. It would be a crime to consign her to the bedsheets and chamber pots as her skills truly lay in the kitchen. She would see about getting another maid in.

Or they would. Would it be "they"? Osborn could prove the same as Castleton in that regard, relegating her to idleness, but she was older now, she had survived much, and she would not live a useless life again. Beatrice stoked the fire until it roared to life up the chimney. The jug was a quarter full of water, an oversight on the part of the footman whose job it truly was not. She set it by the fire regardless; some warm water was better than none.

The furniture had been dropped in place after the duke made his dramatic exit. How lowering that he should do so in front of the household. With greater force than necessary, she dragged a side table across the room to sit next to the dressing table and set one of her small cases upon it. Laying out her brush and comb, her silver-backed mirror and her enameled case full of hairpins, it was as if she was a stranger to her own things. Whoever had been ordered to pack for her had done so with care, and everything on the dressing table in her rooms in Castleton's London townhouse had migrated to the Borough of Waverley. Her powder box and tin of rose lip salve were there, as was the lotion for her hands. The vial of oil she had been exhorted to use every day of her married life was near to empty. Beatrice breathed through a wave of distress as she pawed through the case to unearth the rest of her supply. There ought to have been at least three more... There were not.

Her trunk and valise received the same treatment until her belongings were scattered about the room in her panic; even her precious bonnets had been flung hither and yon. That oil had been a habit she found comfort in, a habit symbolic of hope, for the elixir was meant to increase her likelihood of falling pregnant.

As she was currently inhabiting the disused stillroom, there would be nowhere to make more. Nor was there any point in it as she had agreed to a white marriage—there was no need for the oil at all—but the force of habit was too strong; she decided to use what was left sparingly and dabbed a modest amount on her wrists and neck.

A scratch fell on the door, and Glynis shuffled in with a tray; a cup of tea wobbled upon it. "Now, ma'am, here's a nice cuppa to set you right this morning."

It was on the downward slope from tepid to cold, but who was heartless enough to scold the maid for it when she looked so pleased to serve? Not she. "Thank you, Glynis. How kind of you to tend to my rising."

The maid took in the wealth of clothing spread out over the bed, tumbled like scraps fit for the rag bag. Glynis had not made an impression last evening, keeping to the background, but at the sight of the shambles Beatrice had made of everything from her fine silk stockings, her whisper-thin chemises, and her dresses running the gamut of morning to evening, it was as though a steel rod had gone up her spine. "This is no way for the clothes of a duchess to be treated," the maid scolded as she marched over to the bed. "I'll look out a dresser or two to keep your lovely things nice." She sorted through the pile. "It's not your place to have to mind them."

"Do set them to rights, if you please." Beatrice did mean it to please the maid, and Glynis looked very happy indeed. The mouse crooned her admiration of every garment as she smoothed them out, folding what needed folding and shaking out what needed pressing. "And if you would find me an apron, I would be grateful."

It was shocking what comfort habit could bestow, silly that making a bed or organizing her vanity would settle her. Here she was, by order of the prince regent, married to a stranger in a house close to falling down around her ears, and she knew she was safer than she'd been in ages. She was a grown woman, forced into a situation not of her own making, but she would not be ground down again, erased, stifled.

"Was it the lady of the house who was proficient in the use of this room?" Beatrice perused the dusty jars of crumbling herbs lining one of the glass cases that ranged along the wall.

"No, ma'am, it was Lady Charlotte's mum. She was a member of the Alpha's, er, family—well, not *family* family, as the Alpha's son married her daughter, but yes, well. As such as lived with us." Glynis fumbled several bonnets.

"In the house?" The window was open, and the chill morning air not as pleasing as the cool air of the night. Beatrice drew aside the curtains, tugging when they snagged on the rod.

"Oh yes, ma'am, that's their way. The, er, lords and ladies of this place. They do tend to stay close. Well, the mums and childer, not the males. But now the males, too. Or they will."

Beatrice smiled over her shoulder at the flustered mouse. "Birds of a feather, then." She turned back to the view; there was movement on the grounds, a rustling behind the shrubs.

"Well, no, but yes, in a way. Eh." Glynis wilted under the questioning.

"And did Lady Charlotte live here as well…" Her voice trailed off as the rustling resolved itself into His Grace.

He rose from the weeds and the tangled growth like an Elgin marble come to life. She had made a point in her widowhood to partake in what she'd missed while immured in North Sunderland, and cultural touchstones such as the British Museum had played a part…but the duke was as far from a cold, remote statue as a man could be. His shoulders were akin to those of Atlas, broad enough to shoulder the earth; they made an extraordinary contrast to the fineness of his midriff. She reckoned more than one society miss would wish for such a tidy waist. Beatrice ran her eyes up his belly to his chest and the veritable pelt that lay upon it, a deep, rich brown of a color with his hair, and gazed upon the cut of the muscles beneath…

She'd never seen such a display in her life, statues in the museum notwithstanding. Statues in the museum did not stretch their arms over their heads, did not have arms that appeared able to wrench an oak from its very roots, did not have hands large as spades, with long, strong fingers to scratch over the flat expanse of belly, which flexed as the duke moved forward through the underbrush, closer and closer to exposing—

Beatrice dragged the curtains closed with such vigor they tore from the rope they were swagged upon and fell atop her in a bombardment of dust. Glynis squeaked and hurried over as Beatrice thrashed about beneath the oppressive fabric.

"Oh, ma'am, oh, ma'am," the maid fussed until Beatrice wrestled herself out of the heavy damask.

"I am well, Glynis." She gasped for air and allowed the maid to help her up to standing. "A bath would be welcome, but I suspect the work I have before me will only add to my dishevelment." She coughed as she brushed at her dressing gown. "Do choose what you think best for a day's investigation of the house, and I shall wipe away this grime."

If only she could wipe her mind clean of what she'd seen.

———

He'd handled that poorly, yesternight. He knew when he acted the churl. He wasn't entirely uncivilized.

Arthur sat in his shirtsleeves at table and yet knew better than to sit at table in his shirtsleeves. He knew better than to run out on a lady who was his wife even if she was never to be his *wife*. He had learned how to comport himself; somewhere in the mists of time, he had been schooled in beautiful manners.

Well, if not beautiful, they were at least polished. He could do the pretty with the best of them, but given his oath, which he would not foreswear, what was the point of acting the gentleman when it would lead nowhere?

His oath, which no one knew of but himself. And Ben. And Charlotte. Who would both attempt to talk him round it if they knew he was married, which they would never know. His heart pinched at that, and he pushed aside the kippers he'd vowed to abstain from. Mrs. Porter had laid on a breakfast suitable for a creature of his size, which was well and good, but Freya knew the females of the human species had not the sort of appetites he boasted, and they'd have to work out where they'd put Madam to take her meals.

Such details were the sort he would leave to his Second to organize, but he did not have one and never would. Speaking of never, there would be none of this taking her morning meal in bed like a Mayfair dowager. She would subscribe to their ways, rough and ready as they may be, and therefore—

"We shall break our fast in here going forward," he pronounced as he speared up another rasher of bacon directly from the platter.

"Not our new duchess!" Conlon dropped his serving forks in dismay.

"We've not the staff for to-ing and fro-ing between here and the morning room or whatever it's called." He knew very well it was called the morning room. He would not ask his aged staff to traverse the tangle of halls to get to said room, nor would he countenance cold food. Madam would like it or lump it.

"If she's that high in the instep she'll find it hard going indeed," he grumbled as the staff took to their feet upon Madam's entrance. She raised her brows at the sight of the rasher on his fork; he stuffed it into his mouth. Conlon pulled out her chair, and she sat with the decorum of a queen on her throne.

Arthur sat back and crossed his arms over his chest, for which he received a lingering gaze on his forearms. This was so unexpected he looked down to see what had caught her eye. It was not his coat, for he wore none; her gaze was likely a subtle dig at his disheveled state.

"I have always thought it a pity that more time was not spent around the chief hearth," Madam said as Ciara set a cup down at her place; she then thanked Conlon for the plate of toast and eggs he had, against expectation, dished up with speed. "Although we would not like to interfere with Mrs. Porter's domain."

"It's her domain under your sufferance," Morag began.

Arthur cut her off. "Mind your tongue, woman."

"Your Grace," said Madam, as she spread jam on her toast. There was a world of censure in the invocation of his title. The things the woman could do with her tone and an eyebrow. If he was being honest, it was quite intriguing. An unfamiliar shudder ran through his being, his bear stirring, perhaps.

"Madam?" He stabbed another rasher with his fork and watched her watch him take a bite, like a heathen.

"We shall address one another with respect, if you please." Morag made a face. "All of us, Morag."

"Fair enough, ma'am." The scaldy hen beamed. She always enjoyed being set down after having pushed her luck.

"I for one look forward to taking my meals here, with the appropriate manners exhibited by each and every one of us." Madam took a bite of her toast and hummed with pleasure.

Arthur set his skewered rasher down on his plate. "As I was only saying myself, Madam, it is for the best. I think only of your comfort."

"Do you?" She took a bite of eggs, and Arthur sensed he'd put his leg in a trap. "That is wonderful. For comfort is at the forefront of my mind this morning."

"Do tell." He braced himself for a litany of complaints.

"I am so impressed with the bedding." Oh dear, did Madam want to go down that route? Arthur leaned forward in his chair and folded his arms on the table. A wash of pink appeared at the very top of her cheeks, as delicate as the first blush of dawn as her gaze fell once more to his arms, but she soldiered on. "It is apparent that this house has been maintained with immaculate care." She took another sip of her tea, cool as a breeze, and yet her little finger trembled. Arthur reached out for the teapot and warmed up her brew. The urge to grin at her was almost too much to fight. He hadn't grinned in an age.

"I suggest we dine as a household as well," she said as she added a drop of cream to her cup.

Arthur scoffed. "There is a perfectly good dining room set aside for the evening meal."

"Set aside it is, on the other side of the hall." Morag held low opinions about the layout of the place and never failed to voice them.

"Of course, I have yet to familiarize myself with the house." Madam set her knife and fork down delicately. "I intend to do so, top to bottom, and suspect there is much to be seen to."

"A lick of cloth to master the cobwebs and it is done." The servants gaped at him in disbelief; Madam sailed on as if he had not spoken.

"Once I have gone through," she continued, "I will determine if revising the use and function of several rooms is in the best interest of the household. There is none to say nay."

"Is there not?" As deeply as he revered Shakespeare, teasing Madam was more diverting than watching a wire dancer traverse the Pit in Haymarket.

"I shall do everything in my power to return Arcadia to its former glory." A palpable thrill ran through Arthur's being at her words. "It is my duty. I am the lady of this house." Madam rose and swept out of the room.

Oh goodness, she had *swept* out of the kitchen. Swept, like a girl in a novel, a spirited debutante—who it had to be said often fell foul of the villain of the piece but was always rescued by the hero. She used to sweep out of the schoolroom to amuse Ellie and ruin it by running back in to tickle her to pieces. Beatrice wanted to giggle like the girl she had once been, who had confidence in the future.

That confidence had taken a knock, and bottomless coffers had not restored it, but now she might revive two birds with one fortune.

She continued to sweep down the hall with no notion of where she was headed until she saw the prince's factotum lurking in a doorway.

"Mr. Todd." He cricked his head, exposing his neck. "I have given thought as to how we may make use of your presence here." She had no idea where his talents lay, but he had a bright, clever look about him. "Let us begin by assessing the breadth of the duke's holdings."

"I believe this was the study of the former steward. I took a moment to acquaint myself with its contents." Mr. Todd gestured her in.

Yes, this was very much the study of a steward. The room was small, and bookcases lined the walls from floor to ceiling. The absence of dust proved it was well tended, but despite its spotlessness, there was an air of neglect to it.

Mr. Todd turned to a highboy composed of wide, shallow drawers and opened them one by one until he withdrew a sheet of paper. He laid it on the desk. It was a beautifully rendered plan of Arcadia, the situation of the house, the lands beyond, and the River Wey that ran to the north. Close to the main building were a kitchen garden, a rose walk, a stable yard, and a variety of outbuildings as well as a fair number of cottages; beyond those, a road with an arrow marked it as the way to Arcadia Demesne, which she supposed was the home village. At some distance behind the house was a circular clearing of some sort, with four paths radiating from it like the spokes of a wheel. It was not labeled.

Beatrice ran a finger round the circle of it. "What is this?"

Mr. Todd hesitated. "It is a gathering place for the…family. It has not been in use for some time."

"Does it require attention?" It certainly had hers, mere strokes of a pen though it may be.

"It does."

"Then it shall have it," she decided. "Well done, Mr. Todd. You have made short work in familiarizing yourself with this place. It is no surprise you came to His Highness's attention."

"I am one of many, ma'am," he demurred. "I did as I was bid and nothing more."

Did you? she thought. "I applaud your initiative and assume His Highness would agree with me." He crooked his head again, which she took as a signal he would not elaborate.

Onward, then. Beatrice pointed to the depictions of the small holdings. "Would these be the abodes of tenants?"

"I can say with confidence they would not be tenants as such but members of the..." He trailed off.

"Members of, Mr. Todd?" Beatrice pressed and then remembered the law.

"I do not have permission to use the proper term designating the Alpha species of this place, ma'am," he said. "But these would have been the homes of the members of the group who reside here."

"Will the use of clan suffice?" Mr. Todd nodded and shrugged and grimaced. "I shall refer to it as such until I learn otherwise. Now. As you may know, I have the disbursement of my own funds."

"Yes, ma'am." Mr. Todd nodded. "His Highness alluded to this fact."

Beatrice reached for the quill and ink on the desk along with the handy sheaf of foolscap. Dipping the pen in the ink, she dashed out a few lines, precise in their instruction. A decision made under duress was one in need of revision; she would nurture the potential she saw in Arcadia to its fullest, and that would require funds. "This is the direction of my man of business." She blew on the ink and folded the paper. "I require someone to act as an emissary between his offices in London and Arcadia. I would entrust this role to you."

"Thank you, ma'am." The man looked eager and gratified as he slipped the paper into his pocket.

"I have £10,000 a year." It was an impressive sum, especially to one accustomed to the depleted royal treasury—if Mr. Todd's expression was anything to go by. "I will authorize a steady flow to support the renovations we will require. Please begin with a thorough investigation of such domiciles as the Osborn clan inhabited and what repairs are necessary."

"Very good, ma'am." He replaced the map in the drawer and, if Beatrice was correct, looked around the study with longing before she led the way back into the corridor.

"I look forward to your report," Beatrice said. They left the steward's office, and there was the duke, standing in the hall, glaring at a painting. He had gone to the trouble of donning a coat yet had not undertaken the great effort required to button it.

He turned to her without changing his expression, and she wanted to smooth out the divot between his eyebrows and pinch him at the same time. "And how do you plan to do that, Madam?"

"To do what, Your Grace?"

"Restore this place to its former glory." He swept an arm; the painting fell off the wall, and he kicked it aside.

"With licks of cloth." Beatrice picked up the watercolor, which depicted a group of small beasts peering out of long grass. "By not leaving fallen things on the floor." She set the painting on a nearby table. "With water and soap and lemon oil. And paint and paper and hammer and nail."

"You cannot ask for such effort from my staff."

Beatrice hesitated. "They have told me…what they are."

"They may if they like."

"They are great in age, are they not?"

"They are, and would die of broken hearts should they be pensioned off." His concern for their well-being was clear.

"Therefore, to keep them active and productive, I shall not ask them to do what is outside their ability," Beatrice said. "How you do jump to conclusions, Osborn. One would take you for a frog."

———————

A frog? He would not take the bait. Nor was he a fish.

"I will not be overrun by footmen as Lowell is," Arthur said. "It is well known he has a penchant for taking in the runts of every species and cluttering his corridors with the nation's unwanted offspring."

"How thoughtful of him. I marvel once again that your kind do not seek to emulate his ways." Madam did that thing that made her skirts dance around her ankles. He imagined her ankles were as tiny as her wrists. He was lost musing on this until he realized she was nearly at the top of the stairs.

"Take care!" He caught her before disaster struck. "This tread is unsafe."

"My thanks," she said, breathless, blushing.

He looked at his hands, which of their own volition had grabbed her upper arms to set her upon the landing.

"Mind your way of going," he said, shoving the culprits into his pockets.

Madam turned away. "As I was saying," she continued, "the staff are the sole reason this place is not an utter ruin. As long as they wish to serve, they will. Otherwise, and only if it is their desire, they may be pensioned into one of the cottages that ring the eastern border of the holding. Once they are restored to use. If that suits."

"I doubt it would suit any of them to be exiled to the eastern border." What did she know about his holdings?

"Then they will remain." She stopped before the end of the corridor in front of a room laid waste by Hallbjorn. "This is, as you say, too much for them to make right." She turned and headed back to the landing. "A chore greater than Mr. Todd and I can manage."

"You will not lift a finger." He'd never hear the end of it from Morag should he allow Madam to do so.

"I assure you I am not so delicate I cannot wield a mop."

"I assure you that *delicate* is the last word I would use to describe you."

Madam stopped and looked at him with those blue eyes of hers, those summer-sky eyes.

She *looked* at him. Without the ever-present distance.

She looked at him with warmth, and his chest expanded.

"I am pleased to hear it." Madam climbed the next staircase, and he followed without minding where she was taking them.

The second floor.

The journey ended in a shallow hall, double doors facing them as they stood. Through the doorway lay the long gallery. To the right, the entry to the nursery and schoolroom. To the left…

Unerringly, Madam went in the least favorable direction. Chose the least favorable door, which hung crooked upon its hinges.

Madam crossed the threshold. He would not.

But he did look, and he did see.

The rooms may well have been caught in amber. The layer of dust on the objects and furniture was unlike anything he'd ever seen. Nothing had been disturbed, and despite the gloom and the dirt and the cobwebs, it was as if he shrank and shrank until he was only small, running in from the nursery to complain about Ben or to show off a drawing or to simply sit at his mother's feet as she did what mums did during the day.

Or he could wander in and find his father busy about the work of an Alpha; if Arthur was in the mood to learn how to do whatever it was his father was doing, Papa never passed up the opportunity to show him.

He took one step forward and then two back. This was ridiculous. He was a grown man. These were only rooms. The past was in the past.

Beatrice stood in the middle of the sitting room of what was without question the ducal suite. The liberal use of rich emerald and warm mahogany matched those on the escutcheon of the carriage they'd traveled in, clearly the family colors. Larger-than-life-sized portraits faced across from one another, obscured by years of grime; she could make out one as female, the other male, but nothing more. She could not bring herself to look at them too closely.

She chose not to look at anything too closely, and yet she saw a workbag on the floor near a sofa and a hoop with unfinished work on the table before it. She saw a desk with a sheaf of papers and a quill laid across them. She saw through to a room in which the door of a wardrobe stood ajar, only waiting for its mistress to close it. She saw a pair of boots, one fallen to the floor, one standing tall, their master never to set his feet into them ever again.

Behind her, Osborn took one step away from the doorway, then another.

It struck her that she knew nothing of what had transpired here. Georgie had scolded Osborn for refusing his responsibilities, but he had not said why. "Why" appeared to be driven by pain and loss. Too much pain and loss for one day.

Beatrice stepped out; Osborn stood at a distance down the corridor, tugging on a curtain.

"There is a similarity to the curtains in Arcadia," she said. "I gather they have not been opened for some time."

The duke wrenched the fabric; one side of the hanging tore off the rail, and both finials crashed to the floor. The cloud of dust was prodigious.

"That is one way to go about it," she said once she'd stopped coughing. Beatrice reached out and touched his upper arm, finding it far wider around than her hand could close. "Let us go with care, as we may be able to salvage something from this disarray."

He looked down at the torn fabric in his hands and let it drop to the floor. "As you say." Osborn reached up to the next set and drew them gently off the hooks that held them to the rod. He gave them a shake, and as the dust rose and settled, they exchanged a small smile.

"I propose we repair to the first floor and begin there." She started to fold the curtain, but he took it from her and did so himself. "It will inspire the staff and raise their spirits if the public rooms are brought up to scratch as soon as may be." She indicated a side table upon which Osborn should lay the curtain and made for the staircase.

Out of the corner of her eye, she saw him roll his shoulders and with that gesture lose a bit of the melancholy that clung to him.

"At the same time," Beatrice continued, "I perceive the attics and the maid's rooms are in a dreadful state if the appearance of the roof is any indication."

"You will on no account venture there." The duke stopped at the first-floor landing and poked his finger through the plaster of a wall. "Given the condition of these, I suspect the water damage is treacherous. You are barred from going above."

Was it an argument that was wanted to take his mind from his gloom? Never let it be said she could not rise to the occasion. "I take as my responsibility—"

"As the *lady* of this house." His voice was low and rumbly and abrupt. And teasing?

"—to see for myself what needs to be done." She added another layer of chill as she continued. "One would not expect a peer of your distinction to dirty his lily-white hands."

"My—what? My lily-white—are you having me on, Madam?" He ranted and raved as she glided into a room that contained nothing but a chandelier and a litter of crystal drops on the rug beneath it, and she very nearly smiled.

Beatrice counted her first day at Arcadia as one of excellent progress.

She had a good understanding of the amount of work needed to restore the house (prodigious), was now aware it had been allowed to disintegrate (a mystery), and better comprehended the resistance she was likely to encounter (colossal).

Descriptives applicable to Osborn.

As well as irascible and sardonic and stubborn. If she attempted to lift anything, he was there to do so in her stead; when she reached out to open a door or a window, he shunted her aside to see to it himself. What little furniture they came across was inspected for fitness, and broken objects were set aside as they made their way from room by room.

Osborn balked on the threshold of the largest receiving room, and when she did not exhort him to follow or inquire as to why he hesitated, he took a breath and ventured forward. It cost him, and Beatrice honored his fortitude by being as brisk and snappish as she could manage. He, in turn, was obstreperous and sarcastic. She tested the bell pull, and it came straight down from the ceiling with the requisite cloud of dust. She stumbled back into his chest; he turned her around and stroked the dust off her face, which produced an odd stirring beneath her petticoats, to a disturbing enough degree she dropped the velvet rope and left the room.

So, perhaps not the worst husband she may have found herself forced to marry. Whatever her lack of control that led to being bullied and blackmailed into this situation, she need not act as if she had no say going forward. Good may be wrought from the situation at the end of the day.

There was good to be wrought from her accommodation on the ground floor: it meant a proper bath could be brought in and filled without Glynis or Ciara having to exert themselves too terribly. Morag had promised a bucket line of sorts, and even though

the water would not arrive at its hottest, she anticipated the pleasure of fully immersing herself after the busy, begrimed day. The
door opened without so much as a knock, and she assumed it was
the housekeeper.

"Morag, a closed door requires a warning before—" Beatrice
came around the screen in her dressing gown and gasped.

Osborn strolled in carrying two enormous containers akin to
rain barrels. One was clutched in his fist with as much ease as if it
was a handkerchief, and the other he held balanced on his shoulder. He poured the contents of the latter—lovely, steaming-hot
water—into the copper tub.

"Why did Mr. Todd not see to this?" This was not a task to
be laid at ducal feet, no matter how she teased him about his lily-
white hands.

Osborn gave her a brooding look she could not decipher but
that inspired the rustle in her petticoats again. "This is a job that
requires fewer brains," he replied as he emptied the second, "and
greater brawn."

He threw back his shoulders, and the muscles of his upper
arms…twitched? Parts of his chest also lifted and lowered, and
she could not look away.

Nor did his departure encourage her to avert her gaze. It was
not ladylike to gawk at a man's bottom, not even one belonging to
one's husband, even should he be in name only. However, it was
indisputable that there was no comparison to be made between
the backside of Castleton and that of Osborn.

Glynis and Ciara scampered in after him with a bucket of water
each and an inability to contain their giggles. Out their water
poured, with Ciara adding a few drops of oil from a bottle, and
they toddled away. Twin shrieks of laughter erupted as Morag
came in with soap and an armful of cloths, a duty that, contrary to
her usual style, was executed without comment.

Beatrice stood like a statue in between the bed and the tub and

could not bring herself to fuss with the linens. He'd know she'd
need them after she had been in the water without her clothes and
oh no! Would he be required to fetch the tub after she was done?
She would empty the bathwater out the window, one teacup at a
time, rather than have him return when she was clean and sleepy
and smelling sweet.

The oil was jasmine, and its feminine, heady scent filled the
room; she sniffed at the cake of minty freshness sitting in a dish on
the lip of the tub. Both were fragrant and delicate, in sharp contrast
to her old soap, which like the spare bottles of oil had not accompanied the removal to Arcadia. It was time, likely past time to set
aside the use of both. She would ask Todd where they had got to
but would make no great effort to replicate them.

Osborn returned without his coat and waistcoat and with two
more barrels. The heat rose off the water, fingers of steam wrapping around his arm as he poured out one, then the other, the fine
lawn of his shirt clinging to his shoulders. He flipped away that
thick lock of hair, the one forever falling across his brow. Though
he seemed no worse for his exertion, his skin gleamed in the combination of hearth and candlelight, his shadow casting long and
large against the glass cases.

"Madam. Your bath awaits." The resonance of his voice sent
chills over her skin, and she suddenly felt rather faint. She expected
it was a consequence of the physical work of the day and the resul-
tant fatigue. And the heat of the water. And the fire.

"Should you choose to give up dukery, you make a fit chambermaid." Good Lord, what was she saying?

"I am not, as you may have discerned, adept at dukery." He
seemed amused. Lifting the barrels with much rippling of muscle,
he gave her a sarcastic leg to match her defiant style of curtsying.
"The water will be seen to in the morning. I bid you goodnight."

Arthur replaced the barrels and heard the maids giggling, Odin love them. At their age! Morag sat at the kitchen table and regarded him with censure, while Conlon jibber-jabbered to himself about staff and bathwater and the expectations of duchesses. He walked out in the middle of a thinly veiled scolding concerned with leaving Her Grace alone again and went into the woods to Change.

He remained clothed even as he reached the first cover of the trees to avoid the mistake of wandering back to the house in the nip as he had this morning. What if Madam had seen him? She would have fled for the hills, her shrieks heard for miles around, possibly as far as Lowell Hall.

Arthur picked up his pace as he imagined her naked in the tub, submerged in the water that smelled of jasmine, bathing herself with the minty soap. Her golden hair had been loosened from the severe style that confined it during the day, and the moisture in the air resulted in unexpected waves blossoming around her face, beckoning him to run his thumb over a silky pink cheek. For one as frosty as she, her blush rode very close to the surface, as it would on an innocent. Had she known how the fire shone through the flimsy robe she had donned, she would have hurried back behind the screen. The flames highlighted delicious curves that begged to be stroked and squeezed. His cock stirred in his trousers, and he did his best to ignore it. His wife she may be, but he was only a man.

Well, mostly.

As little time as they had spent in each other's company, he found he liked the salty aspects of her character as much as he enjoyed gazing upon her confectionary qualities. There was none to say they could not rub along nicely as he let her do what she wanted with the house and she left him out of it, none to say that a bit of teasing and firelight-through-the-nightgown gazing could not transpire. There was none to say they could not forge…a polite association. An amicable alliance. A cordial affiliation!

He ignored his bear's incredulous reception of that conclusion, but once he slung his clothes over a handy tree branch, he gave himself over to his essential self.

Well, this was new. His Change had always come upon him easily due to his status of Alpha, sleuth or no. The greater one's place in the hierarchy, the more fluid the surrender from man to beast and vice versa. He knew firsthand how seamless Georgie's Shift became as he grew to manhood, had known his own was a mere step behind. Tonight, however, the segue was unlike any he had undergone in the past.

As a rule, the Change was not easy and was indeed something to undergo: a complete transformation in shape and stance, in skin and bone. The body restructured itself from one being to another, and it was a process not without pain; while not as grotesque as portrayed in those ridiculous werewolf Gothic novels, the pressure of it often displaced itself as air and sound.

This night, Arthur Changed as effortlessly as if he was shrugging out of one coat in preference for another.

It was almost too much for his sensibilities to handle, if he was being honest. One moment he was standing and reaching within for his bear and the next—he was the bear, enrobed in his luxurious coat, his senses sharpened. He fell so fast onto his fours, the bear was equally discombobulated and tumbled over. He righted himself, and for the first time in a long time, since he'd been very small and could not manage his creature's strength, the bear took over.

He shook from head to toe and reveled in the Shift. He wanted to roar and roar—

We shall not alarm Madam, the man said.

We shan't, he agreed. *But we shall* run *and* run.

Claws bit into the cold earth, and with head lowered and hind bunched, the bear leapt forward. Pounding through the wood, he brushed up against trees and shrubs, leaving his scent behind, a comfort for friends, a warning for foes. He ran and ensured Arcadia's boundaries were secure. He sped to the house and lay his scent down there, in the gardens and the lawn, rolling with abandon and heedless of discovery. He wished his duchess—

Whose duchess? said the silly man.

Mine, the bear exulted as he brought them to a halt beneath her window. She was gabbing to that nightingale again.

He scented jasmine and mint and female and a very faint indication of a sweet thing, a salty thing, a season of the year, so elusive but more than was noticeable before, more than he detected in his manskin.

The man was distracted by her chatter with the bird in the tree. She was recounting her day and the plans she wished to embark upon the next.

Does she think we are that nightingale? the man scoffed.

Something is not right, the bear said. *Her smell is wrong.*

The man stopped to sniff. *There's the mint from the soap.*

That is not her. *Is she unwell?* The bear shivered with apprehension.

She is robust, the man said, *robust in her plans and her orders and her—*

The bear sniffed in ever-increasing circles, his nose picking up earth and insects and small creatures and rocks and the rain and—

Hold. When the man took that tone, the bear heeded it. They sniffed a patch of earth too near to the duchess's window for comfort.

That is wrong, the bear growled. *A thing that is not a thing, a smell that is not a smell. Like my duchess.*

They crept away from the window and followed the vagaries of the scent to the southern edge of the park where the glasshouse loomed like a specter, a skeleton of iron, its white struts and beams rent in the front as if a beast of strength akin to theirs had reached out and ripped them apart. Broken glass stuck out of the iron like thorns, and patches of windows were broken on each side as well as the roof, adhering to neither rhyme nor reason.

Even in the low light and from a distance he could see the wreckage within, plants and small trees flung about as if the destroyer had been thwarted in finding what it sought. The floor was torn apart, exposing the stoves beneath, connected to pipes for the distribution of heat to keep the plants alive. Most were dead but for a bed of weeds shored up against the only unbroken wall, a tangle of what appeared to be branches stripped from the trees around it, a variety neither man nor beast could identify.

A bad thing was here, said the bear as they slipped within.

They both scented the air; there was nothing but the soil and the greenery and the hint of a thunderstorm rolling in. It was impossible to discern whether the damage was recent or if it was a relic of the past or—

The work of Hallbjorn, they both mused.

A rustle sounded in the underbrush. For a creature its size, the bear slipped through a broken window sleek as a snake, and headed for the disturbance.

The scent of fox teased his nostrils and he made short work of flushing reynard from its hidey-hole. The sly creature crooked its neck, but it was insufficient to the raging man within. He drew down his *dominatum* and forced the Change on the prince's factotum.

The bear's man was surprised it worked; it was a show of force he had never attempted before.

We had no duchess to save from danger before, snarled the bear.

Todd kept to his knees and crooked his neck. "That destruction is not my work, Your Grace. I sought only to gauge the damage before reporting to Her Grace, er, and to you."

Arthur snorted, and the bear sniffed to spot a lie; there was none, as such. He shook his fur and rose to his fullest height; it was to Todd's credit he did not flee in fear. Came from working for Georgie, the man reckoned.

The man would not let the bear roar and rouse his duchess and frighten her. Instead, he exposed his great maw of teeth and leaned in close to the fox's face. Todd cricked his neck again, and the bear canted his head and indicated the house, to which the factotum fled with alacrity.

They watched him go; the man wanted to search, but the bear knew whoever had been here was long gone, for why else would there be no scent left behind? A drop of rain splashed on his nose; Alpha or no Alpha, he was not about to sleep in wet fur. Swift as a hare, they made for the cover of the wood.

Seven

AFTER SEVERAL DAYS IN ARCADIA, A ROUTINE ESTABLISHED itself. Meals were taken in the kitchen; Beatrice kept a running inventory of works required within the house; her nightly bath was fetched in by the duke. Peppered throughout were arguments between herself and His Grace regarding what he perceived to be her reckless foraying through the dilapidated interior and relentless carping about the funds she was disbursing as freely as Prinny raided the royal coffers.

Not that the latter was any concern of the duke's. She had had the management of her mother's pin money once she'd learned her sums; it was utterly satisfying to put her skills to work for her own ends. It took ready money up front to establish the confidence of the tradespeople she would soon employ in great numbers, and she refused to follow her father's example of holding back payment until the magistrate was alerted. A steward was needed to attend to the books, a topic she would broach another day.

On this day, Beatrice rose and washed and drew aside the curtains to peek out the window. Another evening storm had struck, and she merely thought to look for damage to the grounds.

Not for the advent of a certain duke.

Of whom there was no sign.

Nor was there evidence of him in the kitchen. Someone (Morag) had decided not to put the lord and lady of the house at the opposite ends of the table; Beatrice took her seat, which was set across from what was customarily his place.

Not that he was in it.

Not that it mattered to her.

Morag was off collecting the day's laundry. Mrs. Porter was

kneading a prodigious amount of dough while the maids skittered about, doing the work of three times their number. Conlon stood at attention as best he could, given his ailments. He announced, bless him: "Mr. Todd, ma'am," as the prince's factotum entered the kitchen.

"Do join me, Mr. Todd."

He bowed and remained standing. "I have broken my fast, ma'am."

"Please fetch Mr. Todd a cup of tea, Ciara. We have much to discuss. Where is His Grace?"

Due to Morag's absence, there was no ready answer but for a good deal of muttering.

"Out and about still? Very well." Beatrice spread her toast with homemade blackberry jam, Ciara's work again. Beatrice must find a replacement so the maid could indulge her culinary talents to their greatest advantage. "Before we consult the day's schedule, Mr. Todd, I was curious about certain belongings I did not find amongst those moved here. I am accustomed to using my personal brand of soap and oil. I believe I had at least another six months' supply, and yet there is none to hand. I wonder if you may enlighten me?"

Mr. Todd gave her request due consideration and then said, "I believe any belongings to be found in London have been transported to Arcadia."

"I see. Is it possible to reproduce the blend, Ciara? Glynis?" The maids looked everywhere but at her.

"Do you not enjoy the soap and oil we have laid on?" Ciara asked. "They're from our store, and we made them with such care." Beatrice was not equal to the mouse's pleading eyes.

"I am very pleased with both. New scents for a new start." She took up another piece of toast and a spoonful of jam. "Let us review our tasks for the day. I will require some supplies from the kitchen in aid of what I have planned for myself."

Arthur was ready for Madam this morning. He had taken to lingering beneath her window of an evening. Dare he tease her regarding her nocturnal chats with the local fauna? As if he should be as small as a songbird.

As if she should know what we are without being told, his bear scolded. *Her Grace has nothing to compare us to. Castleton was no specimen, even in his prime.*

I *am a specimen in my prime*, Arthur thought, for what it was worth. The lady had not disputed embarking upon a white marriage, and never let it be said he did not honor his oaths despite the idea of brokering a cordial affiliation growing in appeal—

A nightingale lay on the back step to the kitchens. Its little neck was broken and its wings spread open, exposing its breast, where its heart had been torn out.

"Bloody cats," Arthur snarled. He gently took up the poor creature and brought it around to the churned-up earth near the untended rose walk. He tucked it behind a bush in want of pruning and hoped it wasn't *the* nightingale. No teasing about the bird, then.

Dressing in the laundry, he batted the sheets that hung from the lines drawn crisscross from the beams and winced at the dampness of his shirt despite the ever-stoked fire. They were fortunate the house had a cistern, at least, saving the elderly staff the walk to and from the brook. Even so, they must see about outfitting a vestment hut.

Arthur would see to it. He would, no one else.

Or Todd would. He would instruct Todd to do so.

He stopped Conlon as he passed on the way to the kitchen. "One of the maids will have to bury a bird."

"A *bird* bird?" Conlon asked, his voice trembling.

"Yes, an *avis puri*," he said. Did he need a coat? Men were meant to wear coats around ladies. He put on a coat. "I do not wish Her Grace to come upon it."

The butler smiled like it was Yule and his Name Day in one. "I shall see to it personally, Master Artie."

"I prefer one of the maids do so." He could not let this elderly little man bend his back to shoveling.

"Even *avis puri* set the girls off something fierce," Conlon said.

"Leave it with me, then." Arthur sighed and followed Conlon into the kitchen to be greeted by only one place setting. "Was it not Madam's wish we take our meals as one?"

"Her Grace has been and gone," Morag said, setting down the teapot with a thump.

"It is nine of the clock, Master Artie," Conlon informed him, with subtle censure.

"Our duchess," Morag continued, "is keen to do a day's work."

"As a skivvy?" Arthur snorted.

"Oh, how I dream of having a skivvy," the housekeeper moaned.

"A dream you will continue to enjoy without hope of it coming true." That was a lie. He had to find new staff if only to take the pressure off old joints.

Morag scoffed. "Not if Her Grace has anything to say about it."

Her Grace wouldn't, for this was all for show, was it not? Her interest in Arcadia meant nothing for their union. Well, it was not a union. They were united in name but not in truth. In truth, it was poignant, watching her chat with the little bird. It made his eyes sting, as they would if he'd gazed straight into the sun, and also a little heavy like he needed a good nap. This made no sense as he had slept well. On the ground, it had to be said, not much of a pleasure, not even for his bear, who truly enjoyed his creature comforts. Which did not include sleeping through a deluge and awakening on a bed of soggy leaves, the drip drip drip from the arboreal canopy tormenting him on this fine—

"And where is Madam this fine morning?"

Conlon cleared his throat. "I believe the duchess is up in the attics."

Osborn caught her off guard by charging into the eastern attic; most of the pots and pans Beatrice had ferried from the kitchen crashed to the floor.

"Madam, I believe I instructed you to avoid this area." He stood over her like the dark clouds only now passing over.

"Your Grace." She thought to drop into one of her curtsies but suspected he knew what she intended when she did so, which lessened the effect overall. "It may have come to your notice there was a storm last evening. Steps must be taken no matter how small to thwart further damage to this dwelling." She picked up a pan and set it beneath a drip. "Do make yourself useful if you insist I am not to work unaccompanied."

Beatrice placed a pot beneath another hole in the roof. For such a large house, there was next to nothing in it. Given the state of the rooms she'd seen, it was natural to assume the bulk of the family belongings had been stored away, and yet the attic on this side of the house was empty but for puddles of rainwater.

Osborn set about placing the rest, muttering about *cursory solutions* and *who would empty the things* and then: "I expect you were a headstrong girl." He nudged his last pot under an egregiously leaking eave.

"I became headstrong," Beatrice said. "My mother was blessed by many a happy event, nigh on yearly. I was responsible for my siblings as soon as I reached the age of seven."

"You are one of nine." He sounded proud he'd remembered.

"I am. My mother is now beyond the years to enjoy further confinements."

"And yet—" Even he was not enough of a clod to finish that statement.

"And yet." She called upon Lady Frost and held his gaze. "And yet I have not been so blessed."

At least he had the decency to look abashed.

Let them move swiftly on. "The servants quarters are in slightly better condition." There had been little accommodation made for live-in staff, and she wondered why. Perhaps they had been allowed to stay with family in those rundown cottages? She would quiz Mr. Conlon later.

Beatrice placed the last of her pots and handed him another saucepan. "Shall we proceed?" She led the way across the short hall. "I find myself surprised by the lack of..."

"Belongings? Paraphernalia? Impedimenta?"

"Sofas. Tables. Chairs."

"It is not the way of my...kind to settle in one place for very long. Generally. So possessions are not the apogee of our existence."

"But furniture, Osborn, surely."

The door to the western attics was as idiosyncratic as those throughout Arcadia. Its knob required not so much turning as jiggling and jabbing, so much so Osborn put one of his broad shoulders to use and pushed it open to reveal an entire household of accoutrements.

"Who has done this?" Beatrice looked around in amazement. "As strong as you say Mr. Conlon and Morag are, this cannot have been within their powers."

Heavy pieces of furniture rose to the ceiling like a fortress built of children's blocks, improbably balanced and stacked. A dining table long enough to seat twenty was set on one of its short sides, and in the space between its legs, chairs were stacked in a rickety tower. Four very large wardrobes stood back-to-back and partially obscured a collection of china cabinets as well as several sofas upholstered in beautifully textured and toned fabric. There was a plethora of essentials that would if not fill the house at least fill it out. Every available gap was filled with a comprehensive assortment of footstools. Nearest the back of the chockablock room, a tower of trunks loomed, partially draped in the sort of red curtain found in theaters. A company of mannequins stood near the theatrical ephemera, dressed in the old-fashioned style one expected from productions of William Shakespeare.

In between two bookcases, an enormous mirror sat on a tiny games table. Beatrice edged into the space between as best she could. It was a stunning piece, the work of Thomas Hope if she was not mistaken, and it looked to be the same height as Arcadia's enormous duke. The frame was carved to appear wrought from the branches of a tree, winding delicately around one another, crowned with acorns at the top. The glass required silvering and the frame touching up of its gilding, but otherwise, it was unique and deserved to be admired. She reached out and found it lighter than expected, and as she attempted to slide it out—

Her movements disturbed the delicate balance of the table, which proved unsteady on its spindly legs, and two of them buckled at the unexpected movement. As the mirror wobbled, it tipped face forward in her direction. Her slippers chose that moment to do what slippers did and slid in the dust unsurprisingly thick on the floor between the bookcases. Of a sudden, it was heavier than she'd first thought, and for a breathless moment, it sliced toward her like the blade of a guillotine—

Until it did not. A strong arm caught her around the waist, a large hand reached out and halted the chaos in its tracks, and in another breathless moment, she was out of danger, those two large hands that saved her from the Tread of Danger having now rescued her from the Mirror of Certain Death.

"Blessed Freya, Madam, will you not take care?" The hands moved over her arms, down her back, and she found herself squashed against a chest the approximate intensity of a bonfire. Osborn's heart beat beneath her ear, and against her better judgment, she leaned. She leaned against the heat and heart and allowed herself to feel afraid; now that the reason why had passed, she appreciated how close a call it had been. It was comforting to feel supported, to lean upon something so obviously stronger than herself, solid as a rock. The hands squeezed her around the shoulders and the waist, and a caress slid over her hair. His lips? How strange to find a man's lips so comforting; she calmed as they brushed against her head, and there was solace in the way his nose fit so oddly and yet so well behind her ear. So soothing and yet so petticoat-rustling.

Until the grousing began. "You've not got the sense the goddess gave you. Contrary as a donkey."

"How flattering." Her voice shook, and the arms pulled her closer.

"Are you not flattered? Intractable, yes, but donkeys can be sweet in their way. You have heard of Baron Cuddy, have you not, and his famous drove? He had at least twenty and kept them in the garden of his townhouse in Ainsley Square. Used to walk them daily down Rotten Row until Prince George, that would be Georgie to you, had him barred. There are also some stories not meant for ladies' ears, I am ashamed to say."

"Then do not say." Beatrice took a breath and found that stepping away was not on her agenda. "You are a font of gossip. I suspect you spend your time at society events chattering with the ape leaders."

"If one must endure a Venetian breakfast, one ought to get something savory out of it."

"Or unsavory." One of his hands trailed its way up and down her spine. The beat of the heart and the heat of the chest, the consoling touch and the smell of the freshly laundered shirt—Osborn had eschewed a waistcoat again—combined into a heady mix of comfort that made her heartbeat increase and blood rush to her face. It was nothing more than a casual embrace, and yet... She'd been held in a waltz and taken to the marriage bed but never with such a potent result.

They both jumped at the sound of knuckles rapping on the doorframe. Mr. Todd poked his head in the doorway, took in their stance, and stepped back in an instant.

"Yes, yes, what do you want?" Osborn's voice delved into throaty depths.

"Your Graces." Mr. Todd raised his voice to be heard without being seen. "I have discerned a pattern of disturbance to the grounds and would call it to your attention."

"Her Grace will not be venturing out in this weather," Osborn said.

"Will she not?" For no good reason, Beatrice found it a challenge to remove herself from his hold. She took a breath and made for the corridor.

"I have taken the liberty of redrawing the plan of the grounds and marking it out." Mr. Todd fell back when the duke joined them. "If we were to repair to my—the study?"

Whose study? Beatrice thought, and they made their way below, Osborn's put-upon huffs and puffs sounding like a bellows pumping up a fire.

When they reached their destination, Osborn looked around the room as if he'd never seen it before. On the desk lay a beautifully rendered plan, more detailed and in a tidier hand than its model.

"A glasshouse?" Beatrice indicated the labeled building. "Is that usual, even in a country home?" She thought only the very wealthy could boast of such a thing, and her impression was that the Humphries clan were not among their number.

"They have come into fashion in the human world in the last fifty years, ma'am," Mr. Todd replied. "*Versipelli* have enjoyed their benefits for far longer. Glasshouses are challenging to keep, and it is best if one among the members of the household has a passion for the work and the ability to engage staff to sustain it."

"Plants are not my strong suit," Beatrice admitted. Neither were they Osborn's, as he ignored the conversation and stood enraptured before a globe tucked into one of the bookcases.

"There are many exotic specimens, from as far afield as India and the Antipodes." It appeared plants were Mr. Todd's strong suit. "There are some the purpose of whose cultivation is curious and dangerous to the untutored."

"What is the condition of the building?" Beatrice thought a glasshouse sounded like a lot of work.

"It is standing." Mr. Todd's eyes slid over to the duke, who was engaged in tracing a finger over the sub-Asian continent. "Which is almost too much to expect, given its derelict state."

"That will not do." Beatrice wished she had a little book to write in and a pocket in which to put it. She reached for a piece of foolscap instead, from a pile set in the exact place on the desk one would wish to find it. "Thus, the glasshouse goes on the schedule."

"Schedule, Madam?" Osborn stopped spinning the globe.

"Of what needs doing and when." She jotted down a few notes with the freshly cut quill.

Osborn ranged around the edge of the study, as much as he could given his relative size (substantial) to the room (bijou).

"As we have established, there is no one here to do anything." The duke was like a dog with a bone. "Unless Todd is to accomplish it himself."

"He is not," she said as she dipped the pen in the crystal inkwell and made another note. "Mr. Todd's most pressing task is the refurbishment of the ducal suite, Your Grace." She glanced at the factotum. "If you would inform us of your progress?"

"We have taken the utmost care with the belongings—" Todd began.

"Get rid of them," Arthur said. A beat of silence greeted this outburst.

"If they are packed, they will be ready to be stored," Beatrice said. It was clear the ducal suite held bad memories for Osborn, but there was no call to do away with its contents. "How fortunate that at least one section of the attics is currently undersubscribed. Please continue, Mr. Todd. How may we speed along the process?"

"While the maids are acting with as much alacrity as is possible, the suite is only just habitable at this stage."

"I would think the roof of greater urgency." Arthur opened the curtains draping the lone window and closed them again. At least they did not tumble to the floor.

"I agree, " Beatrice said. "Mr. Todd, I recall asking you to investigate the nearby villages to see if any need gainful employment." She treated His Grace to an inquisitorial eyebrow arch. "What think you, Osborn?"

"You need not speak around me, Madam, as Todd is at both our disposals." He faced her down, and she had the unexpected urge to laugh. He knew she was running roughshod over his ill-tempered dictates, and now she knew he knew, and it was... It was *exhilarating*.

"It is time to swell our ranks," she said. Osborn acknowledged what must have been a victorious look on her face with a tilt of his chin. "If only there was someone nearby who had a surplus of footmen."

Eight

A MERE HOUR BY HORSEBACK DUE EAST, ANOTHER DUCAL breakfast was underway in Lowell Hall, very much later than that enjoyed by the denizens of Arcadia, as this couple looked to be continuing as they'd begun their married life, that is to say, by lingering abed. Well, the bride had; the groom had his duties as Alpha to see to and had only taken his seat when she came down.

Alfred rose as his blushing bride entered the room.

"Your Grace." She curtsied, to the amusement of the footmen. "I do apologize for my lateness." Mr. Coburn rushed to pull out a chair opposite Alfred, who shook his head and indicated the seat to his left.

"I had business in the farthest field," Alfred said as she took her place. "I am only lately returned myself."

The usual complement of footmen ringed the wall, and Coburn tended to the couple's needs, freshening pots of tea and keeping a weather eye on the sideboard's offerings, taking his responsibilities as ducal butler seriously indeed. As Alfred's mate pushed eggs counterclockwise round her plate and failed to conceal another yawn, he opened a letter weighed down with royal seals and made himself familiar with its contents.

"Osborn has wed the Marchioness of Castleton," he announced.

"Beatrice?" Felicity made to freshen her tea but was unequal to their butler's attentiveness. "Oh, thank you, Mr. Coburn. I was unaware she was being courted."

"No one knew I was courting you." He smiled at her and leaned an elbow on the table to gaze at her. She reproved him with a mere glance, and he sat up properly.

"No less a personage than myself knew you were courting me," she countered, and the footmen snickered. "Who is Osborn?"

"Still not up on your *Debrett's*?" Alfred buttered half a scone and put it on her plate. "Arthur Humphries, Duke of. I knew him growing up, he lived in Court with Georgie, big lad, always on the fringes," he said. "He was present at our nuptials."

"I did not notice, I regret to say." They exchanged a fulsome look, and Alfred considered convincing her to delay attendance upon her duties at Templeton Stud.

"Did you not? What held your attention, I wonder?" The footmen giggled, and even Coburn cast aside his dignity enough to crack a smile. "His Highness demanded Bates's company once our vows were said," he continued. "Perhaps he had been called upon to witness theirs. I, too, had my attention elsewhere." He reached back to stroke the spot at the top of Felicity's hip that carried his mating mark.

She batted him away with her napkin. "Does he enjoy a similar, er, status beyond his ducal duties?"

"He is an Alpha," Alfred said. "Although he is not doing his duties. His father was challenged for primacy over their clan and lost. It is past time Osborn took up his mantle."

"Challenged?" Felicity warmed up his tea and administered the requisite two spoonfuls of sugar.

"A usurper of his species fought for the right to command the Osborn holdings. It is an old, old custom of *versipellian* life. George's great-great-grandfather upheld such hidebound notions, but they have largely been abolished." Alfred waved away the kippers proffered by Coburn at his mate's minute flinch.

"Largely?" Felicity added jam to the scone, cut it in half, and put the larger piece on Alfred's plate.

"Most completely. As our kind have become civilized, so have many of our ways, but not all." Alfred applied himself to his meal.

"I do not think Beatrice will countenance violence," she said.

"In fact, I know she will not. I am not apprised of the details, but I can say with confidence her first marriage was not harmonious."

"I have no doubt it was not." He knew only too well what marriage to Castleton would have entailed for the unlucky wife.

"If she were wed to such as he without being any the wiser…" Felicity worried her eggs with her fork.

"Humans have unknowingly wed Shifters and remained in ignorance for the whole of their lives," Alfred said. "I am certain the new duchess is informed regarding our kind, however. As you are now aware, one can tell if one knows what to look for. She held herself aloof to all and sundry, but when sundry was *versipellis*, she was very much on her guard."

He perused the rest of the letter. "Ah. Yes, here, Bates was likely required as a witness, for they were indeed wed directly after we were, in Carlton House."

"Oh! But—" Felicity rose before a footman or three could pull out her chair. "This has every hallmark of an unwanted alliance. I shall write to her straightaway." She threw her napkin down and then picked it up and folded it. How like her, ever striving to make less work for the staff. "Have you their direction?"

Arthur rose and took his *vera amorum*'s hand. "I suspect they have taken up residence in Arcadia, the Humphries homeplace."

"Arcadia. How beautiful it sounds," said Felicity as she ran her hand along his arm to stroke his biceps.

Alfred shrugged. "If it has been uninhabited since his father's time," he said as they left the room, "I suspect it is in a state far less beautiful than its name."

———

"…and after the roof, we shall see to the securing and the cleaning of the glasshouse," Beatrice said. "Although I do not know if there are any present able to take it in hand immediately." Despite Osborn's strictures, Beatrice intended to see the glasshouse firsthand. The sky was clear, and she needed exercise, but there was so much to accomplish indoors, not the least of which was writing a letter to Miss Templeton. No, she must address her as "Your Grace" now.

She turned to Mr. Todd. "I shall revise the schedule and plan for at least ten footmen from Lowell Hall."

"Ten!" The duke left off his morose inspection of the bookcases.

"Too few, Your Grace?" Beatrice asked and was answered with an apoplectic glare. She turned back to Mr. Todd. "I shall require delivery of a letter to the Duchess of Lowell as soon as I have the writing of it."

"Yes, ma'am." Mr. Todd ran a finger along the edge of a bookcase much in the same way a smitten swain tickled his intended's palm. "I will take it myself as I am able for this terrain and will be unremarkable as the night draws in."

"Carrying it in your mouth like a lapdog?" Osborn sniped.

"I trust Mr. Todd will contrive to preserve his dignity." Whatever species the prince's factotum was, he was not making it known to her. Beatrice supposed he trusted her as reluctantly as she trusted him, but Mr. Todd was proving more of an ally in the resuscitation of Arcadia than was the duke, and she suspected she had a reward he would appreciate. Mr. Todd may know more than his fair share about flora, but it was here, at the heart of household order, he wished to be at home. "Please take the time to familiarize yourself with this room, the books and such, and perhaps begin going through the pigeonholes," she said.

Osborn was muttering about *cats that were not cats set amongst the pigeons* when the clatter of a carriage sounded from the drive.

"Are you expecting visitors, Your Grace?" Who in the world would be calling upon them? Good Lord, she was as filthy as a chimney sweep and in no way disposed to greet guests.

Osborn shoved his way to the window. He cursed at what he saw and strode out of the room.

Beatrice and Mr. Todd followed him through the house and out to the forecourt as an aged coach rocked to a stop, an oversubscribed baggage cart halting behind.

There were no postillions; the coachman leaned over to spit in the gravel and made no move to descend from his seat. The door popped open, and a lanky man emerged. He beamed at Osborn, and a small woman, of a height and figure to Beatrice, although brunette rather than blonde, appeared in the doorway. The man swept her down to the ground with a spin and a flourish, which inspired Osborn to make one of his noises, this one akin to coal rattling around in a scuttle.

"Your drive could do with a good raking," called the lady.

"What would you know about a good raking?" The man laughed and pinched her cheek, kissed her, and gave her his arm. Three small children tumbled out of the carriage and raced around in circles, exuberant in their freedom.

"Not that sort, you ridiculous beast," the lady laughed.

"Brother," said the man, voice full of emotion. He embraced Osborn, who returned it with reluctance. Now that Beatrice looked more closely, she could see the resemblance, despite the younger Humphries being leaner in body, brighter in aspect and minus the formidable coiffing of his elder. He laughed with joy as Osborn gave in and turned his face into his brother's neck.

"Sister!" exclaimed the lady, and Beatrice found herself enfolded with surprising strength and rocked side to side. She wormed her way out of the embrace and stood, fingers locked together at her waist to hide her shaking hands. The children joined them and gaped at her with awe, as if she was a foreigner from an exotic land.

"Your Grace," Osborn growled, once he was free from his brother's grasp. "May I make known to you my brother, Garben, and his wife, Charlotte, who have deigned to surprise us with a visit." Charlotte bobbed a belated curtsy, and one of the girls looked mortified.

"Call me Ben," said her brother-in-law; he bowed and then leaned in to buss her on the cheek.

"You are beautiful," Charlotte pronounced. "And your figure is delightful."

"It is exactly as yours is, you cheeky thing." Garben gestured to the children who had gathered around them. "These are Tarben, Bernadette, and Ursella." Bernadette gave her best version of a curtsy and wobbled; Tarben chose not to bow and commenced hopping up and down on one leg.

The littlest of the three reached out a finger to touch Beatrice's wedding ring and then leaned against her leg, small fingers bunching the apron and skirt.

"Oh, there now, Ursella's seal of approval." Charlotte beamed down at her daughter. "She's a shy little bit, doesn't take to many."

"Is she fond of the chill of winter, then?" Charlotte gaped at the duke, and little Bernadette outright gasped. So. She was not alone in finding Osborn rough around the edges and prone to impulsive speech.

Beatrice ignored him and turned to his family. "I am sorry to have greeted you in such disorder and with no preparation." Even to her ears this did not sound apologetic, but rather like she blamed her guests for their presence. The child's fist burned like a brand. "I fear we…the nursery…is not… We have only wrestled one suite into usefulness. It will be a crush for your…your family."

"We are well used to close quarters," Ben said. "It is typical of our kind when the children are this age."

"Then allow me to make you as comfortable as I may." She gently worked her apron out of the little girl's clutches and fled.

———————

Arthur turned to his beaming brother and sighed at the look on his sister-in-law's face.

"Charlie."

"Artie. Felicitations upon your marriage." Only Charlotte could infuse an anodyne tribute with grave censure. The things the woman could convey with a look and a pair of crossed arms. He was surrounded by diminutive women who wielded their gestures like swords.

"I'd no choice in the matter and no way to contact you," he said. He crossed his own arms, which served to intimidate Charlotte not one jot. "And yet here you are, as if my efforts to supply news could ever exceed your ability to gain it."

"How poorly you spoke in front of your wife." That chin! It was like cannon on the fields of Waterloo. "Mannerless clod."

He bent down so she may more easily clout him on the ear. The children shrieked with glee, the two eldest capering about their mother.

"Where did my auntie go?" Bernadette demanded.

"She's my auntie as well!" Tarben was never one to be left out.

"Wherever aunties go when they are sorting out beds for their nieces and nephews," said Ben.

Tarben fidgeted. "Will we sleep in these beds for long? Maybe?"

His brother's family turned to Arthur, hope in the children's eyes and wariness in the adults'. Was there a heart so like a stone to say them nay? Their worldly belongings were lashed on the cart, and while they were clean and pressed, there was an air about Ben's family—*his* family—that spoke of weary rootlessness. What could he offer them that another's roof could not? His roof was little more than a series of loosely joined holes! The place was in rag order, never mind how much Madam had accomplished in so little time. And yet a familiar roof, his brother's childhood home, a sieve as it may be, must serve to provide better shelter than a strange place…

"In you get, and see what you're asking for," he said.

In his rush to the forecourt, he had failed to notice that the foyer was blessedly free of arachnid industry. Its black-and-white-tiled floor shone, the windows were well scrubbed, and the wooden paneling, depicting bears in every posture of hunt and play, gleamed like new.

Tarben eyed the banister, and Bernadette hung her bonnet from a hook on the freshly polished tallboy. Morag stood, hands on hips, in the corridor, and Arthur was surprised she'd not made more of the unexpected visitors. "Take the cubs to the kitchen for spoiling," he directed her. Tarben cheered, Bernadette curtsied at him again, and Ursella... "Where is Ursella?"

She was crouched behind the open door, looking closely at a detail on one of the panels, of two bears fighting. Or at least he hoped they were fighting and not mating. "Up you get, petal," Arthur said, "and off you go."

"She's forever going astray," Charlotte said.

"You won't thank me for ruining their supper," said Arthur, as though it would make them think twice about staying.

"That's what uncles are for." Ben clapped him on the shoulder. "It will be second nature once the sleuth establishes again."

"We are not—" Arthur began and chivvied them into the reception room. The door was still leaning against the wall, and the footstool remained the lone occupant, but the wood of the floor was newly polished to a shine. There were two sofas up in the attics that would look well in here, as would the large mirror Madam had nearly pulled down on herself.

"Have you taken against furnishings?" Charlotte asked.

"There's any number of chairs and such, er..." Ben trailed off.

Arthur bared his teeth. "Was it you, then, stuffing the attics full of the old things?"

"I did what I could when it could be overlooked." Ben was every inch a stubborn Humphries. "I know I had no right in law to be here, but the usurper did nothing more than destroy what offended him before he disappeared."

"Hallbjorn never gathered a sleuth, Arthur," Charlotte said.

"Nor did he mate, nor did he produce young. His time is past. He remained on the fringes here for years, and now none know where he abides. Were he to die without issue, we would be free to do as we wish. If you were to make a challenge—"

"There will be no challenge." Arthur cut off her tirade. "The prince regent has decreed."

"Oh, Georgie," Charlotte scoffed. "Well, if he upholds his decree, then all to the good. Nothing stands in your way. We shall be a sleuth—"

"There will be no sleuth."

"Won't there?" Charlotte mused, and Ben rocked on his heels. "And what thinks your wife? I know she is Castleton's widow, but what does she truly know about us?"

"She knows what we are, in essence, but not in species, and I forbid you to tell her."

"Yes, Alpha," Charlotte said, notably minus the usual obeisance, and then sighed. "Only think to whom she was wed previously. For the love of Freya, she can have no good opinion of our kind."

"I must ask…" Ben chewed on his lip. "Is it usual for *homo plenii* to lack a scent signature?"

"We have not mingled amongst them very much since the children have grown," Charlotte said.

"Is it a product of her humanity?" Ben wondered and then shook his head. "I am sure I recall humans in Court having at least one top note."

"Pardon me." Beatrice stood in the hall, Ursella at her side. "The child was climbing the stairs, and they are not so safe that she can be left unsupervised." She cleared her throat. "We have the ducal suite prepared. Your Grace, if you and your brother would lend Mr. Todd a hand with the beds, then we can carry on tomorrow outfitting it more fully."

"Am I to be demoted to footman?" Arthur could not stop goading her.

"Should it be so beneath your lofty dignity to ensure your family feel at home, they may sleep on the floor," Madam riposted. "Or pile in with me in the stillroom, as I inhabit it alone." She gently extricated her hand from the child's grip and left the room.

Salty little cake with claws—and fangs. Arthur would not be drawn, not by his brother's dismay nor by Charlotte's glare. He would be discreet. His spat with Madam was none of their concern. They need not know—

"We are engaged in a white marriage."

"Are you, now." Charlotte's brow did not arch as elegantly as Madam's, but the effect was the same.

"Why would you presume otherwise? We met a mere sennight ago and married under duress due to Georgie's threats."

"What threats?" Ben let his claws down.

"None of your concern. None of this is your concern." Arthur waved his arms about, encompassing the house and the land and the wife. "Whether or not Hallbjorn failed in his quest to hold this area, it is no longer ours. We are here on our regent's sufferance and no more."

"Nevertheless," Charlotte insisted. Odin's ravens, she was relentless. "There is no call to leave it looking abandoned and derelict."

"She intends to fix this place," Arthur allowed. "She said she'll be about getting in some of Lowell's footmen."

"'She' is Her Grace, you lout," Charlotte admonished, and Arthur leaned down for another smack of her little paw.

"We are wed, not bonded."

"Your wife is not 'she' to anyone, ever. Where are your manners?" Charlotte demanded. "And as to that, are you considering her humanity? You may not be administering the bite or even a scent-marking, but I do hope," and this was delivered in a tone that said she severely doubted such an eventuality, "you are at the very least offering your wife the respect due her in front of others not in the family."

A warm little flame lit under his heart. "You have not changed since the day you were born."

Charlotte blushed. "I am sure I don't know what you mean."

"Fears none," Ben said, proud as punch.

"And is Bernadette or Ursella like you?" Arthur asked.

"Tarben is like me, thank you very much," Charlotte said, "and Bernadette is her own creature entirely. Very high in the instep for one so young."

"Ursella is as shy as the day is long," Ben said, "but she is stubborn. We are hoping she may present as an Omega. What a blessing that would be for our sleuth."

"We are not a sleuth." Arthur suspected this would become a daily refrain.

"What would your favorite playwright have to say about protesting too much? Come, Ben, let us go see how plump our children have become, gorging on biscuits." Charlotte poked Arthur in the belly, did the thing women did with their skirts to convey scorn, and made her way to the back of the house.

―――――――――――

How unlike me, Beatrice thought, *to be so openly spiteful.*

Oh, she knew spite like she knew the palm of her hand, thanks to the antipathy of the *beau monde* and the dishonesty of their social interactions. When she greeted insincere behavior with her characteristic dispassion and an unflinching stare, she found their thinly veiled malice quailed in the face of her implacability; her entire reputation relied upon her ability to repel the slings and arrows of tittle-tattle and importunate suitors.

Yet there she had been, insulted before strangers, nothing new, and she had…lashed out. What an uncivilized impression to make. But it did not matter what Osborn's family thought of her or that she might cause him to lose face before them down to an insult or two falling from his lips.

His lips. Had that happened only hours ago? Up in the attic, he'd held her close, as though she had been in need of comfort and protection. She'd found both in his embrace; his nose had fit so oddly and yet so well behind her ear, and those lips had brushed against her hair…

Let her not think of his lips.

Let her instead address what was clearly the master's study.

Against all odds, the door that lead from the steward's office to this larger room opened unhindered by eccentric deficiency. Like the ducal suite, this room was untouched, the stoppage of time betrayed by an abandoned tea service and the omnipresent dust. Arthur's Alpha, presumably his father, had for the most part kept things to a standard Beatrice admired: books were shelved, drawers were shut, and the arrangement of quill, ink, and paper on the large desk was precise. However, there were signs something ill had occurred: she collected the few pieces of parchment that littered the floor, righted an overturned teacup, reset the fire irons that had fallen in…a rush to leave?

What had happened here?

Lacking anything better to hand, she took off her apron and dusted the desk and then the chair and sat. The letter she had written to Felicity was on its way thanks to the mysterious ways of Mr. Todd. (Was he an owl, to be so confident under the cover of night?) She had not found time to walk the grounds. The ducal suite had been made as accommodating as possible for the family, and their possessions had been brought in. Beatrice wondered if there was anything in the attics Charlotte would find comfortable or if toys for the children might be hidden in a nook or a cranny. She reached for a piece of paper out of habit and found it beyond her grasp. The acreage of the desk was of a sudden too great, and she rose hastily from the chair. It was not her place.

Beatrice did not feel the familiar despair of being in the wrong place. It simply was not hers. She stood to the left of the desk, and there the paper and pen were waiting for her hand. She shook her head at her foolishness and yet—

And yet. She was comfortable standing in that place. Near to what was naturally Arthur's seat of power.

The ink had dried in the well. She went to retrieve more from the steward's office when a knock sounded. She closed the door to the master's study behind her; her instincts told her it was not time for the room to be open to the rest of the household.

"Yes, enter."

Ciara popped her head in. "You've missed your tea, ma'am," she scolded. "We've a cold collation if you'll come along."

She could not face the Humphries *en masse*. "Thank you, Ciara. Has the family been apprised?"

"They are tired from the journey so have taken trays in their rooms."

"Oh dear," she said. "How thoughtless of me to leave them fending for themselves."

"They are at home here," Ciara said. "As is only right."

"I shall take a tray in my room, then." Why should she feel so solitary? It was what she wanted, after all.

"Leave it to me, ma'am." Before Beatrice could protest otherwise, Ciara shut the door behind her.

A few brief notes and there was nothing left but to leave the safety of the office and venture forth. The zest Arthur's family infused in the atmosphere skittered along her skin, a tangible thing, little brushes of vitality. She was so consumed by this, by the life suddenly pulsing around her, she could not be faulted for startling when something brushed against her ankles.

It was a cat. It ceased its ribboning around her feet and leapt up onto an occasional table set against the wall. They regarded one another.

"A cat may look at a duchess as well as look at a king," Beatrice said, and it blinked. "Have you found your way down from the barn? I am not surprised to discover you making free of the main house given the faultiness of its doors."

Beatrice turned toward the kitchen, and the cat hopped down to follow.

"I have put the refurbishment of the nursery at the top of the schedule as it is in a woeful state at best." She looked down at the tabby and found it attending her every word. "Is your lineage as undersubscribed as that of my first husband or even my second?"

"This cat is not your husband," rumbled That Voice. Osborn appeared from who knew where. Why he wandered the halls rather than barricade himself in a study or office like every other peer in creation she did not know. "And if she is anything like her antecedents, she is well able to litter." He and the cat exchanged a glance, and the feline scampered off in the opposite direction.

"A pity then that cat is not your wife." So waspish! Beatrice made to move past him, and he reached out and took her wrist. No matter that his grasp was light and there was no rage pumping off him; she could not help but recoil.

Osborn released his hold without hesitation. "I was not in want of a wife, you or anyone else—"

"It is fortunate I shall not take that to heart," she sniped. Sniped! "Consider me no more or less than a chamberlain—"

"—and yet you insist on acting in a wifely manner."

"Is it the masculine term that offends you?" She resumed her walk down the corridor. "Chatelaine, then. Shall we deem that my role rather than wife?"

He followed her, relentless. "The children were asking for their aunt."

"Have they none that I am such a novelty?"

"None that they come by through their favorite uncle."

"Ah, you enjoy that distinction. Are you their only?" She paused at the green baize door.

"I comprehend what you have done there," Osborn said. He reached up to run a hand over his hair, putting order on curls that routinely threatened to spring free, a habit that made her petticoats feel oppressively tight, which was an impossibility. He considered her and ran his hand over his lush hair slowly. He sniffed and shook his head, confused. "Have you taken to using a new perfume?"

"I am using the soap as supplied by your staff."

"Our staff," he corrected absently. He reached for her wrist again and ran his fingers over her pulse, which skipped like stones over a lake. Which he felt. Which made him squint. "No, this is not mint nor jasmine. This is rather…" He drifted off, lost for words. For once.

"I hazard it is thanks to the lack of mold and mildew," Beatrice said, mesmerized by the fingers stroking her wrist.

"No, it is nothing to do with the house." He stepped closer, and she did not step away.

He tilted his head and stuck out his nose.

He tilted it back again, and she struggled to hold his gaze.

The tip of his tongue appeared between his lips.

She backed up a step and swayed forward two.

He reached out and ran a finger behind her ear.

He rubbed his thumb against a forefinger and then leaned forward, nose very close to her jaw. Now that she was close to him, the scent of citrus was detectable; she recalled overhearing what Ben had said about humans and scents and top notes and wondered if this flood of orange was his or merely his pomade. "What have your relations to say about, about our—this union?" Beatrice stepped back as His Grace seemed content to muse upon her jaw forever.

"They are thrilled beyond expression," Osborn said, readopting his customary scowl. "They anticipate the growth of our family posthaste despite my protestations otherwise."

"We have agreed upon a white marriage." The reminder of this covenant seemed necessary to invoke at this juncture.

"We have." He sniffed her again. "And yet there is no reason to eschew a cordial affiliation."

"A cordial affiliation?" Beatrice asked, incredulous. "What does that entail, I must ask?"

He opened his mouth to explain and once again seemed bereft of words. "It wants careful thought ere I speak further."

Does it? She suspected he hadn't a notion what he was talking about. "Then I can do nothing but await further intelligence, Your Grace." Beatrice sank into one of her defiant curtsies and swished away.

Nine

BEATRICE PAUSED IN HER DAILY PILGRIMAGE THROUGH Arcadia on the threshold of the larger reception room. Its placement at the top of the stairs seemed to beg for its designation as a room for receiving callers, but there was something about it she wanted to keep for their family.

For Osborn's family.

"Mr. Todd." She stopped the factotum on his way past her, a hammer in one hand, a broom in the other. "A word, if you please." He laid aside the broom and crooked his neck.

If only he were as obedient in practice as he was in theory. "The roof," she said.

"Yes, ma'am."

"It is untouched."

"Yes," Mr. Todd said, drawing out his response. "The arrival of the family has disrupted the schedule to some degree."

"Has it? Have you inquired into workmen?" The prince's factotum flushed and showed her his neck again. "Need I involve His Grace in the conversation?"

"You must do as you think best," he murmured.

"I think it best, as I said, that you approach the village for workers." She brushed her hands down her apron. "I could, of course, make my way to Arcadia Demesne myself."

"Again, ma'am, you must do as you wish." There was a twinkling look in his eye, bordering on sly.

The sound of bickering preceded the maids and Morag as they carried in a carpet they had taken for beating. Mr. Todd set down his hammer and came to their aid, which served to fluster the mice. Was he a cat himself? The four of them rolled it out to reveal a gorgeous Axminster, its colors reminiscent of a springtime field of wildflowers. It went nicely with the sofas she had admired in the attic, and the mirror that had come so close to smashing down around her hung in pride of place over the hearth. The room was only missing a few more homey pieces: an embroidery frame, a piano, a kitten to curl up on a lap.

As to that. Beatrice cleared her throat. "I came across a cat last night, and I wonder if it is...a *cat* cat?"

"It is simply feline, ma'am," Mr. Todd assured her. "I suspect it issues from the barn."

"And it will only prey upon mice of its sort?" She glanced at the maids.

"Oh yes, ma'am," Ciara piped up. "They know better, they do."

"Don't stop you running in the other direction," Morag said. Beatrice caught her eye and raised an eyebrow. "Yes, ma'am, sorry, ma'am," the hen muttered.

Beatrice took stock of the room, noting objects whose provenance she did not know; she turned a porcelain vase and wished for flowers to put in it, made an opening move on the draughts board set up on the games table. She straightened the andirons on the hearth and tugged the bell pull in the corner.

It fell out of the ceiling and nearly brained her. The mice gasped, and Morag emitted a guttural sound Beatrice was not certain should issue from a bird. She picked up the rope and held it out to Mr. Todd. "And this task remains on your schedule. Along with having the chimney swept. I shall assume you have not made your way here yet."

He took the rope from her and collected his broom. "Leave it with me, ma'am," he said as he slunk away.

Clattering and whooping erupted from above and swept past as the children raced one another to the ground floor. Ben followed, scolding them lightly as they went. Charlotte came in carrying a lap desk and looked around, approval writ on her features.

"Ben is taking the young out to play. They are nearly able for the Change and have more than their fair share of energy." She smiled and stood, expectant.

Did she desire an invitation to stay? Oh, how Beatrice had dreamed of receiving in her own home. Her mother had not socialized, given her delicate health; she and Eleanor used to pretend to call upon one another, complete with bonnets and pelisses and calling cards. Any hope of creating a circle of her own had died an immediate death once her journey to North Sunderland had been completed and Castleton's true identity revealed. Lady Frost did not entertain.

"I was about to, to sit," Beatrice said. "If you would care to join me."

"This is the most comfortable place in the house, always was. You may have noticed I took the liberty of setting a few things about." Charlotte plumped herself down on one of the sofas.

Beatrice sat with more decorum on the other. "What was the original use of this parlor?"

"It was the family reception room. It is nice to see some of our old things back in the house."

"Had they been above in storage?"

"No, no, we had them in London, uh, when we moved there. I don't suppose Arthur has…"

"Told me anything about his youth? He has not."

"We grew up in Court, which is, of course, no place for children," Charlotte said. Beatrice recalled Osborn's anger at Georgie's threat to take in the family. "When ours were infants, it made no odds, but as they are about to celebrate their seventh birthday—"

"Seven years of age? They are quite robust." She had put them at half a score.

"Yes, this is typical of our kind. Even Ursella, who is smaller than usual."

"She appears healthy." The child was merely quiet, a respite when it came to the liveliness of her siblings.

"Oh, she is, but she is reserved in ways that our kind typically are not, unless they are Omegas," Charlotte explained. "If Ursella designates as such, she will be given the respect she deserves, I don't need to tell you." She did, rather, but Beatrice was not about to say so. Her ignorance of their ways was mounting. "Amongst our sort—oh drat, I do find it awkward, unable to refer to what we are, but—"

"But Osborn has not made himself known to me." *In more ways than one. Which was what they'd agreed.*

Beatrice vowed she could see the words bursting to spill off Charlotte's lips and the effort it took to withhold them. "I must do as my Alpha wishes," she managed.

"Must you."

"Well, mostly." Charlotte winked and set the lap desk on the table. "Meaning no disrespect, of course, as our Alpha's only desire is our safety and happiness." She opened the lid and laid out her writing implements. "It is a great responsibility and the work of the heart rather than the brain."

"The heart?"

"It is where the *sentio* originates and not the mind, as was assumed in olden days."

"This term is unknown to me." Charlotte looked at her with such perception Beatrice rose from the sofa to escape it. "My marriage to Castleton was not…communicative." She moved over to sit in a chair, an austere caned affair, one of several scattered about the room.

"And yet you know what we are."

"My knowledge was gained inadvertently."

Glynis entered with the tea service, her pace as arduous as if trudging through molasses; Mr. Conlon followed behind with enough correspondence to supply a mail coach, piled on a salver. He squinted at every address and handed them over one by one. All were for Charlotte, who exclaimed with pleasure at each.

All but one.

With great ceremony, Mr. Conlon presented the last missive to Beatrice. "From the Duchess of Lowell, Your Grace."

"Oh, dear. Our letters will cross." She slid a finger under the seal.

Dearest Beatrice,

I must begin by insisting we do not proceed "Your Gracing" one another to death now that we are of equal rank. You will recognize this as sheer entitlement on my part. Or cheek. Whichever amuses you the more.

I have been made to understand you are aware of the "unique qualities" to be found amongst the denizens of Lowell Hall and indeed your new homeplace due to your previous situation. Despite this, you must contrive to read between the following lines.

Alfred gives his seal of approval to this approach and sends his compliments.

I am told that Arcadia, while sounding idyllic, may not be as halcyon as its name would indicate and have sent this missive with our speediest messenger, to whom the miles between us are like to nothing. As you may know, it is customary here at Lowell Hall to train those members of a variety of "family types" who are often thought to be incapable of holding their own, as it were, amongst their "sort." Their lives are not held in great regard when compared with their stronger compatriots, but every soul has meaning, and Alfred has made it his duty to preserve these precious lives. As a result, we enjoy a surplus of men willing to work, and I am sending some to you so they may make the best use of their talents.

The "least hardy" of the myriad "sorts" are exclusively male, and as such we have no maids to send. Or, rather, none that meet the presumed gender of one who has a facility for household tasks. There are several lads perfectly adept at the delicate work required in making a house a home and take pride in doing so.

The head footman is Brosnyn. Please call upon him to best deploy each to their gifts.

As we must send them "suitably attired" and with what is needed to do their utmost for you and Arcadia, it will take time for them to arrive. Please look out for them at least three days hence.

Until then, dear Beatrice, I know you will contrive. You are such an inspiration to me. I often watched you turn aside the worst society had to offer with nothing more than a glance, and my admiration for your composure was boundless. You faced down the beau monde *(unlike I, who hid behind the palms without compunction), and I doubt there is anything too daunting for one of such fortitude and heart.*

In sincere friendship, Felicity

In sincere friendship. Beatrice held the letter to her bosom, her first letter, ever, from a friend.

"Thank you," she called after Glynis and Mr. Conlon as they tottered away. Setting down her precious missive, Beatrice poured out, adding milk and the honey Charlotte cooed over. As she accepted the cup and saucer, Charlotte noticed Beatrice's wedding ring.

"Oh!" she cried. She set down her tea and grabbed Beatrice's hand.

"Yes?" The woman's grasp was warm as toast.

"Arthur gave you the topaz?" Charlotte had a complicated look on her face, one of dumbfounded shock with a hint of glee. "Georgie must have kept it for him."

"Is that what it is?" The sherry-gold stone gleamed. "I do not know what it signifies. His Grace is keen to keep his secrets." Beatrice poured herself a cup.

"The better for a dramatic revelation at an inappropriate time," Charlotte said.

"I doubt there will be much call for such histrionics here at Arcadia." Beatrice offered a plate of biscuits. "I do wish to apologize for failing to address you correctly. I presume your husband has a courtesy title? Do you not use it?"

"It is Swinburn. It has done us little good up to now," Charlotte said. She took a breath and continued. "I am sure it is your place to make this request, as you are higher in status, but I shall be bold and ask if I may make free with your name."

"Of course." Beatrice's heart was like a flame in her chest, filling her with warmth. "As, as friends do."

"As family do. And you require a name to be used only within the sleu—er, amongst ourselves." Charlotte regarded her through playfully narrowed eyes. "Beatrice, Beatrice...Bea? Trixie? Beezy! We shall call you Beezy. I am Charlotte, but do call me Charlie."

That was taking it too far, and Beatrice knew her expression showed it. "Charlotte. I shall give it thought."

"Thinking," Charlotte scoffed. "That's getting you and Artie nowhere." She started reviewing her mountain of missives, slotting several to the bottom of the pile.

"I'm sure I do not know to what you refer." Charlotte scoffed again. Beatrice fussed with the sugar tongs. "I trust you will let me know if there is anything else I can do to make you comfortable."

"You have achieved an impressive amount in such a short time. I cannot imagine being cozier than we already are."

Beatrice had to stop herself from scoffing. Aloud, at least. "You say that now, but wait until the next rainstorm."

"One noted the lacework on the roof from the road," Charlotte said, amiably enough. "I did overhear you suggesting Mr. Todd hire workers."

"Yes, I intend to fund the work and, while doing so, build loyalty in the village."

"It's been years since there was money flowing from this seat."
Her sister-in-law was nothing if not direct.

"I have my own."

"I have heard it said that you do." Five letters made their way
into their own pile.

"It is true." There was nothing more she wished to say on that
score. "I have received a letter from the Duchess of Lowell. I wrote
asking if they could spare a few ready hands, and here is Her Grace
addressing the matter herself."

"You share an acquaintance?" Charlotte shuffled three cards
nearer the top.

"She is…" Beatrice thought of those last lines of the letter. "She
is my friend."

"Then you may find yourself playing godmother," Charlotte
said. "She'll be up the duff as soon as may be, I reckon."

"I do beg your pardon."

"The Duke of Lowell won't be waiting to get young." Charlotte
shuffled her letters into yet another formation and thumbed
through the last few.

"Young?"

"It's due to the curse being overturned. Our lot don't palaver
with curses. About whom I cannot inform you," she muttered.

"Curse?" Was Felicity safe?

"That Lowell and their pack would not be fruitful and multiply
until the duke found his *vera amoris*. So he has, and so they will."
Charlotte seemed satisfied with the arrangement of her correspondence and opened the top letter on the first pile. "You would
think he'd have waited."

"Waited?"

"To call in the children."

"Call in the…?" What on earth?

"It's the way of the males of each Shifter species, Goddess
knows why it was allowed. It is the men who determine fertility."

Charlotte scanned the contents of the letter. "We blame the wolves. Their creation tale has become the most widely known among us due to their greater numbers. In their infinite wisdom," and her tone conveyed that it was the opposite, "they deemed it imperative to their survival that their Goddess Diana set the male in charge of fertility." She put aside the first letter and picked up the second. "As all species have mixed over the last century or so, this power has manifested amongst the rest of us." Charlotte tossed her current missive down and sighed. "It is quite tiresome and often requires more breeding than is fair to a female."

This was not news to Beatrice. "It is like that among, um, humans as well."

"As if we haven't other things to do. I adore my cu—children, but Freya forbid Ben take it into his head to repopulate our sle—family ourselves."

"But…" Beatrice blushed. "It is the woman's failure if there are no offspring."

"So say the human doctors. Ha! This is not our belief." Charlotte opened another letter with rather more force than was needed. "I reckon when human ways meet Shifter ways, there will be no doubt as to who prevails. No, dear sister, you will have a child as your Alpha deems it so. Unless you come to a compromise, as Ben and I have. We decided as one, which is the way it should be in this enlightened era."

"Therefore…" If what Charlotte said was true…

"Therefore were I you, I'd have a word with Arthur about keeping his powder dry. There's no rush for the wee ones, you'll be run off your feet putting this house in order as it is, you needn't be chasing after children the livelong day."

"You are all that is illuminating. Please excuse me." Beatrice rose and left the room.

Madam was *looking* at him.

At the beginning of their acquaintance, she'd avoided meeting his eyes most days and subtly, or not so subtly, turned a shoulder away from him when she spoke.

Not so this evening. Throughout the cursory sherries in the footstool room, which was under consideration as a parlor, and during the meal, she'd gazed at him. He'd catch her at it, and she'd not so much as blink.

Arthur drank his wine down in one gulp. He saw she was still regarding him, unblinking, with calculation. Not cold calculation, there was a softness to it—a heat?

A wondering. A thoughtfulness.

The children had eaten and were preparing for bed with Morag. They adored her apparent inability to be impressed, which led them to do everything in their power to dazzle her with their wit and imagination.

The footstool room did not meet with Madam's approval for use after the meal, and she sailed past it with nary a glance in its direction. She led them up to the family parlor; he hesitated before entering, but the balance between what was familiar and new was well struck. The vase, the draughts board brought with them bittersweet images: of Arthur and Ben with their father, learning the game, of mum arranging blooms she'd gathered from the rose arcade. The rug was a new addition as well as several pieces they'd come across in the attic.

"I see you have distributed the furniture."

Madam looked up from the tea service Ben had brought up. "To your approbation, I do hope. For example, these sofas will be more use here than in the footstool room." He barked a laugh. So they were agreed on that, albeit not openly.

They waited for him to bring them in on the joke. He chose not to do so. Madam tilted her head at the mirror. "I also believe the glass is better suited here than tucked away abovestairs."

"Despite the interesting memories attached to it," Arthur said and then wished he had bitten his tongue in half rather than be treated to Charlotte's smirk.

"Making interesting memories so soon?" Charlotte shared out Ciara's latest creations onto plates and passed one to Ben. She fluttered her lashes at Madam. "Do tell."

"Do not, unless you desire half the nation apprised by morning." Arthur snaffled another slice of lemon cake, his favorite combination of tart and sweet.

"I suspect you are second only to your sister-in-law when it comes to knowing what there is to know about society," Madam retorted. "What was it you were saying about Baron Cuddy?"

Charlotte choked on her tea. "Is he still at it, then?"

"The last I heard," Arthur leaned in, "he moved himself and his drove to the Isle of Wight, where apparently—"

The children rushed into the room, freshly scrubbed and dressed for bed. Well, Tarben and Bernadette rushed; Ursella roamed the perimeter, touched the vase and the draughts board before she stood next to her aunt and, as was the child's wont, clutched at her skirt. Madam hesitated and then reached out and ran a hand down one of her plaits.

"Did Morag do this for you?" Ursella nodded and leaned her head against Madam's side. "They are very pretty."

"It is time for our bedtime story," Bernadette announced.

"We want Aunt Beezy to tell it," Tarben added.

Madam blinked rapidly and stiffened. "I am honored," she said, "but it is not my strong suit."

"Everyone knows stories," Tarben insisted.

"They may know them and yet be poor at relating them," she said. Her eyes landed on Arthur again. "I suspect your uncle is far better at it than I."

The children swung around to face him, and he swore he caught a glimmer of humor on Madam's face. Consideration? And now humor? Whatever next?

"I shall start you off, Madam," he returned, and the glimmer transformed into a glare. "Once upon a time, a fair lady was brought to a falling-down castle."

"The lady was fair indeed," contributed Charlotte.

"And she took no nonsense from the mysterious stranger to whom she had been wed against her will." Ben's addition received astounded looks from the adults in the room.

Madam rallied. "This is true, she did not, for she was not nearly as delicate as she looked. She had a spine of steel, like the sword in the story of King Arthur and his court, who contrary to popular belief lived in a borough very near to where we abide." Bernadette looked askance at that, but Madam forged ahead, the result being a confusing tale in which more than one princess, in a nod to fairness for the girls, and a prince, for Tarben, spun straw into gold to appease a trio of wolves who were the size of a thumb. These wolves did not pose much of a threat, and Madam trailed off at the children's growing confusion. She cleared her throat. "I shall endeavor to discover other ways of entertaining you in the days to come."

Their parents struggled not to laugh. "And we shall leave story time to Mum and Papa," Charlotte managed.

"But you must finish it," Bernadette said, looking aghast at such reckless abandonment of common practice.

"Yes, Madam, you must," Arthur said.

"The end." Madam scowled at him.

Ursella shook her head, and Tarben cued, "And they lived…"

Her expression softened, mischievous. "And they lived in cordial affiliation from that day forward."

———————————

Beatrice received hugs from the children before Morag herded them up to bed. Ben kissed her cheek and once again looked puzzled while Charlotte was making faces to rival broadsheet caricatures as they left the room. What were those weighted grimaces regarding?

As if she didn't know. As if she hadn't been *looking* at Osborn.

What if he could "bring in the children," whatever that meant?

What if she dared ask him what it meant?

What if a "cordial affiliation" could be construed to include "marital duties"?

"You need not have told them every bedtime story in one sitting," Osborn…teased? Was he teasing her? Did that fall under the rubric of cordial affiliation?

"I gave fair warning," she replied, and she fought her lips turning up at the ends. As though she wished to smile.

His gaze focused on her mouth. She supposed she must be, then. Smiling. It was such a small thing, but it made his eyelids droop and his head tilt, considering her face and her, her lips.

"Children," she began.

"Yes?" He rose and paused by the draughts board.

"Charlotte said…" Beatrice rose from her seat. She would stand before him and say what she wanted. "She said you can give them to me."

His hand hovered over the board. "Did she."

"She did. The males of your species are in charge of doing so, Charlotte said."

"Charlotte." He slid a black draught forward one space.

"We are on terms."

"You and I are not. On terms."

"Terms are not needed in truth, are they? You are a man. Men wish only to do bed things." Beatrice struggled against the need to wring her hands or else use them to fling a cushion at his head.

"A woman may catch more bees with honey than with vinegar."

"Are you a bee?"

"I am not!"

His expression! If she had been in the habit of laughing, she would have roared with it. "Whatever you are, is it true?"

"That the male brings in the children? Yes. It is some

goddess-forsaken—truly, one would have to forsake the goddess to give the male this power, but yes. If I deem it so, then when my seed…does what it does in your, your womb, then if I—" He trailed off.

"If you what?" How difficult could this be? "Are there words, a ceremony? Need you dance around a bonfire as a heathen would or…?"

"I do not know. I have never called down a child before."

"Shall I ask Charlotte?"

"Do not!" His Grace tore at his hair, which exploded in a profusion of curls. "Sweet Freya, that's all we need."

"If I was to allow marital duties as a part of our cordial affiliation…" Was he going to make her say it?

"You are taking leaps and bounds here, Madam. Even for one such as I, who is not a hare."

"Then I shall put it to you." Beatrice stood as firm as she could. She called upon the spine of steel from her poorly told story. "I seek to redraw our terms. If it is in your power even with one such as I, who has been barren throughout five years of marriage, if your kind can give me a child, then I ask you to give me a child." Ah. There was power in her asking. Did he say nay, her life was no different, but did he say yea…

"I must think on this." He crossed to the hearth to kick the fender.

It was not a "no." "Of course. I did catch you on the hop. Hare or not." Beatrice hid her shaking hands in her skirts. "I shall leave you to it, Osborn." She nodded, and he nodded, and she walked out the door.

"Sleep well," he called as she went down the stairs.

Through the corridor.

Into the stillroom.

Where she closed the door.

And leaned against it.

And breathed.

She sat in her chair, after washing her face and plaiting her hair, and stared at the moon waxing in its heaven…and had hope.

Ten

BREAKFAST WAS AS ENERGETIC ON THE SIXTH DAY OF THE children's arrival as it was from the start. The cubs refused to sit still and seemed to subsist on air, if the effort it took to make them eat was anything to go by. Tarben hopped around the table to the disapprobation of Bernadette, who was skilled in pushing her porridge about to appear she was eating it, which she was not. Ursella slid from her seat to take up residence beneath the table, a little hand waving for scraps of toast, only accepting them if they were free of jam. A pile of rejected slices sat on her chair.

Madam wished to willingly add to this chaos? Whatever her initial discomfort with the cubs, it was long gone as she managed to convince Tarben to return to his seat, encouraged Bernadette to finish her porridge, and ended up with Ursella on her lap, cajoling the child into consuming a rasher of bacon, one sliver at a time.

Arms around the child, she nevertheless had recourse to her inevitable pen and paper and informed the servants and Todd of their tasks on the schedule, or was it Schedule. She reviewed what had been achieved thus far, with great praise for all involved. Arthur noticed that Madam explicitly did not address the fact that workmen, from who knew where, swarmed the roof, and several within were tasked with re-plastering the walls. Nor did she call attention to the veritable army repairing the cottages that once housed the members of his—of his father's sleuth.

Nor did she complain when the children began airing their preferences regarding their accommodation; in fact, she exacerbated their high spirits by transcribing their opinions.

"And have you discovered anything else lacking?" Madam treated this inquiry with the utmost gravity.

Bernadette concluded her long list of items necessary for bringing the schoolroom up to scratch, while Tarben's imagination went in other directions. The absence of their parents allowed it to reach new heights of whimsicality.

"We require a giraffe!" his nephew cried.

"It would come in very handy for retrieving things from the highest shelves." Madam made a note, and Tarben hooted with glee.

"Yes!" He cuddled into her side. "In my other aunt's house, she had a stuffed giraffe."

"Which is in very poor taste when one considers it." Bernadette was truly a matron in the making. Arthur reached out to tickle her and was treated to reluctant giggles.

"We did not like it there," Tarben chattered on. "We were to be seen and not heard. And then when we went to my other aunt's, she did not even want to see us."

"I did not like the beds there," Bernadette added.

"And then at the *other* other aunt's—"

"She was not our true aunt," Bernadette cut across him. "She was a cousin of mum's."

"But we called her aunt." Tarben's voice was rising.

"Only because we could not call her cousin. She was a relic," his sister answered, matching his volume.

"Children," Charlotte scolded. They stopped bickering at one word from their mother. "What in the world!"

"We were telling Aunt Beezy about the giraffe and the meanest aunt," Bernadette said.

"It was a *giraffe* giraffe," Ben explained as he entered carrying two hammers and a bucket of nails. "Not our sort, should you fear as much."

"And then I was going to say about that time we left in the night," Tarben said. "Oh, Aunt Beezy, it was like out of a story of poor wee children escaping an evil sorcerer!"

Madam stilled, and Arthur looked at his brother. How long had they been drifting? And under what circumstances would they need to leave under the cover of night?

"I shall tell Aunt Beezy all about it, but first we must greet what appears to be the contingent from Lowell Hall." Charlotte's voice was light, if her expression was clouded. The children ran out to see.

Madam rose. "If I may have your attention." Everyone in the room turned to her without hesitation. How flawlessly she did this, this managing and organizing and commanding respect. "Upon leaving my room this morning, I came upon a dead creature," she began. The way her gaze passed over Glynis and Ciara encouraged them to infer it was a mouse. "I suspect it is the cat doing what cats do, but I prefer steps be taken to prevent this in future." She waited for the nods of agreement that followed her order as naturally as night followed day. "Now. Come, let us see what the duke and duchess have sent us, shall we?"

The women shared a hand squeeze as Madam passed Charlotte. Ben led out Todd along with the kitchen staff; as was the case of late, Arthur found he must follow.

A cavalcade of carriages and carts rolled up the drive, the Lowell insignia polished to a shine on every conveyance down to the lowly donkey cart. The drivers brought their teams to a halt, and the doors to the vehicles opened simultaneously. Beatrice could feel Osborn's eyes rolling at the demonstration. She thought her heart was going to burst with delight.

No fewer than fifteen men decanted from the carriages, not counting the outriders who joined them as they lined up before her. They ranged from her not-great height to somewhat shorter than Ben. None looked in ill health or in any way deserving of the term *runt*. They stood at attention and vibrated with readiness.

She had written to ask for ten and in return received twenty-five, dressed soberly in dark olive and gray, in livery style but not that of the Lowell holding.

How clever of the duchess, dressing them as though she did not expect them to return.

A thunderous growling rumbled behind her, and she turned to see both Osborn and Ben step forward to scent the air.

"What is it?" she asked even as the duke took her in his arms from behind and turned her away from the footmen. Charlotte widened her eyes at them and then wrapped her arms around herself.

"I expect you have discerned the scent signature of the Duke of Llewellyn." A barrel-chested footman stepped forward. He was on the shorter end of the spectrum and boasted parallel stripes of white in his ink-black hair. "Your Graces, I assure you he is not here," he continued after he proffered the usual obeisance.

"He had better not be," Osborn spat. "I cannot have one of his sort running loose on my land. Nor near the duchess."

"How is it you can scent him if he is not here?" Beatrice tried to wriggle out of the duke's grasp, which resulted in her bum wiggling against him, which created an immediate and unexpected tautness in his falls. It called to mind moments from more than one improper turn around the floor at Almack's, before a patroness could descend to put paid to the unacceptable proximity. She maneuvered again and found herself clutched closer and thrust away and then pulled closer still.

"He is one of the highest predators of our kind," Ben snarled, matching his brother's tone, "and as such his signature is strong."

"He is in residence on Lowell lands," the footman reported. "There is a letter from our Alpha explaining the state of things regarding the Duke of Llewelyn's circumstances, as well as ours." He handed the missive to Conlon, whose confusion over whether to hand it to His or Her Grace was solved by Ben's taking it. "I am

Brosnyn, head footman of this complement, who are entirely at your disposal."

"More fine men to dispose of." Arthur relaxed his hold, and Beatrice gave one more wiggle before stepping around to stand before him.

"On behalf of His Grace, you are very welcome to Arcadia," she said as they gave their obeisance as one. "Brosnyn, Mr. Conlon is butler here, and I will require you to convene with him in all things. This is Mr. Todd." She indicated the prince's factotum. The company assessed him with more than one nose aloft; he returned the favor. "He is here at His Highness, the prince regent's, behest. Mr. Brosnyn, should you or the men have any queries, do direct them to Mr. Todd or me.

"His Grace and I," she continued, "are grateful to the Duke and Duchess of Lowell for sending you here and hope you will find true fulfillment for your talents in Arcadia."

"Where we are going to accommodate these souls is as good a question as any," Osborn groused.

"I have only to consult with you on that matter, and it shall be done according to your will," Beatrice replied without missing a beat. She laid a hand on his arm, appearing amenable and waiting for his law to be handed down.

———

To any who did not know Madam, she would look to be the picture of deference. Ha! "You wish to consult with me about such matters?" Arthur snorted. "That horse has long since bolted."

"Your Grace." He fought a smile as he could feel Madam's nails digging into his forearm. Why he should smile when his salty little lemon cake was veritably sinking her claws in him—

Whose salty cake? his bear wondered.

"Madam?" He looked at her expectantly and took her hand, raising it to his lips.

That's new! his creature chortled.

His lips touched the back of her hand. And Lady Frost blushed.

She slipped her hand from his grasp with less alacrity than he would have expected. "Speaking of horses bolting, I daresay your brother, Lord Swinburn, would not hesitate to welcome your help with his tasks."

"Come along, Arthur," Ben said. "Let us leave this in your wife's capable hands."

Madam's voice rose as she addressed the cohort, as confident as if she did this every day of her life. Perhaps she had; perhaps Castleton had given her authority over his lands and staff. He and his bear snorted in unison at this unlikely scenario. Given she had so many siblings, had she been put in charge of them? That was likely to happen to a girl. This house, as large as it was, burst at the seams with the addition of only three cubs; Goddess knew how thrice that number would fare. And how badly had Ben and Charlotte and the cubs fared over the last years? How much time passed since they'd left their residence in Court? Who had dared treat the cubs poorly?

"Was it Humbert?"

"Who, now?" Ben asked.

"Was it he from whom you escaped under cover of night?"

They reached the barn, big enough to shelter ten horses and sturdy enough, though it did appear to be sagging inward from the sides.

"Oh, Humbert. No, we had not got to that extremity." Ben handed Arthur the hammer and nails as he turned to collect a massive ladder leaning against the main door; he tucked it under his arm with as much exertion as he would a cricket bat. "It doesn't matter. We made a choice, as dramatic as it was, much to Tarben's delight. Holy Freya, he is so like Charlie—"

"Do not turn the topic." A pain in Arthur's chest threatened to take over his entire body, to expand—explode—into the *sentio*. It urged him to offer comfort where it was needed, to shelter his family in its protective embrace. He fought it off as he would an invasive predator.

"Do not dwell on the past. Always your problem, so broody," Ben chided and led the way into the barn. He turned with a grin. "Not that sort of broody, although Her Grace had a look in her eye the other evening. And this morning as well."

"White marriage," Arthur reminded him and cast an eye over the interior. The roof was in fair enough nick, but the beams appeared to be held up by wishful thinking and the inevitable cobwebs.

"Ah, yes, of course. For the best, I imagine."

Now what was that supposed to mean? He was well able to turn a female head did he so choose. He attended every Season Georgie forced him to, shaking off the females if anyone was inquiring. Had they not made their pact, it would likely be the case with Madam as well. "It is, in fact, more in the order of a cordial affiliation."

Ben headed for the furthest beam, which proved to be the most tenuous. "What's that when it's at home?"

"The exact terms are under negotiation, and I would not be so crude as to discuss them behind Madam's back." Arthur took off his coat and threw it unheeding to the ground.

"Ah, discretion, the better part of valor." Ben set the ladder in place and handed Arthur one of the hammers. "Now. We're to ensure the beams and such are secure, as there is concern for the barn's denizens."

The place was noticeably free of equine occupation. "You cannot mean the bloody cat."

"Or cats," Ben corrected. "She or they may be the culprits behind the offerings on your wife's doorstep."

"And so we are to make a palace for them out here?"

"We are indeed. Off you get, affiliate cordially with this hammer, if you please." Ben laughed and ran up the ladder before Arthur could swat him as he deserved.

Footmen tended to the drive, raking the gravel and weeding the verge. They had come with every tool and implement necessary to resuscitate a crumbling manse, inside and out. Brosnyn supplied the names of those best placed to help in the house and was impeccably respectful of Mr. Conlon's dignity. The entire cadre were eager to serve and in many cases suggested their tasks.

Beatrice turned from the window under the newly refurbished eaves, in what ought to be a maid's room. "I hesitate to put either Ciara or Glynis up here," she said, mindful of the many stairs.

"We shall call them the footmen's rooms then," Charlotte said as she ran a hand over the bed covers to settle them into shape. "I suspect the girls would not wish to be removed from the rooms they have made their homes."

"Charlotte." Beatrice sat on the bed, disrupting her sister-in-law's work. "If it is not comfortable to discuss what the children were saying this morning, I understand. But if you would like to speak to another woman about it…"

Charlotte joined her. "These were relations on my side, part of a family group like ours, who had very high standards of behavior. I suspect it is where Bernadette gets it." She laughed; it lacked her usual heartiness. "My children's manners were the cynosure of very discerning eyes, as were my own. Ben came close to blows when I was taken to task before the whole family. We left under the cover of night because I was so afraid he would challenge the head of the house."

"Challenging entails…" Beatrice did not like the sound of that.

"The death of he who is not the victor. At least according to those who abide by the old ways. As that branch of the family still do, given their great age. We ourselves do not." Charlotte patted her hand. "We are adept at packing our bags and moving on, and we fled beneath the pall of my unladylike glory."

"And yet only behold my good self, as little like a lady as you may ever see." Beatrice stood and brandished her dusting cloth. "How the *beau monde* would gawk at Lady Frost now. I am positively melting from the exertion."

"Your sobriquet earned admiration." Charlotte rose and tugged the bed covers flat. "Society assumed it was an aspect gleaned from your years in Castleton's—"

"Care?" Beatrice finished. "I do not think I need go any further in saying it was not care."

"And yet you took your rightful place in society when the time came and faced them down."

Beatrice looked around the room and considered it good. She led Charlotte to the stairs. They had accomplished what she'd designated for the day, and the footmen—dare she say *her* footmen—would be housed in comfort.

"I did, as was my right." She wiped a cloth along the banister as they descended. "With little pleasure. One pined for the peace of the countryside after a Season of whispers, though I could never miss what I found in Adolphus Place."

A footman stood at the door of the family reception room and, when requested, set off with alacrity to fetch their tea. The women took to the sofas.

Charlotte shuddered. "There are none among us who wish to imagine Castleton in the bedchamber."

"It was—" Beatrice folded the cloth in her hands.

"Revolting? Horrendous?"

She looked up. "It was harrowing."

Charlotte leapt from her seat and cuddled up to Beatrice's side. "Oh, my dear." She briskly rubbed a hand up and down the other woman's arm.

"And at the end of the day, I…" If Beatrice could not ask Charlotte, she could ask no one. "I do not believe the act was done properly." She worried at her wedding ring.

"If any were to be improper, I would think it he."

"I am not conveying my meaning. I was, of course, raised in pastoral circumstances." The footman returned, set down the service, and bowed. "Thank you, Brock." He stepped out and pulled the door shut.

Beatrice poured out and tried again. "I have seen the animals. Oh, I mean no offense."

Charlotte divided a scone among two plates. "Did your mum not take you into her confidence before your wedding night?"

"She did, in euphemistic terms. But I discerned the, the mechanics of the act from—"

"The natural world," Charlotte supplied.

"The natural world. My expectation of translating such efforts into the human experience were not met."

"I see." Charlotte drank her tea.

"Do you?" This would be simpler than she'd thought.

Charlotte put down her cup and saucer. "I do not."

Beatrice rent her half of the scone in two. "Mother said there would be blood."

"Was there?" Beatrice shook her head and took a bite of scone. "Did he not breach your maidenhead?" Beatrice shook her head again and shrugged. Charlotte continued. "It is very likely, then, you are still an innocent."

Beatrice scoffed, and to her horror, crumbs flew out of her mouth. "I can think of no one less innocent than I."

"Untouched, then, in any way that signifies."

"But there was… It was not, I cannot call it bed play, but he visited my rooms and came into the bed with me, and…" She could not go on.

"My dear, you are the epitome of refinement, and I shudder to lower the tone." Charlotte took a deep breath and asked, "Did he put his cock in your cunny?"

Beatrice brushed at the crumbs in her lap. "There were, of course, attempts at entry. I do not believe he was successful."

"You'd know for certain if he had."

"There was a sensation of—"

"Of this?" Charlotte poked Beatrice in the fleshy part of her arm down to the bone.

Beatrice gasped at the sharp pain. "Something like, but with far less energy."

"Sweet Freya, did it go in or did it not?"

"His part?"

"Yes."

"No…?"

Charlotte rose and looked about the room. "I would be happy to illustrate the correct effect, only to a certain extent, of course… ah!" She dragged Beatrice off the sofa and over to the mantelpiece to take a candle out of its holder. "Here. Feel this. It is like to as firm as a cock ought to be."

Beatrice grasped the candlestick at the exact moment Ben and Osborn walked in. She dropped it; Charlotte howled with laughter and ran from the room, collecting Ben on her way. The sound of her mirth could be heard diminishing up the flight of stairs.

"Dare I ask?" Osborn's habitual glower lightened.

"You may, of course," she replied. "Nevertheless, I do not recommend it."

"How curious." His voice, always so resonant, achieved a note so plangent it threatened to undo her garters.

"It was such as killed the cat, and you have assured me you are not one." Osborn had brought half the dirt of the barn in with him. She reached out and brushed the arm of his coat. His arm, which was in the sleeve. An arm as solid as an oak, as unyielding as that mighty tree. And yet it was warm, so warm, and it twitched beneath her touch. She ran her hand up and down, up and down…

She ought to stop petting him.

Beatrice buttoned him up instead, her fingers passing over his belly as she did so, causing him to inhale, sharply, and to radiate even more heat than before.

What would it be like if they lay together? She peeked up at him under her lashes; neither moved as she ran her hands over his lapels. She had never willingly put her hands on a man, and it was rather instructive that her touch might cause him to tremble. Additionally, she was not in any way put off by him, which boded well.

Beatrice quivered as he lowered his head to, to kiss her?

No. To sniff her.

"Your Grace," she began.

"Do not scold me, it is what we do." He dipped his head once more. "I do not understand—"

"That I may not enjoy being smelled at?"

"It is what we do," he reiterated. "We can tell our mates from the first fragrance. You do not have one."

She resisted sniffing her wrist. "I am deficient in a new way."

"It is not a deficiency. It is not that you have no scent but rather one that is…" He huffed. "It is not…consistent."

"There are any number of factors that may influence this, such as clothes drying in the sun as opposed to the laundry room, and the amount of exertion a person may undertake in a day's work." This was only common sense, was it not?

"But there is an underlying essence we perceive, much the way one recognizes the color of hair or eyes," he said. Neither had stepped away. "It is like one's characteristics, quick to anger or to blush, for example." His finger lightly touched her cheek. "One may embody an essence as tangible as the sea at dawn or of a Burgundy rose in midsummer or even something as mundane yet homely as…" He spotted the candle on the floor and stepped away to pick it up. "As candle wax."

Her face bloomed scarlet. "Give that here," she said and fumbled it back into its holder.

"You have gone from having no fragrance to speak of to something I cannot fix on."

"I find these comments about the state of my person to be less than gracious."

"They are facts, not judgments, Madam." Why did her skin shiver so when he called her *Madam* in that tone? Did he mean it to sound like an endearment?

"I must ask if this lack is influencing your decision regarding the child." Beatrice set about rearranging the mantelpiece despite it requiring her to handle the candlestick holders.

"As to that—"

Tarben bolted into the room as though shot from a bow. "Uncle Arthur! Papa requires you in the kitchens, but Mum says to leave you and Aunt Beezy alone, but he asked first, and I think I ought to obey things in the order I receive them, what think you?"

The look Osborn gave her was…fraught. Fraught with humor, with warmth, with a world of potential. He took his nephew's hand in his great grasp, and the reluctance in the gaze that passed from the child to her spoke volumes that even in her hopes she hesitated to fully read.

"I have orders to help my nephew fulfill, Madam." He allowed Tarben to drag him out of the room. "We shall consult in due course."

Eleven

WE SHALL CONSULT IN DUE COURSE. HE HAD SOUNDED LIKE A clerk. Their future intimate relations were not a carriage he was considering for purchase or a decision regarding which field to lie fallow.

Madam appeared to hold his comment in equally low regard and presented him with a cold shoulder during the daily allotment of tasks on the day's Schedule. Charlotte was in great good humor regarding Freya knew what, which she had shared with Ben, who kept giggling into his teacup. A brief spat about whether Madam was allowed outside the house was greeted with a reference to the sauce being good for the goose as well as the gander. An order was given for Mr. Todd to communicate Her Grace's desire for the donkey cart to be hitched up, and so it was.

Arthur had no choice but to give over to his bear and follow in the shadows.

Shadows were, in fact, few and far between as green-thumbed Lowell footmen continued their assault upon the grounds. Hedges were trimmed, shrubs were wrestled back from ignominy, and the rose arcade's latticework was shored up, its climbing vines pruned.

He followed along at a distance from the donkey cart. Madam was attired with her typical austerity but for an absurd bonnet, a confection of feathers and tulle in an unlikely shade of chartreuse. The ribbons tied beneath her chin flew over her shoulder as the cart tooled toward the eastern border. Despite the frivolous head-gear, she was a dab hand with the reins, authoritative yet gentle.

Were they to keep the cart and donkey, never mind the foot-men? The carriages that had brought the Lowell runts had been sent back but for one, as well as a team of draft horses large as elephants. How fortuitous that the barn had been restored. But of course it was why the barn had been restored, felines notwithstanding.

Madam attempted to make him read the letter from his peer, which he refused to do, admittedly for no good reason apart from general churlishness. Did Lowell see them as a charity case? The Osborn duchy was not impoverished; he knew what was required to wrench the funds out of His Highness's grasp, which he would not do even if it meant indebtedness to that bloody wolf and to his own wife.

As to that: Why had Georgie chosen this little human for him to wive? There were any number of *versipellian* heiresses who may have served if His Bloody Highness was so keen on increasing ursine solidarity. None were as small and yet self-possessed; some were as wealthy but none so generous. He had only to recall baroness thingamajig, a bird shifter of some species or other who had been so profligate with her wealth, to no one's benefit but her own, even Georgie was appalled. No one else would have clapped eyes on this place and stayed; none he could name would have taken on this challenge with such aplomb and verve.

Here was Arcadia coming back to life, within and without, thanks to one small human woman. She hopped down from the driving seat and handed the reins of the cart to an unknown human—the foreman, he reckoned—as the man doffed his hat and the rest of the crew followed suit. Madam headed for the nearest ladder, and Odin above, if she dared to climb it to inspect the roof—ah. Todd had anticipated her and took to the eaves with alacrity. She would not have…would she? Not in her skirts. Odin *help* her if she started wearing men's clothing as it was rumored the Duchess of Lowell had taken to doing.

His plump little cake in trousers? Odin help *him*.

Todd shouted down his opinion of the work, which expressed high praise.

Madam turned and smiled at the foreman.

It was a small smile, the mere turning up of her lips and yet—

And yet? his bear, bored by the crouching and the lurking, piped up.

And yet she would gift it to a stranger.

He has pleased her, whereas you…

Arthur knew what would please her.

Should a smile be his only reward he may count the game worth the candle.

He and his bear wandered the land well past tea time, noting several disturbances in the landscape that could only have been made by a great predator roaming the boundaries. Perhaps it was only he, the great predator who had been roaming them, but he knew his markings and these were not his. One more thing to protect Madam from, for the love of Freya.

Arthur bathed in the brook, with a cake of soap he had secreted there, the robust scents of orris and oak moss clinging to his skin. He wrapped himself in a cloth and jogged back to the house, pausing when he caught sight of Madam moving about before her window, brushing her hair, an unexpectedly great fall of gold, while she chatted to a squirrel.

He slipped into the laundry and dressed with a view of not being dressed for much longer. Ought he at least put on a waistcoat? He did not wish to be slovenly, but a cravat was out of the question. He put on a waistcoat and a coat, buttoning neither. Or would she like to unbutton him? Must he put on stockings and boots? He must; he would look the veriest tramp, or worse, a louche rake, coming upon her both unbuttoned and unshod.

Half the buttons of the waistcoat, then. Doing them up, he entered the kitchens.

The servants turned to him and quite ostentatiously looked away,

Morag going so far as to leave the kitchen and take the mice with her. Mrs. Porter hung her apron upon its hook with exaggerated care, and Conlon, loyal, devoted Conlon, tilted his head in such a minute obeisance it was the precise opposite of one of Madam's curtsies.

"Taking your cues from Her Grace, I see," he called after them. He joined Ben by the stove, where his brother was calmly stirring the contents of a madly boiling pot. "What are you at?"

"Your wife very kindly asked me for potpourri to freshen the footmen's rooms."

"It smells familiar." It smelled of cedarwood and clover and home.

"It is Mum's old recipe." Ben stirred thrice clockwise. "I am making up laundry soap as well."

"How do your in-laws fare on the Continent?" Thundering Thor, that they should bide so far from home…the shame of it walloped him out of nowhere. So many abroad and away, families enough to thrive on Arcadia's grounds and leave room for more. How Madam would champ at the bit to see them settled.

Ben sprinkled in a pinch of lavender. "They are well, in the farthest north of Germany, near to Scandinavia with many of our kind. They correspond with Charlotte, naturally, and miss the children. We thought to visit twice, but in each instance Ursella objected, going so far as to hide until we missed the ship."

"Why in the world should she do so? And that you allowed it?"

"It was not permissible to leave England, she said. An Omega, even as yet undesignated, is to be heeded." Ben tossed in a pinch of lemon zest. "I encourage you to return and ask me the second question when you are a father."

He might allow a child, but he would never be a father. Would he? "Is there any supper left for me? Has nothing been kept warm?" He poked around the larder and found he was not in the least peckish.

Suffering from your nerves? his bear quipped and was ignored.

Ben stirred the brew counterclockwise thrice. "As the stillroom is occupied, I was given leave to use the hob."

"You need not explain yourself to me, I who have nothing to do with the quotidian workings of this place."

"As is correct, Alpha." Ben stirred clockwise once more and took the pot off the heat. "We missed you at the meal."

"Did you?" Ben did not dignify the admittedly sulky riposte. "What transpired?"

"Bernadette has taken it upon herself to educate Beezy in the improvement of her storytelling, going so far as to transcribe a directive for which events ought to unfold."

"The next Anchoretta Asquith."

"Tarben insisted he too knew how a story should unspool and proved himself to be as lacking in skills as his beloved aunt."

Arthur laughed. "I am sorry I missed it." He truly was. He was sincerely sorry he'd missed that moment. He smoothed down the lapels of his coat, one of his favorites, a deep violet that brought out the bear in his eyes. "I must convey my apologies to Madam for the lack of my company and bid her sleep well."

He left the kitchens to the accompaniment of his brother's muttering, "Is that what we're calling it now?"

The squirrel on the branch tilted its head inquisitively. "Well, you should wonder, Master Squirrel. Had we not inspected each dwelling it would have been rather a different tale indeed. The farther from the first cottage we proceeded, the less attention to detail was to be observed. I bear the builders no ill will. It is the habit of this class of workmen to ensure their patrons remain on their toes." Beatrice left off plaiting her hair—as difficult as ever given its thickness—and idly brushed the ends. The squirrel sat up on its haunches and fled up the tree to hop into another and away. "Until we meet again, sir."

The door opened without even a cursory scratching upon it. Without turning she said, "Good evening, Your Grace. Once again, you prove your expertise at opening doors whether or not it is wanted."

He shut it behind him. "Once again, Madam, may I suggest you proffer honey as opposed to vinegar."

"Do squirrels enjoy honey?" She rose and set her brush aside. He was staring at her hair. She played with the ends of it.

Osborn blinked as though coming out of a trance. "Squirrels?"

"So it was not you with whom I was speaking." He laughed, an enormous laugh that spun along her nerves and set them tingling. He came to stand opposite her, the bed between them. "I heard you laughing in the kitchen," she said.

"I understand Tarben is a rival for your inimitable style of storytelling."

"Surely it is clear I have no skills in that area, and yet the children insist." It pleased her, if she was to tell the truth.

"It is regarding children I am here." He cleared his throat and continued. "Madam, I will lie with you and give you a child. It is within my power, and our cordial affiliation notwithstanding, it need not impact nor change the way we—"

"Conduct a white marriage?" He nodded, and that great curl of hair fell across his brow. It took every fiber of her being to resist rushing around the bed to tuck it back in place. His coat fit him ill, too tight around the shoulders, but was the hue of springtime violets and did appealing things to the color of his eyes. "Will it only be the once or..." Beatrice faltered. "I have heard women speak of the necessity of doing this often until it, uh, takes."

He hesitated and cast his gaze around the corners of the room. "I assume, as with much else in life, it may require diligence and application."

"Very well, then." Beatrice tugged the top cover down the bed and then the next and then the sheet. "There is a pitcher and bowl behind the screen if you wish to make use of them. The water should still be warm." He removed his coat and fiddled with the buttons on his half-done waistcoat. "I assume you can unclothe yourself?"

She heard him mutter *unclothe* as he disappeared behind the screen. She wrestled herself out of her dressing gown and dove beneath the covers. Beatrice pulled them up to her chin—but what if that prevented him from getting in? She lowered them to her waist, and the exposure was too much, as if she was standing in the forecourt in the nude.

Would he expect her to be nude? She never had with…let her not invoke her first husband at this time! Not that Osborn was her husband in anything but name. Well, not for much longer. He would soon be that in deed.

Under the covers, she drew her night rail up over her belly. She shut her eyes, and the candle flame danced behind her lids—

Beatrice leapt from the bed, snuffed out every taper in the room, and returned to the safety of the covers just as he came around the screen. By the light of the fire and that of the moon pouring through the window, he looked like a man any woman would be fortunate to welcome into her bed. He stood beside it, still in his smalls, and what a sight he made. The shadows caressed the divots of his muscles, the flickering light of the flames licked at his skin eagerly, a delicious treat. He tilted his head, unmoving.

Oh. "Shall I move? To the side? Or?" She clenched her eyes shut.

"If you would release the sheet, Madam."

"Ah. Of course." She let go with the hand closest to him but clung to the rest. There was a hesitation and shushing of cloth, good Lord, and into the bed he descended. He lay on his back at her side, exuding heat as if he had absorbed the flames so keen to lick at him. She must not think of licking. She did not know why.

He did nothing for what seemed a very long time until he rolled onto his side, facing her. She lifted her head to get her hair out of the way when he reached for it.

"May I not touch it?" he asked.

"My hair?"

"May I?"

"If you wish?" What had her hair to do with anything?

His fingers lightly stroked the end of her plait; he lifted it to his nose. "Spearmint," he said.

"I used the soap Ciara made. To wash it," she replied.

"Hmmm," he hummed. He released it and slid his fingers to the back of her head and rubbed there. What this touching was about she could not say, but it was very relaxing.

The thought of them relaxing made her tense anew. He murmured softly as he would in gentling a wild creature and edged closer still. His nose ran over her ear, and she shivered. He did it again, and she wriggled.

"Ticklish," he whispered. His fingers ran around the hem of her night rail. How had his hand gotten there? "May I?" he asked.

"May you what?"

"Remove this, or?"

"No, but—wait, I can—" She pulled it up over her belly.

"Thank you," he said.

The backs of his knuckles drew up and down the outside of her thigh. So gently did he do this she felt languorous but also invigorated, an odd combination. A fingertip teased over her kneecap, and she wanted to push into his touch. His hips settled into her side, and his male part in no way nor by any stretch of the imagination felt akin to an inanimate candle.

"Is this pleasant for you?" he asked, and she nodded. He then put his whole hand over her knee. "And this?" She nodded again and sighed when he squeezed it—then gasped when his palm drew up on the inside of her leg.

"No?" he asked.

"No?" she said, unsure, if only because: "Is this necessarily a part of this?"

"Oh, it is." He raised himself over her, and she tucked her head; it was too much to meet his eyes. "If you would allow me?"

———————————

Madam nodded again, and Arthur commenced touching her, lightly, with his fingertips, up one thigh and down the other, parting her legs as gently as he could. Gods, her skin was like silk; he wanted to rub his face all over her body—was her belly as soft? It was, and she was as sensitive there as she was behind her ear. He huffed a pleased little laugh as she shivered under his touch.

He laid a hand on her lower belly, so near her cunny, and wanted to kiss her everywhere, her mouth, her jaw, her belly, the tops of her thighs; do not even get him started on her breasts, which heaved with her labored breath. She writhed again, in resistance or desire? Her fragrance was muted, still, a circumstance that should not be and yet was. Her true essence in ways was withheld from him, and yet he could feel…

He stroked a finger across her honeypot, found the moisture there, evidence of her response even if he could not scent it. Madam made a noise like a perplexed kitten, a little mew of confusion. Did she like it, or did she dislike it? "May I?" He nudged his nose at her ear again. She moved her head away and then back and touched her nose glancingly to his jaw, a nuzzle of his sideburns, as light as a feather, that served to inflame him out of proportion. She nodded, and he added another finger, then another, and stroked and stroked. She moved her head from side to side. Again, desire or resistance? "No?"

"Yes?" she whispered, and if he hadn't been attuned to every twitch of her being, he would have missed the infinitesimal lift of her hips.

Keep hold of yourself, man, he warned himself as his cock, which had responded with interest to the softness of her skin, surged to full hardness at the movement. "Yes?"

She nodded, and he said, "I prefer you to speak your permission, Madam."

"Yes," she said. "Yes."

He set his whole hand over her entrance, and she sighed. His fingers found her sensitive nub and her hips flew up to meet his. He soothed her into acceptance of his touch, and he asked again, and she said yes, yes again. He stroked her ear with his nose, which made her sigh and melt, and he glanced her jaw with his mouth, oh, how he wanted to kiss her. He rubbed his nose against hers and hovered his lips over hers.

"I do not like that." She turned her head away.

"Kissing?" Blessed Freya, who did not like kissing?

"Do not."

"As you say, Madam." He laid his forehead beside hers on the pillow, arched above her, and wished for…things that did matter in this instance. "May I continue? There is no need to go on if you do not wish."

"I wish." She reached out, slowly, and set her hand upon his biceps. "Yes, do. Please continue."

He allowed his hand to rest on her cunny, palm large enough to cover her entirely. He settled himself over her, and she started at the touch of his cock and yet cuddled up to him with her hips. He recited the Nordic pantheon to himself. He traced his fingers over her contours; her breath caught, and her pulse beat like a drum. He whispered nonsense, and if he invoked some of his gods and goddesses aloud, he could not be blamed. She tucked her face against his heart and rubbed her cheek against his chest, and one hand snuck up to rest beside it as the other stroked his shoulder. He shifted her thighs further apart, and she took a breath. "Easy, Madam. Breathe. I am here."

"That is apparent," she muttered, and a puff of laughter escaped them both.

Odin, Freya, Sif, he thought, *Baldur, Loki, Thor, let me be gentle, let me be easy, let me in, Madam, oh gods…* He sank slowly into her heat, her sheath so tight. He met resistance on his way, felt her stiffen, and he halted. He was like to spend before he was fully seated in any case. He fought to keep quiet to prevent further alarm, but it proved impossible when both her hands petted at his sides and her palms settled on his back. What would her little hand feel like on his cock? *Freya, Frigga, Sif…*

Regulating his breathing was a dead loss. If only she would allow kissing, kissing would help pass the time until she relaxed. Speculating as to how previous forays into such behavior had poisoned her against it served to keep him from losing his sense entirely. He nosed at her throat, and she returned the favor, hitching her knees up, and they moaned in concert. He slid farther forward, slowly, and he wrapped his arms around her until, there was no delicate way to put it, he entered her completely.

"Thank you," Madam whispered.

Did she think that was that? "You are very welcome," he murmured, "but we have only just begun."

He reached beneath her, and his hand captured her entire bottom in one palm, and he moved.

———————

He moved, and Beatrice gasped. There had been a pinch of pain, and she'd thought the act was complete, he was fully inside her, surely it was done. But no. There was more, and she was feeling *more*, everything, inside and out.

His skin was…not truly rough but a contrast to hers, making her feel that much softer. He had muscles everywhere, and yet she did not fear being crushed or hurt. He seemed to be doing his utmost to ensure her comfort and honored her wish to abstain from kissing. The heat from his body and the power in it were quite breathtaking, and he was clearly enjoying himself.

Her mind wandered back to when he had touched her cunny and her breath had gone labored and her muscles had turned to water. It seemed unfortunate it wasn't part of the greater effort. Nevertheless, this was far more pleasant than she would have guessed! Beatrice nudged at his shoulder with her nose and then rubbed her cheek against his biceps. She squirmed as he squeezed her bum, and his breath caught, so she did it again, and he growled, and she wanted to laugh, which seemed to be permitted. Given her previous experiences, she was optimistic this was going well enough. She rubbed her nose on his chest and laid her cheek there. It was quite cozy now the odd little pain had passed. She wondered if he would be about this much longer.

He raised up, balancing himself on one massive arm, reached down with his free hand, and—*oh*. Oh, oh—he touched the place again where she was most sensitive, and a rush of feeling came over her, warm and shivery and yearning; as his fingers played, she reached for she knew not what, her entire body was restless and wanting and she didn't know, she didn't know what to do—

Had she said that aloud? For he had left off reciting a series of foreign-sounding names and said, "Let me, let it, here, I can—" and then did something with two fingers and his thumb, and she keened and lifted her hips and wound her legs around his hips. He paused in his stroking, and someone growled, *she* growled and pushed herself into his hand. He groaned and moved within her with greater force; her fingers wound themselves in his hair, and his whole hand engaged in stroking her, and then, and then—

A moment, a pause; Beatrice looked into his eyes, his brown eyes full of purpose and pleading, and her back bowed, and she shuddered and gasped and pulled his hair. Osborn growled and thrust with force, once, twice, and an unexpected heat blossomed within. She gasped and clung and buried her face in his neck even as he clutched her close to his chest like she was precious, like he could not bear to let go.

Arthur wanted to hold her tight. He wanted to slide down her body and rest his head on her bosom, a significant portion of her anatomy he had not even addressed. He wanted to roll over onto his back and cradle her to his chest and stroke her as she came down from her release. He wanted to kiss her so very much; he was parched, and her mouth was an oasis in the desert.

Instead, she stiffened beneath him, and he rose. She turned away when he pulled the covers over her and sought out the pitcher and soap. He gave himself a cursory wash and returned with a cloth to find she had not budged. "Madam, I would inquire as to your state of being."

"I am well." She pulled a pillow over her face.

He nudged her shoulder with the cloth. She squeaked and took it, reached beneath the covers, and in due course reluctantly handed it back. She drew the covers over her head and thus missed his grin. Tossing the cloth in the direction of the hearthstone, he insinuated himself back under the covers.

"Is this necessary?" Madam muttered and rolled to her side.

"Oh, it is." Or so he had decided at that moment. "No child will come if the bed does not contain its father and mother."

She pulled the cover down and glared at him over her shoulder. He shrugged as if it was outside his power to deem otherwise. Her back fully presented to him, she wrestled with the blanket until settling. Her hair streamed over the pillow, a wild tangle of gold he'd only seen in Renaissance paintings or plays. The latter of course were wigs, and Madam's was assuredly not. He reached out and snagged a finger on a tress. One led to another and... "May I?" She humphed and sighed and nodded; he set to unraveling the rest of her plait.

He drew out one length after the next. "How have you been hiding this in that little bunch on the top of your head? Women's fashions. I do not know whom they exist to please. Not the males of the species, I can assure you. Though did you go about with this abundance on display you would cause a melee. So it is the fault of males' inability to behave with decorum that you must hide this in plain sight." He gently combed his fingers through it, from her scalp to the ends. He did it again. And again. "Were you *verispellis*, I would think you a lion. Although that would mark you as male, so therefore, no. There is one in residence at—which is not for me to say. Only see how you make me forget myself, Madam."

He nuzzled the crown of her head. "I hope you do not suffer any discomfort at this moment?" She shook her head and shrugged; he tucked himself closer to her side. "Here, here, allow me," and he stroked a hand from the back of her neck to a shoulder, then around to the other, back and forth, and slipped his fingers underneath the top of her night rail. "Gods, your skin. Had you not had this on during...during, I would have disported myself like a green lad. I shudder to think your reaction had I done so. I suppose I would have earned rather a set-down. But you have been setting me down from the start, have you not, Madam? From the moment you sat in my carriage, beribboned and combative, like a salty little cake. I refer to you as such when I am cross with you. Salty little cake. Sometimes with claws."

Arthur ran his palm down her arm and took her hand. "How rough your palms are becoming. I fear this will result in further demerits to my account. The maids will have some concoction or other, or Ben, as to that. Have I told you the story of what my father did when he discovered his second son was little better than an apothecary? Do not say I have not, as I know I have told you little." He yawned. "Our father did nothing. And by that I mean he did nothing to shame my brother nor to belittle his skills or talents. He merely asked him to devise a stronger tea, as he preferred his brew to be more robust than what was then on offer." Arthur rubbed his eyes. From tiredness, not tears, no.

"I do not imagine myself as a father, but should you give me a child, I would seek to be even half the one he was and call it good." He rubbed his face into the pillow for no other reason than to fend off the possibility of a future itch. "My father, had he the opportunity to lay eyes upon you, Madam, would have taken your guise of Lady Frost as a personal challenge and had you in stitches, likely at my expense, before the clock had turned an hour. And my mother…" Face back in the pillow, a breath. "Mum would have abducted you for a day of who knew what class of feminine mysteries, as she used to do with Charlotte and the other females of the sleuth. Oh, Odin be damned. I am a bear. I am a bear, Madam, and I would not have you fear me.

"I do not believe you have ever been so reticent—ah." For of course Madam was asleep. Thank Thor, she had not heard a word of his melancholy rambling. Nor had she heard him admit to his essential self. Just as well. This was neither the time nor the place for that revelation. With one last stroke of her arm, one last tug on her hair, he slipped out of the bed, gathered up his clothes, and headed into the night.

Twelve

BEATRICE WOKE, LIGHT AS AIR. IT WAS A MARKED DIFFERENCE to any other waking she had ever experienced in her whole life. She woke, and the first thing on her mind was not her schedule of daily tasks. She woke alone and yet... She lifted the blanket and sniffed it, and it was as if Osborn had embedded himself in the fabric, a scent as brisk as midwinter wind and freshly turned earth and gingery biscuits. Was this what he referred to—was this his personal scent? It filled her up, that wind and earth and spice, like the very air in her lungs.

Was that why she was so light? She felt like one of Mr. Graham's hot-air balloons. She imagined herself floating over Vauxhall Gardens and giggled. And then felt an utter fool for giggling. They were not young lovers at long last enjoying their wedding night. It had been very strange and not what she'd expected. Osborn had been cautious and gentle and appeared to be overcome toward the end as if it were not perfunctory, that bedding her was not an enormous sacrifice on his part.

She cuddled her face in the pillow imbued with the manly scents he used in his hair and on his body. He had been rather sweet, like the vaunted honey he suggested she employ. Playing with her hair, bringing the cloth...asking permission before each touch as if her preferences were of importance. And his—his member was rather an eye-opener, though she had not looked at it. She felt it, without doubt, and it was much, much larger than her previous experience had led her to expect. He didn't—he was very—he was both masterful yet gentle with it? Oh dear, as though he was being very careful because she deserved care.

"Do not be ridiculous, Beatrice," she rebuked herself. "He is a gentleman, no matter his shoddy manners. He does not care. It was without any romantic feeling you may wish to attach to it." She dragged the sheets and blanket and wrapped them tight around her, as if the evidence of what they had done could be infused into her skin, to keep safe to think upon later.

At the scratch on the door and the sound of the turning knob, she leaped from the mattress to tear the coverings off the bed. If there was any evidence of her innocence, for surely that little pinch of pain was proof she had been untouched in the most crucial way, she would prefer the entire household be none the wiser. She would launder the linen herself, and no one would know they had lain together.

She bundled them as quickly as she could, for what use it was. Glynis's eyes widened as she shuffled over with the morning's cup of tepid tea. She set it on the dressing table and reached for the sheets Beatrice clutched to her chest. A slight tussle ensued, and Glynis's heretofore unproven strength exerted itself as she removed the linens from Beatrice's grasp with little effort. "There's fresh sheets in the laundry. I'll be back in a trice." She giggled as she left.

Beatrice took refuge behind the screen and cleaned herself as dreamily as a milkmaid who dwelled on the attributes of her lover. Her languid movements stopped.

Osborn was not her lover. He was her husband, and with any luck, thanks to one of those gods he was forever invoking, he would be the father of their child. Her child. The child they made while making—

While doing their marital duties.

They had not made love.

This was a means to an end.

This was not love.

The wait for Madam to appear for breakfast was excruciating.

There was no reason it should be so. They had engaged upon sexual relations as any married couple might. Never mind that somehow Charlotte could tell, which he discerned from the giddy way she was whispering to Ben, which was winding up the children, who demanded to know what the secret was. Never mind that he only made it worse by announcing, "No teasing of Her Grace is permitted," as it only encouraged the cubs to whine and shriek and insist upon the reasons why they should not tease if they did not know what not to tease about.

This edict included him: to call attention to what had happened between them was, for certain, the way to prevent it from happening again. And he wanted it to happen again. Would it?

The children were still bellowing; he made to scold them anew when Lady Frost entered the kitchen and quelled their racket in an instant. Arthur could discern the difference now, and it was very much that personage who sat down at table. She had set aside the informal dress she had sported while cleaning in favor of a very severe, dark dress with long sleeves and a high neck. Despite its plethora of ribbons banding the sleeves and the hem, it gave her the air of a governess out of a Gothic novel. His warnings against teasing were superfluous as Madam's cool demeanor put them in their place.

No, not Madam. Madam was, now he considered it, leagues away from Lady Frost.

Speaking of being put in one's place, her attitude put the last evening's events in perspective. What if he had thought practice might make perfection? Thank Freya she'd slept through his maundering following the sex act.

It was a sex act. It was not lovemaking.

It wasn't—not with the awkwardness and the moratorium on kissing.

She wanted a child from him.

She did not want him.

"Tea, Madam?" he asked and gestured to Brosnyn.

"Thank you, Osborn," she said, and despite her hauteur, she hesitated over his name. Then she blushed. Arthur saw Charlotte's eyes widen; Ben knocked over the sugar bowl.

"Clumsy claws," Charlotte scolded, and the children laughed, explosively out of proportion to the situation. They were roundly hushed.

"There are eggs as usual," Arthur said, "and the blackberry jam you favor."

"I would enjoy some jam," Madam replied faintly as she helped herself to a slice of toast from the rack.

He leaped up from his chair and nearly knocked Conlon down in his fervor to get to the sideboard. "Allow me to dish you up a plate. Do you fancy a kipper?" he asked.

"Kipper? I don't even know her," Ben whispered to Charlotte, who in turn spewed her tea onto the cloth. One arch look from Madam quelled any potential escalation of hilarity.

Tarben took a huge mouthful of his milky tea.

"Master Humphries." Madam very carefully set her cup in its saucer. "Whilst it is well of you to wish to emulate your honored mother in many things, this would not be one of them."

The child swallowed, and Bernadette drew her attention. "Why did you call him Master Humphries?"

"It is the correct address." Madam spread jam on her toast. "Your brother is Master Humphries, you are Miss Humphries, and your sister is Miss Ursella. I was Miss Fleetwood, and my sister—"

"Your sister?" Arthur asked.

"Was referred to by her given name with miss before it, as you would expect." She sliced her toast in two. "Mr. Conlon, will you summon Mr. Todd?"

"If I may, Mr. Conlon?" Brosnyn stepped forward. "I believe he is in the steward's study."

"Off you get, young shanks," the butler said and busied himself setting to rights what Arthur had left in a muddle.

Arthur watched the Lowell footman leave and could not deny the man was a natural diplomat. Only yesterday he'd smoothly evaded a direct query as to the provenance of the workmen on the roof, Brosnyn suggesting Arthur ask Todd without explicitly doing so. Those workmen also counted Lowell footmen among their number. Although what footmen were doing wielding hammers he'd like to know, much less the three hale fellows who now took over much of the maid's work as far as cleaning and fetching and setting fires and beating rugs were concerned.

As the woodwork in the place started to gleam in the sunlight that was now able to cascade through the mended windows, far be it from he to judge who did what, if they went merrily about the business of it.

Quick as a wink Brosnyn returned with Todd in tow.

"Good morning, Mr. Todd." Beatrice handed Conlon a scrap of paper; he in turn handed it to Brosnyn, who handed it to the prince's factotum. "This is a notation on the specific skills of the footmen as yet unemployed with a task. I expect they will enjoy assisting in the work being done on the cottages."

"Never let it be said the Lowell footmen did not enjoy their visit here," Arthur said.

"Their visit?" He found himself on the business end of one of Madam's pointed looks. "I comprehend you have not read the letter from His Grace?" she asked.

"I have not."

"I recommend you make yourself the master of its contents," Madam said. "At your earliest convenience, of course."

"Oh, of course," he huffed.

Madam held her peace until the fullness of his churlishness reverberated around the room and returned to the perusal of her Schedule. "Lady Swinburn and I shall proceed with the finishing touches on the nursery. There is a small drawing room on the ground floor that has been refurbished. It is next to the master's study."

Morag exchanged an empty pot of tea for a full one. "That's no drawing room, that's what was the Beta's study."

"Morag," Arthur said. "Do you never speak unless it is out of turn?"

She appeared to give that her full consideration. "No."

Madam sailed on without acknowledging them. "Let us serve preprandial drinks in that room, Mr. Conlon, if you please. We shall see if formal gathering is its best use. Next, the kitchen garden is ready for sowing. Mr. Todd, were you to oversee this?"

"I was, ma'am," he said. "Four of the Lowell footmen have undertaken its tending and await your verdict."

"It is unfortunate we have missed Disting," Arthur began and then gulped his tea.

"Disting?" Madam asked, her face the very picture of polite inquiry.

Charlotte's eyebrows rose so high they were in danger of sliding round the back of her head. "It is a feast, Beezy," she said, "observed by our kind at this time of year."

"It means 'the charming of the plough' and is a high holiday, as we observe the Nordic pantheon," Ben added. "The word is from an old northern tongue—"

"Do you wish to keep the use of your own old tongue?" Arthur threatened his brother.

"Whose tongue had it tripped off first, so trippingly?" Charlotte asked.

"Nordic?" Madam inquired. "Is that not where reindeer originate?"

Arthur turned to her. "I do hope I misunderstand your implication."

"I would, of course, have no way of knowing whether you are

of cervine persuasion," Madam resumed, ignoring him as the children snickered. "Thank you, Mr. Todd. Now then, on to the morning room," Madam began and parceled out the remaining tasks for the day.

———————

The nursery was in order but for several small details and who was to be in charge of the children. They were quite taken with two of the footmen; would it be too odd to give them into their keeping? Beatrice had heard of no such thing in her life, men minding the young, but the lads were keen and patient and amusing as well as amused by the three, as evidenced by the clapping game they were conducting over in the corner. They would simply refer to Bernard and Christopher as the "children's footmen." Or perhaps the "footmaids." "Nursemen"?

She huffed to herself, which Charlotte misinterpreted as they worked together, folding freshly laundered sheets.

"I do apologize, Beezy," Charlotte said, for once looking truly regretful. "Ben and I tend to joke as children do."

"I am unused to such behavior at table," Beatrice replied. It was a wonder she could not see her breath before her, her tone was so cold. "My own behavior has always been above reproach, offering a reflection of good manners for my siblings that they may follow suit."

"And look how happy it has made you." Charlotte set aside the cloth they'd finished folding.

Beatrice sank onto the window seat. "I was expected to exhibit immaculate behavior and never betray the slightest emotion while my brothers sprawled about the place like a litter of mongrels." She hid her face in her hands. "Oh, I am one grievance away from being no better than a tabbie or a dragon. I swore when I was naught but a green girl, I would never become like them."

"There's never been a society lass I've envied." Charlotte sat beside her. "But for their embellishments, perhaps." She reached out and touched one of the ribbons on Beatrice's sleeve. "I grew up allowed to run wild in Court and often feel the coarser for it."

"Is there no possibility of balance?" Beatrice tweaked Charlotte's apron so it lay flat upon her lap. "I envy your laughter with Garben. Laughing with a husband! Whoever considered such a thing."

"It is not all fun and games," Charlotte promised.

"I envy your bond with him. That you made a love match."

"There's no saying that a love match can't be made over time."

"That is not possible."

"Did it go so poorly last night?"

Oh, the questions she wished to put to her sister-in-law! But the thought of formulating into words what had occurred... No, it would be best if she and Osborn did the bed things again so she may be less overwhelmed and better able to understand what had transpired. "It was rather odd, but I would not be averse to doing it again," Beatrice allowed herself to admit. "It was unexpectedly not terrible."

"Rousing praise." Charlotte's eyes gleamed with devilment.

Beatrice grabbed her by the hand. "Do not tease him with that, Charlie, please do not."

Her sister-in-law laced their fingers and squeezed her hand. "You called me Charlie, at long last, so I shall honor your request." Beatrice suspected there was a caveat in there somewhere, she knew not why. "I do fear for the children's manners. I want them to be free and play but also to be somewhat civilized."

"A governess would fulfill those requirements."

Bernadette ran over and threw herself across Beatrice's lap. "I would welcome a governess," she said. As ever, her brother was not far behind.

"Would you?" Beatrice gave her a tentative hug. "A governess would urge you to sit beside me like a young lady."

Bernadette wedged herself in between Beatrice and her

mother. "I would like to learn more things and also proper manners. I would like to be Miss Humphries."

"Have I not taught you proper manners?" Charlotte sounded cross indeed, but Beatrice saw the twinkle in her eye.

Tarben mimed spewing tea, and the footmen grinned.

"You have taught them many wonderful things, Charlotte," Beatrice said, "primary among them that they are well loved and need not stand on ceremony with their mother and father." Tarben looked relieved Aunt Beezy had not rung a peal over his head. "This is a precious thing, my dears. However, there are a variety of situations in which society may call upon you to behave impeccably." She rose and stood in the middle of the room. "For instance, it is vital to master the appropriate form of greeting your monarch, and I believe I can aid you in this."

"Have you curtsied to the prince regent himself, Aunt Beezy?" Bernadette asked, struck with awe. Ursella appeared as if from the ether and joined her siblings in ranging before their aunt.

"Oh, I have, Bernadette." Beatrice smoothed down her skirts. "I have, indeed, and I would be honored to instruct you."

———————————

With nothing better to do and no task given him explicitly, he followed after Ben and thus found himself in the grove, irritated beyond words. How had Madam known this place existed? He knew she had not wandered this far, and yet Ben had been given the job of tidying the clearing. She could not know what it meant, nor that its disuse was meaningful. Had Ben volunteered to take it on? Did no one think to ask him his opinion?

Hypocrite, his bear snorted.

Your vocabulary broadens apace, Arthur huffed.

"Are you well, brother?" Ben lifted a fallen tree trunk with ease. The central area for the fire was cluttered with piles of ash; trees torn from their roots littered its circumference. "Thought you'd be in better spirits this morning."

He did not miss the lack of privacy that came with living in a—in a not-sleuth. His bear rolled his eyes and then his entire body. "I was only doing my duty," he began.

"Better late than never." Ben tossed the stump onto a pile of others.

"She—Her Grace—wants a cub."

"And when the cub comes?" His brother took up a branch and used it to rake up the smaller branches. "You'll still carry on like this? Without a *sentio*, without the comforts of a sleuth?"

"*This*," Arthur snarled, "is the only way to keep us safe."

"It keeps us apart, for certain."

"You were there, Ben, when our father was slaughtered. How can you expect me to behave any differently?"

"I expect you to do exactly that." Ben gave him his back, a taunt to Arthur's essential self, showing his lack of fear of the great predator Arthur was. "To embrace your destiny, to stand for your family, to fall in love with your wife."

"To endanger each and every one of you." Arthur bent and tossed a clutch of twigs onto the pile.

"We are in greater danger without you."

How could that be? Should they become as strong as they once were, they may fall prey to another challenger, and then what? What if Arthur lost as his father had lost? At least it would not be due to grief, as the wife such as he had would not grieve him but for lack of progeny. As to that, need he dance around a flame like a heathen to call the child down? He dare not ask Ben; he'd never hear the end of it. And why was Ben so keen to have the sleuth reform? Did he wish only for a place to stow his family? He would not stoop so low as to follow the old ways—

"Do not dare to tell me you are looking for a reason to leave," he snarled.

Ben looked up from sweeping ashes. "What?"

"As the males do in a sleuth. Seeing to the succession and then wandering far and wide in search of fresher game?" How dare his brother! "Are you looking to play away?"

As a rule, Ben was slow to anger; when he did choose to express his rage, he did it in an instant. He exploded out of his clothes and into his bear, Arthur a heartbeat behind. Down on their fours, they faced off, rumbling with rage, and threw themselves at each other.

In the shadows, a creature lurked and bared its teeth in glee.

———————

"...and then slide your left leg out slowly—very good, Tarben— and if you can touch your forehead to your knee? Well done!" Having never executed a full court bow, Beatrice gave instruction as best she could by recalling those which she had received. "Oh! And rotate your right wrist, as you would stir a pot of soup."

The girls had taken to defiant curtsying like birds to the air, with Ursella surpassing her sister in execution. This lit a fire in Bernadette, whose stubbornness called Arthur to mind.

"In future, Tarben, we shall supply you with an excessively lacy handkerchief. It makes the wrist twirling far more effective. Now rise, slowly, slowly... It is equally important to show that you rise at your leisure. Oh, children, I am so very impressed." Red-faced, they beamed up at her and then treated her to a battery of hugs. "Charlotte, will you not try?"

"Far be it from me to rob you of your signature move," she said over the cries of her children's insistence. "I suppose it is of your devising."

"Oh yes," Beatrice said. "It was a way to yield without yielding during my first marriage. Or at least in my mind."

"I do not understand." Bernadette frowned.

Beatrice looked to Charlotte, who nodded. How to explain this to a child, to be truthful without being too explicit? "Once upon a

time, a young lady was married to a not-very-nice man," Beatrice
began.

"A beast even as we would deem him," Charlotte interjected.

"It was not entirely clever of her to be so bold," Beatrice continued, "but the young lady discovered that if she gave excessive
tribute, she defied him by appearing to be very obedient. There
was none to gainsay her nor to criticize such deference, and so the
lady won a small victory each time."

"The lady ought to have called upon a knight to rescue her!"
Tarben stabbed the air with an imaginary sword.

Beatrice stroked a hand over his head. "Even I as a human was
aware none may separate a woman from her mate."

"He was not your mate," whispered Ursella.

The men's hard work went undone as the bears fought. Ben's
creature was smaller than Arthur's but rangy, and a history of fra-
ternal fracas kept him canny. The trunks of the fallen trees scattered once more as they wrestled over the ground, the smaller
branches flinging about like shrapnel. Fresh scars were slashed on
the standing trees, and several shrubs fell foul of their battle until
Arthur pinned Ben, teeth gently closing over his throat.

Ben yielded but was a past master at doing so falsely. He
relaxed enough to convince Arthur he was done fighting and
then threw his weight up and around until they rolled through
the underbrush to the nearby brook. A mighty splash and
Arthur drew on his *dominatum* and both Changed back to their
manskins.

They sat in the shallow water in silence until they broke into
a fierce spate of splashing each other. The sun ducked behind a
cloud, and they desisted at once.

"Holy Odin, this is freezing." Arthur contemplated Changing
back into his fur.

"You say that every time we land up in here." Ben looked cheerful enough about it, considering what had led them there.

That was his brother through and through, never one to hold a grudge. Unlike… "Do you recall—"

"When you chased Charlie into this stream?" Ben roared with laughter.

"I've still got the gouge she gave me, I vow." Arthur rubbed his earlobe. "Does it not weary you? The battling and the fighting."

"This is play, brother." Ben splashed him once more. "It is our custom to express our essential selves in such a way."

"It is not all play," Arthur insisted. "It has ever been the hallmark of our world, challenges and bloodshed."

Ben sighed. "None of our generation conform to the old ways. The few elders who do see their power wane with every passing day." Arthur had no answer for that. "Has it occurred to you that Georgie may know what he's doing?" Ben asked. "He is not the fribble the world may like to think him."

"Not always," Arthur allowed.

"What was his approach that night he bid you wed Beezy? Languid wrist twirling or that awful stillness?"

"Awful stillness, mainly." Arthur slapped the water around him. "But he was wearing one of those coats of his. It was embroidered with capering bunnies."

"Jemima's work."

"She was at Lowell's wedding. Bosom friend of the new Duchess of Lowell."

"Ah." Ben nodded as if it was all the answer he needed.

"Ah?"

"Lowell's human duchess who is also acquainted with your new human duchess, who I daresay is not unknown to one of our childhood friends who is *versipellis*. There may be a greater plan that Georgie weaves."

"A spider in his web."

"As is any Alpha, no matter his species."

"We are reducing their number in these parts. Spiders, that is."

"But what selfless work they do, showing us where we have not taken care." He turned and swam for the wider, deeper stretch of the water, and Arthur followed.

Even in their human form, there were no better fishermen than those of ursine lineage. With their bare hands, the brothers scooped up trout as easily as picking daisies. A respectable pile of fish flopped upon the bank until they flopped no more.

"Do you remember when we were young, living in Court, and that sleuth from Denmark came calling?" Ben tossed one last *piscis puris* on the bank and floated, face to the sun, which had pushed aside the clouds once again. Arthur had to admit it was peaceful and idyllic there and lovely to spend time with his brother, to tussle and fish.

"With the view to overthrowing the king? Or forcing Georgie to marry one of them?"

"He was ten years of age and terrifying with it. And he was stronger with us at his back."

"Father had none at his back because of the bond breaking his heart."

"No, Arthur." Ben gave a mighty splash, and Arthur inhaled more than his fair share of brook. "Because he adhered to the old way of ruling, not of mating. How dare you blame Mother!"

"I do not blame Mum. Why in the world should I blame her? I blame the hunters who had strayed where they ought not and took her from us. I blame the worthless cadre Father had assembled, his useless Beta and his feckless Gamma."

"The Beta's mate is the only reason we are alive. She brought us to George and thus to Court and safety." Neither wanted to think what would have become of them had the usurper gotten them in his clutches.

And yet. "That Beta," Arthur said, "who was out and about, engaged upon challenging for his own sleuth."

"He was no Alpha. He was incapable of holding the *sentio*, never mind there were fewer and fewer of us to fight." Ben sank to his shoulders. "Only look at me. I have no role beyond father to provide safety for my children. It is not my place to give them the comfort and protection of a sleuth."

"Guilt, now." Arthur considered splashing to turn the topic.

"Well you should feel it." Ben was calm and yet fierce. "As should all who have treated you as a cub still wet behind the ears. You had no guidance in childhood and were given too free a rein as you approached your maturity. Yes, very well you should be guilty, and further, well you should be grateful for the woman up at that house who is devoting herself to making you a home, you ungrateful, stubborn ass." Ben swam onward again with rather more kicking than necessary.

Arthur admitted to stubbornness, one of his mother's trenchant qualities. He would allow for ingratitude, if he remembered his paternal grandfather correctly. Water was never wet enough for that old goat. He took for granted the assets of character he'd inherited from Papa as well as his erstwhile Alpha's laissez-faire approach to dress. If there was one thing his father never took for granted, it was his bond with Mum. Yet how could it be worth the pain that followed when she was slain? How could it be worth it, opening the door to his brother and his family? As if he could stand to let them wander the earth looking for home when it was—

"Here. You will stay here. At Arcadia." Arthur floated over to join Ben at the curve in the stream.

The sunlight reflected from the water onto Ben's face, his eyes glowing yellow as his brother's bear pinned him in his gaze. "The common mistake that is made regarding Alphas is that they are all-powerful," he said, and Arthur waited for his brother's non sequitur to reveal its meaning. "They are, in their way, yet they require a balance of power given into the correct hands, to form the order required for a healthy hierarchy. Every soul is needed, from Alpha through to Omega."

"Were I to pledge a Beta, Ben—"

"It is not I," Ben said, gentle as the breeze that brushed their skin. "Despite my nickname, it is no mistake I was called Garben. When the time comes, I will be your Gamma."

"Well, who, then?" Arthur kicked at the bed of the stream and stubbed his toe on a larger-than-expected stone. "That fox? Not bloody likely."

Ben pulled himself up onto the bank and backtracked to gather up as much fish as he could carry. "I suggest," he muttered, "looking directly beneath your nose."

Thirteen

BEATRICE WATCHED THE CHILDREN CLATTER AND SCAMPER down the stairs. "Tomorrow we shall learn how to descend with decorum."

"Bernie was not wrong. I know little of proper manners." Charlotte resumed her good-natured acceptance of her shortcomings. "I had no come-out nor a reason to prepare for one, and many of the finer points of civilized behavior are beyond me."

"Charlie." Beatrice stopped her mid-step. "Those children are loved and wanted and encouraged to be themselves with no thought but for what games they will play and how better to battle their mother in their bid never to consume a vegetable. They are free in ways that cannot be taken for granted." Tarben threw himself over the banister.

"No!" Charlotte bellowed with an authority that would not be denied. Her son slid his leg back down and slipped back onto the stairs as if that had been his intention all along.

The moment lasted a little over a heartbeat, and yet it was a revelation. "Does it come naturally, being a…a mother?"

Charlotte slipped her arm through Beatrice's. "It is not without its hesitations and fears, but you will be wonderful. You have clear authority and a warm heart."

"It remains to be seen if I am indeed able." She took a deep breath and dared a question. "Does the seed take at once, or does it require repeated attempts?"

"What did your husband say?"

Her husband. "That like many things in life it may require diligence and application."

"Oh, diligence." Charlotte giggled. "*And* application. Yes, indeed."

They watched as Ursella wandered into the footstool room. "What Ursella said, about Castleton…"

"Not being your mate? Yes, she would know."

"I do not understand how she might."

"Omegas are precious amongst us," Charlotte said. "You are aware of *versipellian* hierarchy?"

"I have heard the terms Beta and Gamma." Bernadette and Tarben raced each other after their sister, and shouting commenced. Beatrice judged it harmless, as did Charlotte.

"The Omega was, in history, considered the least among us," Charlotte explained. "They were perceived to be weak due to their quiet and self-effacing ways, which are contrary to *versipellian* nature. Yet the first clan that allowed its Omega's gifts to develop prospered in ways unknown before. They have recourse to profound wisdom and an ability to calm and manage the emotions of a group without removing free will. They allow the clan to respond rather than react out of feral instinct and fear."

"And to know what cannot be known?"

"To know what is rather than what is thought to be." They paused in the foyer and watched the children wrestle one another off the footstool; even Ursella gave as good as she got.

A great clamor sounded from the back of the house and drew their attention as the women reached the foyer. "Come," Beatrice said. "Let us see what the commotion is."

———————

If it was not one thing, it was another. Furious, Arthur turned in the hall to be greeted by two of the hardier footmen, the cubs and their mother, the duchess in the lead. Ben, arms full of trout, headed for the larder, Mrs. Porter on his tail.

"Madam." The children rushed to stand before him and treated their uncle to a sardonic flurry of curtsying and one exceedingly condescending bow.

"Well done, children," their instructor commended, her eyes smiling. "Yes, Osborn? Is aught amiss?"

He brandished the sticks he held. "I'll have you know the kitchen garden is in rag order."

"Is it?" Her skirts swirled as she turned for the kitchens, while the rest fell into place behind her like a brace of ducklings. "It ought not to be so, as Mr. Todd informed us this morning."

She collected Glynis and Ciara in her wake as well as Brosnyn and three more Lowell footmen.

"This is true, he said as much at breakfast," Charlotte insisted. Arthur joined his duchess—

Whose duchess? his bear wondered.

—joined Madam at the front of what appeared to be the majority of the household except for that bloody fox.

"Only see," he said as they took in the devastation. The fence around the garden was little more than kindling. What had been neat furrows with pea sticks ready to train growing shoots was the picture of wanton destruction, the lengths of wood broken, the strings tangled, and the earth was churned as if there had been a great battle.

In the center of the chaos lay a dead deer: its neck was quite obviously broken and its belly a mass of blood and entrails.

"Children? Oh, where is your sister?" Madam turned to Bernadette and Tarben. "Do find her, if you will. And then back into the kitchen for refreshment, as your perfect application of my lesson earns you first choice of Ciara's latest treats."

They winkled their sister out of a hedge, and Tarben led them cheering to the house with Ciara in their wake. Charlotte followed them at a nod from Madam.

"A word of warning would not have gone amiss, Your Grace," she said and turned to the nearest footman. "Coogan, if you would ask Mr. Todd to join me?" Brosnyn's instructions ensued. "If the men who saw to this initially are not presently intent on a task, do summon them to set this to rights, with my apologies that their hard work was undone." Arthur was next in line. "If you would grant me a moment of your time, Your Grace?"

Her tone boded ill. "Come, let us repair to the footstool room." Arthur offered her his arm, which she eschewed. "It has been set aside for disputations, has it not?"

Madam led the way, past feasting children and gleaming wainscoting. "We shall paint it your favorite color, you have only to say so," she said.

The sunlight from the sparkling-clean windows of the foyer shone upon her hair. "Golden, perhaps?"

"Golden is not a color." She stopped to straighten a painting.

Arthur rolled his eyes, safely behind her back. "By all means, let us argue about what constitutes a color."

Down the hall they proceeded and into the room, which was still lacking the door. She stood next to the footstool and folded her hands at her waist. "I must insist if you have an issue with the work, you apply to me directly and in private."

"Apply to you directly."

"And in private. There was no need for the children to have seen that poor animal."

Arthur scoffed. "The children have a better idea of the cycle of life than you imagine."

"Nevertheless." She stood before him and displayed no fear. "It was unnecessary, and in future—"

"In *future*!" He spat the word like an epithet. "What can the future hold if the simplest of tasks cannot be concluded successfully?"

"Osborn." What had he said that softened her tone? At least she left off addressing him as the scathing "Your Grace." "It is a minor setback, the fault of which can be laid at the door of the natural world."

He swept his arm in the general direction of the garden. "Nothing about that was natural."

Madam searched his face as she would an encyclopedia from which she sought knowledge. "Shall we put the footmen on guard?"

"The footmen!" Alfred's bloody letter! "I would like to know what Lowell was thinking, sending us so many mouths to feed."

"It was the work of the duchess, as the letter informed us. Which I perceive remains unread." He shrugged, recalled Ben's words about being treated like a child and the inference he acted like one. Madam carried on. "I shudder to think what would become of Arcadia without them. They are integral to the reconstruction of your crumbling manse."

"Our crumbling manse." He looked at the ceiling, freshly plastered, at the curtains, cleaned and properly hung, everywhere but at her, as only then was he able to inquire: "I would assure myself of your ease after the events of last evening."

"I am well." Was she? Her cheeks were flushed. Would the room look absurd with blush-pink walls? It may be his new favorite color.

Madam cleared her throat. "And you?"

"I?" Of course he was well. Why would he not be well? Last night had gone...well. "Yes."

"Yes?"

"I am well." They took a step forward toward one another and then backed away as from a hot stove. She pretended to inspect an impeachable swag of curtain, and he inspected her.

Would they lie together again, tonight? After the meal, after the children were put to bed, after gathering for tea and chitchat and Charlotte's knowing glances and Ben's smiling eyes and Madam's nerves, nerves he could see roiling beneath the layer of frost even from across this room. Was that what the frost was for, to disguise the wealth of warmth the woman sought to hide from the *ton*? A wealth that had been thrown away by Castleton? A bounty of kindness that infused every compliment she paid to another on the successful completion of their task, that overflowed when she cuddled one of the cubs? The promise of progress every time she called him Osborn? The hope of growth that would, with careful sowing, produce so much more to be reaped—

Talk of reaping. "I would have an explanation regarding the destruction of the garden, Madam." He brandished the sticks again.

"Why?" That arched brow!

"Why?" He looked at the sticks; they did not yield the answer. "Because I will not countenance such disruption of my land and of my…"

"Of your…?" A head tilt now accompanied the inquisitive brow.

Of his what? His authority? His peace of mind? He laid claim to neither. "To the so-called refurbishment of this place. A place that has known great chaos and ought to know no more. I will put a stop to it." Arthur did not intend that to sound like a threat.

"Do you wish to frighten me?" Madam looked the opposite of frightened. She looked like she might spring claws from her fingertips and fangs from behind that rosebud mouth. "How far would you go to do so? Is it at your door I may lay those poor little creatures who did not deserve to die? If so, you are no better than Castleton, whose lands never played host to anything but predators such as he."

"You may not, as I did no such thing. And do not compare me to that madman."

"Then is it that you wish me to fail?" Arthur stood, struck dumb. She took his lack of answer to be proof enough. "It is well, therefore, I do not make these efforts to garner your favor. I do this because it must be done, and I am well able for it. I will not stand by and live under less than ideal circumstances, nor shall I allow any human or creature to live under anything less than the protection of a sound roof, in full cleanliness and comfort."

"I do not—" What did he "not"? Did he not deserve this bollocking from his tiny wife? Did he not wish for the comfort of his people?

Whose people? his bear wondered.

"Be silent," he snarled and then caught himself, chagrined to have spoken aloud. "Madam, that command was not intended for you."

"No?" Lady Frost was now in full possession of the conversation. "Was it to your creature you spoke so? I wonder what he said to deserve your censure. He may be the wiser of the two."

The beast preened like a debutante. "I did not mean to offend you. I am merely…" *Worried about your welfare, of the welfare of all here. Concerned the changes being wrought are even greater than they appear. Uneasy that you may have fallen pregnant. Anxious you may have not. Distraught you will not welcome me into your bed again, no matter your desire for a child.* "I am merely—"

A knock on the corridor wall interrupted his morose monologue. "It is I, ma'am," came the voice of the fox. "I understand there was a disturbance in the garden."

"If you would excuse me, Your Grace." It was not a request.

Your Grace. That likely answered his question as to whether they would lie together again that night.

———————

The children were abed, none the worse for seeing the destruction visited upon that innocent creature, and the adults gathered in the family reception room. They must devise a less cumbersome name for it. Charlotte and Ben were battling out a game of draughts with subdued hilarity. Osborn had been his usual taciturn self throughout the evening meal. And it was Beatrice's turn to be looked at.

She had been aware of her frostiness upon entering the kitchens that morning and had been powerless to curtail it. She wanted nothing more than to melt at the sight of his eyes, those warm brown eyes fixing on her the moment she entered; the way he stood big as a mountain, the way his hands brushed down his front, his front that had been pressed up against her front… He had gained pleasure from it, had he not? Their argument in the footstool room had been fraught with more than a dispute over the ruined garden. Ought she to have given in to the silly argument? She would not take on fault that was not hers, even if it meant he would not lie with her again. That was no way to go on.

She could not face him if she thought he did not wish to retire with her again.

Would he wish to do that again, tonight?

When he was not pacing around the edges of the room and interfering with Charlotte's moves on the board, Osborn lounged in the chair set catercorner with the bookcase, a chair that had been sitting alongside the chaise longue, which itself had been moved over to the window. Every time Beatrice visited this room, it reorganized itself by some means, which she supposed to be Charlotte or the children. Would she remark upon it? If a sofa was set in place, that was where the sofa remained. Was it a custom of their kind? She thought to ask him, but he was sitting with such… aggression, if that were possible. His legs stretched out before him, trousers taut on his thighs, ankles crossed, one hand propped against his chin, that fat curl lying on his brow.

Looking at her.

"Thank you, Corvus," she said as the tea tray was set before her. She set about doling out treats and tea, Charlotte and Ben abandoning their match for sustenance.

"Ciara has made the lemon cake you prefer, Osborn," she said as she put two slices on a plate and set it down on the tea table. He rose and took it and did not take his eyes off her as he bit into a slice and licked his lips.

Charlotte, her back to Osborn, took her cup as well as Ben's;

before she turned away, she made a show of licking her lips as the duke had.

Beatrice took a sip of her tea and gasped. Osborn rushed to her side and dropped his plate as he did so; it fell facedown on the rug.

"What is amiss? Has the milk gone off?" He loomed over her like an angel of retribution. "Show me your tongue."

Across from her, Charlotte almost treated them to a reprise of her tea-spewing antics.

"I am well, Osborn. It is only that the tea is hot." She selected two more slices of cake and put them on another plate. "I had forgotten it would be so, thanks to our new footmen, rather than the cooler temperatures I have become accustomed to."

"Said the actress to the bishop," Ben muttered, and Charlotte made the least graceful noise Beatrice had ever heard, a cross between a giggle and snort and a bark. It was so rude, it made her want to laugh herself.

"Do not tease," Osborn scolded them. "There is no end of harm that might result from a mouthful of hot liquid."

Charlotte and Ben collapsed onto one another and snorted into one another's shoulders. Beatrice felt a hysterical giggle burgeon behind her breastbone.

"I am sure my tongue has suffered worse, Osborn," she began, which prompted Ben to fold over in half and Charlotte to fall onto his back, both roaring with laughter.

"Compose yourselves!" Osborn demanded. "You guttersnipes, shut your mouths."

"Said the bishop to the actress," Charlotte squeaked, kicking out her feet and knocking over the teapot.

"*Thou cream-faced loons,*" Osborn muttered. To cover her incipient delirium, Beatrice rose to ring for another pot as the duke took out his choler by prodding at the fire.

As the flames rose in the chimney, the room filled with smoke. The hilarity met its end at his bellow, and Ben and Charlotte rushed to open the windows. The heat dislodged a deluge of branches and along with them a dead creature, falling into the flames, only serving to increase the conflagration. Beatrice yanked on the bell pull, and once again it fell onto her head.

Osborn roared; there was no other word for it. He roared and thrust the poker at Ben, who took responsibility for the fire. He roared again, and Brosnyn, Corvus, and three more footmen rushed in, with Mr. Todd close behind. Osborn took the bell pull out of her hand and, much like the sticks from the garden, shook it in his fist.

"Was this not on Madam's schedule to be repaired?" the duke demanded. "And what of the state of the chimney? I distinctly recall it was to be swept."

"It appears a dead *animali puri* played a part in the obstruction," Ben said.

"Who is doing this to defenseless animals?" Osborn sounded apoplectic.

More Lowell footmen poured into the room, Conlon directing their movements in such a way as resulted in them colliding with one another. Charlotte voiced opinions that were going unheard due to the confusion, and Ben waded into the mix with orders that only served to discombobulate the footmen further. Mr. Todd was slinking around the edges of the room and ignoring His Grace at his peril until—

Osborn invoked his *dominatum*.

How curious. Beatrice watched as every being in the room, in particular Mr. Todd, froze in place. She of course recalled Castleton using it, how Georgie's was stronger than his ever was, and how both had affected her, and yet Osborn's did not trouble her in the least. She could feel it pressing, could see its effect on the others, on even Ben and Charlotte, but to her it was not debilitating. It was, in its way, protective, and she was relaxed enough to demand, "Osborn, desist," and clutch his arm.

His arm, banded around her waist. Osborn embraced her, a shield protecting her from nascent peril, and he stroked her head as though she'd been brained by a boulder rather than a bell pull. She petted him on his forearm in appeasement as his whole body shuddered; he released the oppressive atmosphere. It was subtle, less than a shiver of gooseflesh, but given their proximity, there was no overlooking it. The *dominatum* must take something out of him in turn.

"Osborn," she repeated, now clinging to his arm. He took another breath, his chest expanding against her back, his hand stilled on her head. Charlotte took one look at them and commenced herding the footmen out of the room. Mr. Todd eyed the door, and Ben, now sober as a judge, looked to be awaiting instruction. "Mr. Todd, I expect you have some explaining to do," Beatrice said.

"Ma'am," he said, cricking his neck.

She waited for further elucidation; none followed. Osborn made a noise like a rushing river about to crash its banks. "In the morning, after the household breaks its fast, you shall join us in the master's study."

Ben cleared his throat. "It is the Alpha's study, Be—Beatrice."

"The Alpha's study," she repeated, to another rumble from Osborn. She trained her attention on Mr. Todd. "I trust you will present yourself. And you as well, Ben, thank you."

"Ma'am." Mr. Todd bowed and left, Ben on his heels after showing his neck to her, an unusual act on her brother-in-law's part; she did not dwell upon it.

It was tempting to remain in Osborn's arms, even if he was not holding her like a—a lover. The strength of his embrace and his warmth made her knees wobble. Had the chaos ruined her chances of a marital visitation? She found it had had the opposite effect on her; she was rather invigorated. "Mr. Todd could tutor one in how to concede without appearing to do so."

"The Alpha's study?" He released her, and she took the bell rope from him to lay aside.

"Yes. I imagine you know where it is."

"Do not patronize me, Madam. I know where it is, in my own house. My own house which persists in falling around your ears and now attempts to set itself on fire." He went to jab at what was left of the blaze, clearly not having learned his lesson. Beatrice took away the poker. She stopped and saw the creature in the ash was a squirrel.

"Oh. Oh, no." It could be any one of its kind, it did not have to be the one with which she conversed the other night.

Osborn selected a particularly ominous growl from his lexicon. "This was not my work."

"As you have said. I was not about to accuse you." Would she embarrass herself by weeping over a squirrel? "We shall get to the bottom of the matter."

"Then I shall leave you to it." Osborn took the poker back and threw it in with the andirons. He stopped, pinched the bridge of his nose, inhaled. "And we…" He dropped his hand and turned to her. "We shall convene in the morning as you have decreed."

He opened the door and paused with his back to her. "Sweet dreams," he bid her, grudgingly, and away he went.

Thus Beatrice's question as to whether they would lie together again that night was answered.

Fourteen

BEATRICE ARRIVED IN THE ALPHA'S STUDY BEFORE THE OTHERS and used that time to lay certain items on the desk. She had ensured the room was tidied, and it was reordered and pristine. With foolscap and pen to hand on her side of the gleaming expanse, she waited until she was joined by the three men.

Mr. Todd stood before the desk as Arthur took his place to sit behind it; Ben stood opposite to her, flanking the duke. Osborn slouched in his seat, his brow like thunder. He perused the assemblage on the desk and growled.

And yet...for his bristling surliness, he was content to sit. To wait? Beatrice looked at him and felt a tug at her breastbone she did not understand. She had broken her fast with but two slices of toast, so she could not blame a bad kipper, for example, for the disturbance within. Yet it was there, a nudge in her chest, rather like someone tapping her on the arm for her attention or as if a thread, an invisible thread, stretched between herself and Osborn and his brother. She looked to Ben, whose hand lay over his heart. His smile was blinding.

"Garben?" He beamed at her but shook his head.

She worried at her wedding ring, running her fingers over the topaz, and turned to the duke. "Your Grace?" she asked. "Would you like to begin?"

"Far be it from me to tread on your patch." He glared at her as though she was the miscreant.

Beatrice addressed the prince's factotum. "Mr. Todd, you see before you evidence proving you have sabotaged many of the tasks I have given you to the detriment of this house." The bell pull lay there, alongside letters he had been tasked with delivering and the broken pea sticks from the garden.

"To the detriment of your health, Madam," Osborn snarled.

"I had not intended that anyone's health, much less that of Her Grace, be endangered." Mr. Todd cricked his neck at Osborn, whose teeth momentarily took the form of fangs.

"What did you intend, Mr. Todd?" Beatrice asked.

"I was charged by His Highness to obey you in all things and to assist as needed in the restoration of Arcadia." The prince's factotum was as cool as she.

"He had no way of knowing such help would be desired," Osborn huffed.

"I believe our prince suspected Her Grace would take command of such an undertaking."

"His Highness had the measure of you, Madam." Osborn's tone belied his teasing of her.

Beatrice felt the pull again and carried on. "And what else did His Highness require of you?"

This query was met with a twinkle of sly glee. "I was exhorted to make trouble for you and His Grace where I may."

"To what end?"

"The prince hoped that such discord would serve to unite you against a common foe."

"Discord?" Osborn sprang to his feet. "You call it 'discord' when the safety of my—when the duchess is in danger? Look upon these simple objects you have transformed into lethal weapons and know had any ill come to pass it would have gone much the worse for you."

Lethal weapons? Ben tucked his chin to his chest, failing to hide his smile, and Beatrice came as near to laughing in public as she'd ever done in her adult life. "Osborn." She gestured to his seat, and he resumed it. "Have you been in correspondence with His Highness, Mr. Todd?"

A spark of guilt flickered across that cunning countenance. "Yes, Your Grace. As to his wishes, I have been informing him of your progress, or the lack thereof. His Highness wished the adversity to be increased, and thus the minor disturbances within the house."

"And the unfortunate creature stuffed up the chimney?"

"Ma'am, I must say, none of the creatures were my work." His sincerity was palpable. "Indeed, I had taken it upon myself to seek out what could be doing such a thing."

"Took it upon yourself," Osborn muttered.

Beatrice spoke over him. "You have been as a right hand to me over these past few weeks. My disappointment knows no bounds, not so much that you broke my trust, although there is that, of course, but that your hard work was a sham."

"Ma'am, I beg you to believe me, it was not." The prince's factotum showed her his throat. "This place—to have the satisfaction of seeing it return to its former glory, nay, to transcend it—to have had a discernible hand in it…" He dropped his head and whispered, "It went far beyond what one such as I could aspire to. I beg your forgiveness."

"Well you should beg Her Grace," Arthur huffed.

"One as canny as you must certainly infer what your punishment ought to entail," Beatrice said.

Mr. Todd nodded. "I shall right my wrongs and be on my way."

"And how shall His Highness greet that?"

"I—I would not like to say, ma'am."

"With demotion at best, I hazard." Beatrice nodded to Ben, who had yet to cease grinning, and shot a cautionary glance at Osborn. The nudge and pull continued, and it was as if she was following it with her own heart. "I agree that you must endeavor to right the wrongs you caused." He turned to go. "I have not released you." There was no other word for the sound Osborn made but a squeal. "I also say that Arcadia is in dire need of a steward. I would see that she has a champion within and without these walls, one who will strive to serve her in the best possible way for as long as he wishes, having a hand and a voice in her return to glory. I say that man is you, Mr. Todd."

Osborn sputtered and ceased at the lifting of her hand. Mr. Todd took a wavering breath and nodded. For the second time, he bared his neck to her and then bowed. "Ma'am, it would be my pleasure and my honor."

"Excellent." Her heart beat like a joyful drum. "I shall confer with His Grace about the contracts we need undertake to make this so and shall write to His Highness myself, expressing your willingness at my request to transfer your loyalties to Arcadia. I trust that letter will find its way into its intended hands."

"I am all that is willing, and I shall devote myself to you for as long as I live." He paused. "It is my pleasure to inform you I am a fox, ma'am," he said.

"Thank you for entrusting me with this knowledge," Beatrice said. "As such, I suspect you prefer the country to the city. This plan is fortuitous in every aspect."

"You are ensured of my gratitude for the rest of my days." If he bowed one more time, she suspected Osborn would embark on a rampage.

"One more question," Beatrice said. "You say the small crea-tures were none of your doing."

"They were not," said the fox. "If I may borrow a few footmen and walk the lands? We may discover some sign of an interloper."

"An interloper who felled a deer in its prime," Arthur said, "and transported it from the boundaries, in its dead weight, to display in my garden. And who had the strength to climb the roof to stuff a dead squirrel down my chimney."

"I am not one for tormenting *animali puri*. While a deer of such size would be nothing for one even as small as I, I say again it was not my work." As their steward's choler rose, a decidedly north-ern accent slipped into his usually cultured speech. "Regarding the chimney, on my part I stuffed it with several dead lengths of vine from the glasshouse. As to that, my concerns about some of the growth there need to be addressed, given the presence of the children."

Beatrice turned to Ben. "I believe you are the man for that job, Lord Swinburn."

"So I am. Off I get." Ben bowed to his brother, who rolled his eyes, and as he passed her, he whispered, "Well played, Be—Beatrice," and left with Arcadia's new steward.

She turned to the duke, who was engaged in scowling at the blotter on the desk. "Your thoughts, Osborn?"

"Oh, how kind of you to ask my opinion." He glared around the room and flicked a glance at her, her chest. She lay a hand over her heart as Ben had, and it only served to infuriate him further, if his growl was any measure. "You will have your way when it comes to that fox, but you may not have your way in all things."

"Did I not..." Had she not done what was required of her? She could not describe what had transpired, how she knew without a doubt what course to take. The prodding beneath her breastbone had subsided, and yet having followed it, she could not see that she had gone wrong.

"Did you not what?" He rose, his massiveness making an overwhelming impression, as she expected he'd intended.

She hid her fists at her sides, behind her skirt. "I did what the atmosphere in the room asked of me."

Osborn did not greet that statement with scorn nor with hilarity nor with dismissiveness. Worse, he regarded her, his expression unreadable. Finally he grimaced and shook his head. "I will not address this."

"Do you know what I'm referring to?"

Osborn shrugged, mute, and it incensed her as nothing had yet. "Well." Beatrice collected the detritus on the table. "Do you rescind my decision?" He shrugged again. "Then I shall carry on with my day. I suggest you take yourself outdoors where you may unearth better humor."

_____

Being out of doors was a tonic for one such as he, and yet he found taking his Shape did not appeal. He remained in his man-skin and wandered the grounds, noting the newly refurbished kitchen garden and going for a peek at the cottages. The builders fell over themselves in deference, and he was pleased to see, and said as much, that Her Grace's directives had been undertaken. A visit to the barn almost sent the draught horses into a frenzy, and the footman in charge—the stable master now, he supposed—was not backward in going forward in telling him off. It was quite refreshing.

The glasshouse was on its way to complete repair thanks to the veritable swarm of footmen on the roof, replacing broken panes and securing beams. Arthur nodded to Ben and Arcadia's newly minted steward as they convened over the mysterious growths. He did not wish to dwell on what had transpired in the study, which he was certain Ben was keen to discuss. He could see the look in his brother's eye from where he was and hoofed it away.

He would not address it, in the main because he could not explain it. The *sentio* required a ceremony and, yes, a fire to stand around, to open it and unite a clan. It also required the apogee of the hierarchy to be sworn to duty, and that had not been the case this morning.

How, then, could the *sentio* flow? That fox was not his Beta.

Arthur went, without shame, to hide in the rose arcade. He kicked a pile of deadheaded blooms and then guiltily piled them back up again. The place had been his mother's pride and joy; walking down the aisle, he sat on one of the two facing benches she had placed at the end of the path among a cluster of lavender bushes that were on the verge of wholesale rebellion. Charlotte came from the direction of the glasshouse with a basket full of Freya knew what. She caught sight of him and sat on the opposite bench.

"Moping?"

"Why ought I be?"

"Only because Beezy behaved with protocol, unaware she did so."

Beezy, his bear crooned. "Beezy," he scoffed. "That name is apt enough, for she is like a grist of wasps when her choler rises. How the *ton* dubbed her Lady Frost I do not know."

"Do you not?" The benches were close enough to allow Charlotte to set her little slippered feet over the toes of his enormous boots.

"It was Lady Frost who sent me out from underfoot, lest I interfere in the running of my own—"

"Your own?"

"This place." Arthur tugged at a lavender bush, wrenched a handful of the herb, and ran it through his fingers. "This godforsaken place. I never wanted to see it again, I vowed I would not, and if not for Georgie and his threats and his machinations, I would not have done."

"What happened to your father was horrendous, Artie." Charlotte's voice was a soothing balm and yet resonant with her own grief. "And I know you think it was your fault."

"I failed." He leaned over and scattered the heads of the lavender into the trug. Elbows on his knees, head hanging, he let out a breath. "I failed to save us."

"It was not your fault." Her tone brooked no argument. "You were a child."

"I was an Alpha."

"You were a six-year-old child, not yet in full harmony with his creature. Imagine Tarben in your place and tell me you believe him able to take on a full-grown male." A small hand patted his head, and fingers ran through his hair. "You cannot hold yourself responsible for what happened then, only what is happening now."

"What's that supposed to mean?" he groused. Much the way a six-year-old might.

"That child witnessed the most horrific thing imaginable. You must truly grieve it to become the Alpha you are meant to be. That you already are. The fate the Norns wrought was a desperate, terrible thing, and yet here we are, Ben and I and the children, you and Arcadia and Beatrice—"

"Beatrice." He said her proper name for the first time. "Who thinks I am a clod and of no use and an obstacle."

"If the boot fits," she chirped. Arthur glared up at her. "What would happen should you cease to be an obstacle?"

"She will not take care!" He sat up and was aware he gestured melodramatically, like a lesser player in an entr'acte. "She goes hither and yon with no thought to her safety. She will face down any creature with no thought to their essential selves and what harm they may wreak. Freya only knows what she was like with Castleton. She defied Georgie to his face and then curtsied with such scorn! I have never seen such a disdainful thing." He laughed and rubbed his hands over his sideburns. "I have never seen such a thing in my life."

"It sounds as though you admire her."

"Do not put words in my mouth." His mouth, which he wanted to put on Beatrice's mouth, an unlikely and unwelcome impulse that was visited upon him as she stood beside him in the Alpha's study, having woven into a *sentio* that did not exist. Her lips: a darker pink than her blush, akin to the blooms lining the bottom of the arcade, the tea roses that were easily overlooked but were the hardiest of the lot.

"What thinks your bear?"

A yearning growl as he had never sounded in the whole of his life tore from him without volition on his part. Charlotte beamed and tip-tapped her feet against his toes. "Well then," she said and reached out to grasp his hands, which he was by no means wringing like a dithering maiden. "There is no accounting for taste, but I think she fancies your cloddish ways and rather looked forward to furthering your intimacies."

His head came up. "What said she?"

"It is not so much what she said but how she watches you," her voice came over singsongy, "and how she buttons your coat and calls you 'Osborn' when she is pleased and 'Your Grace' when she is cross and orders everyone about for the restoration of your home."

His blood thrilled in his veins. "None of that means anything."

"It means more than you can imagine, you numpty." He tilted his head so she could pull his ear. "Your duchess came to you after years of horror. It is a miracle she allowed you to touch her at all."

"'Though she be but little she is fierce,'" Arthur quoted.

"Do not babble Marlowe at me," Charlotte said.

"It is Shakespeare, you barbarian." They shared a smile at this old joke between them.

Charlotte kicked her toes against his shins. "I never thought to admit this aloud in my life, but I think Georgie knew what he was about."

"Oh, now, Charlie," Arthur moaned and tore at the lavender again.

"Never mind the indolence and profligacy he plays at, we both know he is fit to rule. He strives to change *versipellian* ways for the better. I believe he was not mistaken in his matchmaking."

"There is no way he could have known we would suit so well."

The smile that spread on Charlotte's face was equal parts joyful and devilish. "Do you and Beezy suit? So well? So very well?"

"Say nothing!" His bear was capering in his aura like a fool *ursus puri* in Phineas Drake's Equestrian Spectacular and Exotic Traveling Menagerie. "Charlie, do not, do not say I said that. She and I, we have agreed upon a cordial affiliation—"

"Is that where that came from? The children loathe it!" Charlotte shrieked. She left off kicking him but reached up to tousle his hair as she would Tarben's. "I shall keep my peace. On one condition."

He had dreadful memories of such as she'd wrung out of him in the past. "Go on."

"Tell Beezy what happened."

"Charlie—"

"Tell her." Her hand gave his hair one last, fond scrubbing, and she sat back. "She has known sorrow and fear. She will understand."

Arthur smoothed his hair back into place and rose. He held out a hand, which Charlotte took with great gravity, and he pulled her into a hug. He took her basket and turned them toward the house. "I am going to have to thank Georgie, aren't I." It was not a question.

"Do not lose your sense entirely, Artie." The children, who had been "helping" the gardening footmen, raced to meet them, Ursella predictably distracted along the way. Charlotte pulled him to a halt and into another hug, one of her special ones, the very embodiment of home and safe harbor. "We are only as content as our unhappiest heart," she began, and to Arthur it felt like an arrow had pierced his own. "When we arrived, it was Beatrice's, so like an ember gone cold. It took a falling-down house and friendship and unruly cubs to fan it to flame. And perhaps a certain duke."

Arthur sighed. "My turn then, is it?"

"Mum, Uncle Artie, I planted one hundred tomatoes!" Bernadette exclaimed as the children danced around the both of them.

"I planted two hundred!" shouted Tarben.

"Your uncle needs a squish," Charlotte said, and his niece and nephew turned on him with the same look of devilish joyfulness he'd seen on the face of their mother. Each child grabbed a leg, and Freya bless them, they were *verispellis* children so there was some strength in it. With a theatrical groan, he tumbled them to the ground, the basket spilling its contents onto their heads to shrieks of joy and even stronger squeezes. Ursella turned up as unexpectedly as ever, seemingly from nowhere, and twined her little arms around his neck in a delicate yet inexorable hold. He embraced her in turn, light but steadfast, rolling on his back to amuse her siblings, and let them all sneak into his heart that bit further, deeper and stronger, to the point of no return.

As Beatrice oversaw the removal of the paintings in the Long Gallery—one of the footmen was of artistic bent and assured her they needed to be cleaned and restored—she decided she wanted her way. In all things.

It had been enough, or so she thought, to take charge of the improvements to Arcadia. It gave her such satisfaction to use the money from her first abominable marriage to the benefit of her second and in the fortification of a place she knew would make Castleton spin in his grave.

On from that, it was eminently satisfactory to take on the builders who had no badness in them, just an occupational drive to undermine her schedule and cut corners where they may. Defending Arcadia and herself and their future tenants sent vitality humming down her veins. She garnered respect due to her perspicacity and reveled in it.

Then, standing in the Alpha's study… Managing that undertaking had transcended everything she had done to this stage. If it didn't sound utterly mad, a winding flow of knowing had coursed between her and Osborn and Ben. It was akin to the sensation of words being on the tip of her tongue, of catching sight of something out of the corner of her eye. It was both tangible and etheric, known in both the body and the mind. She knew without question the decisions she made were correct despite Osborn's sullenness.

As she looked out one of the windows, watched Charlotte and Arthur chat in the rose arcade, watched the children hug him and roll around on the lawn, she wanted all of it. The child, the home...

The husband. A true husband. One thrust upon her by fate and Georgie, it was true, but one who might transcend their cordial affiliation and become everything to her. Lover, father... She thought of Ben and Charlotte: and friend. She had more love than she knew what to do with when she thought of having a child of her own, of their own. She had so much already overflowing when it came to Osborn's nieces and nephew—her nieces, her nephew. Would love follow naturally should they make a child? Would they make a family?

While he spoke to Charlotte, he had run a gamut of emotions: despair, laughter, disgruntlement, and pain. She could see the pain he suffered even from her distant vantage. How deep must it run; was it why Arcadia had been in ruins? If only she had the vaunted senses of a *versipellis*, she would have earwigged on Arthur and Charlotte's conversation without compunction.

Was this the first time she thought *versipellis* rather than creature or beast? It must be.

Progress, then, she thought and stood at the window until they were long gone, until the sun set.

She crept down to the stillroom, hoping to raid the pantry after the rest had eaten. At the foot of the stair waited Ursella, who took her by the hand and led her toward the kitchen.

Fifteen

"URSELLA!" CHARLOTTE CALLED FROM THE END OF THE HALL. "Oh, there you are. Bringing us your Aunt Beezy. Good girl."

Beatrice's hand was not released until the child led her to her place at the end of the table. Coogan pulled out her chair, another footman lay her serviette on her lap, another filled her glass with wine.

"Brosnyn has taken charge of the wine cellar, Your Grace," Conlon informed her as she took a sip of the lovely hock.

"Thanks to Mr. Conlon's guidance, of course, ma'am," Brosnyn countered. Beatrice decided then and there he was the under butler and gritted her teeth against saying so to Osborn.

Oh, no. She would not be silenced.

"You make a formidable pair. Mr. Conlon, we shall discuss the appointment of Mr. Brosnyn as your second-in-command," she said, to the delight of both, and only then did she look at the duke. "Osborn," she said, hearing the distance in her tones.

"Madam." He rose. Was he leaving? Because of her? Because of what had happened earlier? Because she had taken another decision without consulting him? He moved down the table and collected her plate. "We are dining French style, if I may tempt you with what Mrs. Porter has so lavishly laid on?"

"You may." She took another sip of wine. "If it is your pleasure."

Charlotte paused in preparing Ursella's plate. "Oh, it is the Alpha's pleasure to serve his—"

"Partridge?" Osborn cut across their sister-in-law and kept his attention fully on her. He quizzed Beatrice on her preferences as he indicated each serving dish laid out from one end of the table to the other. Did she care for the stewed mushrooms or the parsnips?

A spoonful of each? Will he serve up any of the sauces? Jelly or cream? There was yet trout to be had, done in a gelatin mold if she wished? He did not pass a dish that he did not inquire to her desires, and by the time he had worked his way back to her, he lay before her a bountiful plate tailored according to her tastes.

Ben took it upon himself to revitalize the conversation. "The wine was part of our mother's dowry," he said.

"Despite our sort not being great imbibers of wine or spirits. Nor was it a typical inclusion for an English lass," Charlotte supplied. "And yet, of course, the German ancestry was well established on the distaff side. The name was, if I recall, Adelbern, which is not unexpected, considering."

"I did not know that," Ben said, and he smiled at his wife as though she had hung the moon.

"Mum knows everything and everything that happens," Tarben sighed.

"Even before it happens," Bernadette grumbled.

Ursella as ever was quiet, but Beatrice caught her nodding in agreement at her potatoes.

"His Highness would value such intelligence," Beatrice said. The partridge was delicious, as were the accompaniments. She found the peas, when topped with one of the jellies, to be especially tasty.

"Oh, Georgie knows what he'd get in me." Charlotte smiled her thanks at the footman who topped up her glass. "As I have mentioned, we grew up in Court, Beezy. It was a raucous rearing, to be sure, and not one I would recommend."

"There was much that occurred that was not good for the young," Ben admitted.

"Candlesticks as far as the eye could see," Charlotte added.

"How glad I am that your children are here with us now." She eyed Osborn down the length of the table. He had not contributed to the reminiscences, nor did he call a halt to them. He nodded to a footman to remove his plate and stood to take up the bottle himself and see to her glass.

"Yes," Ben replied. "We were let run wild"—a chorus of shouts from the children betrayed their approval—"and while it was not for the best, we were amongst our peers and have made friendships for life. Lowell was often among us, as were the Bates brothers."

"And Lady Coleman, the new Duchess of Lowell's bosom friend," Charlotte added. "Jemima is a clandestine couturier, although there are some in society who have begun to discern her hand in the fashions many are sporting. She is a favorite of Georgie's."

Beatrice wondered if that was protection enough against brewing scandal. It did amaze her, the loyalties Georgie held dear. "What was His Highness like as a child?"

"Much as you see him now," Charlotte said. Beatrice nodded to Morag, who bustled the children from the table and into the care of their footmaid nursemen. "Mercurial, crafty, fashionable, vain. But also intelligent, far-sighted, loyal, and not without playfulness."

"As regards vanity, I would like the footmen outfitted in Osborn livery." She regarded the duke over her wine glass, and something about his lowered lids tickled her stockings. "At the soonest possible eventuality. Is Lady Coleman able to help?"

"Oh, well able. She is swift and not one to quail at a challenge." Charlotte snorted with laughter as Ben shushed her. Was it a quote from Shakespeare, as Osborn was prone to spout?

"I shall see to it," Osborn said, to her utter incredulity. "Are you sated, Madam?" he inquired, silencing Charlotte and making Ben squeak. They looked at each other, incredulous.

"Does he speak with intent, or is he quite oblivious?" she heard Charlotte whisper to her husband.

"Thank you, Osborn, I have had enough to eat." Beatrice rose, if only to defuse the surge of jealousy that swept over her, watching Charlotte and Ben giggle and whisper. "We may repair to the, oh, what shall we call the family reception room? That is so unwieldy."

"Let us call it the den," Charlotte proposed, earning a glare from Osborn. "Ben and I must tend to the children this eve as they will not have their Aunt Beezy for storytelling." She tugged Ben up from his seat. "I believe your time may be best spent in the company of your husband, in your own room."

"I must see to the grounds," said Osborn. "I shall join you anon."

―――――――――

"Anon" proved to be nearly an hour. Beatrice was in her habitual place, the chair at the window, as the stillroom door opened.

"Ah, Your Grace." She looked him over.

He looked down. There was nothing to see there; he was buttoned up for once.

"Not the stoat, then," she said.

"A stoat? Madam, you wound me." Osborn lay a hand on his heart in a melodramatic manner. "If you knew how to spot the telltale signs of a *verispellis*'s essential self, you would hesitate to compare me to a stoat."

"Let us see…" She leaned back in her chair and let her gaze run over him, up and down, lingering in a few places, which had a discernible effect on his composure. "Well blessed in regard to hair. Of greater height than many. Larger in general than most men, and most of your kind, I suspect." She dwelt on his arms, and they did that thing again, that twitching. How tempting it was to ask him to remove his coat and turn around so she may get a look at every inch of him.

Never mind his composure, hers was well rattled now. "I have seen you neither move at speed nor swim, so I know not if you be a greyhound or a salmon."

He smiled, smug. "One's essence may be alluded to. For example, Charlotte spoke rather loosely at the meal."

"Regarding Lady Coleman?" She recalled the odd use of language: quail, swift…ah. "I understand. It would not be well done of me to spread this knowledge, would it?"

"As you say." Osborn stood before her dressing table and touched her comb. "In society I often passed the time wondering what sort of animal a human might make."

"In between cultivating your *on-dits*." Beatrice watched his fingers trace over the back of her brush, swirl in her pot of hairpins.

"During, as I spent so much time with tabbies and dragons and ape leaders." He cocked his head. "And so I have wondered about you." He returned the appraisal to which she had treated him. His gaze was like a brand running over her skin. "A pullet. A pigeon. Or so I thought, that night at the ball. And then I became acquainted with your spirit, your virtual claws like those of an eagle, the perception that would not be misplaced in a hawk."

She exulted in being likened to a bird of prey. And yet: "An uncomfortable companion."

"Far from it. One who would be trusted to see what I could not."

"How unfortunate then I am not one of you."

He pulled over the stool from the dressing table, a pink tufted thing made ridiculously adorable by his bulk as he lowered to sit. "Madam, if anyone could will themselves to change their skins, it would be you."

"I am gratified, Your Grace."

"Are you? I am well aware you only address me as such when you are displeased with me."

That godforsaken curl flopped onto his forehead. Beatrice resisted it as always, wondered what it would be like to indulge in tucking it aside. "It is not so much displeasure as it is deep respect and a compliment for your ducal dignity."

"And yet you have just now presented that compliment to me left-handed." He leaned forward and took said hand. "I know very well how you proffer your respect." He ran his fingers down her own, to the very tips and back. He held it against his, palm to palm, regarding it with concentration. Hers was so small in comparison to his as to be like a child's—

"My father was killed when I was young," he blurted. "Mum had been murdered by trophy hunters, taken from us, and his grief was like to destroy him. He was challenged in the old way by a Shifter from the Nordic countries called Hallbjorn who wanted a stake in England and would take it by force. He had been lurking in the vicinity for months yet came out of nowhere. I was not old enough for the Change, and I could do nothing."

This explained the state of the Alpha's study then, its occupant having left in haste to protect his family. "How young?"

"I had not attained the age of reason."

"Younger than seven, then."

"By a bare six months." Something about that made him laugh. She saw his eyes flash, presumably showing those of his other self, molten gold, fiery yet melancholy.

"And would you have been able to aid your father's cause, that young?"

"I would have tried." He ducked his head to hide his bright gaze.

"And not survived, I imagine."

"Survival." His body vibrated from within, and he snarled. "The be-all and end-all of *versipellis*. Those at the top, predators and princes alike, would do anything to ensure the family names carry on. Or would have done in the past. Parents who were predators strove to ensure the lines did not mix, that lamb did not lie with lion, and yes, they may, in their human forms. You know of Lady Phoebe Blakesley?"

"I do, of course. She escaped my fate thanks to the intervention of her brother, the Duke of Lowell."

"Her parents arranged the marriage so the Castleton name, revered in wolf lineage, would not cease to exist. It takes quite a lot for a Shifter to die of natural causes, and his lineage had been corrupted, ironically enough, by holding to the old laws and eschewing to mate outside their species. His bloodlines were so pure that he was quite mad."

"This is very like the villain in *The Beastly Baron Bardolph*."

"Should you ever meet Mrs. Anchoretta Asquith, you may like to give thought to her characteristics." He managed a cheeky grin.

That was news. "I shall hint as much to the Duchess of Lowell, who would be keen to know."

His smile winked out. "You should not have been wed to him," he said, stroking her fingers over and over. "Georgie should have intervened."

"He was not apprised as he ought to have been, I suspect." The prince had not been present at the ceremony, which had been conducted with both pomp and haste. "In any case," Beatrice continued, "I shudder to think of you as a little boy rushing to defend your pack or clan or what have you. Why was the king not present at this challenge? Are these not matters of state when a title is involved?"

"You are clever," Osborn said. "There was no time to summon him due to the ambush, nor do I believe he would have come. George's father has ever been one to cling to the old ways. Had he been present, it would not have been out of place for him to fight in my father's stead, as the Alpha of all Alphas. We were not important enough to defend."

"Georgie does not think so."

"Despite his antiquated approach to our union, he welcomes reformation that does not directly threaten his power."

"Would he fight in your stead did it come to it?"

"There is no threat. The usurper did not succeed in gaining our clan because it dissolved, the women and children fled, he did not mate, did not multiply. His life is likely over, for if an Alpha does not bring in children in due course, he does not survive. His rights to this place are gone."

"Thus, does it not revert to you?"

"It is…complicated." He nuzzled her palm. "I have said more than I thought I would say and would leave it at this. For now," he assured her. He ran his hand farther up, to her wrist, closed his fingers gently around it. "You relieve me of my secrets without the slightest exertion." He peeped up at her, his eyes solely brown again, a brown like the burnt sugar on her favorite ginger biscuits. She watched as he licked his lips, as his opposite hand cupped her cheek, as he leaned in with the intent to kiss her.

She shook her head. "Please do not."

"Madam, I cannot give you a child out of the mere thought of a child. I find this aspect of coupling to be enjoyable."

"It is not my experience that kissing has anything to do with it."

"Is that so?" His creature flared in his gaze once more, glowing and fierce, no trace of melancholy now. Beatrice reached out and finally allowed herself to tend to that errant curl. It was soft and thick, but she could not get the picture out of her mind, of a small Arthur charging into the vicious melee that resulted in his father's death.

"I find that I cannot welcome your husbandly attention this evening."

"I ought not to have said anything." He made to get up, and she stopped him. Stopped him only as he allowed it.

"Arthur." He looked at her, truly looked at her, without the wry annoyance he greeted her with at first, without the brooding obstinacy her schedule inspired. He looked at her openly, those big brown eyes sparkling with hints of an otherworldly golden hue. They were so close to one another, she was bracketed by his thighs, and her knees were very near the placket of his trousers. His hands had somehow come around her back, and how was it that her fingers were twined in that curl? Beatrice caressed its thickness, so soft, and her heart turned in her chest like a kitten before a fire.

If she knew how his entire body was inflamed by the tentative petting at his hair, she would cease in a heartbeat. Arthur wished he could kiss her, as much as he wished he could cross over to the afterlife and tear Castleton limb from limb. How dared that wolf treat the gift he was given with such disdain?

How dare *he* do so?

"Arthur," Madam began again, "from a young age, almost as young as you were yourself, I was, on the one hand, made to manage my unmanageable brothers and by extension the entire household, barring directly telling the servants what to do. I was to inform my mother what was required, and she carried out my directives. The servants knew this was the case and thus did not trust me. It was unpleasant to be treated so."

"You were only a child." Ah, his foot in a trap, hidden with cunning.

"I was only a child," she agreed. "Nevertheless, as I grew in years, I was then informed I was not permitted to increase my authority in that house, that it was not my place, though my work was in aid of those who flourished there. I ought to prepare myself for a household of my own, as a wife. So I did, with the view of taking what I'd learned and what I wished to correct into my own home."

"And found yourself in no such place." How had their foreheads come to be touching?

"In no such place indeed." Madam ran a finger over his knee, and he thought he might combust with desire. "I found myself in a place in which the lord and master turned into a raging beast at the merest provocation." She related to him the first instance of her knowledge, and his desire turned to revenge. Too little, too late. "I promised myself I would never wed again."

"I promised myself I would never wed at all."

"Only see how well that has gone for both of us."

They shared the tiniest huff of a laugh. How strange, to share a laugh with a wife. Arthur tilted his nose toward her cheek. "Have you changed your soap yet again?"

"I have not."

The peace of a house headed toward slumber settled around them. A log popped in the hearth, and a candle guttered. He sighed and rose, replacing the candle on the hearth, its blaze of light dancing over her golden hair as Madam joined him.

They stood before the hearth, the bed beside them. Neither moved.

"Until tomorrow, then," she said.

He bowed, a mere excuse to sniff at her hair once more before he turned for the door. "*Tomorrow and tomorrow and tomorrow*," he quoted.

"An inauspicious choice of play, Osborn." Did she enjoy the theatre as he did? He opened his mouth to counter, but she cut him off. "Do not paraphrase Horatio in its stead, I beg you."

He laughed. "Then I shall simply wish you the sweetest of dreams," he said. "Madam."

Under cover of the night and the wood, he Changed, with even less effort than before. His bear shook himself from nose to tail, his spirit humming with glee.

What's got you in such a humor?

His creature leapt with grace and descended into peals of laughter. *You'll sniff it out soon enough.*

Sixteen

BEATRICE SUFFERED A FRACTIOUS NIGHT'S SLEEP, AND SHE LAY her disrupted rest fully at Osborn's door. Which was not their door. After last night…after having spoken so frankly and shared their histories, she would prefer it was their door.

And why not? she thought as she finished pinning up her hair in a looser fashion than usual. Why not make the best of a bad situation? Neither of them had wished to wed, and yet there they were, and if it would help her fertility if they were better acquainted, then what of it?

It was not as if she was losing a battle against anything but her former powerlessness.

She was not without power now.

Beatrice asked for what she wanted, and he gave it. It seemed she was able to say what she meant and only good resulted.

It was a state of affairs she wished to investigate further.

So deep in her thoughts was she, she nearly neglected to dab on her oil.

When she reached for it, the vial was empty.

A wash of fear flooded her. What were the consequences of not using it? Even if it never worked in the past?

If that was not a reason to set the ritual aside, she did not know what was, and yet… She tucked the empty glass into her workbag to show Charlotte later or, better yet, Ben.

Beatrice smoothed down her skirts. It was time for breakfast.

It was time to greet the new day.

She passed by the open window as was her habit and looked out into the wood before closing the curtains.

In the wood, the bear stirred and sniffed the air.

"Good morning, Mr. Todd," Beatrice called as she passed the steward's study. The shushing sound of a quire of paper sliding to the floor followed in her wake as the fox stuck his head out the door.

"Ma'am," he gasped. He joined her, utterly perplexed.

"Are you regretting your decision, Mr. Todd?" She found she was sorry to think so. She knew he would excel as Osborn's—Arthur's—their steward.

"No, ma'am, no indeed," he stuttered. "I, er... There is something amiss I wished to bring to your attention. However, it has to do with our sort, and I do not know where to begin."

"The beginning originating deep in the annals of time, I suspect?" Todd shrugged and nodded and grimaced. "Come, take it up with Lord Swinburn, if that suits?" Todd only nodded this time; he relieved her of her workbag, and they continued on to the kitchen.

The man argued with the bear as they left the cover of the wood, lumbering past the clothing folded neatly on a rock.

Beatrice entered the kitchen. As one, the company within froze, like a tableau at a musicale. Conlon, arrested, hovered over one of the warmers. The maids halted in their work, and Mrs. Porter's breadmaking stopped mid-knead. The children as one hushed their morningtide gurning. Ben paused with his fork halfway to his mouth, and Charlotte held her butter knife aloft. Morag gaped, and the tea she was pouring gushed over the edges of its intended cup.

"Morag," Beatrice scolded and fetched a tea towel. Her admonition broke the spell, and while their behavior was unusual in the extreme, she did not comment as she mopped up the spill and sat. "Mr. Conlon, I am in the mood for eggs with my toast this morning."

"Very good, ma'am," he whispered. Brosnyn charged in with two footmen in his wake; they came crashing to a halt and stared.

"Good morning, Brosnyn. And to you, Corvus and Brock." Beatrice set her serviette upon her lap and poured her tea. "Shall we discuss the work of the day?"

———————————————

The bear stopped at the edge of the underbrush and threw his head back. Inhaled.

The man within reeled. Impatient, he drove them forward.

———————————————

"...and as ever, should you have any queries, please direct them to Mr. Todd." She turned to Ben, who was still staring, his fork suspended once more. "Your food will go cold," she said. He blinked and set the utensil down. "Is there any class of ceremony required to invest Mr. Todd in his new role? Something amongst your sort I may not be aware of?"

Charlotte nudged her husband in the side as he remained agog. "No," Ben replied. "There is the *initiatio* for the like of the Beta and the Gamma. Mr. Todd is neither."

"I shall confer with Osborn, for it ought to be marked with some occasion." This received no reaction. Beatrice looked around at the visibly confounded room. "I must ask if all is well?"

"Oh," said Charlotte, in a faint tone, "one hopes."

"Yes," said Ben, who fiddled with his serviette. "One surely does."

A resounding thump fell against the door, making Beatrice jump and gasp.

"Good Lord!" Beatrice made to rise, but Ben reacted with greater speed. "If that is yet another unfortunate creature—"

"A fortunate creature, more like," Charlotte said, and Morag, of all things, of all people, giggled.

The door was pounded upon by what had to be a mighty fist. She heard Ben open it, whisper, and then shut it and rush away. Before she could formulate a query, he hurried back from the laundry, arms full of clothing, and slipped out the door.

It must be Arthur, must it not? If no one else was going to remark upon it, then she would not. Even the children had not roused to their usual vocal heights.

"Let us continue," she said and shuffled another sheet of paper out of the pile.

The kitchen door crashed against the wall, flung open with vigor. Arthur entered and stood, scenting the air. For the first time since they had been under one roof, the company made him proper obeisance, throats bared.

"Good morning, Osborn, we had wondered where you…" Beatrice began as she too made to rise, and he flew across the room to loom over her. He looked wild and disheveled and larger than usual, his curls a riot on his head, his falls hanging by one button. He dropped to one knee, and his eyes—his eyes were glittering and wild and flashed from his warm brown and the fiery golden yellow of his creature and back again. The rumble in his chest resounded like a struck bell and grew in strength and volume; she refused to fear his creature even if she had no idea what it was.

As soon as she thought that, he looked exulted and relieved and annoyed in equal measure. He took her wrist and breathed into her skin. He leaned forward and ran his nose along her jaw.

"Arthur—Osborn! What are you about?"

He answered by drawing his nose up over her cheek, by pausing before her mouth, by rubbing his hand over her neck. "Your

Grace, what in the world?" Her voice wavered, her blush a conflagration on her cheeks.

He stood and fled the way he had come, Ben close behind. A roar and the sound of tearing and Ben returned with an armful of shredded garments. Another roar and then a ringing silence.

All present gaped at her; Charlotte's face bore the frustrated expression that conveyed she had news to impart that fell outside her remit.

Beatrice's hand shook as she took up her tea. There was little in this world a hot drop could not bolster. She gave Charlotte a meaningful look and took a sip. "As I was saying. Let us continue."

Mate, mate, mate, mate, sang his bear as they tore back to the sanctuary of the wood. It was rare he took precedence over his creature when in his essential shape, but at that precise moment, they were equal in power as never before. Perhaps that was the way of things when one—

When he…

When he met his…

Vera amoris! exulted his bear, who took them for a roll into a dell of bluebells.

It was incontrovertible. Where there had been no scent signature, there was now, in full force: of water flowing over the stones of a streambed on a hot summer's day, of long grass lightly touched with morning dew, of salt on the tongue, of sugar on the lips. Of stubbornness, were it possible to scent such, of industriousness as well as softness…

And there was an additional note, an essence that sang between her heart and his, unlike anything in his experience. Not surprising, considering he had not known how his *vera amoris* would convey to him, considering he had kept himself away from any situation in which he may find her, but this, this was unexpected, that each of their elements would be matched by its opposite.

His bear rolled back and forth in the flowers. *There was a scent that was not a scent, and it is gone, and we can scent her, and now—*

Yes, yes, Arthur scolded, *your meaning has been taken.*

His bear snarled and tore at a fallen tree. *How is it you are so... So...?*

Unmoved? Arthur made them run and run around the far perimeter, the bear's joy turned to impatience and anger. They ran and ran until Arthur knew the bear, even with his great strength and stamina, could run no more.

I am not unmoved, he said as they sat on a hill and looked out over Arcadia's lands. *I am perhaps too moved.*

Poxy humans, his bear huffed.

Bloody bears, he retorted. *Snuggling a mate is not the only thing that matters.*

Is it not?

The very fate he had hoped to avoid was now without question unavoidable. He knew not what happened next.

Do you not? his bear demanded. *Next, you do your duty and, in your duty, find your joy.*

Would it be a joy to do his duty? Would the fulfillment of his responsibilities be not arduous but ecstatic?

There was only one way to find out.

———————

During the hours between breakfast and tea, Beatrice reviewed ongoing improvements and gave praise or direction. It was time she had to herself while the family did whatever they did to school and divert the children.

On this day, all five followed her everywhere until she determined it was time for refreshments in the den. The children were staring at her with the same fascination they had when they'd first met. Charlotte was tending to her correspondence without her usual focus and gossipy asides, and Ben was pacing around the edges of the room.

The servants had been incandescent with joy, Morag even going so far as to give her the belated welcome the mistress of the house ought to receive from its housekeeper. Beatrice caught Conlon weeping in the footstool room, which nearly set her off into gales of tears, for what reason she could not discern. To keep herself occupied, she directed several footmen to remove the furniture from the awkward reception room Morag had referred to as the Beta's office and instead instructed them to install a sturdy but elegantly carved rosewood desk, a pair of very comfortable chairs and a tea table, and two bookcases decorated with whimsical figures capering around its edges. She thought to use it as a room in which to deal with her correspondence, as undemanding as it was at the moment. Though that may change as time marched on. There were titles in the locality who would welcome the Duchess of Osborn.

Her breath caught in her chest. For that was she. The Duchess of Osborn.

"I shall save these slices of lemon cake for Arth—Osborn. He is not often about at this time of day and would rue missing out." She covered a small plate, piled high, with a serviette.

"Had Artie left the house very early this morning?" Charlotte asked.

"Rather late last night."

"Ah."

Beatrice met Charlotte's meaningful glance with a shake of her head. "He told me about his…youth. I declined his, er, continued presence in honor of the trust he took in me."

"That's one way of putting it," Charlotte huffed.

"Charlie! I could not." She tilted her head in the direction of a candlestick. "Not after learning such a thing."

"What thing?" Tarben was indeed very like his mother.

"Children, I would consult with your mum in private," Beatrice said. "Do show your papa how well you curtsy and bow."

Bernadette and Tarben went off with determination. Ursella gave her a long look and meandered after her siblings.

"I suspect there is little to nothing you can tell me," Beatrice said, "regarding the events of this morning."

Charlotte laid down her pen and did not meet her gaze. "I cannot say a word, even were it permitted, without becoming..." She withdrew a handkerchief from her sleeve. "I will become emotional, and it would not be helpful at this moment."

"It is terrible? What happened at breakfast?" She had had such hope...

Hope she saw reflected in Charlotte's eyes, along with tears. "The absolute opposite of terrible. It is wonderful, wonderful. Oh, you are my sister in truth, and I could not be more pleased." She sobbed, once, loudly, and fell into Beatrice's unprepared arms.

The commotion their mother made naturally drew the children back.

"Mum is not upset," Beatrice assured them. "These are happy tears due to, to—"

"To how Uncle Arthur behaved at breakfast," Bernadette said.

"It is very exciting," Tarben said at his usual volume.

"It is because you smell, Aunt Beezy," whispered Ursella.

"You didn't before, and now you do!" Tarben bounced up and down.

"Was there a change you made recently that may have affected it in the past?" Charlotte sat up and blew her nose.

"I had oil I was told by Castleton's housekeeper that I needed to apply daily." Beatrice dug the vial out of her workbag and held it out to Charlotte, who passed it to Ben. "I used the little that was left yesterday."

Ben removed the stopper and held it up to his nose. "Neem oil," he said and exchanged a look with his mate before explaining to

Beatrice, "which has no scent of its own once it meets the scent of another, if that makes any sense."

"It does not."

"It is used to mask one's natural signature so none may discern it," Ben explained. "Such as *versipelles* who wish to hide their essential natures, for example. I have known it to be used as a lark for a masquerade but never with long-term intent." He sniffed the vial again. "You say Castleton's housekeeper gave it to you?"

"Upon arrival," Beatrice said. She glanced over the heads of the children. "I was told it would ensure the succession."

Ben's expression darkened. "The exact opposite is true."

"I am stunned to hear it." How truly friendless she had been.

"That lot. Intolerant and shortsighted," Charlotte growled, a very large sound coming out of such a small woman. "They would not have countenanced anyone less than *versipellian* aristocracy as their Alpha female. They had no notion what they had in you."

"The oil served to suppress your scent as well as your ability to fulfill your marital obligations regarding offspring." Ben looked fit to be tied.

"All due to the application of a little oil." And the soap, which she suspected had been made of the same stuff. "And now that my essence is discernible?"

"It is how *vera amorum* know one another," Ursella piped up. The authority in her little voice belied her youth. "And so if you had no scent your true mate could not tell if you were his."

"Artie was reacting to the revelation of yours." Charlotte waggled her eyebrows. "And your fragrance is, eh, affecting him."

"This is as far out of the realm of polite conversation as I have ever dared." Beatrice took in the hopeful faces around her. "Is the effect due to, due to..." Was she Arthur's true mate? How could that be?

"It is not for us to say," Charlotte said as she put her hand over

Ursella's mouth. The child's shoulders dropped as she heaved a weighty sigh.

"Then there is only one way to find out." Beatrice rose as the family—*her* family—bared their necks to her. "I shall seek out the duke."

Seventeen

ARTHUR COULD NOT REMAIN AS HIS BEAR INDEFINITELY, AND yet he chose to wander the edges of the land.

His land.

He could not fight the *sentio*, not now. When and how it would be done… *If it were done when 'tis done, then 'twere well it were done*…properly. Quoting the Scottish play again? As Madam said, not the most auspicious choice.

He did not dispute the feeling rising in his heart for his mate… and thanks to that had such compassion for his father's grief it was as though his papa's heart beat in his chest. He now understood the depth of his Alpha's despair at the loss of his mate, the mother of his children.

In experiencing that loss, in empathy for his father, he knew without a doubt he would welcome his true mate with open arms. The fear of loss was not greater than even one moment of the euphoria the bond would bring. He understood not only his father's desolation but his father's joy. The notion Arthur would sacrifice even one moment of that reality was the height of absurdity.

He understood the child's grief as well and knew it was time to set it aside.

To trust. To dare. To lay himself bare.

To the bond. To his mate.

True mate! his bear sang as they splashed through the brook.

His bear, whose great sensitivity allowed him to deeply feel the breeze ruffling his fur, to perceive the beauty of the blossoming spring, to inhale deeply the scents of the earth, his earth, his land, to admire the beauty of the changing light as the day waned. He climbed the sturdiest tree in his copse to watch the sun paint its nightly farewell over Arcadia and welcomed it—this place, that woman—into his heart. His heart, which would soon no longer be his own and in turn would be so much the stronger for it. A shiver ran up his spine as he scented his mate on the cooling breeze, turned to see her walking toward him unerringly through the wood, without hesitation, head held high. And beyond his comprehension, his heart expanded even further.

———

Beatrice followed the path she had seen Arthur walk that first morning. The way carving through the wood was broad yet careful of the flowering shrubbery and mindful of the saplings straining for light and growth. It led to a clearing surrounded by dead stumps scored by claws and soaring trees forming a canopy. She would have continued on had she not seen the branches of the largest oak flutter.

A small boulder at the edge of the clearing would serve as a place to rest.

She sat. She took a breath. She spoke.

"According to your brother, I was given an oil made of neem that masked my scent. I was exhorted to use it every day without fail by the housekeeper of Adolphus Place, whom I considered an ally. The oil's purpose was not to ensure Castleton's succession, as I had been led to believe, but rather to prevent it." Beatrice sought him in the branches, but he was well hidden. "I went from one abode in which the staff distrusted me to one in which I was universally disliked and thwarted. I presume they did not want a *homo plenis* as the Alpha female? I would be gratified if you could shed some light on this."

He was awfully quiet for one she must assume was of great size. "I used the last of it and so… I gather I have an odor? And it is causing a reaction in you?" Beatrice asked. "You must appreciate how impossible it is for a lady to converse about the scents of her person, made somehow worse by your lack of response."

Impatience gathered, and behind her breastbone, her heart flared. "How glad I am I practiced on smaller beasts. Although I am not so much conversing with you as I am with this mighty oak." Another flutter of leaves greeted her pronouncement.

This would not do. "Osborn, show yourself," Beatrice demanded. She rose to move closer to the tree. "Arthur. Please."

A bear dropped down from a height, which was not so very great as he was very, very large. He towered over her like the tree itself, his massive shoulder well over her head, the hump of his neck adding to his bulk. His coat, a rich brown, was the color of Arthur's hair, and its—his—eyes were the brightest gold. He snarled, baring his teeth in a fashion Beatrice supposed was meant to send her screaming for her life. She would admit to a quiver of unease, but she had not been called Lady Frost for no good reason. She folded her hands at her waist and held the bear's gaze.

It chuffed, then growled, then roared up into the canopy; the leaves swirled as if blown by a gale. He lowered his head, glared at her, and pawed at the earth. She went so far as to yawn.

The bear slowly reached out with his nose and snuffled the pulse on her neck.

She giggled.

He Shifted.

She shrieked and covered her eyes. "Clothe yourself!"

"Are you having me on, Madam?" Beatrice peeked and saw Arthur's hands planted on his hips, inexorably drawing her attention there, doing nothing to calm her nerves. She covered her eyes again. "Here you are, facing down the largest bear on this island, and when confronted with a bit of skin—"

"More than a bit, you heathen," she muttered from behind her palms. She peeked again. "Larger than His Highness?"

"What larger?" His voice was as silky as stockings drawing up her legs.

"Your bear! Not your…parts."

"Both larger." Could a man his size snicker like a boy? "Additionally, I feel I must point out, you are not unfamiliar with my mighty oak."

"I have not been required to gaze upon it." She turned her back.

His warmth and size were like a bulwark without being over-whelming or overpowering. "Do so, if it pleases you," his voice at her ear. "It is your right."

———————

Madam turned her back on him. He, Arthur Humphries, Duke of Osborn, one of the few truly fearsome predators at the top of the hierarchy in the whole of England, and she turned her back on him with as little thought as if he were a goldfinch or a snail.

He moved closer, let his heat wash over her back. Paradoxically, it made her shiver.

"We have lain together," he murmured against her ear. He inhaled her unleashed fragrance; he was intoxicated.

"We have," she said, her tone acerbic and yet…possibly only in an effort to keep up frosty appearances. "In the dark, under the covers. Not out in the open, like those dippers down in Brighton."

"Dippers? In Brighton?"

"The Bawdy Bathers of Brighton." She went so far as to send an incredulous glance over her shoulder and got caught, in a manner of speaking, in his chest hair. He flexed his pectoral muscles; rather than blush as he thought she might, Freya help him, she moistened her lips, the little pink tip of her tongue dragging along her plump lower lip, and he lost track of what—

"The *what* now?"

"They are women and men bathing in the sea together, in the, in the—"

"In the *nip*?" He knew he sounded gleeful. He had never heard of this, and he heard of everything. Well, not nearly as much as his sister-in-law did, to be fair.

"Ask Charlotte, I am sure she will provide you with chapter and verse." Her gaze slipped down to his belly, and she turned fully away again.

"And here you said you do not like gossip."

"This is not gossip, it is factual information as you may find in a newssheet or a ladies' magazine."

"If this is what lies between the covers of *La Belle Assemblée*, I shall take up a subscription posthaste."

"You will not find articles on how to woo your intended *en plein air*."

"Shall I woo you despite the barn door closing behind the horse?"

"I hope I might have more distinction than to be, to be taken on the ground."

"Madam." He laid his hands on her shoulders and stood as close as he dared, given his state of arousal, which had sprung up, pun intended, in a heartbeat. "I would take you everywhere and anywhere and always assure your comfort in every case. Come, now," he purred, yes, he would admit it, like one of those bloody cats she pampered. "Shall we not look upon one another and see ourselves as we truly are?"

"I am not truly Lady Frost," she whispered.

"Oh, that lady. I find her to be intoxicatingly capable," he whispered in return. "I find when she melts, she reveals a fierce little creature who is delicious." He rubbed his nose against her ear. "And delightful." She shivered; he did it again. "I am not a ravening beast with no thought to your pleasure or comfort."

"I find when the beast rumbles and grumbles, he reveals his desire for me."

Ah. "My desire for you is incontrovertible and was growing

before your status was revealed. It is not merely due to *versipellian* custom I desire you. But due to it I know we will suit, forever."

She dropped her head, exposing her neck, and he was done for. He reached out and placed his palm gently alongside it, and she tilted her head to rest her jaw on his fingers. If he was not mistaken, she brushed his knuckles with her mouth.

"I have had your family—our family clinging to my skirts all day."

"Our status is the epitome of a *versipellian* dream come true."

"I did not mind." Her breath warmed his fingers. "This evening, however, I would prefer we found some privacy. I propose we dine together in the stillroom."

"As ever, an ingenious solution, Madam."

Madam nodded, for it was her due. "Until tonight." She sniffed his knuckles, which he had to admit was rather ticklish. She tipped a small glance over her shoulder and left the way she'd come, head high but with a spring to her step.

Beatrice lit the last candle and straightaway thought to snuff them all again. It was her third attempt to light them and leave them ablaze; she backed away from the mantelpiece and took in the transformation of the stillroom.

The household had been busy in her absence, obeying an instinct to set a scene tonight. A walnut inlaid table had been brought in and set with service for two, a cold collation of meats as well as due consideration given to the sweets, weighted heavily on the side of lemon cake and ginger biscuits.

The sheets had been changed, fragrant with lavender and cedarwood and clover, and the bed hung with curtains beautifully embroidered with bears rambling from top to bottom. She supposed they would have been her first clue if they had been in place upon her arrival. What looked to be the household's entire collection of pitchers and vases were full of flowers of the wild variety, some with the roots still attached, betraying the children's hands in their gathering.

She was freshly bathed and the water and tub removed by a parade of discreet attendants. A delicate nightgown embellished with lace had been laid out on the bed with a dressing gown to match, neither of which had previously been in her possession. Her hair was brushed and plaited into a fat braid.

The fire was low as the weather was warming, so it was not chill air that made her shiver.

When the knock fell on the door, she expected it was another footman with yet another offering, but it was in fact—

It was in fact her husband.

Her husband, freshly groomed and buttoned up.

"A knock on the door?" Beatrice said. "And a cravat?"

He jerked his chin up against its tightness. "One of the footmen is quite good at this sort of thing."

"Ducal valeting?" Despite the tidying up, he appeared ready to explode into dishevelment in an instant. "We shall put him entirely at your disposal."

His expression was less than enraptured. "I suppose we are keeping them? All this talk of livery and such?"

"Your Grace," she began.

"Oh, no. Do not address me that way." He glared at the bed hangings. "I shall read the bloody letter."

"You reading it will serve as my bridal gift."

"I shall contrive to do better than that." He slipped a finger under the cravat and began to loosen it.

"Well, then." Beatrice gestured to the table. "There are cold meats and cheese and bread rolls," she began, as he prowled toward her. "And cake."

He smiled, a predatory thing that frightened her not at all. Rather, it made her feel hot all over; perhaps she ought not to have stoked the fire. "I will have my cake first, my salty little cake, and then we shall see what Ciara has prepared."

"To what do you refer, Osborn?" It was a challenge to retain an imperious tone when stalked by so handsome a beast.

"Osborn. My night improves." He stood before her and undid her braid. "You, Madam. I told you all about it the first night we lay together, but alas, you fell asleep. You are my cake, and I am keen to devour you."

She ran her hands over his lapels, which for once did not require her attention. A salty cake? What nonsense. "I am sure I do not know what to say."

"Then let us speak no more." He took her chin in his hand.

Beatrice knew what such touch signified and turned her head. "As I have said, I do not like kisses."

He dropped his hold immediately. "You do not like them in general or Castleton's in particular?"

"Castleton did no such thing." She shuddered. "I was kissed once or twice during my only Season, and it was unpleasant."

"Show me."

"What on earth can you mean?"

"Demonstrate." Arthur opened his arms. "I am yours to do with what you will."

Beatrice took a moment to consider his proposal and then grabbed his face and smashed her lips on his. Teeth crashed against teeth, lips ground against lips.

"You cannot convince me that is appealing." A pity kissing wasn't nicer, for the feel of his mouth against her own had not been as terrible as she'd expected.

"That is quite disagreeable. Here…" Arthur took her hand and raised her palm to his lips. "If I may in turn demonstrate?" He brushed his mouth over her hand, and her pulse leapt.

"You may." Oh, dear.

Arthur opened his mouth and ran it along her palm, his lips

warm, his breath hot but not unpleasantly so. Was it pleasant? *Pleasant* did not begin to describe it. It was gentle yet invigorating; it weakened her knees and made her feel hot and tingly between her thighs. He ran his nose from the center of her palm up her longest finger and then followed it back to her wrist with his lips. He nibbled on the fleshiest part of her palm and repeated the circuit, nose over her ring finger this time, lips lingering, slow, back down to her wrist. He took her hand in both of his, treating it with the reverence he would accord a precious artifact in the British Museum. He kissed the back of it, gently sucking on her knuckles.

"Does that…" she began. He looked up at her without ceasing in his task. "Does this approach work on the mouth?"

"It does. May I?" She nodded, and he pulled her closer, did that thing he did with his nose and her ear until shivers rippled through her core. "It is best to begin like a hummingbird supping from a flower." His lips hovered over hers as that bird would over a bloom and settled, removed, brushed, settled again.

He took her very breath with each caress.

Beatrice had forgotten to apply her salve and was certain her lips were dry as dust; as she moistened them with the tip of her tongue, it coincided with another touch of his mouth, and his groan inflamed her. His hands gripped her hips, and she snuck another lick.

"Madam," Arthur groaned, adding in approximately ten more syllables than required.

"Is that not done?" He did not sound like he objected.

"Oh, it is done. It is doing me in." He slid his hands down her back, and she reached up and stroked his face, petted those sideburns, and sank her fingers into his hair. She licked her lips again, and he hauled her up against him and ravaged her mouth.

It was mutual ravaging, leavened by the taste of toothpowder and arousing discovery. Beatrice spared a thought for those poor young bucks who had no notion how to kiss and those poor girls who had no idea what they were missing. She twined her arms around Arthur's neck, and he lifted her straight off the floor, her feet dangling somewhere around his knees, one of his hands cupped beneath her bum.

She intended to pay better attention to the act this time, with less fear and greater participation, but this was so unlike their first foray she was swept up, in his arms and in the moment. She twisted in his grasp until he set her down and proceeded to lay waste to his cravat. She shimmied his shirt out of his trousers while he made short work of the tie at her waist, the robe soon decorating the floor. She ran her hands up his back, and the growl this inspired was prodigious. She laughed, breathless, and wrestled at his coat.

"Madam, wait, wait," he panted, "Here, I can—" and he tore at the coat, wrapping himself up in the sleeves and struggling to extricate himself as she lay back on the bed and drew up the hem of her nightgown, uncovering her body as a gift, with pleasure. Arthur tore aside the sleeve that would not release him and wrenched his shirt over his head.

Beatrice sat up to remove the gown, and he batted her hands away. "Here, here," he chanted, raising her to her knees and removing it himself, his fingertips playing over every inch of skin they found; the nightgown joined the growing pile of abandoned clothing. He swept his hands from the crown of her head, down her back, squeezed her bum, tickled her ribs, and then halted below her breasts.

"Here," she said, pulling his hands up to cup them, and she gasped, dropping her head to his chest. He moved a palm to her nape and drew her head back for another kiss, even as he did not release her breast, until she trembled against him.

He too shook; the notion that she had the power to affect him like this intoxicated her. She applied herself to his falls, and he left off kissing and touching her to see to them himself. Buttons pinged onto the floor, and a seam rent as he tore them off.

"We shall have to see to a new wardrobe, Duke." Beatrice kicked aside the duvet and the top sheet and pulled a pillow under her shoulders.

"I shall keep you in the nip." He ripped his stockings to shreds, and his smallclothes were next to be rent into scraps. He crawled up the bed to hold himself over her.

Beatrice caressed his forearms. "The Bawdy Bride of—"

"The Borough?" He hovered his mouth over hers.

"I shall keep you in the nip," she murmured, "for I have much of you to acquaint myself with."

"I am at your disposal," he whispered and took her mouth once more.

Given her newness at bed play, Beatrice still lacked the courage to look at his…his part. Perhaps she might use her hands rather than her eyes? She ran her fingers over his chest, through that glorious pelt of hair, and rubbed her hands over his nipples, which elicited an interesting response. He countered with his hand on a breast. She parried by reaching down to stroke his hips with both hands and then slowly, lightly, took him in hand.

"Who is Baldr?" He was muttering those foreign names again.

"The god of my only hope of not exploding in your palm." He took her hands in his and held them by her head. "I cannot give you a child if I do so."

"I want more than a child from you." Oh, what had she said? He froze above her, and oh no, it was a mistake, she was mistaken in speaking so plainly.

"Under normal circumstances, a man will say anything to procure the paradise laid before him," he said. "But know this for truth when I say I will give you everything, Beatrice. My mate."

Beatrice rose, and Arthur lowered, and they joined and, overwhelmed, stilled. He held himself as close as he could without crushing her, keeping his weight off her while surrounding her with his strength. She basked in it now that she knew it was there for her protection, that it was hers to draw upon, to trust rather than fear.

In trust, Beatrice lifted her hips to draw him in deeper and wrapped her legs around his hips. He raised up on his knees and slipped one of his massive hands beneath her. She kissed him everywhere she could reach, and he did the same, curving that great back and nipping at her earlobe, running his tongue down her neck, mouthing at her collarbones, and as the feeling within built and built, she set her teeth on his biceps and tightened the grip of her knees. He left off beseeching his gods and goddesses and whispered her name, over and over, until they clung to each other through their release, one after the other.

———

"Do not fall asleep on me again, if you please." Madam had thrown her shyness aside and lay sated in the candlelight, allowing him to bathe her with the soapy cloth.

"I cannot help it if your diligence is so thorough I am done in." She ran a little foot up and down his shin.

Well, that was as pleasing a thing as he'd ever heard. He demonstrated this by snuggling them up in the sheets. Ah, a reprise of shyness: she tucked her face into his neck, and he tilted his cheek to lay it on her head.

"Arthur." She ran her fingers through that lock of hair she preferred. "Am I truly your mate?"

"You are. My bear is in alt, and the family will soon be."

"They already are." She took a breath and glanced up at him. "I thought you had to—"

"Had to?" She certainly wasn't referring to—

"Bite?" Madam wiggled against him with fervor, so much so he was in danger of hardening again. "I thought there was a bite?"

"There is." How to explain this without sounding like a barbarian?

"Castleton attempted it once or twice."

He reeled back. "Attempted?"

She hid her face again. "It did not take."

"It must have been horrific." Arthur sat up to lean against the headboard and pulled her into his lap.

"It was." Madam settled her chest against his and rested her cheek on his shoulder. "Worse, Georgie demanded proof I had not been bitten, for whatever reason."

The snarl that burgeoned in his throat was so strong, it brought on a burst of *dominatum*—for which he received a fierce tug on his forelock.

"None of that, thank you very much," she said. "I insisted a lady be appointed to inspect my person. I gather the bite may lie anywhere on the body?"

"Do not discuss this as though we were discussing stockings and garters."

"I would not show Georgie those, either, for what it's worth." She sat back on his lap and set about petting his sideburns again.

"How dare he," Arthur snarled, but his incipient rage was no match for her comforting touch.

"He dares as he is the highest among you and me, in both our natures." Beatrice combed her fingers through his curls, idly, like a gesture of long habit. "I held his gaze through the request and through the aftermath. I can assure you, he regretted it."

He could well imagine. "Had you done so while holding one of those curtsies, I could only count it even better."

"Why should he wish to see was I unmarked?"

Arthur ran his hands up her back. "Had you not known the Shapeshifter secret, he would have assumed you were not aware of what the mark signified. Your wealth would have been his, and you would have been doubly his subject, as a human and the mate of a Shifter. You would have been given a portion, a mere fraction of what he took, immured in a cottage in the marches, and lost to society." He came over shy of a sudden. "Dare I hope you feel you escaped a terrible fate?"

She hummed, teasing him. "I feel fortunate, when all is said and done."

"I fear we will have to be grateful to Georgie, when all is said and done."

"We shall, in our own good time."

"I suggest we engage in activities more pleasant."

"Do you indeed, Your Grace?" She slid over to his side, and her salty tone did nothing to flag his desire and, if anything, aroused it. "Pleasant is far too anodyne a term."

———————

It was very well that Tarben knew what flowers meant, but Ursella knew other important things about them that he did not.

She knew, for example, the flower best suited to mark a true mate bond was orange blossom. None grew near the house, and it would not feature in the kitchen garden. If they were following the traditions of the bears, the blossoms would have been harvested at Disting and dried. She would tell Uncle Artie it was time to mind the ceremonies now. Even if Uncle Artie didn't think they were a sleuth. (They were.)

Orange blossom was not a meadow flower or a wood flower like bluebells, so she would not venture out to Uncle Artie's spot in the copse. The only place she could think to find it was the glasshouse. As she made her way there, the underbrush rustled with *animali puri*. Was it hedgehogs and bunnies making the bushes rustle and dead leaves crunch? It was hard to tell, for she could not scent a thing, which was awfully strange.

When she reached the glasshouse, she saw the broken pieces were fixed and the door was new, and yet it creaked as she opened it, which was frightening but in the way a story might be frightening. The moonlight shone through the glass, and the plants and trees within cast looming shadows. As she paused at the end of the center aisle and did not find what she sought, one of the shadows detached itself from the others and found what it sought.

Her.

Eighteen

WITH *VERSIPELLIAN* HEIGHTENED SENSES IN MIND, BEATRICE made her way around the chamber as soundlessly as she could. She donned her night rail and dressing gown, retrieved a note that had been slipped under the door, poked at the fire, quiet as a mouse.

It mattered not, for Arthur slept like…well, a bear in hibernation.

She tidied up the remains of their supper, such as it was, for Arthur's appetite was prodigious. In all things. Yet despite his size, despite his Shape, he was gentle and careful in his actions and movements…but at the same time, determined upon his objective. He did not hesitate once the way was made clear to pursue his pleasures. She did not feel merely a convenient figure, but that her pleasure was as important as his. Not a means to an end but the end itself.

She pulled aside the curtain: the sun had risen, and they would miss breakfast if they tarried any longer. It was past time to join whatever a collective of bears was called.

It was time to rouse her husband.

"Arthur." No response. "Osborn." Not even a groan. "Your Grace!" He pulled a pillow over his head. "Come and bathe," she said, and he groaned and grumbled and mumbled.

"Bathe?" he demanded of the pillow slip. "How do you suggest I fit in that wee tub?"

"The laundry has been prepared to accept us."

"Us?" A big brown eye blinked up at her.

She held up the note. "There is a receptacle of adequate size to contain the Alpha and his, his mate. Ben saw to preparing it for us."

He scrubbed his face against the pillow to slough off his sleep. "What hour is it? Surely you may allow yourself a day of rest, Madam. This is like to be our honeymoon."

"It is nearly past time for breakfast, Your Grace. You have eaten all the food provided for us, and we have whiled away more than one hour—"

She whooped as a large hand pulled her onto a larger body. "'*Those hours, that with gentle work did frame,*'" he quoted, "'*the lovely gaze where every eye doth dwell—*'"

"Not every eye, and nor shall every eye," she muttered, turning her nose to his neck. "We are to bathe and clothe ourselves and join the family, as I am told it is necessary we present ourselves as a bonded pair. Or nearly bonded."

"It is required." He squeezed her in a hug his kind were prone to. "This bed is too small."

"What shall we do about the ducal suite?" she asked. "I cannot feel good about removing Ben and Charlotte."

"There is another suite on the first floor." He stretched, and his muscles were put on display to their best effect. "They were the staterooms, which I propose we do not make hospitable and thus prevent a protracted stay from our regent."

"Let us take them for ourselves," Beatrice mused. "We may call them what we like."

"'*A rose by any other name,*'" Arthur intoned through a mighty yawn.

"Your comprehension of Ben Jonson is impressive," she teased. Her robe was removed in a trice considering the slumberousness demonstrated up to that point, and those hands slid underneath her nightgown, up her back, and down over her hips as she was rolled beneath him.

"There are scholars who would take that out of context and supply it with a bawdy explanation." His fingers trailed over her cunny. "For this is a rose by another name, and its sweetness I vow

I shall never tire of. Let us refer to our rooms as the Rosalia Suite, perhaps."

"I may have been happy with that before you have—oh." He found what he sought, and her bones turned to water.

"We may call it the Crimson Suite if your blush is anything to go by. This may be my favorite color yet."

She gently moved his hands away and cuddled into his side. "My favorite color—"

"Is?" He contented himself with carding his fingers through her hair.

"I cannot fix upon one. It may be brown, but two different hues appeal. Or it may be golden."

"I have it on good authority that golden is not a color." He grinned, looking youthful and happy.

Beatrice saw his eyes flash, molten with pleasure, his essential self showing his joy. "Brown, then," she decided. "A color not considered appealing amongst the *ton*, but to be truthful, their opinion has never mattered much to me." She ran her fingers through his luxurious hair and reveled in his gaze. "Brown is a warm color, and warmth is safety, and safety is to be sought under a repaired roof and within uncommonly strong arms. Yes, it has much to recommend it, does brown."

"Madam, you take my breath away."

Oh, kissing. When done correctly, it truly was a prodigiously wonderful thing, and she discovered an appetite for it. How would she keep her mouth from his, going forward? She sighed against his lips, and he rumbled his displeasure as she withdrew. They must learn how to discipline themselves, and there was no time like the present.

"Come, husband, our bath awaits."

———

Beatrice hoped the staff would not be too cross about the water puddled on the floor of the laundry.

She and Arthur appeared in the kitchen and were greeted with applause from the gathered servants; the uproar assured that those within hearing distance soon swarmed into the room. As they were Shifters, that was the entire household. Beatrice returned Charlotte's embrace with her whole heart and Ben's kiss to her cheek with one to his. Tarben leapt around them like a frog, and for once Bernadette left off her decorum to let loose a few hearty cheers.

"Now then," Charlotte said, "I do hope that was not unexpectedly terrible."

"What are you on about, Charlie?" Arthur scowled.

"A private jest between herself and her husband, I am certain." Beatrice pinched her sister-in-law, and both laughed.

"Blessed Freya," Ben said, "these two with their heads together will be our undoing."

"It will be the making of you—" Charlotte objected just as Beatrice said, "It will be the making of us all."

"We are doomed," Arthur muttered.

"If this is doom," Beatrice countered, "then I invite it in." She smiled up at him, and his face fell, not in dismay but in, well... She had no idea what his expression conveyed. No one had ever looked at her like that before. His eyes were soft, and they drank her in as if she was an oasis in the desert. Was it because she was smiling? She reached up to touch her lips, and he took her hand, kissed her fingertips, held her hand to his heart, and kissed her before the assembly. The roar released by the entire company was like to tear off Arcadia's newly fortified roof.

Flustered, she pulled away, but not without a squeeze to the great paw enveloping her hand. "But where is Ursella?" Beatrice asked as she looked about. "Have the children taken their breakfast in the nursery?"

"Oh, that child," Charlotte groused. "How could she be missing this? It was all I could do to keep her from spilling what she sensed."

"Ursella!" Ben called.

There was no response. "She is never far when we call," Beatrice said.

"Ursella?" Charlotte called, her tone puzzled.

"Have you seen her, Bernadette?" Beatrice asked. If one of the children were to notice, it would be she.

"Last night, we picked flowers for the stillroom," Bernadette began.

"I know what the flowers mean!" Tarben tugged Beatrice's skirt. "I know red roses are for love and blue hyacinth are for constancy and peonies are for—"

"And then we came back and went to bed." Bernadette looked troubled.

"Ursella only found daisies, which mean loyalty," Tarben added. "She was cross because I knew something she did not and *she* is an Omega and thinks she knows everything—"

"I scolded you three up the stairs and into the nursery, squawking like the little rattletraps you are," Morag said, offering up her taciturn joking for the children's sake.

"We had no story because Mum said you were otherwise occupied, Aunt Beezy," Bernadette said.

"We checked on them directly," Charlotte said, struggling to keep her voice steady, "and that was that."

Beatrice leaned against Arthur as a tremor ran through her. She was not the only one who experienced a quaver in the atmosphere, and fear settled over them like a heavy cloak.

"This is my fault," Arthur whispered. "No sooner had I been so arrogant as to claim my place than disaster strikes." He tore at this hair, and a thunderous rumble built in his chest.

"Arthur, come, let us keep our heads." She laid a hand on his arm and addressed those assembled. "We shall look over the house and see where she may be hiding. If, as you have told me, Charlie, she is prey to the emotional well-being of our, our—" She looked to her husband.

"Sleuth," Arthur said.

"Of our sleuth," she continued, "then it only follows that even joyful emotions are taxing." Beatrice took stock of those before her. "Morag, if you would organize Glynis and Ciara and the household footmen to search the ground floor and then mind Tarben and Bernadette in the den. Mr. Conlon, please direct Mr. Brosnyn as you see fit in dispersing footmen on the first and second floors and as well the attics. Bernard and Christopher may take the nursery and the schoolroom." The footmaid nursemen appeared dismayed beyond comprehension. "Once we have concluded our searches, we shall reconvene if we have not discovered her hiding place. Mr. Todd, please remain behind. Thank you."

She waited for the servants to embark on their assignments. She had a delicate question, but there was no time for hesitancy. "I must ask why, if scenting is among your powers, you cannot detect Ursella's?"

Mr. Todd looked at Ben, whose expression conveyed sheer dread. "Mr. Todd drew to my attention a disturbance in the glasshouse, a great growth of neem in the southernmost corner."

"It is not a varietal suited to our climate, and given its growth, it has taken years to cultivate, if I judge it correctly." Mr. Todd's demeanor said he did so. "It would not have been suitable for use until earlier this year."

"Who would seek to conceal their signature?" Beatrice asked.

"Do not." Arthur's voice trembled with suppressed fury. "Do not tell me you were withholding the possibility Hallbjorn was here." His *dominatum* vibrated around them, threatening to explode.

"The usurper? Who killed your father?" Beatrice wished she had power the opposite to this oppressive force, to spread peace instead. Which she supposed was Ursella's gift, and the child's absence pained her afresh. "Why should we think it was he?"

"Who else would have a stake in this place?" Arthur railed.

"Who else would seek to undermine what little authority I can call mine without having done anything to make us a true sleuth? Who else would wait until we were at our weakest—"

Charlotte reached out and grabbed Arthur by the hand. "Artie, please open the *sentio*."

"I cannot do that and fix this." He was adamant but took Charlotte's hand in both of his. "If he senses the connection has opened, he will be able to call us to himself, and it would not be within our power to resist. We escaped the first time because my father's heart was broken and with it the connection. Had it not been, the result would have been horrendous."

"What is the *sentio*?" Beatrice asked.

"Now is not the time, Madam, to further your indoctrination into matters *versipellian*," he snapped.

"Then when, Your Grace?" This was no use. "In the amount of time it took to speak that speech, you could have explained the concept."

"It is the connection within the collective of a clan." Mr. Todd fell on his sword. "It allows every soul to feel the strength and care of the Alpha and to aid one another through him."

"It will endanger every soul here as it will be too new to have any useful strength except for the usurper to command us through it," Arthur insisted.

"How is it he will be able to connect?" Was this what she had felt in the Alpha's study?

"It is attached to this place, and he is still Alpha here."

"I find it hard to believe," Beatrice scoffed, "that he would still hold sway."

"I am certain that his lack of offspring prevents it," Charlotte said. "Artie, please."

"When all is said and done," Beatrice said, "it is Georgie's responsibility to deal with the usurper."

"The sins of the father, Madam?" Arthur huffed.

"The sins of your kind you say you wish to eradicate." She was overwhelmed, not in a way that paralyzed but rather galvanized. It was not fear that flooded her but fury. Here was another old man who expected the world to turn on his antiquated, vengeful, self-centered ideals. And here was her noble husband caught in the web of meaningless protocol.

No. This would not do at all. "Arthur, we must proceed methodically. You and I shall go through the ducal suite and the staterooms. Come, come." She slipped a hand in Charlotte's and stroked the other down Ben's arm. "Idleness will not serve. Let us go over the house, and then we'll know if indeed further action is necessary."

Over the next two hours, calls rang throughout Arcadia from top to bottom with no room overlooked, no cupboard left unopened. How fortunate they were in their coterie of footmen and in the diligence of the original servants of the house. Beatrice kept one ear out for a triumphant call; it did not come. She led the way back down the stairs, exchanging shaken heads with those she passed. Arthur had left her to take the staterooms himself, and she made her way alone to the kitchens, where the searchers reconvened.

She looked about for Arthur and Mr. Todd, who were not present. No matter: the rest turned to her for guidance. She stood at the head of the table, where she found a scrap of fabric.

"What is this?" she asked, even as she feared she knew the answer.

Brosnyn cleared his throat. "I discovered it on the doorstep, ma'am."

"Ursella's pinafore," Charlotte moaned.

Ben took it to scent. "Nothing," he said. "No scent other than her own, no hint of who she is with or where she may be." He looked at Charlotte, helpless. "This is my fault."

"It is the fault of he who is perpetrating this outrage. Let us reach out to the friends of the Osborn sleuth," Beatrice said and headed for the so-called Beta's study. "We shall send word to Lowell Hall and Carlton House for help. Who will take the messages?"

"I am a peregrine falcon, Your Grace." Faulkner, one of the gardening footmen, stepped to the front of the group following her.

"Ma'am." A dark-haired, large-eyed household footman joined him. "I am a bat."

"You are the faster, Wybern," said the falcon. "I shall make for Lowell Hall."

"And I for Town," said the bat.

"If the note is precise, you may carry them in your mouths. Is that a satisfactory solution and not an insult?" She opened the door to the Alpha's study. "Your Grace?" He was not there. She cut through her study and down one door to the steward's office. "Mr. Todd? Where have they gone?" How could they believe disappearing was a wise choice? She did not have the time to dwell upon it. "Let us assume they have taken on an aspect of this search best suited to their skills."

Beatrice turned to her brother-in-law. "Ben, I cannot fathom your despair at this moment, but I have several questions, and I require answers. Now."

―――――――――

Curled into as small a ball as she could manage and tucked up against a tree, Ursella watched the bad man walk back and forth, talking to himself. All through the rest of the night until dawn, he muttered and moaned and growled.

"...I shall once again prove my greater strength by challenging and winning. They've no right to be here—lost, lost in fair battle. Paid good money for the mate to be taken. The son of the king, a fool, a fribble, his father weak. Ought I challenge for the highest sleuth in the land? Think on it, think on it..."

She knew the story of her grandfather who had been killed in a challenge. What her parents didn't know she knew was that her grandfather's heart had not been in the fight. He'd tried his best, but he'd been so sad, and the *sentio* so broken, he could not prevail. That she had this insight was as much a part of her lineage as was the color of her eyes, as the way that Tarben was like Mum and Bernadette was an old dowager like their great-great aunt on Papa's side.

This was the beast who'd killed her grandfather, and she would not allow him to kill anyone else.

"My uncle is not my grandfather," she said, against the voice of her mum she heard in her head telling her to hush.

The beast rounded on her and loomed, like a specter. Only this was no ghost; no, he was very real, flesh and blood and bone.

"He will soon meet the same fate." He bared his fangs, and she shivered, more from the cold than fear. This one would not do anything to her. He could not touch her, for if he did, his fight was forfeit before it began. "I traveled far and bided my time. I have done so again and killed the small creatures and will challenge the big creatures, and I will keep my hold, and then I will prevail for eternity."

"This is not a good story. Aunt Beezy's are like this." Ursella waved her hand around and around. "Mixed up and they end in the wrong places." She sighed and tried to find comfort against the tree root. "I'm hungry."

"You do not hunger until you have known the hunger I have suffered from this rebellion of this sleuth—"

"And I'm thirsty."

He struck out as if to throttle her; he thought better of it, but claws appeared at the ends of his fingers. "No, no. I will not forsake my rights to this place, witless child. How glad I am I had none of my own to whinge and demand and cry."

"I am not crying." Ursella was not, and she would not, no matter how he snarled and sprang his claws. "I am shivering because I am cold, you mean old man."

The creature growled, incensed, pushed to the limit of his patience. He Changed, fell forward, and revealed his ursine self to her.

And Ursella smiled.

Nineteen

WITH THE BAT AND THE FALCON ON THEIR WAY AND HAVING NO notion how long it would take for aid to arrive, the search for Ursella continued out of doors. Armed with Ben's knowledge and due to Arthur's absence, Beatrice struck out on her own. Charlotte implored her to take one of the footmen, but the tug in her chest returned; whether or not it was quite ridiculous, she trusted it and followed her instinct to go alone.

If it was not quite, quite ridiculous to think it, she understood Arthur was on a mission only he could execute, and she must carry on at home in his absence. Compounding the potential foolishness, she muttered to him as if he walked by her side.

"You may like to know having footmen in numbers is quite handy when one's niece goes missing. And footmen with a difference as well, though their noses will not discover many clues if Ben's suspicions about the use of neem are true. I suppose they may look for tracks upon the ground as hunters do? It is well past midday, although I doubt a lack of sunlight would prove an obstacle." She felt a tug on her heart. Was it affirmation? It must be this *sentio* Arthur spoke of, though how it could work without danger or without having been officially opened she did not know. "You had best undertaken a worthy task or I shall know the reason why."

She shivered. "I set off with no thought of a coat for Ursella. If she decided to go for a wander under her own power, I hope she dressed herself accordingly. In any case, I have my shawl. I may at least offer it should I be the one to find her."

After making her way through Arthur's copse, she found herself drawn to a newly cleared path. If her memory served, it led to the circular space of no name... "Or a name not made known to me. I suspect it is significant enough to have remained unlabeled on a map and the sleuth knows it without naming it."

The presence in her heart turned both warm and warning. "Its importance may prove to be the usurper's undoing. Your brother has told me of your ways in this regard, and I am certain Hallbjorn will be no match for Lady Frost." Beatrice jutted out her chin, not that Arthur could see it. "I feel I must gently remind you of my proficiency at goading decrepit *versipelles*. It took little effort to push Castleton to his limit. Whenever he revealed himself, his pack did so as well, seemingly against their will, increasing my knowledge and hold over them. Why they did not kill me I do not know. I imagine the punishment for killing one's Alpha female is quite harsh. All this is to say, I am well able to provoke a Change in his Shape and therefore..."

The connection was useful insofar as the response she received from the other end was a cacophony of emotion. How helpful it would prove in the future. "I am here," she said aloud, and her voice summoned the creature from the trees surrounding the circular grove.

A creature it was: though greater in size than Castleton's wolf, this bear was similar to him in many ways, none of them salutary. Its skin was patchy and discolored and hung from its gaunt frame. It looked underfed and unwell. Its mouth hung open and displayed jaws underpopulated by teeth, and it was in possession of only one fang. Its eyes were mad, unfocused, filmy. Nevertheless, she did not fool herself into thinking she could defeat it physically. Words would have to do for now.

"You have forfeited any chance of victory ere you have begun," Beatrice said. "As I understand it, the challenge must be made in human form and only then may the essential selves of the combatants engage in the battle for primacy." She called upon every shard of ice Lady Frost possessed. "Show me the child."

"Here I am, Aunt Beezy." Ursella stepped around the creature into view.

"Hello, Ursella, it is wonderful to see you," Beatrice said. "I am sorry you are without your coat. You must feel the chill."

"It was cold in the night," the child said, "but I am well."

How was she to ask her niece if she was entirely unharmed? "I am glad to hear it. Your sleuth has been searching far and wide. It is my privilege to have found you."

"They would have come straight here, if they could scent me." Ursella glared at the creature. "He made me rub my hands and my neck and even my dress with a weed."

"It is a plant called neem, and its primary property is the masking of scent. Well, we shall simply wait until the household has exhausted every option and arrives here. Should either of us come to harm, then this creature's challenge is well and truly lost."

"He is called Hallbjorn." It swung its head around to glare and growl at the child. "I know what he has done."

"Do you? You are clever." How fortunate she had such practice maintaining a cool facade; Beatrice fought the urge to grab the child and run. "I am curious how you fell into his hands?"

Ursella had the grace to look chagrined. "We went up to bed, but I wanted to find a very special flower for you and Uncle Artie. He brought me here and made me sit and listen to him." She scowled, unafraid, and rolled her eyes.

"Oh, how dreadful." Beatrice marveled at the child's composure and vowed to do it honor by matching it with her own. "The whole night long you were made to listen?"

"It was, and I was." Ursella pouted. "He said the silliest things. About how we were not a proper sleuth and never will be, as my uncle has no second or third or anything. That my uncle was weak as my grandfather is weak and he would fall in a fight. I know this is not so as Uncle Artie does not wish to encourage such old-fashioned behavior as challenging. And he knows if I come to harm it will go the worse for him, and not only at my uncle's hands but my aunt's and my mum's and my papa's. He is a coward."

The creature had snarled throughout Ursella's speech, and Beatrice chose simply to speak louder over the din. "I have never met anyone as strong as your uncle," she said.

"He is strong," Ursella agreed, "but he is also stubborn."

"I must claim that fault amongst my own." Beatrice sighed. "I do like to think I am only stubborn when my heart is at risk."

"That is very like Bernadette," Ursella said. "She does take everything to heart."

"Your papa told me about how important the heart is to your sleuth."

"Our sleuth," the child corrected her. "*Versipelles* need the *sentio*, no matter their clan."

"Am I correct in thinking, therefore," and they continued to discuss this as if chatting across a tea table despite the vocal rage of the creature, "without the *sentio*, there is no claim?"

"Yes, Aunt Beezy," Ursella said. "It is well that Uncle Artie waited to open it up again until it was the proper time to do so."

"To wait is a form of strength," Beatrice said. "Knowing when to choose one's time is a gift."

"A great gift indeed," came a voice. "One that your husband, ma'am, and your uncle, child, used to best advantage." George, Prince Regent of England, stepped into the grove from one of the four paths leading into it. He was dressed without his typical magnificence, which was nigh on a greater shock than the fact of his presence.

Opposite him appeared Alfred, Duke of Lowell. From the third path prowled Alwyn, Duke of Llewellyn, and finally, finally, into the grove strode Arthur, Duke and Alpha of the Osborn Sleuth. For that was what he was, and that was what they were, as all in the family and in the house followed behind: Ben and Charlotte with Bernadette and Tarben, the footmaid nursemen, Mr. Conlon and Brosnyn, Morag, Mrs. Porter armed with a skillet, Glynis and Ciara and every single footman. They ringed the edge of the grove, strong in their numbers and so close to complete in their hearts.

"The Duke of Osborn is wise and good, in himself and in his sleuth." Georgie caught Beatrice's eye. "Do not, ma'am," he commanded, and she ceased the descent into her distinctive obeisance.

Charlotte made to retrieve her daughter, and the creature growled, and Beatrice had had quite enough.

"Arthur," she said, "do fetch your niece."

"Cousin," said His Highness. "Your wife has spoken."

Sweet, holy, *blessed* Freya and all her Valkyries. Was Madam attempting to ignore Hallbjorn to death? For the conversation she was conducting with their niece was as leisurely as one conducted around the hearth nibbling marzipan. He picked up his pace, not caring that his regent's directive was they should appear at the grove as one, like performers on a stage; nevertheless, Prinny had his way as he and the three dukes appeared at the heads of their respective paths simultaneously.

Madam rose from her curtailed curtsy and took in the aid he had gathered, her eyes smiling. Even as Arthur moved to fulfill his wife's decree, Hallbjorn bunched to attack. Ursella gave the creature a wide berth and held up one little hand as she passed. "It is time for beddy-bye, bad man," she said, and like a marionette whose strings were cut, he collapsed and commenced snoring.

"Well done, Ursella," Arthur said. Madam lifted the child in her arms and made to pass her to Ben, who had rushed forward with Charlotte, but the child held fast.

Ursella patted her mum's cheek and then cuddled into Madam's shoulder as she reached out to clutch Arthur's coat. "Oh, Uncle Artie, he was so mean, and he said he was going to make us be his sleuth, but I could see that he is very, very old and not at all well."

"Not at all well?" He reached out and ran a hand down her plaits and then took both the cub and her aunt within his embrace.

"No." She shook her head. "Not in his heart or his head. He thought I would be frightened, but I was not."

"What a brave girl you are." And the Omega to their sleuth. What a blessing.

Ursella nodded, solemn as a bishop. "I see things as they are, and so I am not afraid. And I felt you in my heart, even if the bad man thought we could not." She moved her hand to set it on Arthur's heart. "When this is better, we all will be."

He leaned in and kissed his niece's forehead. "Very soon, my fierce little cub. Freya would look upon you and shiver."

"I do not fear the war goddess. Mani will mind me." She yawned, and once handed over to her father, she flopped into sleep.

"Who is Mani?" Madam was never one to pass up an opportunity for enlightenment.

"Goddess of the moon and patroness of Omegas, so there's our answer, not that there was any point in posing the question." He exchanged a look with Ben and Charlotte and nodded.

"We shall take her in with the footmaid nursemen," Charlotte said, "and leave you to it." The women embraced, and Ben hugged his cub as if he could take her into his own body; they left with the rest of their brood and several attendants. A parting glare from Morag alerted Arthur to the consequences should he fail to follow through.

He would not fail.

For love was never failure, and right thinking never faltered.

"Custom decrees I can only honor my father's memory by avenging it," he said, addressing his prince, his peers, and his people. "Look upon this creature and ask yourself did you stand in my place, would you see such a challenge through?" The beast was in dreadful condition, and his bear was appalled to the same degree as he pitied it. Should they choose to fight, it would be over in an instant and would leave a dreadful burden on their conscience. "This is not the picture of a healthy Alpha, one to follow, one to trust in his inner circle, one to hold a *sentio* able to bond any, much less many." Arthur shook his head.

"How has there been no challenge for this place from elsewhere?" Madam asked.

"The knowledge Hallbjorn did not hold it was suppressed," Georgie said.

Madam huffed. "After all this time?"

"When I deign a thing is not to be discussed, ma'am, it is not spoken of." Georgie's awful stillness descended, and Freya deliver them, Madam was as unimpressed as that fortuitous evening in the Montague conservatory.

"So, therefore, if it was not known there was none to hold Arcadia, then it could not be taken," Madam observed.

"Truly, none support these archaic ways in our modern times," Arthur assured her.

"In law, it lay within my power to prevent the knowledge of his incapability to become common currency." The prince's inherent majesty drew down around him like one of his extravagant cloaks. "How I longed to resolve this issue. As I am not King, there was only so much I could do. Arrange a marriage, for example. One that would reestablish the *sentio* in these lands so strongly, it would inspire this rogue to show itself and thus bring about the resolution I desired. A thriving sleuth, lead by a vibrant Alpha pair, with no chance of disbanding as the cubs will soon follow."

The creature roused. "Thus are we resolved?" Madam's tone betrayed her desire to see this travesty concluded.

"The rules of engagement have been forsworn," Arthur said. "Hallbjorn's fate is neither my concern nor my responsibility."

"As the Alpha of all Alphas present here," Georgie intoned portentously—he did not get nearly enough opportunities to do so—"I shall shoulder this burden. I take responsibility for this blight upon our kind. While I regret he has not found salvation, he cannot be allowed even the slightest hold on Arcadia from this day forward." His Highness gestured expansively. "Ask what you will of me, Osborn, and I shall make it so."

"I cede this ill-begotten rogue to you," Arthur said, "and ask that you remove him from my lands."

"You may have apprehended the gravity with which I approached this situation." His Highness gestured to his frame. "I appear before you, dressed drably as I am so the ensuing sacrifice will not be so great." Hallbjorn, sensing his impending fate, began to retreat. In the blink of an eye, His Highness Changed into his bear, great in size and presence but, it was true, that bit smaller than the Alpha of the Osborn sleuth.

Regardless, he was fearsome as he rose on his back legs and roared like to rend the moon from its heavens. He landed on his fours, bunched, and leapt for Hallbjorn.

And as written by the great man himself: *exeunt, pursued by a bear.*

Twenty

A FIRE BLAZED IN THE DEN'S HEARTH, AS MUCH FOR COMFORT as for heat, and its smoke curled unimpeded up the chimney. Warm baths, delicious biscuits, and innumerable cuddles later, the children were ready to retire despite the sun having only set, and they demanded a story from their Aunt Beezy. If that was what was wanted, then that was what they would receive, along with her signature ending to the tale. "…and they lived—come, children, as one."

"In cordial affiliation from that day forward." The chorus was ragged and lacking in enthusiasm.

"What's a corjul fillishun?" Tarben asked.

"A question for the ages, Master Humphries." Georgie stood at the threshold and paused so all within might comprehend his magnificence before he came into the room.

The children looked at Beatrice, who nodded. In impeccable harmony, they bowed and curtsied to their regent.

The royal sigh was windy indeed. Some class of princely edict trembled on his tongue when Charlotte rose from the sofa.

"Georgie."

"Charlie." If Beatrice did not know better, she'd think the prince swallowed in trepidation. "Worked out in the end, eh?" he said, and did he attempt a chuckle? If he thought to dare, it died in his throat as Charlotte prowled toward him. While one of his status would never tremble, his fist did convulse around the elaborate hankie in his grasp.

"To what do you refer?" she asked. Her children, who knew well what that tone entailed, were caught between horror and glee and took refuge behind their footmaid nursemen. "To the marriage you forced dear Beezy and darling Artie to undertake, with threats to the well-being of my family?" She stood before him, and his placid expression twitched. "Or do you refer to the abduction of my child, our Omega? The abduction that did work out in the end, very little thanks to you, in your failure to inform us the usurper was a threat. Or is it regarding the usurper himself, whose fate I shall not inquire after as it was very, very nearly too little too late?"

"I believe you have spoiled His Highness for choice, Charlie." Against protocol, Beatrice took the prince's arm. "Your Highness, shall we be hosting you this evening?" *Let us hope not*, she thought. The staterooms were in no way prepared to accept a royal personage, and she had become quite attached to the notion of making them hers and Arthur's, sooner rather than later.

"I shall abide at Lowell Hall until the ceremony, though it is mere hours away." He sniffed. "Lowell and his duchess will remain, as Her Grace wishes to visit with you and the duke will not be parted from his wife. Miss Tabitha Barrington will be your guest as well."

"What a competent butler you make, Georgie," Charlotte spat.

"Charlie, if we may take our leave of you? Goodnight, children," she began and was hugged thoroughly by the cubs, Ursella no worse for her harrowing adventure. Indeed, she was very much herself as she wandered off to drag an ottoman beneath a window. "Your Highness, we shall detain you no longer as Your Presence was undertaken in great haste and I am sure you wish to avail of time spent in relaxation and peace."

She steered him out of the den, and they paused on the landing. A precision of royal footmen lined the stairs down both sides, one to every second tread. And Arthur thought Lowell was extravagant.

"Your timing was impeccable, Your Highness." Her gratitude, she feared, would ever be seasoned with annoyance at his interference in her life.

"Your husband wasted no time in demanding my assistance."

"I am cognizant of the sacrifice you made, sir." Honestly, would this man accept thanks or not?

"As I said, the ensemble I wore was easily sacrificed."

"Georgie." His expression vacillated between indignation and one very like fond amusement. "If what Ben told me is anything to go by, making a stand was a delicate yet deliberate choice, and I insist upon expressing my gratitude."

"What had Garben told you?"

"That the challenge would be forfeit did Hallbjorn not make it in his manskin. That should a member of the royal family choose to intervene, it sets a precedent onerous to sustain."

"And so you sallied forth to inspire enough rage in Hallbjorn to force his Change and sent word to me that I do my duty posthaste. Deliberate and not so delicate."

"This is the product of your orchestrations, sir." Beatrice would not relent.

"And as I said, it worked out in the end." He looked around him with longing. "I spent one summer here, when Arthur was quite, quite small, little more than a babe in arms and not in the least bit entertaining. He will not recall this. It was the most idyllic season I have ever spent. I was free to roam and Change and feast on wild strawberries and honey from the comb. I was minded by Arthur's mother with as much care as she minded her own, and his father gave me a pattern upon which to base my behavior—well, some of it. It does my heart good to see Arcadia restored and its chatelaine and Alpha female to be everything it deserves and more."

"Georgie!" Arthur bellowed from below. "Get your great hairy arse down here, there's work to be done."

"Your Grace!" Beatrice gasped. Relaxing protocol was well and good, but this was a step too far.

"Oh. Madam." Contrite, he popped his head around the end of

the staircase. "Didn't see you there. Your Highness, we beg your company as we prepare for the proceedings at dawn."

"Proceedings?" This was not on her schedule.

"I leave that for your husband to relay." Georgie bent over her hand and processed down the stairs. Halfway, the footmen behind him fell in, giving an impression very like a waterfall, taking their place guarding his back, those at the fore leading the way.

"For Odin's sake, Georgie, do you practice that in your spare time?" she heard Arthur grouse.

Brosnyn appeared in the wake of the royal phalanx. "Ma'am, the Duchess of Lowell and the Honorable Miss Barrington await you in the footstool room."

"Thank you, Brosnyn." As odd as it was to receive guests so late in the day, Beatrice was thrilled to see her friends. "If you would show them up?"

Arcadia's butler shuffled out ahead of the women, Felicity in particular solicitous of his great age. "Mr. Conlon, please assemble the housekeeping footmen and prepare the Sorrel Suite and the Verona Chambers?"

"It is being done even as we speak, ma'am," he replied.

"You are a treasure." The little turtle beamed and toddled away.

"The Sorrel Suite? You have been busy," Felicity said as she attempted a decorous ascension up the stairs. She failed about halfway, and Beatrice found herself in an embrace that rivaled the bears' for strength.

Tabitha's hug was as fierce. Another friend made on the fringes of the *beau monde*'s ballrooms, Miss Barrington had only returned to society after living abroad with her brother Timothy. The willowy lady had a passion for apothecary matters and was said to be as knowledgeable as a man on the subject. She certainly spoke with as much confidence as did a man, a quality that inspired censure from the arbiters of manners in the *beau monde*.

"I find the naming of rooms to be sufficient reward for tending to their refurbishment myself," she replied. "Come, let us repair to the den. It was known as the family reception room, but we found it unwieldy to say that every day and night. It is a term that has, em, meaning for the Humphries clan." She caught herself in time before revealing anything she ought not before Tabitha. "I am afraid there is an inconsistency to the names. They do not share a theme, as in being called for flowers, for example. Even at this early stage I fear it is too late to change them."

"They are idiosyncratic, then." Felicity and Tabitha took in the room, and Beatrice found herself on edge waiting for their response. "This is a wonderful setting, Your Grace."

"We were not to 'Your Grace' one another to death if I recall your letter correctly," Beatrice reminded Felicity.

"It is very homely," Tabitha said, "but an open window or two would prove healthful."

"I will direct a footman to do so as I have no trust in my ability to open them myself. I vow, I required Arthur to exert his, uh, superior strength on every door in this place. The ones that were not already off their hinges, that is."

Brosnyn hovered on the threshold. "Ma'am, Mr. Conlon wishes to know your desires regarding refreshment."

"Let us have tea for four, thank you." Beatrice dragged the chaise back to its place near the tea table. "My sister-in-law, Lady Swinburn, is seeing to the children up in the nursery and will join us directly. There." She settled the chaise into place and fetched a cane-backed chair to finish off the grouping. "The furniture moves about willy-nilly, none will admit to it. I do not know if it is another family idiosyncrasy or if His Grace is keen to raise my ire."

"Beatrice, have you been taking one of my tonics?" Tabitha touched the back of her hand to Beatrice's forehead. "I have not heard more than five words from you in one sitting in our entire acquaintanceship, and here you are, as bubbly as a brook."

"She has had a tonic," Charlotte quipped as she joined them. "Applied by her husband."

"Charlie, do not!" Beatrice scolded her and then made the introductions. Three footmen followed with tea trays, and once ensconced behind the pot, Beatrice's joy was complete. Her own home, her staff, and, when it came down to it, her teapot. She could ask for little more, except…

"You look radiant," Felicity said.

"In the first weeks it was due to an unladylike glow of exertion," she joked as she poured out.

"Her Grace did more than her fair share to rejuvenate Arcadia," Charlotte added.

"If only you had seen it when we first arrived," Beatrice said. "Shattered windows, the roof like a sieve, wind howling through the walls. It was like something out of one of Mrs. Anchoretta Asquith's novels. Oh, Felicity! Oh." She caught herself with a glance at Tabitha and faltered. "I heard something about that good lady and recalled I do not like to gossip."

"It is not gossip if it is common knowledge," Felicity said.

"I am aware that Mrs. Asquith is, like many here, able to change from one Shape to another," Tabitha said. "His Highness took me into his confidence." This statement, made by any other in society, would have been delivered with no little pride. Tabitha mentioned it as though it was of no greater consequence than reporting that the coal bin had been filled.

"Miss Barrington has been put in charge of the rehabilitation of His Grace, the Duke of Llewelyn, who now resides in Lowell Close," Felicity informed them. Beatrice had recognized the duke from her nuptials in Carlton House but knew nothing of his past. "She was on her way to settle there but met us on the road to Arcadia. Her brother, Mr. Timothy Barrington, is our new tutor and has gone on ahead."

"I was gratified to see Llewelyn lending his aid to your cause,"

Tabitha said. "It is promising to see him extend himself. He will not achieve wellness by lurking around the edges of humanity nor of *versipellian* society."

"You must know his history, Miss Barrington." Charlotte's face was the picture of censure.

"I do, Lady Swinburn, and my heart goes out to him," Tabitha assured her, "but so does my mind. My intellect tells me the refusal to embrace his new circumstances will not aid his healing."

"What was done to him was unconscionable," Charlotte spat. "One cannot fault him for struggling to regain his health."

"What was done to him was the height of barbarity," Tabitha agreed. "But I believe your kind tend to collapse into your feelings. No offense intended."

"I am tempted to take it, Miss Barrington." Beatrice had never seen Charlotte nonplussed; Tabitha's forthright persona had that effect on people.

"That is your prerogative, of course." Tabitha held out the plate of biscuits to Charlotte, who took one out of ingrained habit. "As it is of His Highness. He takes offense with aplomb and frequency."

"A characteristic common in princes, and in dukes," Beatrice muttered, and Felicity laughed.

"I shall negotiate the contrast between what I think is required for the benefit of his health, as well as respecting Llewelyn's choices," Tabitha said, and Charlotte appeared mollified. "He will be quite the challenge."

"Oh, indeed," Felicity said, her voice brimming with amusement. "We are very eager to witness the evolution of Miss Barrington's plans for His Grace."

═══════

A muffled rustle in the underbrush would have eluded ears less acute than those of a *versipellis*. "Llewellyn, show yourself," Arthur called as the motley crew of Shapeshifters entered the grove. "You are welcome to join us if you require a formal invitation."

The rustling stopped, the concealed one poised. There was an explosion of movement, and they heard him flee.

"His reserves were sorely taxed by merely standing in the presence of so many this night," Georgie said.

"He moves with great speed as a human," Ben remarked, hackles showing. "I cannot fathom how fluidly he must move as his essential self."

"You have heard he does not Change?" Georgie asked. The men nodded.

"Does he consciously fight against it?" Arthur could not imagine doing so.

"It is a natural response to his captivity," Bates said. "And not all of us are as much at home with the animal within as others."

Arthur perked up at that. Was Bates not in harmony with his wolf? Was that why he was content, earl's son or no, to be Second to Lowell?

"Miss Barrington will have the care of His Grace's recuperation," said Lowell. "It was His Highness's notion to have my duchess do so, which will not transpire. My wife is rather occupied with her new enterprise. Among other things."

And what was that smug look on His bloody lupine Grace's face? Yet another innovation to cast the rest of them in the shade? As if he weren't setting enough precedents left, right, and center.

"Shall you not engage in the efforts you wish accomplished, Artie," Georgie said, "or are you content to stand about like a wallflower?"

Arthur threw his coat over a branch to the horror of both Georgie and Alfred. Ben mocked the faces they made behind their backs as he did the same, and Their Royal Highness made his degree of involvement clear by spreading an overlarge handkerchief on a boulder and sitting in a huff. Bates as ever took the middle ground: he removed his coat but folded it with the care of a valet.

Speaking of valets. "How good of you to send me more mouths to feed, Lowell."

"I did as my wife bid," Alfred replied, unperturbed, "in honor of her friendship with your wife."

"And my wife," Ben added, "is well pleased with the two lads who have the care of our cubs."

"This talk of wives," Georgie said. "How tiresome." Any implication of marital harmony was in the worst taste given the dire state of the prince's own mating, and Arthur swiftly turned their attention to the task at hand. When he was an Alpha cub, setting a bonfire was one of the first things his father had taught him. Ben and Bates, arms full, lugged branches into the clearing, while Alfred kicked and rolled a large stump forward.

"That will do well for the center, Alfie," Arthur said.

"That nickname is not for your use." Lowell called up another smug smile and explained no further.

"Fair enough," Arthur said and slapped him on the back. He drew Ben's attention to Lowell as he turned away: an imprint of his mucky hand showed clear as day in the center of Weston's finest. Bates rolled his eyes but neglected to inform his Alpha of the alteration to his ensemble.

"Alfred, in all honesty." Arthur heaved another sturdy branch onto the arrangement. "Am I meant to keep the footmen?"

"They are presently arrayed in your livery," Bates said as he dumped another load of twigs at the base of the structure.

"Which you organized, brother," Ben added. "You hired Lady Coleman yourself."

"Will you not allow me to torment His Grace the Duke of Lowell? *Pap'r-faced villains.*"

"Is he still invoking the bard?" Georgie moaned.

"He quoted at me on my wedding day." Lowell rolled another

log into the clearing. "Osborn, it is the pleasure of those in my care to work with the gifts they discover. I cannot employ each and every one to best effect. I am pleased they have found places here."

"And with ten more on their way. Or is it twelve, Lowell?" His Highness sounded smug indeed.

Lowell refused to be goaded. "I shall remind my duchess to alert Lady Coleman about the requirement for more clothing."

"Or will Bates do so?" Ben looked innocent, a sure indication that he was scheming.

"Ah?" Arthur sniffed more gossip in the air.

"No baiting Bates, if you please," Georgie said. "It reflects ill on the lady."

Ben groused as he moved to his brother's aid. "I can't be the only one in these parts seeing to the succession."

Felicity turned to Charlotte. "I trust your daughter is well after her ordeal?"

"She is, thank you," Charlotte replied. "Our cubs are resilient in their own ways, and it is difficult to knock Ursella from her perch."

"She is our Omega," Beatrice announced, her pride as great as if the child were her own. "Even at her young age, she was more than a match for Hallbjorn."

"I understand His Highness has resolved the issue?" Felicity asked.

"He has, although I have yet to discuss Arthur's plan in retrospect as he did not inform me of it beforehand." Arch looks were shared around. "And I leave His Highness's methods to his discretion."

"A duke in general and a *versipellis* in particular is not always as forthcoming with their plans as we would like," Felicity said.

"Your diplomacy is breathtaking." Beatrice laughed. "I try to set a good example through my own behavior in devising a daily schedule for the household. I have yet to discern its influence on Osborn."

"Beatrice, are you well, truly?" Felicity took her hand. "I must admit to trepidation when I heard of your nuptials, and under such circumstances."

"Thank you, I am well." Beatrice busied herself with the detritus of the tea table. "I was not at first, as you may well fathom."

"A woman of wealth forced into a marriage with a stranger," Tabitha said, "presents more than one challenge to overcome, I suspect."

Beatrice nodded. "Yet I was fortunate to discover upon my arrival at Arcadia a purpose tailored to my abilities, one I was pleased and eager to undertake. And it served to establish common ground."

"Yes." Felicity folded her serviette into the smallest square she could contrive with the thick cloth. "Common ground is quite necessary."

"Indeed." Beatrice had a notion her friend referred to bed play. "Some ground was more common than others. And in certain instances, if such a mission was not up to my abilities, I discovered my husband's talents in tutelage."

"Is that what we're calling it?" Charlotte rolled her eyes.

"My sister-in-law has not met polite discourse she hesitates to circumvent." Beatrice took Felicity's serviette and threw it at Charlotte.

"I agree with Lady Swinburn," Tabitha said. "Euphemism does not serve us. We must speak frankly amongst ourselves if we are to profit from one another's knowledge and experience." She softened her typically assertive tone with a brilliant smile. "Beatrice, despite being an unmarried woman, I have a breadth of knowledge to convey, do you but ask me."

"Thank you, Tabitha, I believe I shall." Beatrice went to the door and called out to the attending footman. "Corvus, do fetch the decanter from His Grace's study. And four glasses."

"…and then she nigh on decapitated herself with a mirror." Arthur carved a sturdy branch into what would be a torch. The men lounged around on the ground, apart from, unsurprisingly, Georgie and Lowell. "Nearly drove me to drink."

"But all is well between them, in any case," Ben said, "and I do mean all."

"Then we will await the news of your expectation of a happy event." Lowell sounded satisfied.

"Yes, well…" Arthur looked around him at the fathers seated in the clearing. "She's wanting cubs as soon as possible. She knows it is up to me. I don't know how to go about it."

"Oh, my brother. Let me be your guide." Ben sat up, his face the picture of seriousness. "You see," and he took up two innocent objects, one circular in shape and one straight, whose benignity was soon compromised. "When a mama and a papa love each other very much—oof!"

The others roared with laughter as Arthur tackled his brother and tussled him to the ground. "It's the 'calling in' nonsense," he continued, once the roughhousing was done. "Is there an invocation or a ritual or…?"

Lowell cleared his throat. "Wolves have only to invoke Diana, and it is done."

"What, you say 'Diana, give us pups, please and thank you'? After or during or when? Hush, you boil, you plague sore!" Ben rolled around in hysterics while Alfred hemmed and hawed and Georgie, out of character, blushed.

"It is a combination of wish and will." Ben regained his composure. "The words you think or say, they are what suits each male to his nature and that of his mate." He smiled, in memory of his own cubs' conception perhaps. "I believe the female ought to have a say, obviously, given the nature of my beloved wife, and I would not have it any other way."

"I have been asked to bring them in," Arthur said, declining to say at which stage he was so importuned. "It is the wish of my duchess."

Ben cocked his head. "Are these new terms in the cordial affiliation?"

The company gaped as their regent broke into gales of laughter, such as they had never heard in their long lives. It rollicked on and on until tears ran down his face, to the degree he was required to rise, use his hankie, and replace it on the stone.

"I am a genius," he said. "You owe me endless gratitude, Osborn."

"A cordial what now?" Lowell looked up from the branch he was struggling to scrape into a suitably torch-like shape.

"Our beginning was fraught," Arthur smiled to himself, "but we have found our way."

———

"…and men often need direction to that sensitive area."

"And this is the seat of the, the…" Beatrice faltered.

"The female erotic function, yes," Tabitha said. Felicity blushed as easily as Beatrice did, and Charlotte snorted into her brandy. "It is thought in order to conceive, the male and the female must experience release simultaneously."

"And release is the…fluttering?" Lacking occupation for hands that wished to wring in discomfort, Beatrice lifted the decanter to pour out another dram. Felicity did not partake, but Tabitha seemed to be well on her way to making up the duchess's portion.

"As the flame on a candlestick often flutters."

Beatrice shared a hearty laugh with her sister-in-law, who said, "Your husband, the Shakespeare aficionado, may call it 'fading' or 'to die.'"

"As the French would have it: *la petite mort*," Tabitha said, her accent not what it could be, considering her years spent on the Continent.

"And you say humans deem it necessary that both male and female experience this simultaneously to be successful in procreation? I find this a rarity despite the diligence and application of my husband's efforts," Charlotte said, dodging another serviette launched her way.

"There is little experimentation to strengthen these claims and no circumstances under which to investigate them," Tabitha replied. "I believe it is through repetition, as well as the diligence and application you mentioned, that the desired outcome is achieved."

"It is said the female is at fault if there are no children," Beatrice said, hesitant. "It is what the man-midwives say."

"One would be better fixed by listening to a female midwife," Tabitha said. "Much common wisdom is not confirmed by science, and it may be simply that science is unable to compel common wisdom to conform to its methods. One anticipates a day in which we combine what has always been known by our ancestors and what is yet to be known through scientific inquiry. It is a balance, I believe, that may be struck through the unity of intuition and observable knowledge. And once women are as prevalent in the field as are men."

Beatrice kicked off her slippers and curled her legs beneath her. "Do speak more of this balance, Tabitha."

"Do not! I have engineered this precisely!" Arthur batted Lowell away from the scaffolding of branches. He collected his coat and shoved his arms through the sleeves. Lowell seemed inclined to fuss over it and set it just so about his shoulders, muttering about the line of the thing. The small woodland animals, their only witnesses, were unlikely to be bothered by a poorly hanging garment.

"I hope you will treat the *initiatio* with the decorum it deserves," Lowell said, giving one last yank to the coat's hem. "One would expect full regalia, if you even possess it."

"I have the appropriate garments, for the love of Odin." He was almost certain he had. "That Todd creature His Meddling Highness made us employ is seeing to it."

Georgie huffed. "You are the recipient of every aid required to fully step into your role of Alpha due to the good offices of those around you without the lifting of your littlest finger, and yet you gurn."

"Always up for a good gurning, is Artie," Ben teased.

"Is that what you're calling it?" Bates quipped, and Arthur chased his brother over hill and dale, leaping boulders and crashing through shrubbery until both were breathless and Arthur ended up laughing at the sky.

"I am fortunate." He stood and faced them: his brother, his cousin, his neighbors. "I thank each of you, here and now and without the formality of ritual speech or fire, and proclaim my gratitude as boundless, just as you say, Georgie. In this place, at this moment, know that I thank you from the bottom of my heart."

"And that heart will open tomorrow to include us in its gratitude and strength." Ben looked proud and overcome. "What a day it will be when the Osborn sleuth takes its rightful place once more."

Arthur embraced Ben and rocked them side to side. Next was Lowell, and the two turned it into a playful competition. Bates and he shared a manly handshake and exchanged slaps on the back. Georgie arched a brow, but Arthur would not be put off as he all but threw himself on their prince. Who among them embraced their regent with the wish to connect rather than to kowtow? What Georgie had said was true and according to His Highness's design: without Beatrice, Arthur would not be here, and the honor due his prince was, if not boundless, at least comprehensive.

"My thanks," Arthur said, once more, and turned for the house.

"And felicitations on the taking of your rightful place, Beta," Bates said to Ben.

The brothers exchanged a smile. "I am the Gamma, Matthias," Ben said.

"Not the Second?" Ha! Lowell's Beta appeared astounded. Arthur had got Bates on this one.

"No," Arthur said. "There is another."

Twenty-one

ANOTHER NIGHTGOWN SHE WAS NOT AWARE SHE POSSESSED had been laid out on the bed. It was white, as sheer as a breath on a winter's day, and tied in a rather suggestive fashion at the tops of her shoulders with ribbons as fine as spiderweb. The accompanying robe was cobalt velveteen, and the hue made her eyes sparkle like sapphires. As much as she appreciated it, the ensemble deserved to be admired by another party—

"Beatrice." Arthur called her name from outside her window.

Without hesitation, she threw her legs over the sill and was lifted into his arms. He set her down with care and, taking her hand, drew her toward his woodland sanctuary.

"I was there the night Felicity met the duke, you know." Beatrice took a deep breath of the fresh night air.

"Were you?" Arthur laced their fingers together. "I heard he carried her away through the Countess of Livingston's garden."

"He did. He swept her up in his arms and spirited her off at speed."

"Is that a dare, Madam?"

Beatrice hesitated one heartbeat too long: he lifted her with as much effort as he would an apple, and off he sped, into his copse, achieving his goal in less time than she had to draw two breaths. He stopped at the entrance, set her down, and gently spun her around to face a bower of cushions and blankets, the velvet curtain from the attics hanging as a backdrop from sturdy branches. Lanterns were scattered about, light playing over the rich colors of the fabrics, and a hamper sat to the side, spilling over with sustenance. The setting was made even more exquisite as it meshed so well within the sumptuousness of nature, the stars and the moon peeking through the canopy of trees.

Beatrice leaned against him, tucked under his chin. "Did you find inspiration in *La Belle Assemblée* after all?"

"I did not." Arthur huffed. "It was, in fact, *The Lady's Monthly Museum*."

"It never was!" Beatrice laughed.

He turned her in his arms and took her face in his hands, marveling at her expression. "'*Loose now and then a scattered smile and that I'll live upon.*'"

"Your facility for quotation and this setting," Beatrice said to his sternum, hiding her face from his besotted look, "betrays a love for the theatrical."

Arthur nuzzled the top of her head. "My mum loved the theatre, and Arcadia Demesne was known far and wide as a place traveling players could settle and perform before their feet itched for the road. We provided them with room to store their various properties and welcomed them back with open arms upon their return."

Beatrice led him onto the stage he'd set, kicking off her slippers to curl her toes into the plush rug and smiling at the candles in their holders. Hidden creatures rustled in the underbrush, unafraid, and she looked up as a light breeze ran through the branches above, a bird call sounding overhead.

Beatrice turned to him. "'*The clamorous owl, that nightly hoots and wonders/At our quaint spirits.*'"

"Madam…" Arthur fell to his knees. "You take my breath away."

She held his face in her hands. "I hope I may live up to what the theatre manager intends."

"I assure you, there is no one better for the role."

Beatrice cast her costume aside as Arthur leapt back to his feet to toss his clothing around the copse, his shirt dangling from a nearby branch. She laughed as he pulled her to him and dropped them gently to the ground, rolling on his back to sit her almost directly onto his…his manly part. "I believe I mentioned I do not like to ride," she chided.

"I believe you once did not care for kissing." Arthur slipped his fingers down her belly and teased her with his thumb. The now-familiar sensation came over her, the paradox of turmoil and languor, and she rolled her hips, his cock hardening against her thigh.

"Oh." Beatrice moved again, and he moaned, gripping her hips. She wanted to giggle at the way she rubbed along him like a cat but thought he might take her laughter ill. She rose on her knees and felt like one of those goddesses of his; small she may be, but what power she had to make him growl so. She took his hands in hers and stroked her face with them, drew them down over her breasts, settled one on her hip, returned the other to her cunny, laying his fingers in the best place to convey pleasure. She leaned down and braced herself on his chest, and both gusted sighs of contentment and impatience. "I see. This is indeed a class of riding I foresee enjoying, Your Grace."

"Do not—ah!" He gasped as Beatrice reached down to touch him, to run her fingers over him as he did her. He throbbed in her palm. The strength he called upon to set a leisurely pace was apparent in the sweat gathering on his brow.

Beatrice moved and through a combination of instinct and pure luck brought him to her entrance. She looked at him from beneath her lashes. "Arthur. Show me what to do."

He showed her by doing, rearing up gently and sheathing himself in her heat. She lay her hands on his shoulders and rocked. He braced his feet and lifted his hips in tandem, ran his hands from her shoulders to thighs, up her sides, ran his fingers through her hair, the golden strands luminous in the candlelight. He set one hand at the back of her neck, gripping her nape as her movements settled into a rhythm she deemed best, if her breathing was anything to go by. With his other, he teased her most sensitive place to her approval and her censure when he slipped it away.

As much as he desired the release that awaited them, he did not wish to rush their way to it.

Could he feel pride when he was feeling so much else? How well she took command of their pleasure, having not known it before. How quickly she discovered what was best for her fulfillment and for his and sought to give them both the joy of this act. If he'd had any doubts she was his match they were gone—and on the heels of that thought, his ability to think clearly as she found a movement—*Baldr, Sif, Loki, Odin, sweet Valkyries*—that made him shudder with deepest arousal as she squeezed around his cock and moved, over and over until his blood sang in his veins. He wrapped his arms around her, his mouth worshipping every inch of skin he could reach, inspiring her to further heights of passion as she writhed in response. The tingling in his balls threatened to draw it all to a close, but not until he made them one in truth.

"I would bond with you now," he murmured.

"Where shall you bite?" She playfully nipped at his shoulder.

Arthur struggled to keep his voice discernible above a growl. "It is often in a private place known only to the bonded pair."

Beatrice gripped him with her knees, holy *Freya*, the better to glare down at him. "I want it to be seen. I want all to know you are mine."

He sat up, keeping her tight to him, huffing at her little giggle at the sudden change in position. They kissed, and he scented her beneath her jaw, trailed his tongue around her earlobe. She tilted her head to his chest and moved her hair away from the side of her neck. He licked it and nudged it with his teeth, and she nodded. As their passion mounted, his fangs lowered, and with as much care as he could muster, he bit.

Their ecstasy exploded, and Beatrice shook in his arms, tightening around him as she found her release, goading his own. As naturally as if he had done it an infinite number of times, as easily as he called Her name every day, when he came he invoked Freya;

he said please and thank you and let him give his wife, his beloved, the child she yearned for. He gently laid his mate down on the soft layers of their bower. Arthur embraced his duchess, his lover, and ran a hand over her belly, imagined, and believed.

———————

Beatrice wrapped herself in a silken coverlet as Arthur took care to fold the gossamer nightdress before he set it aside. "Have you had Lady Coleman make me a new wardrobe?"

He looked at her, slightly abashed. "This is from the players' store."

"A costume?"

"Desdemona, I fear." He grimaced and offered her a sugared plum in consolation.

"Your beloved dramatist's heroines do not enjoy pleasant fates." She took a bite of the treat and started. "Did you know him?"

"Who? Shakespeare?"

How she adored making him scowl. "I know you lot do not age as we humans do."

"Madam, I object." He shook out a cloth and laid out a selection of victuals. "I am not two hundred years old. In Shifter years that would make me…" The math appeared to be beyond him. "Very, very old. As old as Conlon, for Odin's sake."

"There is much I do not know." Beatrice stroked the bite at the back of her neck and shivered.

"Now that we are bonded, you will no longer age at the rate of the rest of humanity, and as a consequence, I have sacrificed my years to match your own."

"That is generous of you, to lose those years."

He sat and pulled her into his lap, his fingers finding her mark. "Those years are wasted if I do not have you to give them to."

"Even if they are given to Lady Frost?"

"A glorious challenge, that lady. I find I would miss her did she go."

"Oh." Arthur played with the ring on her finger, and she held out her hand. "Charlotte made one of her faces when she saw this and would not tell me what it signified."

He cleared his throat and said, "It is the gem of office for those whose task it is to resolve all dilemmas and right all quandaries, and I will say no more about it at the moment."

Beatrice had another question at any rate. "I was surprised to see it set in silver. Is that not anathema to *versipelles*?"

"Bloody wolves." Arthur scrubbed his hands over his head in agitation, with the delightful result she needs must comb her fingers through it to put it in order. "Their lore states they become powerless when silver is applied to their person, as in jewelry or when used as a weapon. This is a ruse, for it is gold that harms all Shifters and confines them in their essential forms, catskin or bearskin or duck feathers. As little as an ounce of gold is able to trap *versipelles* until they are free of it."

"Then what of Lowell's curse?"

"In fairness, that is not an exaggeration," he allowed. "If the Alpha of any species does not bring forth young, then the pack or the sleuth or the herd disbands. It is something of a curse as it means the rest, the followers of that Alpha, will not reproduce."

Oh, dear. "Arthur, I fear you have been unfortunate in your spouse."

He cupped her face in his hands, his massive, warm, loving hands. "Beatrice, that creature did not take you successfully to wive, and I swear on my true essence and by Frigga and Odin and Freya and Thor, you will have as many cubs as your heart can love."

"I anticipate prodigious diligence on your part."

"And I on yours. As my brother and his wife decided together, so shall we, when you wish."

Beatrice had wished for it from the start of their bed play, for what it was worth. "I am rather disappointed there will be no dancing under the crescent moon in the nip."

"I did not say that, did I?" he teased. "I look forward to introducing you to our ways. We have a number of ceremonies and observances to be undertaken as a sleuth."

"Disting," she recalled. "In the spring."

"And in the summer, Lammas to celebrate the first fruits, and Haustblot in the autumn, and of course Vetrnaetur."

"Oh, of course. Let us not forget Vetrnaetur." Beatrice stumbled over the pronunciation. "Will we... Must we let everyone know the bite has taken, or is it enough it will be seen?"

"There are one or two things that require we gather, and the sooner the better. We will meet the sleuth at dawn."

"Will the bite help us call in the children?"

"It cannot hurt. But are you? Hurt?"

"No." Her eyes sparkled. "But I am doomed to high-necked gowns for the rest of my days. Much like Viscountess Wallace."

"Oh ho, you are a gossip when it suits you, I see." Arthur's eyes shone with delight.

Beatrice wrapped her arms around his neck. "You suit me."

"And you, me." And kissing suited them both very well.

Beatrice found herself bundled back into strong arms and deposited on her windowsill well before the moon set. She stole another kiss to add to her store, an infinite space larger even than Arcadia's attics.

"So," Arthur said once his breath had returned. He laid his forehead on hers, and she played with the lock of hair she claimed for her own.

"So?" Beatrice prodded. "Are we to cavort around a fire at dawn?"

"Not as such. But we are to meet at dawn, and there will be a fire. You need your rest."

"Will you not stay?"

"I cannot." He took her hand in his and stroked his thumb over the topaz in her ring. "For I have a request to put to you and would leave you to think on it."

Twenty-two

BEATRICE STOOD IN THE GROVE BESIDE A BONFIRE, UNLIT torch in hand, waiting for the correct moment to set it aflame. The night was at its greatest depth, and the whole world held its breath before the rising of the sun. When Arthur had described what she needed to do, in the warmth of his embrace and after hours of lovemaking, it had promised to be exhilarating. Now, in the darkest moments before the dawn and despite the roaring bonfire, waiting proved lonely, and her mind raced.

She stood, clothed in yet another new garment, a gown in the Osborn colors like the livery the footmen sported thanks to Lady Coleman. Arthur had truly seen to that task. She could cross it off the schedule.

Her schedule was the least of her worries as she waited to be welcomed into the sleuth, as its Alpha female and its—

Would they come? Or would she be left here to stand alone, alone as always? She told herself the sleuth would welcome her, despite her humanity, despite her taking on a role that set her over them. It seemed they had already done so, but would this cere-mony only serve to point up her frailty as a *homo plenus*? And thus, as a consequence, reject her appointment as—

It was too good to be true, too much to be believed.

And yet she must believe. She must trust. She wished to serve as Arthur asked her to serve. She had already proven she was worthy and able. But were her directives to the staff followed out of fear or out of respect? She was certain she had not done anything to inspire trepidation despite her lofty title. Had anyone asked her if she had garnered the household's good opinion, she would have thought she had.

But what of those moments when she drew on the mantle of Lady Frost? Who loved Lady Frost? No one. Oh, but…Arthur said she was a challenge, a glorious challenge. But who wanted such a challenge? It sounded tiresome to her, and tiring. He would tire of battling the ice, of melting the rime. He would decide he preferred an amenable mate, never mind the bite—

This mental chaos would not do. In fairness, yesterday had been as if an entire fortnight passed in one day. Between the emotional strife and the lovemaking in the copse and the bite, it was no surprise she was less than mentally acute, standing in the chill of the earliest hours of the morning.

She was Arthur's mate. She bore his mark. She was herself, Beatrice, with a soupçon of Lady Frost. She was Aunt Beezy, she was Madam. She was a salty little cake, apparently. Beatrice closed her eyes and took a deep breath, then another. She was soon to be even more as well as Arthur's wife—

Ah. There. She opened her eyes and her ears and, most importantly, her heart.

It felt as though every heart she held near and dear beat in her chest. She stood now in anticipation and—yes, there it was—the exhilaration she hoped for.

In the dark, around the edges of the clearing, people took their places as they had the previous afternoon when they gathered to support Arthur. As many souls as resided beneath Arcadia's pristine and impermeable roof, those gathering sounded greater in number. Before she could wonder why, a figure approached the path that roughly led from London.

"I commence the *initiatio*." His Highness, Prince George, Regent of England, stood at the end of one path, holding his unlit torch as indifferently as he would a quizzing glass. "I stand as a representative for the elders of our kind. Despite my youthful good looks. And my *au courant* fashion sense."

Beatrice lit her torch from the bonfire, and the flame flared high. In its light, she discerned many a familiar face. "You are welcome, Your Highness." Not a quiver in her voice. *Thank you, Lady Frost.* And yet a smile threatened despite the adoption of that trusty persona. "In accepting this light from me, you light my way forward in the role I have been asked to fulfill to the reproof of none."

"I accept," he said. She touched the fire to his branch, and it took. She turned her attention to the next path, which lead from the cottages, where the heart and soul of the sleuth would abide, where its families would thrive and grow in number.

"I stand as a child of this sleuth." Ursella stepped from that path, her torch sized for her little fist.

Beatrice fought incipient tears. Behind the child stood her siblings and her parents, beaming at her like they had swallowed the sun. "You are welcome, child. In accepting this light from me, you light the way forward for the young."

"I accept." It was not her imagination, was it, that this flame sparkled like fireworks over Vauxhall Gardens? She thought it must have done so, for Ursella gasped and her brother and sister whooped.

"Well done, Ursella," she whispered.

"And you, Aunt Beezy," the child said, dignified in her great responsibility.

The next path led from greater England and Wales and Scotland beyond. A familiar figure stepped from this direction. "I stand as a friend to this sleuth," Felicity said.

"You are welcome, friend." They shared a look of joy and awe, that life should find them here. "In accepting this light from me, we agree to show the way for one another always."

"I accept." The light blossomed, and behind Felicity stood her duke; his Beta, who grinned at her; the Lowell Omega; and several others from that esteemed pack she had yet to meet.

One remained, and jubilation sang through the grove. Her skin shivered with gooseflesh; buoyed by the expectation of all present and her own thundering heart, she turned to the final path.

"I am the Alpha of this sleuth." Arthur, her husband, her Alpha, stepped forward. She had never seen him in ducal raiment: he was in full rig-out, his linen immaculate, his ceremonial sword gleaming in the firelight, his sash snug across his chest, the entire ensemble topped with nothing less than his coronation robes, crimson velvet draped with the four ermine tails denoting his rank. He looked down at her from his great height, his eyes rich in the firelight, mercurial as they flashed from his own to his creature's, golden and warm.

"You are welcome, Alpha. You are welcome, my love." Her heart bloomed like a rose. "In accepting this light from me, I, in turn, accept the role you seek to bestow upon me."

"I accept." The flame that flared was the largest yet. "I recognize Beatrice, Duchess of Osborn, as my *vera amoris*." The flames on both their torches roared higher. "Our nuptials were rather rushed, and even now we are behind the times. There are words our people speak when they pledge their hearts before the sleuth, much as the humans do. But I had no sleuth, then, or would not admit to one." A gentle wave of laughter swelled around the circle. "Someone wise once said that we are only as content as our unhappiest heart"—Beatrice heard Charlotte squeal—"and had I known it was mine, I would have denied it. And yet it was. My heart had broken many years ago, and I had done nothing to mend it. Little did I know it was not a job for one, but for two, for five, for tens of those willing to open their own hearts and let me in.

"But there is one whose care I will place it in forever, as my *vera amoris* and my mate, my confidante, who I shall argue with and grumble at and dig my heels against—and entrust with your hearts as well. I entrust her with your well-being and your peace of mind, and I entrust her with the future of Arcadia. As Alpha, I appoint Beatrice, Duchess of Osborn, as my Second, the Beta of this sleuth."

"I accept." She turned to Ben, who had joined them; both lit his torch with theirs. "As to my Alpha's wishes, I invoke the *initiatio* and appoint Garben Humphries, Lord Swinburn, as Gamma." They exchanged a smile as Ben, in turn, lit the torches held by sundry attendants, and soon the grove was full of light. Arthur took his and her torch, and with a boy's glee, chucked them into the fire.

Beatrice turned to Arthur. "Your Grace." He grimaced, and she laughed. "Osborn?" He shook his head. "Alpha." She reached out and laid her hand on his heart. "Arthur, it is my duty and my joy to bid you fully open the *sentio* of the Osborn sleuth."

Ursella ran up, and Arthur swept her into his arms. "You are not of an age, Ursella, to fully take on your role in assisting me," he began.

"If I may." O'Mara, Lowell's Omega, stepped forward. Ursella reached out to clutch at a lapel of the Irishwoman's swan-tailed morning coat and was gifted with one of O'Mara's rare smiles. "It is never beyond an Omega's powers to serve her clan as she wishes and, indeed, as she must," she said, "but it is the privilege of one like her to lend her aid."

———————

In the end, it was the work of a moment and required more effort to keep the connection closed than allow it to open. Arthur looked down at his wife, his mate, his duchess; at his niece, their Omega; at O'Mara who supplied just enough support to allow Ursella ease. He laid his hand over the tops of theirs and—let go.

The limited experiences he'd previously had with the link were nothing as it opened and he was flooded with the heartbeats of his people. *How lucky it is that I am so large*, he thought, and his bear, content to observe quietly until that moment, roared with gusto. The power of the *sentio* was enough to knock him back on his heels; through it flowed a colossal wave of love and—yes— affiliation, cordial and more.

The sleuth took a breath as one, released it as one, and as the sun rose, it rose to their unity and celebration.

And then it became a party. Mrs. Porter and the mice and the kitchen footmen had ferried food and drink to share out among the sleuth and their guests. It was Arthur's pleasure to serve his mate and hers to serve their people.

They separated and each took a side of the grove through which to circulate; Arthur did not think it was by chance his contained a crowned head of state.

"A human female as Beta. This is unknown in our lineage," Georgie pronounced. "I shall take full credit."

"Rest assured, the first child of our union," Arthur said, "will not be named after you."

"Cousin, how unkind." His Royal Highness pouted into his champagne.

"Truly, Osborn, how thoughtless you are," Lowell said.

"You may make up for it yourself, I suspect," Arthur quipped and left a blushing duke the prey of an inquisitive prince.

He came upon his mate (*mate!* crooned his bear) in conference with what was likely to become an unholy alliance between herself, Lowell's duchess, Charlotte, and the Barrington female. "*'When shall ye four meet again?'*" he paraphrased.

"Artie!" Charlotte dug a knuckle under his sash right up into his ribs.

"I adore the Scottish play." Miss Barrington beamed, even as she moved off to intercept Llewelyn—and where had he come from? Something needed to be done about that duke. His history was horrific, and all due respect he even survived it, but who knew what he might get up to, and as for setting a human as his keeper—

"Is she able for him?"

Beatrice looked after Tabitha, but it was Her Grace of Lowell who spoke up. "Surely you have learned your lesson about underestimating the female of the species?" She swanned off, and Beatrice giggled.

"I underestimate human females least of all species," he called after her and soon found himself drawn away with his wife. "But honestly, his is a fearsome case."

"It was Georgie's wish." Beatrice took his empty glass and handed it to a footman. "He is doing rather well in matching human women and male *versipelles*."

"He is not taking credit for Lowell, is he?"

"Felicity said he claims his lack of intervention was intentional." Beatrice was steering toward home, but he stopped them at the opening of the path that led there.

"Is there another ritual to observe?" Beatrice looked over her shoulder at the bonfire and laughed.

Arthur took a breath, searched his store of quotations, and... "The Bard himself cannot do justice to your laughter or to the light in your eyes when you are full of joy. I hope I may add to it." He turned her toward the path, and out of the night came not a multitude but something even better. "When you were given the neem oil and told it would help you increase, it was not out of spite it was done so. Well, not only.

"The staff conspired for their liberation, you see. For Castleton died without an heir and failed in his duty. As he had no young, the pack was released." In the faint light of the still-rising sun, shapes became apparent, of figures on foot making their way to the grove. "When Hallbjorn won this place, it was an empty victory, as you know, for the sleuth fled his rule. Without females, he could not mate, and without mating, he produced no young. And no female would entertain him, for he had nothing to offer. He had lands but no sleuth, and he had no sleuth because our own would not join with him as long as he lived. Those who survived scattered until—"

"Until?" Beatrice's voice shook.

"Until you. Behold, Madam, your bride gift. All these souls to make at home."

Arthur felt her tremble at his side and then step forward to welcome those who had been in hiding, those who had been without a true home, those who had been tossed to the four corners of the earth. More would return from further afield, but for now his wife, his Beta, embraced the women and kissed the children and shook the men by the hand; they gave her obeisance and in turn gave it to Arthur, and he wove them into his heart, one by one. Tears were shed as greetings were exchanged and friends well met; even Georgie was seen flourishing his hankie.

As the last entered, an extremely elderly male who Arthur recognized as Conlon's brother, they stood and gloried in the reunion unfolding before them.

"Your Grace." Was there a trace of Lady Frost who looked on? Beatrice's voice broke; oh, dear, she called upon the ice in order not to cry. "I shudder to think what may have become of our people had proper preparations not taken place."

He made a show of lowering his brow. "It is well you took it into your own hands to fund the renovation of the entire eastern border. We have cottages going begging."

"How fortunate." Lady Frost melted, and Beatrice's smile rivaled the sun now fully risen over Arcadia.

Arthur raised her hand to his lips. "How fortunate indeed."

FIN

Read on for a taste of more enchanting
Regency shifter romance from Susanna Allen

a
Wolf
in
Duke's
Clothing

Available now from Sourcebooks Casablanca

One

February: the Season, London

IT WAS A VERITABLE CRUSH.

In the year 1817, with the Napoleonic Wars well and truly
won and the American Colonies well and truly lost, nothing
less than an utter squeeze would do, not when the hostess was
the Countess of Livingston and well able to put the wealth of
her husband's earldom on display. The ballroom was spacious,
framed by its gilded and frescoed ceiling; impressive with its
shining wall of mirrors; fragrant from the banks of hothouse
flowers set about the vast space; and yet... Nothing about it was
unlike any other ballroom in London, where hopes and dreams
were realized or dashed upon the rocks of ignominy. Packed to
the walls with the great and good of the English *haute ton*, the

society ball was as lively and bright as any before it and any that would follow.

Despite having traversed a well-trod path of lineage and reputation all their lives, the guests gave themselves to the event with an abandon that appeared newly coined. They came to the dance, and to the gossip, and to the planning of alliances and assignations with the energy of girls fresh out of the schoolroom and young lords newly decanted from Eton and Harrow. Those undertaking the lively reel threw themselves into it as though it were the first opportunity they had to perform it; the watchers congregated at the sides of the dance floor observed it as though they'd never seen such a display in all their lives. Though the room was lit by more than two thousand candles in crystal chandeliers, shadows lurked in the farthest corners; the gloom was not equal, however, to the beauty of the silks and satins of the ladies' gowns or to the richness of their adornments. As the multitude of jewels and those eddying skirts caught the light, the setting looked like a dream.

Unless it had all the hallmarks of a personal nightmare. Alfred Blakesley, Seventh Duke of Lowell, Earl of Ulrich, Viscount Randolf, Baron Conrí, and a handful of lesser titles not worth their salt, found the Livingstons' ball to be an unrelenting assault of bodies, sounds, and most of all, scents. This last was a civilized term covering a broad range of aromas that encompassed the pleasant—perfumes, unguents, and those hothouse arrangements—to the less so, among them the unlaundered linen of the less fussy young bucks and the outdated sachets used to freshen the gowns of the chaperones. If he wouldn't look an utter macaroni, he'd carry a scented handkerchief or, in a nod to the Elizabethans, an orange studded with cloves. Whilst either would save his sensitive snout from the onslaught of odors, it would defeat the purpose of his presence this evening.

As usual, said presence, after an absence of five years, was causing a flurry of gossip and conjecture. With jaded amusement, the

only amusement he was able to muster these days, and without
appearing to do so, he eavesdropped on the far-ranging theories
regarding his person that were swirling around the ballroom, much
as the dancers spun around the floor itself. If the gossips only knew
how acute his hearing was, they might hesitate to tittle-tattle…

"My Lord, he is divine," last year's premiere diamond of the
first water sighed.

"That chiseled face, that muscular form." Her friend, at best a
ruby, fanned herself vigorously.

"If only my dear Herbert would grow his hair until it touched
his collar," Diamond said.

"If only my Charles would pad his jacket. And his thighs. And
his bum!" Ruby laughed wickedly.

"I doubt very much that there is any padding on the duke's
person," Diamond said.

Ruby peeked at him over her fan. "If only he would stand up
with one of us so we could get a hand on those shoulders."

Two bucks of vintages separated by at least twenty years waited
out the current set. "He may be among us, but he will not stay as
much as an hour. My valet would thrash me did I not pass at least
three hours allowing the entire *ton* to remark upon his prowess,"
the aging young buck opined.

"And yet, he is dressed to a turn, his linen pristine, his coat of
the latest cut," the actual young buck replied.

"His linen may be," scoffed his elder, "but there is something
queer in the lineage."

"Lineage!" One old gent bleated to another as they made their
way to the card room. "Hodgepodge more like. A ragbag of depen-
dents of no known origin, a mishmash of retainers, a mélange
of—"

"Yes, yes." His companion flourished his cane. "My own family
claims quite a healthy acreage near to Lowell's shire, and ne'er the
twain shall meet, I can tell you."

"I do not take your meaning," Gent the First said.

Gent the Second put his hand on his friend's arm and leaned in. "My nephew's housekeeper's brother's wife's granddaughter is from the neighboring village and says there is never a house party, never a ball, and never a need for outside help. And we all know what that means."

"Penury."

"Not a groat to his name."

Along the mirrored wall, an older matron rustled her organza. "He is rich as Croesus, although the origins of the fortune are suspect."

Her bosom friend gasped. "Surely it does not come from trade?"

"He keeps no sheep, he tends no crops—well, he has no people to do such things. Even he is not so far gone to propriety to engage in animal husbandry firsthand."

"Some say the entirety of his holding is a gold mine, a literal gold mine." Bosom Friend looked ecstatic at the notion.

"Hardly," Matron replied. "There's not a nugget of gold on this island; the Scots mined it eons ago."

A merry widow and her ardent admirer lingered near the drinks table. "No one I know has had him, and I know everyone who has had anyone of import," Merry grumbled.

Ardent moved closer. "Is he…?" He gestured to a group of *very good* male friends clustered in the corner.

"*Quelle tragedie*, if so," said Merry. "It is true that he is seen nowhere without his steward, Bates, by his side."

"He, too, is a favorite amongst the ladies."

"No one's had him, either."

And so the ton *sups from the same old scandal broth*, thought Alfred. He'd heard every word without having moved so much as an inch from his place near the entrance to the ballroom. No creature with hearing such as his would need to do so. The rumors and speculation built in strength the longer he did not take a wife, but it was not merely a wife for whom he searched.

Searched he had, far and wide, all across Europe, as far as the Far East, a duke of the realm wandering the earth like a common journeyman—but it had to be done, for no one could find his lady for him, identify her for him, take the place of her. He found himself back in England after five years of endless travel, thwarted yet somehow not disheartened despite being here again. Here, almost to the man and woman, were the same faces he'd seen upon entering society after coming up from Oxford, faces that were beginning to resemble one another; he feared they'd all been intermarrying rather too closely for comfort.

His own family line was a different breed, and to explain his clan's uniqueness to most in this room would result in panic, fear, and an atavistic desire to obliterate any trace of him and those like him, for all time. To expose their distinction would put all under his care in the most perilous danger—a paradox, as that difference made him more powerful than any human being.

Yet, here he was among them, bracing himself for the possibility that the one sought by him and his inner creature, his essential self was of their number. His wolf stirred within him, impatient, vexed by the delay in finding their mate, held in check when all it wanted to do was hunt and hunt until they found the one whose heart and soul called to them, belonged to them, whose presence would set things right at Lowell Hall.

"Your Grace." His steward, Matthias Bates, appeared at his shoulder.

"Animal husbandry…" Alfred murmured, and Matthias gave a low laugh. Alfred regarded his closest friend and right-hand man—the perfect second-in-command, aligned with him in thought, yet with enough independence of spirit to challenge Alfred as needed. Bates stood as tall as he, at several inches over six feet, although the steward was blond where he was dark, lean where he was excessively muscular. None of the gossips had gotten around to that criticism this evening: What well-bred male of his status sought to gain such brawny proportions?

"I believe the *haute ton* needs to stop marrying itself." Alfred began to wander, Bates at his side.

"Indeed," Bates replied. "And it is, of course, a discussion relevant to your own situation."

A sigh soughed through Alfred's entire being. "It is enough to make one wish to take a ship and sail far, far away—had I not already done so and visited every corner of the globe."

"There are always the Colonies."

"The United States of America," Alfred corrected. "I am not well acquainted with any of our sort from out that way, despite their being one branch from whence we all came. My sister has not written to me of discovering such, in any case."

"One imagines such outliers to be as poor a choice as one of these women."

The air around the two men became oppressive, as though all the heat of the room had coalesced to envelop Bates. He struggled for his next breath, and his body trembled as he fought an outside force for control of it. It did not affect Alfred, as this elemental energy generated from him; known as the *dominatum*, it was the ultimate expression of his power as Alpha of the Shifters of Lowell Hall. This power was his and his alone, the essence of his authority, the manner in which he held sway over the beasts within his people, the way in which he protected them from outside aggressors, and if need be, from one another. To him, it was akin to the dynamism of the Change: held entirely within and called upon with a thought. Its use was judicious, never mindless, but in this instance, it was excessive; he blamed his wolf, who was surging under his skin, seeking release. Even the slightest insult to his future mate was enough to incense them both, and at this precise moment in time, when the search looked to be a failure, he did not need the reminder that his true mate was no longer likely to be one of his kind.

Bates was not the only one to experience the potency of the emanation. Though invisible to the naked eye, it had an intensity akin to a lightning strike; the ladies who had ventured closer, hoping to catch the eye of the duke, came over rather faint and repaired to the retiring room. Nor were the men unaffected: the more delicate youths swayed as though they had visited the punch bowl several times too many. Alfred's face showed no effect or exertion but for the tightening of his jaw and an increased ferocity in his gaze.

"Your Grace." Bates managed a stiff bow and turned his head, baring the side of his neck. "I misspoke. We will welcome any female you bring to us as your bride, regardless of her provenance." He held his posture until the pressure receded but still did not meet Alfred's gaze.

"What must be done, must be done," Alfred said, and they continued their perambulations. "The issues that arise when lines too closely related produce offspring is, in the case of the *ton*, a weakness that expresses itself in illnesses of the body and of the mind. This is happening far too often amongst our own branches of society, and it must be addressed. The bloodlines of our…family must be strengthened, and our only hope may be found by my marrying one of 'these.'"

"Which will endow permission to do so for those among us who also wish to marry and to be, er, fruitful," Bates replied.

"Permission must be endowed sooner rather than later. Enough time has been wasted in my jaunts across the Continent. The continents, in fact. My wish to marry one of our own is not to be. I despair I have wasted time and endangered our people in trying to do so. I wanted my ma—my wife to be of our lineage."

"Alpha—" Bates dropped into another bow. "Alfred, that is to say, Duke, Your Gr—"

"Matthias." Alfred reached out and touched his steward on the arm, bringing him back up to full height. "If a secure future for our people is achieved through marriage to a society lady, then any sacrifice will be worth the cost." He swept his glance around the room and met a domino-effect of lowering glances. *How difficult this undertaking will be,* he thought, *if she won't look me in the eye... But surely the one meant for me is as strong as I, no matter her genus?* "My entire existence walks this fine line between our ways and the ways of society. The paradox is that in choosing my bride from the *ton*, I will have to hide my true self from her, regardless of our customs."

"Impossible," said Bates. "You will no more be able to hide your true self from your wife than the moon could fail to draw the tide."

"That sounds almost romantic, my friend," Alfred teased.

"Certainly not." Bates's offended expression inspired Alfred to indulge in a short bark of laughter. "It does not fall to me, thank all the Gods, to subscribe to this fated-mate nonsense." He coughed and lowered his voice. "But the notion you could spend a lifetime pretending to be something you are not? The expense of energy this would require?"

"I have neither the time nor the energy for romance."

Which he would feign, like it or not. His interactions with the ladies of the *ton* had always been marked by a social duplicity that was anathema to him: the little white lies, the sham emotions, the manners that in fact betrayed a lack of gentility and integrity. But there were far too many in his care, and they had gone too long without a strong sense of cohesion and community for him to indulge in stubbornness. He must lead the way, though it seemed unlikely he was to find happiness on his path.

Happiness! Had he ever thought happiness was in his future or was his birthright? In every clan he met, of every breed, he saw what a world of difference it made when they honored the ways of their kind. When a pack or a clowder or a flock were led by an

Alpha pair who were *vera amorum*, they thrived, and it pierced his heart with regret, even as it strengthened his resolve. His mother and father had lied about their status, claiming one another as true mates, and the reverberations of that falsehood were still serving to hurt his people and endanger their future.

"I will do what is needed, whatever that may be." He took the glass of champagne that Bates offered, and both pretended to drink. "I will find a lady before the Feast of Lupercalia, and we shall go forward from there."

"Your Grace, I must remind you of what O'Mara made plain upon our return to England. Nothing less than a love match will satisfy your people." He sounded dubious; since puphood, Matthias had scorned the tendency of their breed to mate for life. "As well, you will have to proceed as a male of the *ton* and observe the customary formalities."

Alfred half listened to Bates prose on as regarded the necessity of *billets-doux* and floral tributes and wooing and instead assessed the women who came close, but not too close, to him. They treated him as though he were unapproachable when all he wanted was to be approached; unlike the majority of the young aristocratic males in the room, he yearned to marry. A failed pairing could destroy the morale and robustness of a pack—he had only to look at his parents: the disaster that was their reign had all to do with disrespecting Fate and allowing their ambitions precedence. And yet, he dreaded the notion that he might not find her by the Feast day and would thus be consigned to searching one ballroom, one garden party, one Venetian breakfast after another, for another year, all in the hopes of discovering—

He thrust his glass into Bates's hand and froze, nostrils flaring. There. Where? He let his instinctual self scan the ballroom, his vision heightening to an almost painful degree even in the soft candlelight, his focus sharp as a blade. He fought to turn without the preternatural speed with which he was endowed and struggled to align the rest of his senses. His ears pricked, such as they could in this form: he heard laughter, a note of feminine gaiety that made his skin come out all over in gooseflesh, a sound that landed into the center of his heart as would Cupid's dart. His inner self rolled through his consciousness, eager to explode into life, and he held it at bay.

The set concluded; the next was to be a waltz, and the usual flutter of partnering unfolded around him. That laugh rang out again, and he turned once more in a circle, uncaring if anyone noted the oddness of his behavior. It was as if every one of his nerve endings had been plucked at once, as if a bolt of lightning were gathering its power to explode down his spine. He scented the air again, and between the candle wax and the overbearing scent of lilacs, he divined a hint of vanilla, an unexpected hint of rosemary, a waft of sweet william…

"We are very near the wallflower conservatory," joked Bates as he set their untouched glasses aside. "Shall you pluck a bloom from there?"

Alfred held up a hand and focused on the wall of palms screening the corner in which the undesirables mingled and hid, homing in on a bouquet of fragrance he'd despaired of scenting, a combination of familiar elements he may have experienced singly but never before as one, not with such rapturous force. He turned to face the greenery; Bates moved to protect his back. He inhaled, and yes, there it was, a collection of mundane notes that combined to create a glorious symphony of attraction, desire, lust, yearning, and possibility; a concoction of lush skin, that hint of sweet william, fresh air, horses—and an excessive amount of lemon? His heart beat like thunder, and as the violins tuned for the upcoming dance and the crowd's murmur built into a roar, he swept, heedless, through them to reach the source.

Two

IT LOOKED TO BE A VERITABLE CRUSH, AT LEAST FROM THE VIEW behind the palms. It had taken the Honorable Felicity Templeton far longer than usual to claim her place away from the superior gaze of society. As she had resolutely edged around the dance floor, she nodded and distributed faint smiles to those who exerted themselves to obstruct her path. Did the Incomparables and Corinthians and rakes force her to arduously achieve the anonymity of the fronds out of spite? They certainly cut her, if not directly, then with just enough acknowledgment of her person to imply that her person required very little acknowledgment at all.

She had held her head high as she maneuvered past the simpering maidens and their vigilant mamas; past the knowing widows and their fluttering fans; past the tabbies and the tartars and the dragons clustered in strategic positions around the dance floor so no one and nothing would escape their notice; past the leering elderly gents keen on finding their umpteenth wife; and past the young bucks who insinuated their bodies against her softer parts without fail or shame. She was no one, after all; there was no one to give redress.

And yet, they gossiped about her. The *ton* would gossip about a fly on a wall, never mind an oddity that debuted at the grand old age of twenty and after five seasons had failed to secure an offer, much less a husband, a young woman with only an uncle and two cousins to her name—and were they first cousins? She'd best marry one of them, should they be further removed along the bloodline, as beggars could not be choosers, even if they were Cits. She had, of course, tragically lost her parents one after the other, but that didn't excuse her sad lack of style. Her uncle, Ezra Purcell, must have the funds to hire his niece a decent companion. It was a scandal she went about with no companion at all!

What would they say if they knew that every misstep she took was made with purpose? That she was on a mission to remain unwed? They would collapse in a heap of disbelief.

Once installed in the area meant to screen the less fortunate ladies from the gaze of their betters, Felicity let down her guard, safe for the moment from the talk and the laughter and the whispers; from the overwhelming colors and scents; from the vertiginous sensation of the dancers swirling near to her and then away; and from the sensation of being surrounded, about to be drowned in humanity. She was also secure in the company of her friendship with Lady Jemima Coleman, who had run her own gauntlet to escape the protracted notice of the *ton*.

Both ladies had collected as many cups of lemonade as they could carry so that they might be refreshed throughout the interminable evening without needing to leave their camouflage. Felicity sipped from her second serving, cautiously. "This tastes rather unusual."

"I believe it has been concocted from actual lemons," Jemima replied. "As well as with a touch of honey, as my grandmother used to make it." Her robust Northumberland cadence, earthy and rough around the edges, came as something of a surprise from as petite and delicate a lady as she appeared—a surprise the year's swains did not find enchanting.

Nor did they find Felicity's strapping, sun-kissed person to be in any way intoxicating. Standing eye to eye with most of the men of her class, Felicity was not suited to the high-waisted, wispy fashions of the day, which did not show her bosomy figure to its best advantage. The short-capped sleeves made her arms look positively muscular, and the roundness of her face was exacerbated by the severity of her topknot. Such fashionable deficits would send many a maid weeping into her pillow at night, but not she. If anything, she ensured that her dress and toilette were done to her disadvantage as rigorously as possible.

For Felicity had a plan, a plan that would turn into a dream come true.

"Do you yearn for your homeplace?" She rearranged a few fronds to shield them further from the gaze of the ballroom's denizens.

"I do not." Jemima delicately sipped from her cup. "Most especially not since having made your acquaintance."

"We are friends, Jem, for the love of—galoshes."

"We are, we are," Jemima replied. "And it's grateful I am for it. I have received the welcome to be expected for a nobody from near enough to Scotland to be vulgar and uncouth, and yet it has transcended even the worst of my imaginings."

"The slightest intimation of difference sets this lot off like hounds on a hunt." Yet, Jemima was everything Felicity herself was not, far closer to the *ton*'s ideal of femininity, and she couldn't imagine why her friend had not "taken." Fine-featured and slim yet with an ample bosom, pale-skinned, with smooth, dark-brown hair, Jemima's appeal was perhaps undone by her gray eyes: too perceptive, too observant, and thus disturbing, as there was oh, so much that was required to remain unseen in high society.

"I can only imagine the things they're saying about me." Felicity waved her cup airily toward the crowd. "'Why, she's as sturdy as those columns she prefers to hide behind—I wouldn't give even the tweeny one of her gowns—that hair of hers is positively red—I do believe she has been out in the sun without her bonnet!'" She sighed. That hadn't been as amusing as she had intended.

"If they knew the truth about you, their tongues would fall out of their heads from wagging." Jemima reached out to touch Felicity's elbow. She was demonstrative and a frequent giver of soothing pats and bolstering squeezes.

It had the desired effect. Felicity smiled and could feel the vitality of her vision surge through her like it was a living thing, a thing that was strong of spine and stance, beautiful and glorious and fierce. The mere thought of her passion filled her entire being with life and hope and joy.

"Bedamned with them," she said, with conviction.

"Your language becomes dangerously coarse these days, friend."

"Due to frequenting the stables and the sales." Felicity smiled into her cup, hoarding the dregs of her treat.

If the *ton* only knew how conversant Felicity was in matters regarding the stables and the horseflesh sales. What would her parents have thought, were they alive? But were they alive, she would not be on this path. She would have been brought out at the proper age of seventeen, when she was still dewy and naive; perhaps dewiness and naivety would have garnered her a decent match, but as time went on, Felicity doubted she had ever been as fetching and credulous as any of the debutantes she'd come across.

Her parents' marriage hadn't been in the usual run of things: they had fallen in love at first sight and damned the consequences—one of which was Felicity, born rather hale and hardy for a child delivered at seven months. Had they truly known each other before they'd let their fascination for one another sweep them away from family and friends? Upon their elopement, her mother had been cut dead by her family for a time, which had amused her father, as it was the aristos who indulged in that sort of nonsense. For Felicity's mother was the daughter of a merchant, and her father a baron, and the twain had met, heedless of all societal strictures, for better and for worse.

She'd also been aware of her father's dislike of her mother's horse madness, of her mother's laughing disdain of his fears, but when she'd died due to that passion, the grief proved too much for her remaining parent, and he soon followed his love to the grave.

Two bereavements hard upon the heels of each other had forestalled any chance of a debut, and as the years passed and her heart healed, Felicity was certain she had missed her chance. It had been a dream she had shared with her mum in happier times, just before it was time for her to lengthen her skirts and put up her hair: of standing at the top of a sweeping staircase, clothed in a diaphanous, white gown, waiting to be announced, all the while turning heads and smiling down upon the beaux who swarmed to meet her as she descended.

That dream was long gone. Notions of a match made locally were scotched thanks to her father's dramatic decline into debauchery following her mother's death, and she lost face with the neighboring gentry despite being of the highest status in the locality. Or so they were in their part of Kent, at any rate; her mother had spoken of a duchy over the border, but Father had no interest in taking hat in hand and pursuing an acquaintance. For what had the Quality ever done for their family? They had looked down upon his wife and laughed at him for daring to have wed beneath his station, choosing love and passion rather than lineage and bloodline.

Ironic, then, that all that Felicity cared about now were bloodlines. For years, she'd thought her legacy consisted of a pittance doled out from her late maternal grandmother's estate and the harem of seven high-strung mares her mother had collected. Eight years on, their blood ran true and made them difficult mounts even for the most experienced of riders. With the skills she'd learned at her mother's knee, Felicity had such experience and also the ambition to found a line from a cross with sturdier stock under her own auspices. When her maternal uncle Ezra had inexplicably decided she would make her bow at the ripe old age of twenty and had taunted her with what he considered would be the devastating conditions of the inheritance left for her in her father's will, she had found a new lease on life. She would focus only on her aims. She would indulge in the joy she found in those stables and at those sales, and she'd be *damned* if they took that away from her.

"I learn more and more on every visit," Felicity said. "And that scheme of yours worked a treat. I move without restriction throughout Tattersalls dressed in the widow's weeds you created for me. No one is the wiser."

"And how does your stud?" Jemima asked, sending them off into snorts of subdued laughter.

"Himself is still refusing to cover my mares." More snorting, which in Felicity's case ended in a frustrated sigh. "Delilah near to kicked him into uselessness." She raised a hand. "Do not say it. I am aware that he is not entirely useful at the moment, but he is what I envisioned. His conformation, his lines, the heaviness of his bone…"

Jemima once again placed a hand on Felicity's arm, offering the comfort of a friend able to read between the lines. "You will succeed. It is a noble Undertaking, and the realization of a Dream is rarely straightforward." A devotee of the Gothic novel, Jemima's speech often gave the impression of being riddled with initial capitals. "The pursuance itself is an Art."

"The breeding of horses is indeed an art," Felicity replied, "but there is science involved as well. Biology, in fact." More snorting, this time behind their fans. "You are the true artist between us, Jem."

"If only you would accept the wardrobe I have made for you, then you would honor that art." She plucked at the drape of Felicity's gown, an uninspired, pale peach that clashed with her complexion. "This *peau de soie* has not been cut correctly, and it is puckering like a toothless old woman. And the waistline is far too high. If only you would wrap a sash around your waist, your figure would show to great advantage."

"That is not the plan, Jemima." Felicity was gentle with her friend—dressmaking and all that went with it was the lady's consuming passion. Jemima was a genius, and her own understated but cunning frock was a testament to her talent: despite adhering to the style of the day, Jemima's use of fabric and embellishment was striking, too striking for the sticklers, who found her garb to be bordering on salacious in a way they could not articulate.

"When your plan comes to fruition, you must look the part," Jemima insisted. "In fact, you ought to look the part before it does. You must lead the way, Felicity, be the inspiration to others like you, like us. The way I would dress you...none of this straight drapery and insipid palette and fussy sleeves and lace and wisps." She moved around Felicity like a bird of prey. "Bold blues and violets and greens, rich textures, a tight waist and deep décolletage, shawl collars and tiny diamanté buttons and ribbons threaded through, perhaps, perhaps..."

Felicity was both enthralled and slightly frightened. "I do not have the countenance to carry off such a departure from the norm." Not as regarded her figure, in any case. "I have neither the influence nor the infamy attached to my name."

"May I at least gift you with a new style of hat I have created? It would suit you down to the ground. It dips low over one eye, rather along the lines of the Paris Beau."

"A man's hat? You shock even me, Jem." Nevertheless, the notion thrilled her to her core. "It sounds quite dashing."

Jemima's hands fluttered, almost dislodging her fan and reticule. "It is infinitely dashing. Yet feminine. You are my inspiration for it, Felicity, as you are both."

"I will remember you said as much, the next time I feel less than either." She took a small notebook and stick of graphite out of her reticule. "'Jemima insists that I am dashing and feminine.' There. That's on my list to remember when I am covered in muck and hay and despairing of ever getting my stud to do his duty."

"I have a notion to make a clever little holder for graphite and suchlike." Jemima took the stick of lead wrapped in cloth and turned it around in her hands. "Something perhaps that has a chain to connect it to the notebook so it is always to hand."

"It's only a book of my lists, but I do like to keep them near."

"This one is almost entirely crossed through. Is that promising?"

"It is not, I'm afraid." Felicity took back the graphite and thumbed over another page. "I have been seeking a solicitor who might review my father's will for me, but none will consent to meet with a mere woman. Even the widow's garb only gets me so far. And I cannot secure a response from the firm that originated the document, which is peculiar and worrying."

"Perhaps they have disbanded? Shall we hire a hackney and call upon them in person?"

Felicity reached out to squeeze her friend's hand. "Thank you for offering, but a subtle querying of my cousins has revealed the address to be in the stews, of all places. I would not risk our safety in such environs, nor can I expect my cousins to accompany me without having to explain the reason for the journey. Why would my father consult in such a low place?" She picked up another glass of lemonade. "How infuriating this is, to be so uneducated in the ways of the world. I must discover how the terms will be made good, as I am so close to my twenty-fifth birthday. It is in less than a fortnight—eleven days, in fact."

"Many, many happy returns." Jemima snapped open her fan for emphasis.

"I shall accept your congratulations on the day itself, with a champagne toast to coming into my freedom and womanhood." Felicity closed her eyes at the thrill of it. "And then I shall begin to wear those gowns of yours. I promise."

"What is the first thing on your list you will do? When the terms of the will are met?"

"Which list?" Felicity laughed. "I have many, many lists."

"The whimsical one." Jemima flapped her hands as a demonstration of frivolousness.

Felicity shook her head. "I have no such list. My wishes to eschew marriage and motherhood are eccentric choices as they are."

Jemima set her delicate jaw. "Why must we choose? Why must we have only one thing and never the other? Why should my art and your craft prevent us from havin' a man and wee childer?" She caught herself descending into her rustic dialect. "It is unfair. All of society's dictates show preference for the man's lot over the woman's."

"I...regret I will not have a family," Felicity said. "It was once my dream, as any girl might have. My intentions now preclude me from such, for no man would support the business ambitions of his bride. But surely your dream is not beyond the pale?"

"Because it is mere fripperies and trinkets? Woman's work?" Jemima scoffed. "I do not merely huddle on the floor with pins in my mouth. I create! And as such, I am too much for a man who seeks a broodmare. No offense intended."

"None taken." Felicity took a turn in touching her friend's arm. "I myself do not believe we can have both. And since we are both considered the Antidotes of the century"—at least this made Jemima smile—"we must not devote even one iota of our passion and vision to something that cannot occur. While we may not know what will happen in regard to our dreams, at least we will have the capacity to adjust and change them. People are not so easy to change. May I present as exhibits Odious Rollo and Querulous Cecil? My cousins and keepers, navigating the shoals of society with little grace and much dissipation."

It did not surprise her that Rollo had gone down the road to ruin, but that Cecil, who had once been her friend, was so lost to sober behavior...it was deeply disappointing. In their youth, their families had briefly reconciled, and they had become fast friends but had not met again until her debut. She had hoped they would renew that friendship, but Cecil's loyalty was entirely with his father and brother, despite the ill-treatment he often received at their hands. "Neither honor me as a relation, much less a woman.

I know how to school a horse," she concluded, "but I have no idea how to deal with the likes of them."

"I am imagining them with bits in their mouths," Jemima joked.

Felicity let out a hearty peal of laughter—yet another fault in the eyes of the young bucks. "Indeed! And I am holding the reins in one hand and a long whip in the other." She laughed again, and she and Jemima toasted with their last cups of lemonade. "I often marvel that we are related," Felicity said.

"You may be of their bloodline," Jemima said, "but you are of different stuff altogether. A weave runs true in the hands of the weaver, not in the thread or the wool."

"We will make of ourselves what we choose," Felicity concurred, "and the dev—the doodle take the hindmost."

Suddenly, the usual murmur and shriek of the ballroom reached an almighty roar, like the sound of the sea at high tide in a hurricane, and was remarkable enough in volume to reach the ladies in their secluded corner.

"Must be rather a big fish swimming about," Felicity said, bestirring herself enough to part the fronds. "Thank heavens the supper dance is next; then I shall spirit myself away for another night. Eleven days to go…" she whispered.

Jemima peeked around a palm. "Oh, dear, is that Querulous heading this way?"

"Blast! No, that is Odious, about to introduce another one of his prospects." Felicity stashed her cup in the pot of one of the palms and considered fleeing through the French doors.

"I admit I yearn to waltz," said Jemima.

"If I thought you were lurking here on the fringes in order to keep me company, I should be very cross indeed," said Felicity, yanking her gown into an even more unflattering aspect.

"Perhaps it is you who are keeping me company." Jemima waved her fan about like a tiny wing. "I have no chance of acquiring a partner. This is why it is known as yearning."

Odious and his companion went in and out of sight as they wove through the crowd, which was feverishly pairing up for the final dance before the meal.

"It makes no sense that my cousins insist on matchmaking. They have no right to my money, so why should they be so intent upon my marriage?" Felicity groaned. "And look whom Odious is bringing me. Waltham! His nose will be level with my bosom, and he has pustules on his scalp. Rollo is a beast, if that is not an insult to beasts."

Jemima's throaty laugh rang out, full and with an undercurrent of roughness, like the grit in an oyster crafting a pearl. Felicity found it infectious; she turned her back to laugh into the wall so she would not be perceived to be amused by her cousin's attempt to fob her off on Waltham. As she composed herself, giggling and sighing, she turned to her fate and ended up face-first in a Cravat of Perfection.

IT HAPPENED IN A HEARTBEAT: ONE MOMENT SHE WAS nose-deep in a neckcloth that smelled of starch and sunshine, the next she was being led into the ballroom, a strong hand at her elbow, a warm, deep voice sounding well above her ear. Along with the scent of clean linen, she caught a whisper of vetiver, of soap, and of male—male? What was *male*? It wasn't a fragrance she could recall identifying before, but if masculinity could be bottled and sold on Bond Street, it would be redolent of this man.

As she fought against the slight slide of the marble floor under her slippers, she managed to sort through further sensory information: the sound of Odious's protestations, of Jemima's gasp, of Waltham's blathering, contrasted with the current silence in the room, a silence pregnant with astonishment; she shuddered, and the hand gripped her arm with authority. Chills cascaded through her veins; the hold did curious things to her person. As did the heat coming off the body that was turning her to face it; as did the feel of the muscular shoulder under her hand as she took the proper position, with her other hand engulfed in a firm grasp; as did the knowledge that this man, whoever he was, was tall enough to be looking down at her. All this hurtled through her mind and body before she had so much as taken a glance at him, all this before she had managed to look up into his eyes.

Icy-blue warmth. A paradox, to be sure, but his eyes were the hue of winter light and yet burned as they gazed upon her. Who would have fancied that eyes such as these would look upon the Honorable Felicity Templeton and burn? It was almost too much to bear, and she sundered the contact to focus upon the Cravat of Perfection. His hand flexed around hers as though…crestfallen.

This made no sense. Why should she be able intuit a complete stranger's emotion through as mundane an action as the squeeze of a hand? She felt the urge to assuage the disappointment and so lifted her chin and looked him in the eye.

The hand flexed again, the thumb stroking her knuckles with relief. It was a ridiculous conclusion to draw, but she was as certain of it as she was of that burning gaze. The entire situation was absurd, that she should be standing up with the likes of him, so far above her touch—whoever he was. Felicity was about to say as much when the violin drew its first note. His right hand nestled itself on her upper back, and she was swept, with elegance and authority, into the waltz.

God—galoshes, he was glorious. His clothing was in the first stare of fashion, yet he didn't give the impression of having been wrestled into his coat. The broadness of his shoulders was unheard of in a nobleman—did he toss cabers as a pastime? His dark, unruly hair would torment even the least haughty of valets, but it suited the hewn quality of his face. She, who never took vapors, felt exceedingly vaporous. It was time she asserted herself.

"We do not have an acquaintance, sir." She congratulated herself on her observation of the proprieties, however delayed they might be.

An effortless turn took them around a corner. "Had you been longing to gaze upon Waltham's pustules?"

She refrained from smiling, much less laughing, as she yearned to do. "I do not know to what you refer."

"He is famous for his scabrous scalp. Has been since Eton."

"I find it difficult to believe you and he are contemporaries." *Much less of the same species*, she thought. "I would hazard he is greater in age than you are."

"Not at all. Perhaps the disparity in our apparent youth or lack thereof can be accorded to the possibility that my family's exquisite breeding has nullified the occurrence of erupting carbuncles."

Felicity fought to turn her giggle into a cough, but then thought coughing was unrefined and ended up making a noise that sounded as though a fox was being drawn through a wringer.

He didn't smile, not in the conventional sense, but his eyes shone as if she had given him a marvelous gift. He drew in a deep breath through his nose—had she examined his nose in detail? It was the pattern card for an aristocratic appendage, straight but very large and yet appealing. If she didn't know better, she'd think he was *smelling* her. Her horses exhibited the same flare of nostril when they were making olfactory investigations of their surroundings. But he was clearly a lord of some stripe and likely didn't go around sniffing strange women.

What to say, what to say…did not the burden of chitchat fall upon the lady? If only she had social graces! If only she'd had a governess or a companion…or her mother. Her breath hitched with sadness, and the hand at her back gave her a comforting pat. What in the world was happening?

"Quite the crush, sir, I am sure you will agree." There: benign, with a touch of frost. Impersonal. A comment any of the other ladies in the room might deliver.

"Your Grace," he said, executing another flawless maneuver around the next corner.

She snorted and consigned to oblivion any chance of being confused with a lady. "I am not a duchess."

"But I am a duke."

Bloody hell! "Of?" There: even chillier, and disdainful. As if he were a duke of no account at all. She didn't know what she was doing or why she was doing it, but there was nothing to be done but to brazen it out.

"I am Lowell."

"I am unfamiliar with the name." Which wasn't a lie.

"Haven't memorized your *Debretts*, then?" He sounded pleased.

"I am shocked that I am unfamiliar with the name of a duke of the realm." As if it were his fault.

"I do not go about indiscriminately in society," he replied.

"I am not indiscriminate in my going about, but the notion that one of the highest in the land would be unknown to even one of the lowest would be ridiculous on any account." *What* had she just said?

The hand that had caressed her upper back now laid itself on her side and slid up a fraction, and back down. "If I may make myself known to you, I am Alfred Blakesley, Seventh Duke of Lowell, of Lowell Hall, Tandridge, Surrey."

"Tandridge? Surrey?" This could not be… "My family home is in Kent, near to the village of Edenbridge, which marches along the border of Tandridge."

"Of course it does." The hand caressed her side again. "And all my efforts these past five years were an exercise in futility." He swung her around a corner of the dance floor. No explanation followed.

"I do not know of what you speak."

"You will, ere long," he murmured, nostrils flaring once more.

"Sir! Your Grace. I must object to this repeated inhalation of my person."

And then he smiled—oh, not the kind of smile that a jolly person might assay, full of teeth and creased eyes, but the merest, slightest quirk of the lips. Had she examined his lips? It seemed outrageous and unfair that a man would have a mouth like that, full and plush and yet chiseled and manly. The smile teased out crinkles at the corners of those breathtaking eyes, which made Felicity misstep and fall against his chest—had she examined his *chest* in detail? She couldn't bear to, it was all too much: the glorious handsomeness, the effortless dance… She swayed, and he bolstered her, without exertion, and the first part of the set came to an end.

All at once, she became aware of her surroundings, of the susurrations of gowns and the murmur of voices around the room as innuendo was sown hither and yon. Self-consciousness descended upon her like a heavy cloak, and she wanted nothing more than to flee. How dare he do this to her, make a show of her in front of what she was coming to believe were not the cream of society but the dross? The only thing worse than being made a spectacle of by another was to make one of herself, and so she remained, even as the duke's hands tightened on her person, as if he sensed her impulse to abandon him. The next set began; he swept her around again, and Felicity refused to be powerless.

"Quite the stir you've created," she said.

"Have I? Created a stir? A stir, of all things." His mellifluous voice betrayed mirth.

"Oh, yes, well, may you be amused, Your Grace," she replied. "As you do not go about, you may not know I number among the most legendary of Antidotes that the *haute ton* has ever seen."

"I have often thought little of the opinions of society," he said. "I find no reason to revise that impression, under these circumstances."

"Which are?"

"Dancing with you. Holding you in my arms. Feeling your heart beat"—he drew her closer, and a wave of whispers threatened to capsize her composure—"as we move through the waltz."

She, who had taught herself to waltz based on illustrations in *La Belle Assemblée*, who had never expected to make use of that knowledge, was floating around the ballroom as though she had enjoyed instruction from the *crème de la crème* of French dancing masters. Lost to the music, to the feel of his hands holding her rather closer than was permissible, she took a turn in breathing in his scent, and her old visions of ballroom triumph reawakened— until she looked about her, just for a moment, and saw the spiteful smiles and the fans concealing mouths that dripped venomous *on-dits*.

"I suppose it's an interesting strategy." She pretended to muse, looking away from the crowd and focusing on his perfect cravat, a vision of enviable elegance.

"Strategy?" He brought her even closer to That Chest.

"You have done your duty standing up with a wallflower, have made a beneficent showing, and can therefore take yourself off without falling into the grasp of the fortune-hunting mamas or the wily widows. After all, no one would believe"—she made herself laugh—"that you have an interest in me. I am Miss Felicity Templeton, if I may make myself known to you. An honorable, of which you would not have been aware unless I told you. Which I have. Had you any curiosity as to who I was?"

"I know who you are." He growled in her ear. Growled? In her *ear*? She pulled back but moved only as far as he allowed. Rather than take fright, she became angry. That half smile, the single most charming, delirious thing she'd ever seen, only served to infuriate her further. It appeared he could divine her feelings as she did his, and the more fractious she became, the more pleased he seemed.

She bristled. "If it would not create even more of a scene, I should leave you here in the middle of the dance."

"Should you? Dislike the odd scene now and then?"

Were dukes always this impertinent? "I have had quite enough of this, Your Grace, and I do not appreciate being made to be a figure of fun, or worse."

"It is not my intention to do so, I assure you."

"And who will assure the *beau monde*? On the very rare occasions I have been led out, it has been with partners culled from the worst of the *ton* by my cousins, who seem determined to make a mockery of me. They fill my dance card with the halt, the lame, and the aged to highlight my inability to attract partners for myself, though I have no desire to attract any at all. None of these likely fellows ranked higher than a baron, and on the occasion they'd fetched me an earl, the gossip lasted for a fortnight. How dared I reach so high? But perhaps you have done me a favor. I have plans to remove myself from society forever, and I believe you have made my exodus that much simpler."

"*Pardon* me?"

"I shall be nothing less than a laughingstock, and receive the cut direct for daring to dance with a duke. I must thank you, Your Grace." Her voice dripped with sarcasm and the tremor of failing bravado. "You have made me notorious."

He sighed. "Oh, my dear. I can do much better than this."

Again, without volition, Felicity found herself being taken elsewhere: no longer on the dance floor, headed for her erstwhile hiding place.

Acknowledgments

Being fortunate is a theme of this novel, and I am extremely fortunate in the team that supports my work: my agent Julie Gwinn, my editor Deb Werksman, the design, copy, production, and marketing departments of Sourcebooks. Thank you all!

As a former theatre critic who often rejoiced when a production went seventy-five minutes straight through with no interval, I'm not sure how I would have managed during the Regency Era: five-act plays followed by a comic pantomime? It is true that in the absence of cell phones and YouTube, this was a reasonable amount of one's time to devote to an evening's entertainment, and back then people were more likely to actively socialize while the play was going on than attend to the performances. I suspect this drove Arthur mad, because despite my partiality for plays of short duration, I love the theater with my entire being and gave him my passion for it.

I express my heartfelt gratitude to Arthur's favorite playwright, William Shakespeare, for having a line to suit almost every occasion and facial expression. I've drawn from *As You Like It*, *A Midsummer Night's Dream*, *Macbeth*, *Othello*, referred to *Hamlet*, and could not resist the opportunity to use theatrical history's best stage direction from *The Winter's Tale*.

A theatrical tidbit I was pleased to learn was that George IV's first mistress was the actress Mary Robinson, who he first encountered when she played the part of Perdita in (wait for it) *The Winter's Tale*; she also blackmailed him as did my Beatrice. Despite their reasons being different—Mary sought her promised annuity after years of mistressing—I am happy to be able to back up that Georgie could be put on the back foot by a determined woman and thus a historical liberty was not taken.

And in case you were wondering, as I was, the Scottish play has been a locus of superstition from its first production in 1606 and the invocation of it in the confines of a theater done only by the very brave.

About the Author

Susanna Allen is a graduate of Pratt Institute with a BFA in Communication Design and counts *The Village Voice*, *New York Magazine*, and *Entertainment Weekly* as past design experiences. Born in New Jersey, she moved to Ireland for twelve months—in 1998. She is the author of *Drama Queen* and *The Fidelity Project*, both published by Headline UK, and *That Magic Mischief*, soon to be re-released via Ally Press. Susan is living her life by the three Rs—reading, writing, and horseback riding—and can generally be found on her sofa with her e-reader, gazing out a window and thinking about made-up people, or cantering around in circles. She loves every minute of it.

SEASON OF THE WOLF

Next in Maria Vale's extraordinary series:
The Legend of All Wolves

For the Alpha, things are never easy. The Great North Pack has just survived a deadly attack, and Evie Kitwanasdottir is dealing with new challenges, including the four hazardous Shifters taken into custody. Constantine, the most dangerous, is assigned to Evie's own 7th echelon.

Constantine lost his parents and his humanity on the same devastating day. He has been a thoughtless killer ever since. When Constantine moves under Evie's watchful eye, he discovers that taking orders is not the same as having a purpose. In Evie, he finds a purpose, but there is no room for small loves in the Pack and Constantine must discover whether he is capable of a love big enough for the Great North.

"Prepare to be rendered speechless."
—*Kirkus Reviews*, Starred Review, for *Forever Wolf*

For more Maria Vale, visit:
sourcebooks.com

BEARS BEHAVING BADLY

An extraordinary new series from bestselling author
MaryJanice Davidson featuring a foster care system
for orphaned shifter kids (and kits, and cubs)

Annette Garsea is the fiercest bear shifter the interspecies foster care system has ever seen. She fights hard for the safety and happiness of the at-risk shifter teens and babies in her charge—and you do not want to get on the wrong side of a mama werebear.

Handsome, growly bear shifter PI David Auberon has secretly been in love with Annette since forever but he's too shy to make a move. Annette has noticed the appealingly scruffy PI, but the man's barely ever said more than five words to her... Until they encounter an unexpected threat and put everything aside to fight for their vulnerable charges. Dodging unidentified enemies puts them in a tight spot. Together. Tonight...